# Matthew's War

*The Terra Prime Series*

## Book Two

Terry A. Hurlbut

ISBN: 979-8-9856407-6-2 (paperback)
ISBN: 979-8-9856407-5-5 (ebook)

Published by Conservative News and Views.
https://www.conservativenewsandviews.com/.
Cover by Andrew Dobell - Creative Edge Studios.
www.creativeedgestudios.co.uk.
Printed in the United States of America.

To Andrea

# Contents

# Chapter 1

"**M**r. Prime Minister, Members of the Cabinet, *Rav Aluf* Marcus, *Aluf* Levi, and Members of the *Knesset:*

"I am here, at the invitation of the newest officer in your Defensive Army, to tell you what you already know—and, I hope, tell you something you did *not* know.

"Allow me to introduce myself. My name is Matthew Morrow. Until recently, I held the permanent rank of Lieutenant Commander—that's *Rav Seren* in your rank structure—in the United Systems Navy. I have defected from that power. Today I am an officer without a country. Before, I was one of my society's most promising officers. In fact, I was, and am, the prototype of what was to be an army of invasion. And now I am in exile—a state you know only too well."

Murmurs began until Prime Minister Yitzhak bin Avram raised his gavel and brought it down.

Matthew Morrow, wearing a lieutenant commander's uniform of the United States Navy, regarded his hosts for several seconds. "I am in that exile for two reasons," he said. "One, I discovered a very ugly secret of the security services of my society. Two, I discovered my true purpose. My society intended that I eventually lead an army of invasion against the United States—and against yourselves. Either that or they intended that someone else assume that leadership role. They are very patient, these planners. I have worn this body of metal and plastic for, to the best of my knowledge and recollection, fifty years, to one significant digit. I have had a career in my Navy that originally seemed to hold great promise. Then, fifteen years ago, I made the discovery that led to my arrest, imprisonment, and languishing for fifteen years in a medically induced coma."

That provoked, not murmurs, but gasps. Again the PM brought down his gavel.

"Happily, for me and, I hope, for all of you, a striking young lady brought me out of that coma and helped me to escape. That young lady is, in fact, your newest officer. Give your hand to *Segen* Ayelet Cohen of the Defensive Army of Israel!"

Applause broke out. Beside him, Ayelet, looking as lovely as ever, though now she wore the dark khakis of the *Tzahal,* stood up and waved her right hand. Her raven-black hair caught the lighting of the cavernous meeting hall. This time, the PM let the applause continue for half a minute before once again gaveling the assembly to silence.

"I do not exaggerate," Matthew went on, "in saying that she saved my life. Only later did I come to appreciate that fully. Since then, she and I have taken part in three major actions. These included the liberation of a 'game preserve' in which children were the game." Angry murmurs greeted that, but, as before, only for a moment. "The last operation was the decisive battle that led to the removal from office, on impeachment for and conviction of *treason,* of the President and Vice-President of the United States." More gasps.

"The United States is in the hands of an acting president," Matthew went on. "And—more to the point—the United States is now at war with the United Nations and the United Systems."

More angry murmurs broke out but didn't last long. Matthew could tell that these parliamentarians were hanging on his every word now.

"I need not tell you how the United Nations betrayed you," he said. "I suspect I need not tell you, either, how the United Nations betrayed the very nation-state that founded it. But I *do* need to tell you that, in these treasons, the United Nations had help. *Extraterrestrial* help. For the race we call the Elves, who hail from the planet Tau Ceti e, intervened in the war that is variously called the Great Climate War, the Re-Wilding War—or the Second War of *Diaspora,* as I believe you call it."

The gasps now were of sheer surprise.

"It has taken me a relatively short time span," he went on when the PM had restored quiet yet again, "to realize that the Elves *are not* the friends of humanity they pretended to be. They have willfully withheld from the nominal leaders of my society—leaders they themselves installed—several technological secrets. *And they are responsible for that pedophile game preserve. And at least six others,* which the Third Cavalry Regiment of the United States Marine Corps is now attacking."

A second round of applause greeted that announcement. Matthew waved both hands for silence, and this time the PM didn't even need to move his hand toward his gavel.

"Your Prime Minister, your Chief of Staff, and your Director of Intelligence have all received full briefings on this matter," Matthew went on. "I attended, and indeed took part in, many of these briefings. Much of what I have told you, I have shared with them. They agree with me that you, too, ought to declare and wage war against the United Nations and Systems.

"But what they could *not* tell you, because they might not grasp the implications themselves, is that your position is far more advantageous than you suppose.

"No doubt you are asking yourselves, 'But what can we do, with the relatively primitive weapons we know how to make, against a society that boasts directed-energy weapons and bombs that could create magnitude-ten or stronger earthquakes?' Well, let me answer. They *dare not* use the second sort of weapon, else they would have done it long ago. This happens to be the headquarters world of the United Systems. It would not do to start seismic or even tectonic events on this world. *Especially* not when they recently fought a long, bitter, and costly war against an enemy halfway across the galaxy, and *now* must fight some of their own colony worlds, who have declared their independence! And *that's* why they built me, and hoped to build hundreds of others like me, to come down here, into these Caves, and into the American caves, and root you all out.

"But what, then, of the powerful energy weapons they possess? Well, I could say that your friends, the Americans, have by now acquired samples of these weapons and are working out how to duplicate them. I could say that, but that would be of no moment. *Because you, and they, already have far superior battlefield weapons!* The simple method of projecting an object by expanding gases from a chemical explosion in a confined space was one method upon which they need never have tried to improve. Energy weapons are *highly* overrated on the battlefield. In a space battle, maybe they have their place. On land, they perhaps have greater range. But at close range—ladies and gentlemen, I took part in three battles after my defection and escape. In the last action, friendly and enemy forces used both kinds of weapons. And I can tell you straight: yours are the better weapons. And as for the energy weapons, I can give you the secret of an absurdly simple defense against them—an electromagnetic force field, like the one I personally can generate at need.

"All of which to say this: *fear not!* I have taken the measure of your enemy, and I tell you, he is weak, hard-pressed, and his soldiers would crumble in an instant when facing your weapons. A great flash of light is *nothing* compared to thousands of tiny metal shells flying at them." *As I know only too well,* he didn't say. His body shield proved too weak against an onslaught of such tiny shells. If Ayelet had delayed a second longer with the reinforcements she had brought, he would be dead. The repairs his generous hosts had made shortly afterward did not erase the memory of that event.

"So as you deliberate, as you ponder how much longer your exile need last, remember the example of the many leaders who have vanquished seemingly superior foes. Otnyel. Yehud. Devorah. Gideon. Yiftach. Shimshon. And, of course, the incomparable David."

*That* name brought the *Knesset* members to their feet or set them drumming on their desks for a full minute.

"Will you, therefore, follow their example?" he cried out to them. "Will you take back what is rightfully yours and help restore freedom and justice to this world, and, by extension, to a galaxy?"

"*Ken! Ken! Ken! Ken! Ken! Ken! Ken!*" The chant went on for a full three minutes until the members ran out of energy. The Prime Minister then took over and called for an immediate vote. Matthew didn't have to guess: the vote was unanimous: for war.

After that vote came another unanimous vote to adjourn. And, after taking that vote, someone broke out in song. Quickly the other members took it up.

*"Kol od balevav panimah, nefesh Yehudi homiyah,*

*"Ulfa'atey mitzrach kadimah, ayin le-Tzion tzofiyah.*

*"Od lo avda tikvatenu, ha tikvah ha noshana,*

*"La'shuv le-eretz avoteynu, le'ir ba David, David hana.*

*"La'shuv le-eretz avoteynu, le'ir ba David, David hana."*

* * *

"And where did you learn all those names?" asked *Rav Aluf* Caleb Marcus, the chief of staff.

"You may thank your newest officer, *Segen* Cohen, here," said Matthew. "She introduced me to your *Tanakh*. A most inspiring work. My society has nothing like it."

"Or perhaps they have forgotten it," said Ayelet. Then, to the chief of staff, she said, "I can assure you, sir, that my Zealots have the *Tanakh*."

"They have a digital copy of the Dead Sea Scrolls," the lead General said. "Thanks to you and your family, of course—and for that alone, I ought to decorate you. But *Rav Seren* Morrow, here, did not know it—until, if I understand him correctly, you introduced him to it."

Matthew and Ayelet both nodded.

"And I *still* don't know this work," said Hospital Corpsman Andrea Riley. "I can see how important it is to everybody, and now I'm frightfully curious."

"So am I," said Chief Information Technician Barry Sutton. "Is this history, or philosophy, or what?"

"A little bit of each," said the General. "And more to the point, *Rav Seren* Morrow, you spoke those names as though they were your own heroes."

"They are," said Matthew. "Each of them fought a war similar to the one I wage. I noticed that at once when I read of the *Shoftim*."

"But how could you possibly read a work as complex as the *Tanakh* so quickly?"

"My auxiliary processors, to say nothing of my secondary memory, allow me to read any bound volume as quickly as I can turn its pages," said Matthew. "But I take your point. You ask how I could come to such an understanding so quickly. I will say only this: stories of heroism and strategy against impossible odds have always resonated with me. I've never known why, but that is the truth."

"Well," said *Aluf* Levi, head of the Institute for Intelligence and Special Operations, "I never met a *goy* who understood our *good book* half as well. As much as our American friends tell me how much they revere it, with you, it's different. You treat it with a respect with which I could wish our own, younger generation could treat it."

"You flatter me, *Aluf* Levi," said Matthew. "Though, I still don't *quite* understand all of it. The Deluge, for example. For what can that possibly be a metaphor?"

"I assure you, that's no metaphor," said the Intelligence Chief. "Oh, I suppose everything in the *Tanakh*, even events, are metaphors for something or other. The Eternal is like that—symbolism means everything to Him. But if you're wondering whether the Deluge ever took place—I assure you, it did.

"But perhaps I am not the one to educate you along that line. You really need to talk to those who can."

"The Academy of the Hebrew Language?"

"As good a group as any—though, I definitely would recommend the Sanhedrin to you. I don't suppose you have with you the photographs of that Elfin transport you stole?"

"Don't forget, *Aluf* Levi, that I need no photographs," said Matthew. "I have graphics processors that can help me render into graphic-file form the image of any person or object I see. I can record everything I see and hear—as still pictures or as motion pictures. And store any text I read as machine-readable text."

"Remarkable," said the General, almost in a whisper. "I look forward to receiving the Academicians' report. But first: we have been remiss as hosts. You and *Segen* Cohen will, of course, join us for dinner."

"Almost a *state* dinner," said the Prime Minister, speaking for the first time. "For *I* shall play host. Though, I have never played host to a … Forgive me…"

"Machine?" Matthew smiled a crooked smile. "Well, strictly speaking, I *am* mostly machine, except for my central nervous system and spinal and cranial nerves. Nevertheless, my builders did not neglect any of the senses. They left me taste and smell, as well as touch, sight, and hearing. I shall very much enjoy your dinner—especially since it doesn't come out of a printer."

Matthew's last remark actually set everyone else present to laughing.

* * *

"And what exactly is this 'printer' that my husband was trying to tell me about?" asked Leah bin Avram, the Prime Minister's wife.

"I'm not sure you would wish to know, ma'am," said Matthew to his hostess. "I certainly would not deliberately insult such a good cook as yourself."

"Now, don't you hold back on me, my good man. I still want to know what a printer is."

"Well, I don't think you would care to imagine a machine that can prepare a dinner plate, laden with food, almost as quickly as any of your own printers reproduces a document."

"Ugh," she said, her face reflecting a moue of disgust. "How can your people so degrade themselves by eating a meal that comes out of a machine like that?"

"By sacrificing quality for convenience," said Matthew. "And that's even allowing for this being a *kosher* meal, fit to eat by a higher standard than most I've seen."

"I'll vouch for that," said Andrea Riley. "Everything at your table has been excellent, and much easier to digest."

"Furthermore," Matthew went on, "the printers cannot last in our former society. They are making mistakes. Already it is making food taste a little worse every day."

"Tell them about the promazine derivative," said Ayelet.

"Oh, yes," said Matthew. "The printers leave a foreign substance in all food and drink they produce. And that substance is an antipsychotic medication."

"*Oy, gevalt!*" cried the Prime Minister. "Why didn't you mention it at our conference with the American acting President?"

"It did not seem to matter then."

"But I should think it does! If we're going to face an enemy with their bodies full of something like that, then we have even *less* reason to fear."

"Not after I send out a virus to cancel that part of every printer's program."

"Eh?"

"That's right, Mr. Prime Minister," said Barry. "Matthew wants to stop the printers in our society from drugging everyone's food. Because he wants the people themselves to rise up in revolt."

"That's very wise, Prime Minister," Marcus said. "Remember that it is not war only that *Rav Seren* Morrow wishes to wage. It is revolution. That means defeating the enemy from within. And rousing the people themselves to take up arms. Those people will be our allies."

"I still don't understand," said bin Avram. "Why do you want to make revolution? What drives you?"

"Simply this, Prime Minister. I cannot trust the leadership of my society any longer. They built me to attack an inoffensive target. They arrested me when I discovered something about their activities they wished to keep secret. And, several times, they have tried to destroy me. Now, I can either try to make my case to a sympathetic authority—which is useless because we have no separation of powers like what you, Israelis, have, or the Americans have. Or I can make revolution. I choose revolution."

"Your service rank name does not do you justice, Matthew Morrow," said the Prime Minister. "Even though it is the rank you had achieved, or as near enough to it as will translate into Hebrew. I would like to propose a higher title for you. You ought to call yourself *Shofet* Matthew."

The comparison actually shocked Matthew. Could he really compare himself to a *judge*? And not just any judge at that. The *Shoftim* were more than judges. They were great heroes and military leaders who rose to challenges almost none of them thought they could meet.

So he asked the obvious question: "Can I truly take my place beside men like Otnyel, Yehud, Yiftach, and the other leaders I named?"

"Why not? You have a strength that Shimshon himself would envy, and a self-restraint he never had. You have the dedication of Gideon and the heart for justice of Yiftach. And, you have the matter-of-fact directness of David. True, they called him *Melech*, not *Shofet*. But Shmuel, last of the *Shoftim*, declared David for what he became, so David did have a connection to the *Shoftim*. And believe me, young man—for you *are* a young man in my eyes, even with your machine body—you are everything an ancient *Shofet* was and embody everything the *Shoftim* were all about."

"You have paid me a great many compliments, Prime Minister," said Matthew. "I'm not at all sure I deserve them. I began my warfare, if you will, to ensure my own survival—and happen to have met a lot of friends along the way. Like Ayelet here, and Chief Sutton and Corpsman Riley. And some very brave children whom I helped liberate from … Well, perhaps I oughtn't to mention that in front of a lady."

"Don't worry about that," said Leah. "My Yitzhak told me all about those horrible places."

"Then you understand," said Matthew, inclining his head to her. "In any event, Prime Minister, I'm only trying to do justice as best I can. As I told you, the stories of the *Shoftim* resonated with me. I'm not sure I'm entitled to have you remember me as one of them. Not yet. Not until I can earn it."

"And when might that be?" asked Yitzhak bin Avram, suddenly sounding more solemn.

"I might not be able to tell you that," said Matthew, "until the war I must fight, is over."

The group finished the meal in silence, after which everyone agreed that they should rest. Matthew retired to a room that had a makeshift charging alcove—another favor everyone seemed to know to do for him. But it also had a regular bed—and sure enough, Ayelet joined him in that room.

"I trust this arrangement won't be awkward for you?" Matthew asked.

"Of course not!" said Ayelet. "Why should it be awkward? You're a very special friend to me. In fact: *Shofet* Matthew—the more often I repeat it, the better I like it."

"Please don't repeat that," said Matthew. "I do take your point. But can you take mine?"

She opened her mouth—closed it—and finally said, "I do, Matthew. If not for the modesty you are now showing, you wouldn't be the special friend that you are."

"Thank you."

"But seriously, your own history matches so many of those of the *Shoftim*. For example, Yiftach lost out of his share of his father's estate because his mother was … well…"

"Not his father's lawful wife?"

"Yes. And Gideon had to face the resentment of his own people after he took action against a practice he saw and recognized as wrong. And the Prime Minister was right—you are far superior to at least one of the *Shoftim*—Shimshon. You have his strength but none of his weaknesses."

"But as I say," said Matthew, "I can only hope to distinguish myself half as well as did any of those ancient leaders."

"You already have—at least in my eyes."

"Now *that* is quite a compliment, coming from the leader of the Zealots."

Ayelet suddenly frowned.

"Did I say something wrong?" Matthew asked.

She stayed quiet for five seconds. Then she said, "No, Matthew. It's just that the Zealots haven't actually done more than recruit up to now—and provide intelligence for at least one of those operations you mentioned in the *Knesset*. Now they have to do much more. And … Oh, Matthew, you worry about deserving an ancient title? *I* worry about whether my movement will be worth anything—now that the time has come for action!"

Matthew needed only a split second to know what to say. He moved toward her and took both her hands—and felt the tension in them as he did. "Ayelet," he said, smiling, "look at me."

She did.

"I'll repeat to you what I told the *Knesset*," he said. "You saved my life back in the Harper's Ferry cavern. Before that, you made the difference between mission success and failure at the pedophile camp in the Lucketts District. More than that, you took on a challenge, not even knowing whether you would succeed or fail, but because it was the right thing to do. That was true of most of the *Shoftim*, and of *Melech* David, too. *You* deserve the title of *Shofet* more than I. And you shall have it. Your Zealots will rally to you when the time comes—and you, and they, will know it."

He felt a slight change in the conductivity of her skin—not the mark of a liar, but the effect of one realizing something new and amazing about herself. She smiled back at him—a warm, radiant smile. "For one who never heard of our law, prophets, or writings," she said, "you have paid me the most profound compliment you could have paid. And I believe you meant it."

"As surely as I stand here, in Mara Israel."

"Thank you, Matthew," she said. "And you're right. I will do what—well, what *Shofet* Devorah did. Wait for my opportunity, knowing it will come."

He released her hands. And before he could react, she reached up with her right hand, cupped the back of his head, and brought his head down so she could touch her lips to his.

The kiss lasted only a fraction of a second. But in that moment, he remembered again the last woman to kiss him. *Natalya*. With an effort, he stopped the flow of tears to his eyes.

Then it was over. Ayelet stood before him, displaying her usual mild impudence. "Come," she said. "We both need sleep—even you, as I know perfectly well. We have a big day tomorrow."

"Oh?" he asked. "And what have you planned for tomorrow?"

"First, I need to show you at least two places that hold some of my people's memories—not all of them pleasant. Then we will meet a delegation from the Sanhedrin. And *HaAkademiyah LaLashon HaIvrit*. Members of both these organizations definitely want to talk to you. And you should talk to them."

"I look forward to that. All of it."

The rest of the evening didn't last too long. Matthew prepared himself for the charging alcove, while Ayelet disappeared into the bathroom attached to their room and emerged wearing what appeared to be makeshift sleeping fatigues, for lack of a better term. They said little to one another—besides wishing each other a good night. As she had when they had shared a room in the Cumberland Caverns, Ayelet composed herself for sleep—but Matthew read the odd mixture of peace and anticipation on her face. Then he willed himself to sleep. At least he could do *that*, knowing that it was only temporary. He had no wish to return to the enforced sleeping state in which he had languished for fifteen years.

* * *

"As I'm sure you've heard many times before, welcome to Mara Israel," said the leader of the three-man group who greeted Matthew and Ayelet. Each of these men wore the same kind of civilian dress to which Matthew was still trying to accustom himself to seeing. Except, all three men wore black-on-white outfits, topped with black broad-brimmed hats. They also sported full beards and moustaches. "These two gentlemen are Rabbi Reuven Lapid, Vice-Chairman of the Sanhedrin, and Eliezer Perel, Dean of the Academy of the Hebrew Language. And I am Rabbi Shmuel Govan, Chairman of the Sanhedrin. And on behalf of all of Israel, we offer you our profuse thanks."

"And I thank you," said Matthew. "Now, I hope I can earn your thanks. Thus far, I have done little but make speeches."

His three hosts laughed. Rabbi Govan said, "Your reputation for modesty precedes you," he said. "And what impression have you formed of us?"

"You are certainly a very brave people," said Matthew. "No one should underestimate you. I have just come from a tour of Yad VaShem. A most enlightening display—and a tragic one. I have seen very few stories of wrongdoing on such a massive and ugly scale. And I commend your people for preserving historical evidence."

"We tell ourselves, 'never again,'" said Rabbi Lapid in a solemn tone. "But I have to observe: our ancestors of the twenty-first century did succumb to a false sense of security. As tragic as the Shoah was, the Second Shoah and Diaspora was even more tragic—and infuriating. First, our people had to burn incense on the *bamah* of high technology—true enough, that was our chief export in those days, but it was as seductive as a priestess of Astarte in the days of *Aluf* Joshua. And I refer, of course, to the 'immunizations' against the Novel Corona Virus. One-third of our people died that way, and another third were so befuddled in their brains that they could not fight the United Nations Climate Forces when the time came.

"And yet, the Eternal has heard our cry and raised Him up a *Shofet* for our modern age. It hasn't been quite as long as was our time in Egypt, but long enough."

He felt Ayelet take his hand and give it a quick squeeze. It was on the tip of his tongue to tell these men that they should honor Ayelet with that title, not him. However, he sensed Ayelet wouldn't consider herself ready for that. But someday…!

Aloud he said, "Yes, I've read your *Tanakh*. And was able to confirm much of it at the Israel Museum, which I have also seen."

"I must say," asked Dean Perel for the first time, "that your Hebrew is *mo'ed tov*. Where did you have time to learn it?"

"Oh, as to that, I studied that early in my career, and have studied it all my life."

"*Really?*"

"Why not? Don't you know that Hebrew is the root of all human language?"

"And who among the *goyim* would admit such a thing?"

"No one, of course," said Matthew. "But it's only logical. Every root in every other language traces back to Hebrew, directly or indirectly. That's the simplest theory I could construct for the similarities I observed. But I did make one oversight."

"And what might that be?"

"Failure to notice the similarities between Hebrew and Elfin."

"Ah, yes," said the Dean. "*Aluf* Levi of *Mossad* told us about the extraterrestrial race that actually speaks a variant of Hebrew, which is why I was so glad to receive the invitation of these two learned men to meet you. Have you a sample of Elfin writing that you can share?"

"Let me interface with one of your network consoles," said Matthew, "and I can at least share part of a document I have seen."

"We have one right here," said Rabbi Govan. "By all means, proceed."

Matthew did so. When he did, the Dean took his time to read it. Then he said, "*Aluf* Levi is correct! This isn't *exactly* Hebrew, but it is a variant. A branching that has simply 'aged' in a different way. A very early branching—earlier even than the Sanskrit and Oriental branchings."

"About how early, would you say?"

"Why, I wonder whether this branching came earlier than the Deluge! But if it did, it would be literally fantastic. No one is supposed to have survived that, except Noach and his family."

"*Aluf* Levi mentioned the Deluge," said Matthew. "He insists that it took place, exactly as the *Tanakh* describes it. But he also suggested that you could enlighten me further."

"Indeed I can!" said the Dean with an enthusiastic air. Then more soberly, he said, "I suppose we are the only ones left who keep that legend alive. According to it, the Eternal was sorry He had made human beings and also had to scour the earth of a hybrid human-demon race that was abroad in those times. So He released a flow of water that drowned every land animal, and every human being—except for a family of eight, and several breeding pairs they carried." Having warmed to his subject, the Dean narrated in detail a passage from the *Torah,* describing the event. Matthew recognized it at once.

"You do realize," he said to the Dean, "that this passage you just quoted reads exactly like a ship's log, as I should know. I signed hundreds of them as the second officer on two Navy ships."

"Really!?" cried Rabbi Lapid, delighted to hear the comparison. "But of course. This is the log of the *Thevah*—the Life-ship. Noach, the Shipwright, built and commanded her, and his three sons kept this log."

"About those 'hybrids,'" Matthew asked next. "What did they look like?"

Rabbi Govan cradled his chin in his right hand for a few seconds. Then he shrugged. "No one knows," he said, "apart from pure speculation. Noach never drew any pictures. Neither did his sons. Or if they did, those pictures are lost. Even *Yovhelihim*—Jubilees—doesn't have them."

"But surely a flood of that magnitude would have crushed all the plant life beneath it," said Matthew. "I don't understand why we don't see its evidence today."

"Are you sure?" asked all three men in chorus.

"Well, you tell me," said Matthew. "How did the plants grow back? How did an olive tree grow back so that a turtledove could pluck off a compound leaf and bring it back to Noach's ship?"

"Reseeding, of course," said the Dean. "And as for the pressure you mentioned … Tell me this, *Rav Seren* Morrow—or I should say, *Shofet* Matthew. Does any civilized world, besides this one, have such abundant quantities of petroleum, natural gas, or coal?"

Matthew didn't even have time to reflect embarrassment at these men urging that title on him, yet again, for what he felt was utter astonishment. Because he realized that no other world had anything like the "fossil fuels"! They didn't even have deposits of radioactive ores, nor did their crusts exhibit background radiation. And the only isotopes of lead or any lighter metals were the most common that one could find on Earth. The dizzying variety of light, heavy, and even radioactive isotopes was unique to Sol d. After a considerable silence, he admitted as much.

"Of course," said the Dean. "I would expect the Deluge also to be unique to this world. The fossil fuels are its products, as are the radioactive substances in this world's crust. The crushed forests and jungles of the world of the Deluge became coal. And the dead animals, some of which were very large, became petroleum and natural gas."

"And the radioactive and other odd isotopes?"

"Products of piezoelectricity. Centuries ago, an American engineer named Walter T. Brown worked this out. You see, the Deluge involved the escape of an ocean from beneath the crust—more than sixty miles deep."

"I thought only the Americans used the mile as a unit of great distance."

"We use it, too, and have ever since the Second Diaspora. The only difference is that we describe it as three thousand five hundred twenty cubits, not five thousand two hundred eighty feet. But it still represents a thousand paces, and we have a treaty with the Americans establishing the 'pace' as a unit of length with a common definition."

"And that subcrustal ocean—would that be the 'fountains of the deep'?"

"Just so. And this event produced earthquakes the like of which had never happened before, and never happened again. And when they acted on the buried quartz deposits, they produced electromotive potentials measurable in billions of volts—SI volts or American Patriotic volts, which doesn't matter much. Enough to produce elements with atomic numbers greater than 180. These split at once to form the two most abundant radioactive elements, uranium and thorium. And in that highly charged environment, these would decay—very rapidly—to produce all the other radioactive elements heavier than lead."

"And the light isotopes?"

"Beta decay products from radioactive isotopes of the next lighter elements, of course."

"And where did all these come from?"

"From the same source that produced the heavy isotopes. All that activity I mentioned, the formation of such incredibly heavy elements, followed by their fission or cluster decay, released uncountable neutrons. If the *Thevah* hadn't been floating on the water that now covered all the land, those neutrons would have killed Noach, his family, and all their specimens. As it was, the cluster decay created an isotope of carbon that pervades all life, and shortens all life spans."

"Yes," said Matthew. "I had wondered why, beginning with Shem, the life span of human beings declined ninety percent in eleven generations. The Elves, I note, did not have this problem.

"And it explains something else. Ayelet, maybe you know what I mean. On every origin world of every species except humanity, industrial development went directly from beasts-of-burden to biofuels, and from there to hydrogen-oxygen and eventually to photovoltaics and solar-thermal. With no intervening step using fossil fuels—because those societies never had them. Nor nuclear fission, for that matter, and by reason of a similar lack. I'm surprised they developed nuclear fusion."

Ayelet nodded. "And that's how the Elves could have their appeal to the original UN," she said. "They didn't have to pretend to be disdainful of a fossil-fuel-based economy or nuclear reactors. Because they never had either."

"The Elves might be a special case, however," said Matthew.

"What makes you say that?"

"First, as I told you, they live longer than any other hominid race. Second, their technology has always been vastly superior to that of any other race. And their physiognomy is significantly different from that of the others. Their pointed ears set them apart from everyone else. And their anatomical dimensions are up to one-half larger than those of any other race."

"One-half larger?" asked one of the rabbis.

"Does that suggest something to you?" asked Matthew.

"If not for those pointed ears, I could almost take them for … No. Too fantastic."

They said no more about it. But Matthew noticed that the two rabbis left that meeting with more than usually thoughtful expressions.

"Ayelet," he asked, as they took a taxi back to a tube station that would take them back to the Prime Minister's residence, "do you have any idea what the Dean might have been talking about?"

"You mean, about who the Elves might actually be?"

"Yes."

"There *is* one possibility, and I'm almost afraid to mention it. But you have to go back to the *Tanakh* to find it. The *Tanakh* might have two names for them."

"And those would be?"

"*Anakim*, and *Nephilim*."

"The 'mighty men of old, men of renown'? But I thought the Deluge destroyed them."

"Maybe … or maybe not. The verse you just quoted said the *Nephilim* were abroad in those days, *and even afterward.*"

"Dean Perel is right," said Matthew. "Too fantastic, and those pointed ears tell against that. But still … Why should they speak a variant of Hebrew that is older even than the Hebrew you and I speak now?"

"That's the central riddle, isn't it?"

"Yes," said Matthew. "But it's also another riddle to solve another day. All I know, especially after what you and I saw in that second operation we fought together, is that they are enemies pretending to be friends. If that theory is at all correct, then it might explain their enmity. But, since I already know all I need to know, that can wait."

"For what?"

"For me to acquire any more evidence on this point. That is, when I'm not fighting a war … Excuse me." The Personal Digital Device the US Navy had issued him had just throbbed. He pulled it from a pocket of his uniform and answered it. "*Rav Seren* Morrow here," he said by force of habit.

"Here, Yitzhak," said the voice on the other end. "I just had a message from your acting President. He requires your presence back in the Cumberland Caverns as quickly as we can arrange it. It seems certain persons are about to come to trial, and he requires your testimony. Yours, and that of *Segen* Cohen."

"We're on our way back to your compound, Prime Minister," said Matthew. "I apologize for having to depart on such notice, but duty does call."

"All of us understand perfectly. Your other companions will be waiting for you when you return here. And again, from all of Israel, thank you."

"And I thank *you*, Prime Minister, for the welcome and the opportunity. I'll see you later." He closed the contact, then turned to Ayelet. "Thinks are moving fast back in the American caverns," he said. "Trials, the Prime Minister said. I can well imagine—treason trials, criminal trials, and courts-martial. They'll want our testimonies. You, Andrea, Barry, and me."

Ayelet stiffened—only slightly, but still. "I'll be ready, Matthew," she said.

# Chapter 2

"**W**hat is your name, rank, and affiliation?" asked Rear Admiral Sean Vincent.

"Captain Rodney Coleman, United Systems Special Security Forces," said the defiant prisoner. "And you, *sir,* are in deep…"

Before he could utter what obviously was on the tip of his tongue, the American Director of Naval Intelligence brought his gavel to the table with a loud *crack.* The prisoner fell silent.

Admiral Vincent, sitting at a broad table with Matthew Morrow to his left and his nephew, Major Ian Vincent USMC, to his right, regarded the prisoner with a quizzical eye. Matthew, wearing the blue suit of the United States Navy, complete with ribbons representing the Purple Heart and the Distinguished Service Cross, could guess what his newfound friend was thinking. Here was their prisoner, lashed to a straight-backed armchair, telling his *captors* that *they* had reason to fear. Of Matthew himself, the prisoner had taken no notice at all, thus far. More futile defiance, Matthew knew. After all, Matthew himself had captured this man and brought him here, though it had been … difficult.

Admiral Vincent resumed his interrogation. "You would do well," he said, "to take better stock of where you sit."

"And *you* would 'do well' to let me go while the letting-go is good!"

"And if we don't?"

"Then you will die—all of you!"

"Who is Captain Folsom?" asked Vincent abruptly. *Good,* thought Matthew. *Change the subject.*

"She is none of your business!" snarled Captain Coleman. Then: "On second thought, maybe I'll make her your business. She's the one who will lobotomize all of you. Except for you, *Matthew Morrow.* Of you, she will take a *very* special interest."

"And what interest would that be?" Matthew asked, deciding to join the conversation.

"That's for me to know and for you to find out."

"No, Captain Coleman, it is for you to tell us," said the younger Vincent, speaking for the first time. "Again: you would do well to take better stock of where you sit—literally and figuratively. A military tribunal has just convicted you, on the testimony of unimpeachable witnesses, of aiding and abetting kidnapping, aiding and abetting criminal endangerment of minors, accessory to attempted murder—and crimes against nature involving minors. Not to mention espionage against the United States."

"Convicted, hell! By a kangaroo court, with no counsel of my choice…"

"You will not speak without permission. The tribunal offered you counsel, but you refused. You chose to act on your own behalf, which is never wise. A court consisting of officers similar in rank to yourself convicted you.

"And then the court granted you a singular mercy. Offenses like yours once rated life imprisonment without the possibility of parole. You *have* the possibility of parole. And your parole board could, in theory, release you to a place of relative freedom, though, also, a place of exile."

"But there are two catches," said the elder Vincent, resuming control. "The first is that *I* will run your parole board—I, the Director of Naval Intelligence. The Judge Advocate General of the Navy has signed off on that. Second, you will never see that exile until *all of us* can leave these Caves any time we please. That will require victory in the war that, as we told you, the United States Congress and the Israeli Knesset have now declared against the United Nations and United Systems. So it's up to you, Captain Coleman, but in your place, I would help us prosecute that war. Because you don't go free until we win—or you die a natural death— whichever happens first. Do you understand?"

The prisoner hawked up and spat across the room. The wad didn't land very far—six feet, and he was fifteen feet away. How odd, thought Matthew: I can actually *think* in these "American Patriotic" units of measurement my hosts use. Before today, I would have judged that distance to be two meters—not that it matters very much.

But the prisoner wasn't done. He cast a baleful eye on Matthew. "Traitor!" he shouted. "Is this what you signed on for?"

"I did not *sign on* for being *used*," said Matthew, slowly and deliberately. "I did not *sign on* to have my central nervous system transplanted into this body of metal and plastic I now wear, just so your superiors could eventually have an 'ultimate warrior' to attack these people for no good reason. And I certainly did not *sign on* to be subject to arrest, imprisonment, and a fifteen-year medically induced coma after spotting that little 'recreational facility' of which you were chief of security. So don't you *dare* talk to me about treason."

The prisoner, wearing a sullen face, said no more.

Admiral Vincent spoke to the helmeted Shore Patrol Chief—whom Matthew remembered. This was that Chief Carter who had led the SP Squad that helped Matthew face down an attack by the corrupt former President's Secret Service contingent. "Unbind the prisoner and escort him to his cell," the Admiral ordered. "This court will now go into executive session."

Chief Carter escorted Captain Coleman out, whereupon the DNI looked at his two companions in turn. "Well, gentlemen?" he asked. "Your opinions?"

His nephew threw up his hands and sighed. "We told him," he said. "He's been under confinement for a week and a half now. I thought it rocked him when we tried him as swiftly as we did—I think that's one of the fastest courts-martial on record, and that's saying something. But it's almost as if he thinks this is an elaborate game."

"Which, apart from the deaths of his men, his commanding officer, and the Elfin Ambassador, it would be," said Matthew. "What do you think I concluded when the Seventh Cav Squadron's Recon Platoon discovered me and my fellow escapees from Bethesda Naval Hospital? *I* thought it was a game. In his service they play that kind of game all the time. He has simply raised his psychological defenses."

"I asked for your recommendation, Commander," said the Admiral. Then he added, "My apologies. I did not intend to speak to you as I would to a subordinate." He meant, of course, that Matthew now had a remarkable distinction—that of a military ally. That came with his defection to this underground society, its declaration of war against the United Systems, and the treaty he now had with his hosts. And now, of course, with the Israelis.

"That's of no moment, Admiral," said Matthew. "In fact, I *do* have a recommendation."

"And that would be?"

"Expose the prisoner to something he would fear greatly. Specifically, sudden changes in acceleration."

"I don't follow."

"Admiral," said Matthew, "our society has total gravity manipulation. He's used to riding in a conveyance that adjusts itself so well to changing acceleration that he feels as though he's sitting still. He's never experienced the slightest stress from launch or braking. So let's expose him to these things."

"Where?"

"Your society has an abundance of amusement centers," said Matthew. "Use one of them."

The two officers at the table next to him stared at him in openmouthed astonishment. Then the younger man asked, "Are you sure it can be that simple? After all, our citizens and lawful residents enjoy such facilities all the time, and they don't have problems of that kind."

"That's not exactly true, son," said the Admiral. "You wouldn't catch *me* on any roller coaster at my age. And I speak for a lot of adults."

"More to the point," said Matthew, "*he* has never done so. He has probably filled his head with lurid visions of the stress of abruptly changing acceleration, and the harm such stress can bring."

"And where might he have visited, to do that?"

"The United Nations Educational, Scientific, and Cultural Organization took over several amusement parks on the surface. These parks belonged typically to some very large joint-stock corporations with names like Walt Disney Enterprises, Six Flags, Anheuser Busch, and Cedar

Fair Entertainment. Today UNESCO maintains them as museums, all to show the people how 'profligate' you Americans were before the Great Climate War."

Instantly Captain Vincent's eyes lit up. "Would that include Kings Dominion, in Doswell, Virginia?"

"Yes," said Matthew. "You know about that installation?"

"I should hope so! Kings Dominion is legendary in Virginia. But you're sure Captain Coleman knows about it?"

"Considering where we captured him, he's probably toured that facility often. But he would never dare or even imagine taking any of its rides. No one in my former society would."

Even as he said that, he knew it was not true. For another memory came to him—a memory of an earlier visit he had made to the Kings Dominion Amusement Museum. Only, he wasn't on shore leave at the time. In this memory, he was just *a boy of four*. His parents had taken him— so he *did* have parents once. They had spent their time in the children's area of the park, a place named after a character in a twentieth-century comic strip. Every attraction in that area repeated the theme. But in the distance, he had seen another attraction—a very tall double-tracked red arch resting on yellow columns. As he watched, a train of ten cars, each black as jet, rode up to the top of the arch at a forty-five-degree angle— then plunged down the other end at an eighty-five-degree angle. He had stared and breathed two words. "Some day…" But he then had turned to look at his mother—and caught a look of white-hot fury tinged with terror in her eyes.

Then the memory cut out, and he was back in the present day, just in time to see Ian Vincent grinning wolfishly and saying, "Then let's oblige him."

"Now hold on a minute, Ian," said the Admiral. "Do you seriously suggest capturing the original Kings Dominion and subjecting the prisoner to 'enhanced interrogation' there?"

"You betcha—sir."

"But why? Why not simply strap him onto a roller coaster down here?"

"It wouldn't be as effective, sir. He knows Kings Dominion but *doesn't* know any of our facilities. He's had time to scare himself about Kings Dominion's roller coasters, which in any case are probably a lot taller than anything we've ever been able to build. Right, Commander?"

Matthew answered, "I can't vouch for how tall your tallest roller coaster is in these Caves. But in Kings Dominion, the builders had the advantage of the open air—and one coaster, in particular, rises to a height of three hundred and five feet."

"Which is half, again, as tall as the tallest coaster we've got in the Caves."

"We'd have to crash the barrier, wouldn't we?" the elder Vincent asked.

"That would not present a problem," said Matthew. "Chief Sutton could get us in." That, of course, would be Chief Information Technician Barry Sutton, one of his three original fellow escapees. "Besides, I know the layout. I, too, have visited the Kings Dominion Amusement Museum, and often, on shore leave. It cannot have changed much since my last visit. UNESCO makes no attempt to redevelop it. When I last visited it, it was at the same state of development as when UNESCO took it over, in…" (here he paused to convert to the Gregorian Calendar the Americans used) "…2035.

"Furthermore, the Barrier near the Museum has a gate. We will 'crash' it."

"I take it you have a particular program of enhanced interrogation in mind."

"Indeed I have, Admiral. And there's more. Kings Dominion's communications center has a direct connection to the main information network. That makes it the perfect place from which to distribute propaganda videos—or the software 'upgrades' I talked to your nephew about, to stop the printers my society uses from drugging everyone's food."

"It's still a hair-raising campaign," the Admiral went on. "Such a thing should be a diversion for a much larger operation."

"I cannot recommend that at this time," said Matthew. "But I *would* remind you that this operation will inspire Ayelet Cohen's Zealots, and anyone else willing to make revolution."

"Let's ask Colonel Campbell in for a conference," said the DNI.

* * *

"It's crazy, sir," said Colonel Campbell. "In fact, it's just crazy enough to work."

The conference had moved from the interrogation room to another room much better suited for planning a battle. Those in attendance now included the Marine Commandant, the Marine G-3 (Chief of Operations), and the staff of the Third Cavalry Regiment, including Major Vincent and Major Frank Jellicoe, the Regimental S-3 and commander of the Seventh Cavalry Squadron.

It also included Matthew, the DNI, and all three of Matthew's companions. These last included Chief Sutton, now of the United *States* Navy instead of the United *Systems* Navy; Hospital Corpsman Andrea Riley, now transferred to the United States Navy; and *Segen* Ayelet Cohen, now of the Israel Defense Forces.

The G-3 asked, "Then you approve of Commander Morrow's battle plan?"

"Without reservation, sir," said Colonel Campbell. "And to the point Admiral Vincent raised, as I understand it, about diversionary tactics: as a matter of fact, I *have* been thinking about a main action we ought to think about taking. Commander Morrow, am I correct in assuming that, pursuant to the Great Environmental Reset by UN Secretary General Gunilla Thorsell, the UN truly did eliminate all uses of—do you understand what *aircraft* were?"

"Craft that used their bodies, or some parts of them, to generate aerodynamic lift?"

"Correct. Well, did they eliminate such craft from use?"

And Matthew saw the point at once. "Indeed, yes, Colonel Campbell," he said. "And if your next question is what do they use instead: well, they *don't* use gravitomagnetic transports as a rule. They transport everything by rail, in underground evacuated tubes. The UN built several, following, as nearly as possible, great circle courses."

"As I thought!" cried Colonel Campbell, warming to his subject. "And where do those tubes run?"

"The longest, and perhaps the backbone of the tube system, runs from Rio de Janeiro in Amazonía, then northwest toward the narrow strip connecting that continent with the larger continent of Aztlán, and from there through Antigua (which they once called Guatemala Ciudad, as I understand), Mexico Ciudad..."

"And then through Los Angeles, San Francisco, Portland, Vancouver, Juneau, and from there across the Bering Straits and through Siberia, Manchuria, and then…where?"

"To Ho Chi Minh City in Vietnam, by way of Beijing," said Matthew. "Branch lines from this line serve all the major population centers. The one of your former States that this network does not serve is Hawaii—which the UN reorganized as the Kingdom of Hawaii, transformed to *status quo ante* the arrival of the first American settlers, and left to its own devices."

"Commandant, do you understand the opportunity we have?" said Campbell. "Can you imagine what we could do if we tapped into those tubes, anywhere between Los Angeles and San Francisco? We'd have instant access to all their population centers! But to do that without detection, we need to distract the enemy. And that's easiest done at Kings Dominion. We stage an overland assault, capture it, and defend it with what looks like everything we've got. Of course, we really mean to abandon it. But while we're doing that, we press toward our underground objective—which is probably at or near our level anyway—and, well, I'll let you guess what we do next."

"Now you're talking about an even more hair-raising campaign," said the G-3. "You're saying to expand this to more than just a brief expedition. And to begin with, you want to capture this amusement park with just *one* squad?"

"Yes," said Matthew. "The pedophile game preserves were each better defended than Kings Dominion will be. Strictly speaking, I captured the Lucketts preserve with the aid of two archers."

"Yes, I heard about *Private* Zachary Radner," said the Operations Director drily. "But you won't have him at your side this time."

"Why not?"

The G-3 almost choked on his coffee. "Are you … *serious!?*" he blurted.

"I am," said Matthew.

*"But he's just a kid!!"*

"This *kid* has accepted Marine training." Out of the corner of his eye, Matthew noticed Colonel Campbell nodding and the Commandant smiling. "Besides, I want him. And several of the others."

*"You want to use kids on a major military operation!? What the … for!?"*

Calmly, Matthew explained: "To interrogate Captain Coleman effectively, I will need a staff of adolescents, or pre-adolescents, uniformed as twenty-first-century Cedar Fair ride operators and attendants. And those 'kids' would be just the cadre I need. They might not all have been old enough three hundred eighty years ago. But they certainly look it and act it today."

"You'd ask *them* to take part in a thing like that?" asked the G-3. "After all they've been through? To say nothing of their lack of training for an intelligence operation?"

"General, if I may," said *Segen* Cohen. "I think you'll find those kids would jump at the chance. Sweet revenge. And it might give them just the catharsis they need."

"She's right, sir," said Major Jellicoe. "I remember how well some of those kids fought at the Battle of Harper's Ferry. Two of them saved the Commander's life in that engagement."

"Yes, after Commander Morrow here took a fusillade of bullets for one of them," the G-3 answered. "As I recall, that particular kid was standing way out in the open. Bad form, to say the least. And Private Radner didn't even fight at Harper's Ferry."

"But that's only because he was awfully busy doing something else: helping *Segen* Cohen here fly that Elfin VIP transport to deploy my platoons to two other adits. He'll want that catharsis as well as anybody. It's not exactly pleasant to remember this, sir, but I attended some of the courts-martial and treason trials and other criminal trials, at which he and others testified to what they endured."

"And I," said the G-3, "presided over many of those courts-martial, as you know very well. *Segen* Cohen, you were originally a psychiatric nurse. Will you give me your professional opinion that those children will benefit from taking part in this operation?"

"Without hesitation, sir," said Ayelet.

The G-3 paused. Finally, he said, "All right. Against my better judgment, I agree to this plan."

"Good," said the Commandant. "And you and I need to start drawing up plans for a wider assault against the UN. For now: Colonel Campbell, the assault on the KDAM will be your baby. You will co-ordinate with Commander Morrow and his staff."

"And I," said the DNI, "would like an interview with *Private* Radner and anyone else whom you recommend take part in this operation."

"I'll arrange that," said Ayelet.

"But I also want to repeat to you, Commander, my invitation to avail yourself of the services of Vincent Neurological. If they can enhance you—as my nephew thinks highly likely—you're going to need all the enhancement you can get."

"I'll accept your invitation."

"Good. Then I'll leave you other officers to it. I have some reports waiting for my attention."

With that, the Admiral, the Commandant, and the G-3 excused themselves. Colonel Campbell took over the meeting and called it to order. "We will now take up operational planning," he said. "Hospital Corpsman Riley, you're excused—unless you feel you can contribute in any way."

"I took a few shore leaves at Kings Dominion myself, sir," she said. "I'd like to contribute a few mites if I could."

Ayelet smiled. "In my new country," she said, "a *mite* is actually worth something."

"Yes, I've read," said Andrea. "One Troy pennyweight of copper. But yes, if I may remain?"

"I'll vouch for her," said yet another voice: that of Captain Stephen Robinson USMC. He was now the S-2 of the Seventh Cav. "Her service was invaluable during the Lucketts raid, so she definitely knows her stuff. And, for that matter, those kids."

"Then that's settled," said the Colonel. "Let's begin with the lay of the land, as it were."

Matthew called upon one of his favorite sets of "extra circuits" that enabled him to draw free-hand as precisely as a draftsman might draw with table, drafting arm, compasses, and so on. *Remarkable that this society has revived the use of such tools. A good thing,* Matthew thought, *it gives their industries greater precision.* Within five minutes, he produced a full and accurate map of Kings Dominion. This included the backstage area that would be their immediate objective.

Chief Sutton confirmed Matthew's precision. "That gate will yield easily," he said, grinning.

"And my old Recon Platoon can take care of that guard force with no problem," said Captain Robinson.

"I hope," said Colonel Campbell, "that your replacement as leader of that platoon will do half as well as you might have done."

Suddenly Steve Robinson felt a little uncomfortable. "Well, sir," he said, "I'm counting on the new Platoon Sergeant to lead that platoon. I agreed to break in a new warrant officer, under instruction from the Officer Candidate School."

"You're telling me that you're going to send that platoon in, with an untried, not-quite officer, to lead it?"

"Actually, if I may, Colonel," said Matthew, "command of this operation will effectively fall to me. So three points. One, I'm confident that I can handle any senior officer candidate whom the OCS cares to send. Two, as is true in my old service, sergeants have as much to do with leading platoons as their nominal leaders. To this same point, I know Sergeant Jameson from our earlier operation together. I will personally vouch for *his* ability to lead that platoon, with or without a nominal leader. Three—and possibly most important—I know the members of that platoon. That will be vital in bringing this operation off. If I have to go in with an 'untried' platoon leader, with as good a platoon sergeant as Peter Jameson to back him up, that's a small matter."

"You are correct," said Colonel Campbell. "This will be your operation, just as the Lucketts raid was your operation. So let's get down to detailed planning. How do you plan to go in?"

"Through the barrier gate, with Chief Sutton's help, then through the delivery gate here, and then to capture this blockhouse." Matthew pointed to the single blockhouse that, he knew, housed Park Operations, Communications, and First Aid. "That's where the guard force has its headquarters."

"How big a guard force do they have?"

"Six altogether," said Matthew.

"*Six?* That's not even a squad! How do they cover all that terrain?"

"With wireless networked cameras."

"Cluster…! Where's your element of surprise?"

"That's another place where I come in," said Chief Sutton. "I can spoof those cameras to light up their screens with perfectly ordinary and unoccupied vistas. Those guards won't even know we're there until we hit the blockhouse. Piece of cake."

"'Funnel cake,' Chief?" asked Matthew, unable to resist that bit of wry humor.

Major Vincent and Captain Robinson both burst out laughing.

"What's so funny?" asked Campbell.

"Sorry, sir," said Robinson, still smiling. "But 'funnel cake' is a signature Kings Dominion confection. Obviously, Commander Morrow, here, knows the objective very well."

"I take the point," said the Colonel. "Apart from that guard force, do you expect to find anyone else in the park?"

"No, Colonel," said Matthew. "It's off-season, so the guard force will be the only ones present when we make our assault, which I plan to make at two zero hundred hours. By then, the sun should be well set. In the original period during which the park operated, that might not be true this time of year…"

"But since we abandoned Daylight Saving Time, having no use for it in these caverns, that will definitely hold," said Campbell. "What other resources and personnel will you need?"

"If I may suggest," said Matthew, "we'll need at least two autonomous omnibuses. Do you have a cavern under NRD-01-VA-Doswell?"

"We have, if I understand that Nature Reclamation District reference correctly."

"Then let's bring those buses up from there. We'll use that as our primary staging point."

"We can do better than that," said Campbell. "If we start now, then in four weeks, we can bore an adit to pop out not far from that gate. Right into the I-95 depression."

Matthew knew that depression well. In fact, it ran next to the park, on the associates' parking side—right where he would need to be. Remarkable that the depression still remained after all these centuries. Thank lazy UNCLIFOR for that—for though they had torn up the highway, they never filled in the depression. Vincent Tunneling should easily be able to bore a ramp to come out into it. Matthew wouldn't care to drive a bus up the embankment. But one of their AFVs could make it easily, even with one of those buses in tow.

"I'll agree to it," said Matthew. "That will definitely make logistical support easier."

"Now, once you get in, you want to stage a scene, right? That means you'll need a ride crew, and they'll need outfits."

"I'll ask Cedar Fair Properties to help us out," said Matthew. "UNESCO still maintains the old post-exchange-cum-quartermaster store called 'KD Central' in the old Human Resources building, right here, next to the Team Check-in Gate. They'll have most of the uniforms in all the old color schemes. HR will have the equipment for forging authentic-looking employee identification cards and magnetic name tags. I'll also want Cedar Fair to lend us some ride trainers. My younger force needs to operate at least two of the rides in a realistic manner appropriate to the twenty-first century."

"That," said Major Vincent, "will make quite a show. But we have another thing to consider now, don't we?"

"We certainly have," said Major Jellicoe. "Now that we've broached the subject of using this as a diversionary action, we have to defend Kings Dominion. I'm sure those Special Security Forces will respond as fast as they can to take it back, right?"

"Right," said Matthew.

"Then your command will need to mount an effective defense, but not *too* effective—and still manage to evacuate. Quite a tall order, wouldn't you agree?"

"Not necessarily," said Matthew. "Chief Sutton and I could, I'm sure, collaborate on how to create a fully automatic defense and an equally automatic means of recording everything that happens."

"Recording? What's the point of that?"

"Not only recording," said Matthew. "Streaming it out from the communications center. It will have propaganda value."

"To whom?"

"To my Zealots," said Ayelet, now grinning like a she-wolf. "They will definitely draw the moral. But I'd like to suggest something else, and I hope you won't mind."

"Go ahead," asked Jellicoe.

"When I was last in Mara Israel, I had time to examine some of their battlefield weapons. I don't know how to say this, sir, except straight-out, but…"

"I'll say it for you," said Jellicoe. "You're wondering whether the Israelis make better weapons than we do. Well, it's always been an open question, whose weapons would be better. Suppose the three of us—you, Commander Morrow, and I—make some direct side-by-side comparisons. Then we'll select the best weapons we can get from American and Israeli armorers."

"Agreed," said Ayelet.

"Then that pretty well covers it. All that's left are details."

That discussion took another hour, after which the meeting adjourned.

* * *

"I'm starving," said Ayelet when Matthew and his three companions were alone. "Can any of you suggest a good restaurant? Or do they have those here? I've eaten nothing but commissary food since I came back to give my evidence. Good food—better than anything I ate at Bethesda. But still."

"They have restaurants here," said Matthew. "Unlike our old society, these Americans did not get rid of their restaurants. They almost did—during the Coronavirus affair."

"Don't remind me," said Andrea. "I've just got through a lecture on that—about how the infamous Dr. Ottavio Fausto engineered that virus, with help from the Wuhan Institute of Virology. And how half the governors of the original United States accepted his recommendations— with disastrous results. So did the State of Israel—and the result was the Second Shoah. If they, and we, had followed the example of the Swedes, they wouldn't have suffered as they did. As it is, it's a wonder any of their travel service industries survived. It's a wonder *we* survived."

"But of course, these Americans revived their hospitality industry as soon as they established these undergrounds," said Matthew. "And yes, I know a place where we can all go to eat discreetly. In fact, it's a kosher restaurant, too." Out of the corner of his eye, he saw Ayelet's face light up at that prospect. So did Andrea and Barry.

Reaching the restaurant didn't take long, and the restaurateur knew Matthew by reputation, as nearly every American did, especially here in the Cumberland Caverns. Within minutes he had seated the four at a private table; within a few more, they had given their food orders.

As the table waiter left with their orders, Ayelet said, "And to think that these people are all used to waiting for someone to prepare proper food. In the good old United Systems, only the elite eat anything like that. And even that was a compromise by the Five Ladies and the foundation for a New World Community."

"I heard about that, too," said Barry Sutton. "'You will own nothing, and you will be happy,' they said. And they got their wish—but only when the Elves came to this world. I still have trouble wrapping my mind around what the Elves did. I grew up thinking they were *friends* of humanity."

"Which they clearly are not," said Matthew. "Without the Elves, UNCLIFOR could never have prevailed; the Five Ladies would be political also-rans…"

"And ironically, human society would have achieved a lasting prosperity while *still* addressing the environmental concerns they *thought* people were neglecting," Barry finished. "Look at Leon Vincent, whose name is so famous down here. That guy even *believed* their hype about how a 'runaway greenhouse effect' would turn this world into another version of … well, Elfhaven, where the Elves come from, though no one knew it at the time. Leon Vincent changed the world's automotive industry all by himself, producing vehicles that could use the energy they had more efficiently and without polluting the air around them. These Americans *still* use his ideas because they're ideal for this kind of underground living. The Israelis, too. But look at what the Five Ladies nearly did to him. *And* how the Americans took care of him. He wasn't even a natural-born American citizen, and yet these Americans rescued him after Francisca Ordoñez-Pizarro had him thrown into … What was the name of that prison?"

"Sing Sing," said Matthew. "In what is now NRD-01-NY-Ossining. They didn't even retain all the cities in the polity that became Nuevo

Aztlán. Only the academic and major sympathetic administrative centers remained. But enough of that. Barry, how are your studies coming at the Naval Technical School?"

"Fantastic," said Barry. "And thanks for thinking of me for the assault on Kings Dominion and those programs for automated defense and camera feeds. I already know my professors at NTS will be delighted to have me work on that."

"Maybe you'll have another project," said Ayelet. "Vincent Neurological is going to enhance Matthew here. In fact, I think I'll suggest that I second myself to them as a staff nurse. They'll need somebody who knows you."

"Thank you, Ayelet," said Matthew. "I'm sure that will be very helpful."

"While you're getting enhanced," said Barry, "get them to move some of your fighting skill and other routines onto permanent Read-Only Memory chips."

"I'm not sure my body can hold much more."

"Matthew," said Barry, grinning, "you don't know the half of what these people can do. They can pack ten times the information we can into a ROM chip. While you're at it, get a full listing of their *Encyclopedia Patriae*."

"Their equivalent of the *Encyclopedia Galactica*?"

"You got it," said the Chief. "Among other things, it will come with a full set of values for the Seven Constants of the Universe. Remember the trouble I had using one of their multimeters? It's because when they decided to get away from the metric system, or *Système International d'Unités…*"

"Which we now know as *Système Interstellaire*," Matthew said, interrupting.

"Right. Well, these Americans wanted even to get away from using the first units for electrical and magnetic quantities, plus chemical quantities and those having to do with light. So, in addition to going back to the foot, the slug, and the Rankine, for length, mass, and temperature, they *also* redefined the units of electric current, which they call a franklin, after

Benjamin Franklin, plus amount-of-substance and luminous intensity. Ayelet and Andrea, you might as well know: they use a much larger Avogadro number than we're used to. I'm having to learn all new units and variations for physical quantities like electromotive potential—that's voltage—electrical resistance, power, capacitance, inductance, magnetic flux—all across the board. And all new chemical units, too."

"Why'd they bother with all that?" Andrea asked.

"Are you kidding?" said Ayelet. "After the way the UN did them, they'd want no part of the old units."

"But still, electric current and amount-of-substance don't have anything to do with time, length, mass, or temperature."

"Actually," said Barry, "they do. The original definitions the UN used, back before the Great Convention of 2019 that gave us the Seven Constants, derived the last three base units from the first four. The original unit of electric current, the ampere, depended on lengths and forces, expressible in SI units. One mole of a substance was originally its 'formula mass' in grams. In the American Patriotic system, it is the formula mass in drams."

"I see," said Andrea, her face registering her enlightenment. "They did that to maintain coherence."

"Coherence?" asked Matthew. "What's that?"

"Coherence is when you can derive a unit from others without having to use some arbitrary multiplier as a constant for no better reason than the historical. In this case, if the Americans had merely retained the old ampere, mole, and candela, they would have had to use arbitrary constants to bridge the gap between these quantities and the other four fundamental quantities. To avoid that, they created new definitions of current, amount-of-substance, and luminous intensity."

The conversation had to break off then; their food orders had arrived. Even Matthew had ordered a meal. Besides his being able to appreciate taste, he found it much easier to partake of a meal in the presence of others while having a dinner table conversation with them.

As they started to eat, Barry said, "I did notice one thing. Their 'foot' is a lot smaller than our 'meter.' That's quite an exception to our finding that their units are larger than ours."

"Not entirely," Matthew reminded him. "The Rankine is a smaller increment of temperature than the kelvin in SI."

"True. But the length unit might be significant in another way. The meter was originally one-ten-millionth of a half-meridian on Earth. Which, come to think of it, makes it specific *to* Earth—not exactly appropriate for the *United Systems,* is it? I wonder why people missed that."

"That kind of hypocrisy is rampant in the United Nations and Systems," said Ayelet.

"Yes," said Barry slowly, "I can see that. But the point I wanted to make is that the foot derives from the average length of a person's foot. Yours, mine, anyone's. And for that matter, a morgen foot, or a Neo-Inuit foot—just about anybody's average foot—except one species."

"The Elves," said Matthew. "We go right back to them. I wonder what Dr. Girard would say?"

The Chief laughed. "You have to remember, Commander, sir, that we lowly chiefs don't get to speak to Surgeons General, even if they have offices in the same building."

"I might, someday," said Matthew. "Because she was once my ship's chief surgeon."

"Really?" asked Andrea. "Débora Girard was the ship's surgeon on *Bonaventure VI?*"

"Yes," said Matthew. "I'm surprised she didn't intervene in my case."

"Maybe they keep your presence secret from her," said Andrea. "Remember, that was a Special Security Forces operation. And we know how chilling they can be. By the way, this meal tastes very good. Even by the 'real food' standard in this society. Where'd you find this place?"

"After Ayelet introduced me to kosher food—shortly after the Harper's Ferry incident—I made sure to find a restaurant she and I could both enjoy."

"Speaking of enjoyment," said Ayelet, "I can't wait to talk to you about what I have discovered."

"What time is it?" Barry asked abruptly.

"Thirteen-twenty-three hours Central Standard Time—or thirteen-twenty-three Sierra as we say in the Navy."

"Sorry that I have to eat and run," said Barry. "But I should be getting back to the NTS."

"And I have my own school to go to," said Andrea. "Chief Hospital Corpsman's School. They want me to help run Sick Bay on one of their old battle destroyers—USS *Elmo Zumwalt* DDG 1000. A lot of new things to learn." She stood up, as did Barry. "Ayelet, Matthew, it was lovely seeing you again."

"Likewise," said Barry. "Now, where do I 'settle up'?"

"I'll take care of it," said Matthew.

"Maybe someday you can brief me in greater detail on this thing called *money*," said Barry. "These people are like Merchantmen, except a lot more honest. Anyway—permission to leave?"

"Granted," said Matthew.

After Barry and Andrea left, Ayelet smiled. "That was awfully considerate of them, giving us this time together. How've you been, Matthew? I find it so hard to go without seeing you."

"Is that why you volunteered to sign on the Vincent Neurological during my enhancement?"

Ayelet smiled more sheepishly. "You can always see right through me," she said.

"And you," said Matthew, smiling back, "are far more obvious than you know. But that's part of your charm. You told me I was your special friend. Well, the feeling is mutual."

"Thank you," she said. "And that still goes." As if to reinforce the point, she reached across the table and put her hand on his.

* * *

For the next three weeks, Matthew put in full days. Vincent Neurological gave him something very like a private hospital room while they examined him every day. Ayelet did sign on as a staff nurse, an arrangement to which the *Tzahal*—the Israel Defense Forces—readily agreed.

Gradually the examinations gave way to discussions, and after that, some interesting repair sessions and even two neurosurgeries. Among other repairs, Vincent Neurological's engineers followed Barry Sutton's advice to move as many of his capabilities as possible to ROM chips that would hold them, even if the worst happened to his memory. And he did receive the *Encyclopedia Patriae*, in parallel to the *Encyclopedia Galactica* he already had on board. The Library of Congress expressed immediate interest in receiving copies of the Galactic Encyclopedia, for historical curiosity and the other information it held, to which the Americans, being underground, would not have access.

And every late afternoon—for him, neurosurgery was an outpatient procedure—Matthew would talk earnestly with engineers from Vincent Aerospace. They were, of course, most interested in duplicating his body shield—and the Elfin cloaking device from the captured Elfin ambassadorial transport that now rested on the ground above them, still projecting the image of a low hill.

Once, Matthew, Chief Sutton, and Hospital Corpsman Riley traveled to a *very* secret installation, the location of which their hosts did not reveal. There, they saw the two modern ships of the American Navy—USS *Elmo Zumwalt* DDG-1000 and USS *Michael Monsoor* DDG-1001. When he saw these two vessels, with their inward-sloping hull designs, Matthew agreed: these two ships could definitely use the cloaking device and the electromagnetic shield.

And on another occasion, Matthew, Ayelet, and Frank Jellicoe traveled to Mara Israel, bringing several American weapons along and some of the best Marine weapons instructors to test them. The Marines and the IDF held a series of "meets" because all agreed the only way to test battlefield weapons, apart from actual battle, was in competition. To no one's great surprise, the Americans conceded the advantage to the Israelis. Jellicoe ordered three mortars, eight Israeli-made UZI submachine guns, and the latest IMI Negev mounted machine gun from Israel Weapons Industries for use in the upcoming Kings Dominion operation. He also said he would ask the Commandant of Marines to talk to *Rav Aluf* Marcus about active IDF participation in the other operation he was planning, namely, the breach of the Great Spinal Four Bore Line.

And in the evenings, Matthew enjoyed the company of Ayelet Cohen. Part of that included frequent tours of some of the more interesting "attractions" in the caves. These mainly included many museums of art, including life-sized sculpture and statuary, and the natural and political history of the United States of America. Most of these, Matthew's hosts told him, their ancestors had relocated to the Cumberland Caverns from many places above ground where they once stood. Sadly, his hosts told him of incalculable losses of some of those works of art, even more than a decade before the Re-Wilding War had finally broken out. It gave Matthew a fresh appreciation for the value of art.

In the third week, Chief Sutton turned in his greatest "special student projects." These included a routine Matthew could use to crash the gate at Kings Dominion, and the "autonomous television director" and "autonomous company commander" programs he would use to direct the propaganda feeds and automatic defenses once he held Kings Dominion.

In the fourth week, Rear Admiral Vincent asked to see Matthew—and Zach. In private.

"Good news and bad news," he said. "The *good* news is that we do have an upsloping tunnel that opens into the I-95 Valley. Really, every time I think about that, I wonder why a river doesn't run through it."

"Neither source nor adequate depth nor outlet," said Matthew. "And several real rivers cut the depression in several places. In Virginia alone, you have the James, the North and South Anna Rivers, the three tributaries to the Mattaponi—all of which required bridges to cross them, and those bridges are now gone. So—no water channel."

"As may be. Now the bad news. There's something we three have to face right now. You two cannot afford capture. Or rather, *we* cannot afford to allow your capture."

Matthew didn't need the Admiral to tell him why. "Betrayal of information?" he asked.

"Correct. And you each have to face what you will do in that event."

"I will die first," said Zach, lips tight. "I told Commander Morrow that when I first met him."

"That," said Matthew, beginning to feel the odd glow from having a new idea, "might not be necessary." He went on to explain what he had in mind.

The Admiral swallowed hard. "I've often wondered," he said after ten seconds, "how it would feel to send a man into … well, never mind. Who else has to know about this?"

"A very select cadre at Vincent Neurological," said Matthew. "But if I may suggest, you should brief General Levi at Mossad. Before he tries to find out for himself."

"Why the … would he do that?"

Matthew shrugged. "General Levi once shared with me the story of Jonathan Pollard," he said.

Admiral Vincent winced. "You're absolutely right," he said. "That aside, our Israeli friends have a right to know. I'll brief him myself. How about you, young man? Do you understand what you're getting into?"

"Yes, sir," said Zach Radner. "I'll take the risk."

"For the record," the Admiral asked, "why?"

"Anything to help a friend, sir," said Zach. "Or, as in this case, a lot of friends."

* * *

A knock on his door made Matthew look up. Odd. He'd left orders that no one disturb him. He crossed to the hallway door and put his eye to the small eyepiece in the centerline of the door.

Ayelet stood outside. But he could plainly see she was upset. Her hazel eyes were bloodshot, and that raven-black hair he liked so much was matted. Quickly, he opened the door and let her in.

She came in, but did not speak. He reached for her, and she flinched and drew away.

Matthew closed his door. "All right, Ayelet," he said directly. "Just tell me what the problem is."

She didn't answer.

"You must know," said Matthew, "that I will wait as long as I must before you tell me."

She turned and looked at him—just stared, without speaking. And then she did speak—or rather, shouted. "How can you men be such *jerks!?*"

He smiled—and quickly raised a hand to intercept hers gently. "At least you tell me I *am* a man," he said. "I greatly appreciate your regarding me as a man, not a machine."

"Oh, I wish you *were* a machine just now!" cried Ayelet—and she really *was* crying. "Then it wouldn't hurt so much! But you're *not* a machine. You have a man's brain, so you're a man. A man I … I…" She broke off.

"What exactly are you trying to tell me?"

"Oh, as if you didn't know!" she shot back—and now he saw the tears in her eyes. "I'm in love with you. Andrea knew it, that first day. That's how she could goad me into switching you on. And now you've set yourself up so that I might never see you again!"

That made Matthew angry clear through—but not at Ayelet. "Did *Aluf* Levi talk to you?"

"Is *that gonif* involved!?" she fairly shouted. "No wonder the doctors made me sign a Non-Disclosure Agreement!! Oh, Matthew, did you forget that I was on the staff at Vincent Neuro? Do you really think they could keep a secret like that from me? They didn't even try! They told me what they're going to do, and…" And she covered her face with both hands and sobbed.

Matthew had never known the meaning of the word "awkward" before tonight. He said, "Ayelet, you are an officer. You've joined the IDF. You know the risks if I should fall back into enemy hands."

"Oh, how can you be so *cold* about it?"

"That kind of coldness keeps me alive," he said. "It has saved other lives, and missions, and too many to count."

"That's not it, Matthew," she said, lowering her hands. "You can't fool me. You've had some other woman in your life. A woman you lost—and you still feel that loss. I know the signs as well as anyone. But do you have to take your sorrow out on the living? Is that fair?"

He turned to stare directly into her eyes. The tears flowed more freely than ever. And he found himself moved as he had never been before. "Sit down," he finally said.

That seemed to make her angry all over again. "Don't you dare try to con me…"

"Sit down, Ayelet. Please. What I have to tell you, you need to be sitting down to hear. I speak from experience." For that matter, *he* had to sit down to tell it.

She sat at the small table holding the laptop the company had lent him. He sat down next to her, pushing the laptop aside.

"Her name was Natalya Fyodorovna Bronskaya," he began. "I first met her when we were both assigned to PCU-81, the future CV-81, USS *Bonaventure VI*."

"*Bonaventure VI?* Then would that be the Marine Lieutenant who died in action on Rigel g?"

"The same. I was second officer aboard *Bonaventure,* as you know. And she commanded the strike force. Which, again, as you know, is a full company of Marines for ships of that class. The strike force commander is *also* in charge of security for the ship—because when they're not fighting an action on the surface, a ship's Marine strike force doubles as its security force. And, given that role, the strike force CO has access to the 66-1 and other files on nearly everyone aboard.

"And *I,* as second officer, had access to *her* 66-1. Some very interesting information in that file. Do you remember I told you that I once knew a witness to the failure of the Novy Mir colony on Kepler-438 b?"

Ayelet gasped. "She was *there?*" she asked.

"Yes, and she was that witness," said Matthew grimly. "Born on that world, raised on it—and a child of sixteen when the colony degenerated into an orgy of looting, gang warfare—and some other things that Natalya kept hidden behind a privacy block.

"Anyway, USS *Napoléon Bonaparte* drew the assignment to pacify Novy Mir. Her Marine contingent practically rewrote the book on urban ground warfare in that action. They found Natalya, and had more than a little trouble getting her to trust them. She must have made an impression that was at least halfway favorable because they actually sent her to Marine Base Quantico. Where, to the surprise of a lot of people, she enlisted."

"Probably wanting to be as strong and skilled as possible," said Ayelet, who was actually starting to relax—somewhat. "So she could take care of herself. I assume you later found out what else happened to her on Novy Mir?"

"Yes," said Matthew. "Things I'll never tell a living soul."

"You don't have to," said Ayelet, with feeling. "We, psychiatric nursing officers, learn all about Novy Mir as a model for post-traumatic stress disorder. But please—go on."

"She graduated near the top of her class. After three years, she'd made sergeant, then was selected for Officer Candidate School. She finished in six weeks and then, as a fresh second lieutenant, was leading the platoon tasked to guard the Ambassador Extraordinary/Plenipotentiary of the United Systems in his peace negotiations with the Morgenetic Empire. Her file is sketchy on this next point—but you might recall that someone tried to assassinate the Ambassador. She figured it out and stopped it. For that, she received a decoration and a promotion—and her assignment to *Bonaventure VI*, moving up from platoon leader to company commander."

"Quite a service record," said Ayelet. "But how did you two become— do you understand what 'being an item' means?"

"I can guess," said Matthew. "It happened on a shore leave we took together—not at any fleet base, but in a liberty port. Not just any liberty port, either—it was a Merchantmen's world. You understand the sort of establishments the Merchantmen like to build to gain the confidence of United Systems Naval and Marine personnel on shore leave. For reasons I never did learn, she took me to a casino. We didn't gamble, but she did order several rounds of double drinks. I remember getting seriously intoxicated. So did she. The only other thing I remember was that we somehow wound up in bed together."

Ayelet stared back in openmouthed astonishment. Then she said, "I've heard of women trying something like that to get over that kind of trauma," she said. "But this is the limit! I hope you didn't put her on report?"

"And compromise myself?" said Matthew, smiling an ironic smile. "I'll tell you this much, though: she taught me, in that one episode, more about women than I had ever learned before. I'll confess something to you: I was still an adolescent—in fact, I think a pre-adolescent—in an adult body before then. After that, I knew what it felt like to be a man. But she found the episode dreadfully embarrassing. Do you know what she told me the next morning?"

"What?"

"She said, 'About last night—it never happened.'"

"'*Never happened*'?" said Ayelet. "Whom was she kidding? Did she *want* to go on report?"

"For disrespecting a superior?" asked Matthew. "Odd—that never occurred to me."

"Why not?"

"Because the entire wardroom treated me that way. Sure, I had the nominal permanent rank of lieutenant commander. But my fellow officers, I must tell you, did not all treat me as someone having authority over them. The Captain certainly treated me with the respect and the expectations due to and from an officer. But the others … It was almost as if I were their special project."

"Sounds disgustingly condescending," said Ayelet. "No wonder you didn't want to carry the title of *Shofet*. Did you ever get past that condescension?"

"Actually, yes," said Matthew. "The ship went on other missions, and gradually the condescension went away. In fact, I made four very good friends. I won't say that of the Captain—because ship's captains can't afford to be 'friends' with any of their officers. But the exec officer, the ship's surgeon, the ship's psychiatrist, and the engineering officer all became my fast friends.

"Natalya, though, was a special case. We drew another special assignment together—one that the JAG Corps handed to us, in fact. On that occasion, she finally apologized to me.

"Then she said … sorry…" Matthew apologized to Ayelet as tears, coming back afresh, blinded him.

"Take your time," said Ayelet—and not sounding like a psychiatric aide, either. "I told you—I know the signs."

"Thank you. I … I'm all right now. Anyway, she said she still had feelings for me, feelings she hoped I would understand. I didn't, of course—I still had an emotion-blocking chip in my brain. But I could still feel respect, and treat her with the respect she deserved. And that's when she told me those other things she had suffered on Novy Mir."

He paused for fifteen seconds. Then he said, "I'll likely never know why she, herself, had taken such an interest in me. Nor did we ever have time to explore any possibilities. Because—well, you see, Rigel g happened not long afterward. And I … I was not able to mourn her passing for another six years. That's when Dr. Girard and engineer Shaka worked out a plan to remove my emotion-blocking chip. *Then* I could mourn—and I did. Not only losing a friend—but losing an opportunity she and I could never have again."

"You didn't try to drown your sorrow in alcohol, did you?"

"Oh, no," said Matthew. "That would have been impossible. You see, after that shore leave—after she said 'it never happened'—I asked Dr. Girard to enhance my organic intake processors. I was never going to let ethanol, or any other intoxicant, affect me that way again."

"I don't blame you," said Ayelet. "Oh, I can't imagine what you've been through. All your adult life, you've been someone's science project—first this Dr. Frankel, who put you together; then the Naval Academy; then the officers of *Bonaventure VI* and *VII;* then the psych department at

Bethesda—and now those people at Vincent Neurological. And … me. Oh, may the Name help me, I've done it to you, too." And she turned away from him.

"Don't blame yourself for that," he said, turning her back to face him. "After all, I consented to most of it, especially from you. You did me a great favor. I have a high ideal to serve, higher than I've ever had before. And I have you to thank."

"How can you brush it aside so easily?" she asked. "Matthew, there's a human being under that golden shell you wear. I have come to know that man. Sure, you can be hard—when you have to be. But you can also be kind and gentle—and you can enjoy being alive. All those trips we've taken since we came to this underground—I know you enjoyed them as much as I did.

"And I have this horrible feeling that it's not going to end well for you this time."

"Your … concern for me touches me greatly," said Matthew. "You were telling the truth, then."

"Matthew," said Ayelet, "I do not lie about such things. And I will never, never lie to you."

"I thank you for that," he said. "That means more than you know."

She suddenly seized both his hands and held them tightly. "Then know this," she said. "I don't care, just now, about missions, or protocol, or any of it. I care about the man I have come to love. And if it wouldn't break discipline, I would very much like to … to … Oh, please, Matthew, do I have to say it out loud?"

"No," he said. Then he stood up, drawing her up with him.

And at last, she smiled. She was still smiling as she let go of his hands and slowly put her arms around him. Her starting to remove his tunic was all the clue he needed.

Naturally, Ayelet stayed the night. The next morning, they said goodbye to one another. He could see the tears in her eyes again. Just barely—because tears filled his own.

"Thank you—for one thing more," he said.

"What's that?"

"For not telling me 'it never happened.'"

"I would never say a thing like that to you," said Ayelet. "Especially after last night. Oh, Matthew, if you knew how badly I've wanted that experience, you'd probably write me up yourself. And it would have been worth it. If we never see one another again, last night was the most wonderful experience I ever had."

Matthew could only nod. They embraced one last time and then left, each going his and her separate way.

* * *

When Matthew joined the Recon Platoon of the Seventh Cavalry, Sergeant Jameson winked at Matthew. Chief Sutton, who accompanied Matthew, wore a more solemn expression.

# Chapter 3

**"S**o this is Kings Dominion?" asked Jameson. "This place looks dead."

"That's because," said Matthew, "the regular season ended two weeks ago."

"Can anybody see us?"

"No," said Matthew. "The park has cameras to cover every nook and cranny. But UNESCO never extended that to that depressed highway bed, nor even to this area we're in.

"Mr. Walston, are you ready?"

Officer candidate and Chief Warrant Officer (CWO-5) Ben Walston nodded. "Yes, sir," he said. "Sergeant Jameson has the platoon in hand, and I have the battle plan. We'll be ready at H-Hour."

"Good. Then perhaps you will be good enough to sketch it out."

"Fire Team Charlie will go in first, through the delivery gate, and attack the blockhouse from the admin parking lot. Then, once Park Comms is in our hands, we signal Fire Team Delta to bring in the prisoner and escort our 'auxiliaries.' The latter we will process in  the HR section of the KD Central building, and also outfit with uniforms."

"And the prisoner?"

"As ordered, he is under the appropriate conditioning, using a regimen of  phenylcyclohexylpiperidine. Fire Team Delta will use a ketamine injection to sedate him before we bring him into the park. They will also open all the interior pedestrian and vehicular gates so that we can make our way to Intimidator Plaza unimpeded."

Jameson broke into a smile that grew into an ear-to-ear grin. "I can hardly wait to see the look on his face…!"

"I can well imagine," said Matthew. "But what's more important is what I make *him* imagine."

"Will those rides be in operating condition?"

Matthew nodded to Mr. Walston, who said, "They will be, Sergeant. UNESCO makes dry runs with them by way of demonstration. Which, of course, is the main attraction of this park today. If we find anything wrong with the rides we want to use, we get the tools we need from Maintenance. Cedar Fair Entertainment lent us a few ride mechanics for that work if required."

"And the rides we will use?"

"Flight of Fear, Intimidator Three Zero Five, and, if necessary, Delirium and Tumbili."

"And the guards?"

"We send them back to the Doswell Adit on one of those two buses we'll have." Candidate Walston was obviously well-versed.

"How do we treat them?" asked the Sergeant.

"With the customary treatment of prisoners-of-war, of course," said Matthew.

"Our star prisoner isn't exactly getting that kind of treatment."

"But he's more than a prisoner-of-war," Matthew reminded him. "He's a convict."

Jameson swallowed hard. "Don't remind me—sir," he said with feeling.

* * *

The operation went as smoothly as Matthew could have wished. The Park Ops blockhouse yielded easily—and, thanks to the other functions the building served, Matthew's little attack force now had a ready-made dispensary and a comms center.

The first thing Matthew, Chief Sutton, and Warrant Officer Walston did was to see to the preparation of the blockhouse and the administrative parking area to withstand a siege. At Walston's order, Sergeant Jameson selected the best weapons experts in the Recon Platoon to install the big IMI Negev in the comms center, facing outward and ready to fire.

Those same experts then mounted the roof of the long two-story building that flanked one side of International Street. On this side, the ground level featured restaurants and merchandise shops. The second level, with openings only on the rearward or "backstage" side, housed the administrative, training, and operations offices of the live entertainment and rides departments. And on the roof over these offices, the weapons men installed the three mortars. They also, here and in the Canteen, the Maintenance Shop, and KD Central, installed the eight UZI submachine guns. Then, for good measure, they installed eight DEW long guns beside the UZIs. And to all these weapons, except the Negev, they attached automatic systems that would aim and fire them on remote command.

And while the weapons men were doing this, the other members of the Recon Platoon modified all the surveillance cameras to take remote commands from the comms center, and specifically from Barry Sutton's autonomous "television director" program.

As soon as Matthew and Chief Sutton adapted Park Communications for his purposes, Warrant Officer Walston sent the signal to Fire Team Delta. They appeared at daybreak, escorting the two electric buses on loan from Vincent Tunneling. They bore Zach Radner, Tom Jameson, Sandy Rossini, enough of the other older children to make a complete ride crew, and their "training officers." The fire team brought the prisoner in their vehicle—unconscious and sleeping rather uneasily.

Fire Team Delta entered the park and opened the pedestrian gates. Matthew and Walston led the auxiliaries into KD Central. There, they opened the "uniform store" and issued khaki trousers all around—Zach and his crew already had authentic shoes and socks from the era—and the red-and-black short-sleeved tunics of ride crews. Matthew himself donned the white-and-dark-blue uniform emblazoned with SUPERVISOR across the back. Finally, Matthew broke into the HR part of the building, where he found the cameras, old-style printers, and laminators he needed to forge identity cards and magnetic name tags with the original Kings Dominion insignia.

As soon as Fire Team Delta returned, Fire Team Charlie—now wearing some of the uniforms they had stripped from the guards they had captured—entered the park with their prisoner. Walston, who was looking more like officer material with every passing hour, put those guards on the bus and sent it on its way—autonomously—back to the break-out point. The DNI's special SP force would take charge of them.

While Walston took care of that detail, Matthew entered Training Room One and addressed his crew.

"You all received your training, of course," he said. "The time for training is now over. In your vernacular, it is showtime. Are you ready?"

"Yes, sir!" they all said in unison.

"Very well. Now our bus should be back by now—completely autonomous, same as the vehicles to which you might be accustomed. As you can see, our American hosts are at least as advanced as we are, if not more. In fact, they invented autonomous driving before the Great Climate War. We will board the bus so we can be at station by the time the prisoner awakens. Once you take station, remember to act the part, and *do not break character for any reason.* Not without specific direction from myself and myself alone. Do you understand?"

"Yes, sir!"

"Good! Then let's move out."

He led them out of the training room and along the hallways back to the Associate Services part, then outside. The bus, having delivered the other prisoners, had returned. Matthew nodded to Zach, who, as the "crew lead," led the teenagers aboard. Matthew climbed aboard last, then silently signaled the bus to proceed. The bus rolled through the wide-open vehicular gate (which UNESCO normally kept closed for complete verisimilitude). It passed the one-third-height replica of the Eiffel Tower and rolled down the Central Walkway. They passed a large analog clock and turned down Candy Apple Grove toward Jungle X-Pedition. On the way, they saw the tallest and bulkiest pendulum any of them had ever seen—a thick rod, with a disk at one end bearing several seats with ride straps, hanging from a four-legged frame. The gaudy DELIRIUM legend identified it.

The bus passed it, then went under an imitation bamboo arch labeled JUNGLE X-PEDITION. Matthew glanced briefly at the imitation thatched-roof and bamboo buildings to either side, housing restaurants, merchandise shops, and the like. Then, in the distance, he beheld this area's tallest and most complex attraction: a green double track, with bamboo-painted steel joists to support it, that rose straight up, then bent over and described four serpentine loops with three sheer vertical drops. He read the name TUMBILI on a support near the top track. Now *there* was a wild ride, Matthew decided. And aptly named—for the word meant *monkey* in Swahili. Too bad their prisoner wasn't awake to see it.

The bus moved through this area toward a hangar-like building. It sported the emblem of a fictitious agency—Bureau of Paranormal Activity—and the number 18.

When the bus stopped, Zach led the "crew" out and into the building. Matthew got off, then sent the bus back into Jungle X-Pedition, out of sight of this particular complex. Then he walked toward Fire Team Charlie, who were guarding the prisoner.

"How is he?" he asked.

"Just beginning to stir," said Sergeant Jameson.

"Good," said Matthew. "Now send your vehicle out of sight. It's an anachronism here."

It was done just as easily as Matthew had sent the bus away.

Captain Coleman moaned and turned his head.

"Can I help you?" said Matthew, now affecting the tone of a park supervisor as well as the uniform.

"Whuh—where am I"?

"You're outside the Flight of Fear building. And now you're going for a little ride."

"*What!?* You're crazy! I'm not getting on that thing!"

Matthew smiled his most ingratiating smile. "Why, Captain Coleman," he said, "we at Kings Dominion don't like to disappoint a guest. Do we?" He directed that last at Corporal Jameson and Fire Team Charlie, who smiled and shook their heads.

"Come on," said Matthew. "Get him on his feet. A little turn on Flight of Fear will be just the ticket."

They picked him up—gently, as Matthew had trained them—and started to move their prisoner toward the queue railings. As soon as he knew where they were frog-marching him, he balked. "I said, I'm *not going on that thing!*"

"Easy, now," he said—just short of the sign that said FLIGHT OF FEAR SAFETY GUIDE and bore a list of safety rules. The sign sported a "thrill rating" symbol in the upper right-hand corner: two black diamonds, slightly overlapping, with the white number 5 in their center. As if that weren't hint enough, the sign bore this legend under that symbol: AGGRESSIVE THRILL RIDE.

"No!" cried Coleman, now genuinely struggling. The Marines held him firmly and pushed him along. "No! What do you think you're doing!? *Stop!!*" But they would not stop. They kept pushing him along, taking every turn in the back-and-forth serpentine ride queue passageway. Coleman screamed louder than ever as they entered the building and turned toward a stylized mock-up of a flying saucer. Along the way, they passed a poster listing ride statistics, including the maximum speed of the ride, the number of inversions, and the ride time—approximately two minutes.

As the party entered the ride loading station, and the prisoner beheld the ride train waiting for him, he began to plead. "Please don't do this. You can't. This is inhuman. Can't you see I'm panicking? A man can die from panic! Don't put me into that thing! Oh, please! Please! PLEASE!!"

Matthew nodded, and now Sandy, smiling grimly, took over. She and the other "ride attendants" took hold of him, forced him into a seat in the front row, and carefully strapped him in. Then, almost lovingly, Sandy checked the restraint system to ensure he would stay in place.

Now she turned to face Zach, who was standing in the control booth. She raised her right arm, hand doubled into a fist, but with the thumb sticking out instead of tucked in—the "all clear" signal. Zach nodded, inserted an operator's key into the panel before him, and turned it. Matthew couldn't see his feet, but he assumed Zach was fitting his right foot into the "dead-man-switch" pedal. Then he switched on the old-style hard-wired microphone and blew on it. At once, the public-address speakers spoke with the sound of his breath.

"Welcome to Flight of Fear," he said. "Please keep your hands, feet, and all other body parts inside the ride at all times. If you are having any difficulties, please raise your hand, and an attendant will assist you."

"GET ME OUT OF HERE!" cried Coleman. Sandy ignored him.

Zach smiled just as grimly as Sandy had and pressed two buttons on his panel at once.

A recorded voice started a countdown.

"PLEASE! STOP THIS THING! DON'T SEND ME IN THERE!"

The countdown voice continued—then stopped as if in confusion.

And without warning, the ride train shot forward and into the darkness beyond.

"AAAAAAAAAAAAAAAAAAAAAAAAA!!" from the prisoner, who continued to scream as the ride train wound its way along the tracks. Matthew knew from earlier inspections of the ride that it sometimes shot straight up.

He dispatched Fire Team Charlie to the exit room, where he knew the ride would leave the dark part of the hangar. Flight of Fear was unique in Kings Dominion for unloading in a different room.

"Six, this is Charlie," squawked the old-style radio at Matthew's hip.

Matthew picked it up. "Six," he said.

"He's out now," said Jameson's voice. "But he's befouled himself and the seat."

"As I expected," said Matthew. "Break out the rubber gloves. Take him off the train, clean it as we discussed, then send the train back here."

"Ten-four."

Matthew called to Zach. "As soon as that train comes back," he ordered, "go through the full shutdown checklist. Then get yourself and your crew to Intimidator Three Oh Five and open that up."

"Ten-four," said Zach with a jaunty wave of his hand.

Matthew left Zach and the crew to themselves while quickly making his way to the exit room. There, he found the prisoner—and caught the sharp, pungent odor. He hoped Fire Team Charlie were wearing their nose filters. From the looks on their faces, they were.

"Now," he said to the prisoner without preamble, "are you ready to talk?"

"Go to hell!" said Coleman, though a little less sullenly than Matthew remembered.

"I thought people like you always said there wasn't any such place," said Matthew. "Never mind. We'd like to recommend another ride for you. This one is the tallest ride in our park and a heavy favorite among our guests."

"NO! NOT THE INTIMIDATOR! NO! NO!!"

"Yes," said Matthew, smiling again. He nodded to the fire team, who took hold of the prisoner and marched him out of the building and into the open air.

With Matthew leading the way, the team half pushed, half dragged the prisoner toward a tunnel-like passageway into another open-air space. There, the face and some biographical information on one Dale Earnhardt, a stock car race driver who had died on the track, greeted them.

And beyond—there it was! Exactly as he remembered it from when he had first seen it as a boy of four. The bright red-and-yellow track reared up before them: a forty-five-degree ramp rising 305 feet into a bright, sunny sky, then plunging earthward at an 85-degree angle. But *had* he seen it at that age? He must have—and forgotten that, with much else, long ago. He didn't trouble himself with why he should be remembering things like that today. They had happened, but that could wait.

Coleman took one look at that tall ramp, and his eyes bulged anew.

Further along, another "Safety Guide" with that same double-diamond symbol greeted them. Next to it, in a plastic sleeve, stood a multi-colored pole. Tom Jameson got up from the chair in which he was sitting, took out the pole, and "measured" the prisoner with it. "Good to go," he said with a smile as the fire team dragged Coleman along another queue passage. Toward the end, they carried him past a fork labeled "Front row only."

"PLEASE! DON'T DO THIS! I'LL DO ANYTHING! DON'T MAKE ME GO UP THERE! NO! NO! NOOOOOOOOOOOOOOOOOOOAAAAAAAAAAAAAUUUUUG HHHH!"

Again Sandy waited for them, with four of the burliest of his former victims. Together they wrestled and fastened him into a seat in the front row of the first car on the train—with the bulging imitation engine compartment with the number 3 painted on its crown.

Once again, Sandy raised her arm in the "all clear" signal. Again Zach pressed a button to start a canned spiel about ride safety. As Coleman continued to scream, Zach clearly placed his feet into a dead-man-switch stirrup, then pressed two buttons on his console at once.

"GENTLEMEN! START YOUR ENGINES!" shouted a man's first-tenor voice.

"NOOOOOOOOOOOOOOOO!!"

A motorized set of catches caught the ride train and hauled it up the ramp.

Coleman alternately cursed and pleaded all the way up.

The ride train topped the rise—and started down the chute.

"AAAAAAAAAAAAAAAAAHHH! HWAH! HWAH! HWAH! HWAAAAAAAAHHHHH!!"

The ride train plummeted down the track, then abruptly turned level and to the right, racing along the track at ninety miles per hour.

As the ride train rode up, then down, then made abrupt turns and shot through *very* tight spaces, Coleman never stopped screaming. He was still screaming as the train made one last turn, past a strobe light mounted toward him on the left side of the track. Finally, after making one brief dip, the train leveled out and slowed to a stop. Then it returned to the station.

Matthew said not a word. Sandy and the crew unfastened the prisoner. Fire Team Charlie, having crossed to the other side, dragged the prisoner along the exit ramp.

The ramp led under the track, then to the small photo shack at its end. Matthew preceded the prisoner into this shack, then walked behind its counter. Again as he'd ordered, the consoles were already active. And an overhead display depicted the prisoner, mouth wide-open and eyes bulging in terror, in his front-row seat.

"Here's your photograph," said Matthew. "We thank you for coming to Kings Dominion. Ride on." Then, dropping the pretense again, he asked, "Now—are you ready to talk? Or shall I have this team take you to Delirium? Or perhaps Tumbili, which is on the way—or Berserker." Then he lowered his voice further, saying, "Or maybe I'll take you to Xtreme Sky Flyer, suit you up, rig you, and haul you up twelve deck levels to the top of one of its two stationary cranes. Of course, it's actually seventeen deck levels in the original dimensions of buildings of the period. And you can hang up there until you finally pull the ripcord to send you swinging out over Candy Apple Grove—if you don't freeze, in which case, you can hang up there forever, for all I care."

"NO! I'LL TALK! I'LL TELL YOU ANYTHING YOU WANT TO KNOW! JUST—PLEASE—NO MORE!!" And with that, Coleman began to sob.

"Take him back to Central," said Matthew to Sergeant Jameson, "and get him cleaned up."

"Aye-aye, sir," said the Sergeant. He and Fire Team Charlie took the prisoner away.

Now Matthew addressed his "ride crew." "Ladies and gentlemen," he said, "your performance has been exemplary, and you have earned a rich reward this day." Then, beckoning to the actual Cedar Fair personnel who had come along on this mission, he said, "You know the sorts of attractions that made this place famous. These people have kindly consented to give you a proper tour."

A supervisor in the more modern Cedar Fair uniform stepped forward—and smiled broadly. "Who's ready for some fun?" he asked in a hearty voice.

Everyone in Matthew's ride crew shouted at once.

All but one. Sandy Rossini got that impish smile on her face again.

"What?" asked the supervisor.

Now Sandy grinned openly. "I want to see *him* on The Intimidator!" she said and pointed straight at Matthew.

Matthew was astounded. He knew Sandy would be a handful—she almost threatened him with insubordination on the way into Harper's Ferry. But this…!

"What do you say, Commander?" he heard someone ask.

What *could* he say? In truth, he didn't know what to expect. Calculating derivatives of distance with respect to time, to the first (speed), second (acceleration), and even third level, including acceleration due to gravity, was one thing. But to *experience* it…! For a fleeting moment, he felt the same fear Captain Coleman must have felt.

But if he said "No," he would lose the command presence he had carefully built with these children.

And then that memory came back. Matthew, as a boy of four, staring at this very ride and silently swearing that, someday, he would ride it, though the laws of his society strictly forbade it.

In the end, this decided the issue for him. "I'll do it," he said. And he led the way back past the Dale Earnhardt shrine and into the queue partitions, finally taking the Front Row Only path. Abruptly, another member of his crew broke from the crowd and stood to join him. Tom Jameson.

Matthew said nothing. He silently nodded to the boy and walked on. The others took the other queue path for positions further back.

The supervisor and two other members of the actual ride crew crossed the track. One of his companions disappeared into the control booth. The other stood ready to strap Matthew and his fellow passengers in, along with a crew member who had *not* crossed the track.

As he took the left seat in the front row of the first car—the seat Captain Coleman had taken, now freshly cleaned and sanitized—he waited for young Tom to join him. Then he whispered to him, "Why did you do that?"

"An officer shouldn't go anywhere without an escort, sir," he said.

Matthew said nothing more as he reached up and hauled down the swinging chest pads, thrusting his head through them, locking the assembly down, and securing it with a single canvas strap. Out of the corner of his eye, he saw Tom doing the same thing. The two ride operators then made their way down the length of the train, checking restraint systems for all aboard—for Matthew had sensed rather than watched as the train filled up with the members of his own "crew."

Now the two operators raised their fists, thumbs thrust out, to signal readiness.

The supervisor himself took the controls and activated them.

Again that first-tenor voice cried, "GENTLEMEN! START YOUR ENGINES!"

And again, the pull chain caught the train and hauled it up. Matthew leaned back, resting his head on the headrest behind him. Out of habit, he calculated precisely how many seconds must pass until, at last, the train came to the rise ... and topped it.

He found himself staring down a nearly vertical section of track.

The train started down.

And Matthew did not find this frightening at all. Nor boring. He found it exhilarating.

Never before had he fully appreciated speed. Gravity compensators were crutches! *All* flying cadets should experience powered flight without them! It would make them better pilots, Matthew was sure. And a ride like this would be the perfect introduction to the sensations of speed and acceleration.

As the train flared out at the bottom—again, to calculate speed, and compare it to the rate of the train on its last run, was one thing. To feel it take the sharply inclined turn, then make a steep climb, then descend so rapidly he was almost in a *weightless* condition…! This was what flying ought to be about. He had known it when he first watched this train make a dry run decades ago.

A right turn, then a left turn through a space so tight he instinctively leaned over. What a powerful thing instinct was! Even his calculation that he would easily fit through the space could not stop it. Then another abrupt right turn. Then up a hill, then down, then up and to the right—and past that strobe light, which went off several times, taking everyone's picture. Then one portside dip and the train righted itself—and stopped.

Everyone aboard except Matthew gave a loud cheer as the train started again and returned to the loading station. And he knew two things. First, he had fulfilled a dream he had long forgotten. And second, he now commanded more respect from these adolescents than he had before.

Before leaving The Intimidator, he made one last visit to Dale Earnhardt's shrine. There, he touched the face of the portrait and held that pose for five seconds. The supervisor, wearing a "Team Member" hat, doffed it and bowed his head. He obviously knew when someone was paying last respects.

Matthew and his crew then tried Flight of Fear and The Dominator. Now *there* was a real flying cadet's ride: a positive loop, an Immelman turn, a right bank, then a split-S, and two barrel rolls, before the ride finished with a sharp bank to the left, then to the right, before leveling off and returning to base. Then Delirium, then Tumbili, then a truly wild ride called "Twisted Timbers." That's when Zach and Tom expressed interest in the Xtreme Sky Flyer: a tall metal arch, two cranes, and a cable assembly designed to haul a person or group 240 feet into the air, then drop them so they would swing to six feet above ground, then up almost as high. Only a few dared that attraction—but those who did indicated they might want to join the Marines and become paratroopers.

* * *

"Is everything in order, Mr. Walston?" Matthew asked upon arrival at KD Central.

"Yes, sir. The showers in the men's head did need repair—but per your suggestion, we took some tools from Maintenance and repaired them."

"I see you know how to get things done. Well done. The prisoner will need cleaning up. See to it."

"Yes, sir," said Walston, saluting. Now Squad Two (consisting of Fire Teams Charlie and Delta) brought their quivering, sobbing prisoner to that shower, together with a change of clothing, and cleaned him up. As they did so, Zach Radner let himself into the costume shop in that part of the building.

"It's a shame we couldn't have scared him with some of these outfits," said Zach, grinning. This was the most garish wardrobe Matthew had ever seen. "What did they do with these?" Zach asked.

"In that era," said Matthew, "they celebrated a holiday called Halloween—or Samhain as the ancient Druids in England once called it. In 2001 CE, Kings Dominion inaugurated a celebration of their own, which they called Haunt. The entertainment department set up several scare scenarios, in blockhouses or other buildings or sections, along with several walkways. You might have seen a set of vertical pipes along the Administrative Parking Lot. That's another of the mazes, or at least how it looks when they don't fasten dry corn shucks to those pipes to simulate a cornfield.

"I thought about that, but we wouldn't have had time to do that kind of job properly. I needed something that would scare him right away. The roller coasters did the job."

Just then, Sergeant Jameson emerged from the head with the squad. They half-carried the prisoner, now with his hair still damp but no longer exuding that sewage smell.

Matthew led him to Training Room One in HR, where he held the interrogation. During the entire session, Matthew sat where he could watch prisoner and interrogator. Warrant Officer Walston sat next to him. He made sure to record everything in his secondary memory.

Zach opened the session with questions about the pedophile network—how it spotted and acquired prospects, how many camps existed, and how many children had gone into it (thousands over the last thirty years) and come out of it (none). Sandy questioned him further about the kind of VIPs who would visit the camp. The Elfin Ambassador turned out to have been a regular visitor since he took over the post more than fifteen years ago.

Sergeant Jameson questioned the prisoner next. It didn't take the non-com long to confirm what they all suspected—first, about American complicity with the pedophile network, next, about a "reservation" for Americans on Botany Bay.

The time had now come for the last part of the interrogation. "Mr. Walston," he said, "your conduct has been exemplary, and I will gladly recommend that you continue your officer training. But I must ask that you leave me alone with the prisoner at this time."

"Security, sir?" Walston asked.

"Semantics being what they are, yes, security considerations definitely apply here."

"Understood. Your orders?"

"Take charge of your platoon. I will have further orders for you after I finish here."

Walston saluted smartly and led everyone else out.

That left Matthew alone with Coleman.

"Captain Coleman," he said, resuming his seat behind the table, "who is Captain Folsom?"

"Who?"

"Don't play coy with me, Captain, or I'll have you winched up on Xtreme Sky Flyer."

"No!" said Coleman, the horror returning afresh. He took a deep breath, then went on: "Her full name with titles is Brianna Belle Folsom, MD, PhD. She is Chief of Psychiatry at Botany Bay."

That was the control question since Matthew already knew her identity. "And why," he asked, "would she take a 'special interest' in me?"

"Because she has another specimen just like you on her research ward."

"What do you mean 'specimen'? Who?"

The prisoner sat mute.

"Tell me what I want to know," said Matthew, "or I will use certain means I have discovered here to create in your mind a living nightmare from which you will never, *ever*, wake up. *Who is the other living specimen on her ward!?*"

"Lieutenant Natalya Fyodorovna Bronskaya, USM, late of *Bonaventure VI.*"

Matthew shot to his feet so fast his chair slid away from him and struck the far wall behind him. He stood where he was for about five seconds—and found himself counting every clock cycle. Then, very slowly, making every effort to keep himself in control, he walked around the table and toward the seated prisoner. Placing his right hand feather-lightly on the prisoner's left shoulder, with thumb and forefinger bracketing his neck, he almost whispered, "Tell me right now why I should not snap your neck clean, Captain."

"I'm telling you the absolute truth, Commander. Lieutenant Natalya Fyodorovna Bronskaya is on Botany Bay—and she is now just like you."

"Lieutenant Bronskaya," said Matthew, still struggling with his emotions, "died twenty-five years ago, in action on planet Rigel g."

"That's what you thought," said Coleman, a hint of his earlier triumphal insolence beginning to return. "In fact, the then Chief of Psychiatry was seeking to replicate Dr. Erich Frankel's experiments. Dr. Folsom did her fellowship in psychiatry with Dr. Tildblad, until he died. That was five years ago. She inherited the project and has carried it on ever since."

"And you know this—how?" asked Matthew, doing his best to feign mystified disinterest.

"What do you mean, how?" asked Coleman. "I was stationed there!"

"As Dr. Folsom's security officer?"

"Congratulations! You just won the kewpie doll."

Another confirmation of truthfulness. "All right, I'll bite," said Matthew, taking his hand off the prisoner's shoulder. "Who am I to Dr. Folsom that she would find me so interesting?"

"You might be the one person who can bring Lieutenant Bronskaya out of her blue funk."

"And what do you mean by that?"

"I mean," said Coleman, "that she has been—I believe Dr. Folsom used the word *catatonic* to describe her. She will neither move nor speak."

This had to stop now, or he would kill the prisoner out-of-hand—and he could still be useful. "Thank you, Captain Coleman," he said with an effort. "That will be all for today. Mr. Walston!"

The young warrant officer re-entered the room.

"Here are your orders," said Matthew. "First: send Privates Radner, Rossini, and Jameson to this room; I shall have further orders for them. Second, take charge of the prisoner. Have Fire Team Charlie bring him back below using the new adit we dug. Third: send that Doctor in here to back up my memory. Fourth: get a message out to the DNI that he should imprison Captain Coleman *securely*, and to expect more information from human sources. Fifth: send the doctor and Privates Rossini and Jameson back below with orders to proceed by the best available transport to the Cumberland Caverns for a full debriefing. And last: get yourself, your platoon, every auxiliary except Private Radner, and all our vehicles back below, using the new adit and the Doswell Adit at your discretion. Report back to OCS. I will send a briefing of my own to give you a definite up check. Do you understand all that?"

"Yes, sir," Walston said. "Do I take it you will not be returning below?"

"You do indeed," said Matthew. "This operation has taken a new direction. Everything will be on a need-to-know basis."

The officer candidate nodded. "Yes, sir," he said more soberly. He saluted and left the room.

Zach, Sandy, and Tom came back into the room while Fire Team Charlie took away the prisoner.

"Sandy and Tom," Matthew said, "you will return with the other auxiliaries. Ask to speak with the DNI—and with *Segen* Cohen. Tell them both everything you saw and heard today. *Everything.* Then mention the name Natalya Fyodorovna Bronskaya. *Segen* Cohen will recognize that name. Tell her I'm going to give a propaganda show from here. She'll understand what I mean by that. Do you understand what I want you to say?"

"Yes, sir," said Sandy. Tom nodded.

"Good," he said. "Find Mr. Walston. He knows what to do."

The two filed out, leaving Zach and Matthew alone.

Zach waited for Matthew to speak. Seeing that, Matthew said, "I thank you for your courtesy to me right now. I'm sure you understand that I am clearing for action, as we used to say in the Navy."

"Yes, sir," said Zach. "It makes perfect sense."

"You should go back with Sandy, Tom, and Corporal Jameson."

"Maybe I should," said Zach. "But I'm not going to. Where you go, I go."

"You do realize that you are volunteering for the most hazardous service you can imagine."

Zach smiled. "Yes, sir," he said. "But I'm now equipped for it, same as you. Besides, while you and Lieutenant Cohen were taking in the historical sights, I was soaking up another kind of history."

"What kind might that be?"

"Popular culture in America before the Re-Wilding," said Zach. "And earlier revolutionary history. Some people smelled the rats long before. Their fellow citizens didn't listen to them then. Maybe we can make a few United Systems subjects listen now."

Matthew opened his mouth—then closed it. There was really nothing more to say. He held out his hand and let Zach take it. He knew that someday he would remember that handshake for the rest of his life, however long—or short—it might be.

Matthew looked up at a knock on the door. He turned and recognized Dr. Harrison.

"Come in, Doctor," he said. "You and I have a last bit of business to transact before you head below."

* * *

"Hello, all you good people of the United Nations of Earth," he began. "I am Lieutenant Commander Matthew Morrow, United Systems Navy. I have something to tell you that I'm sure the authorities will seek to deny.

"Your rulers have been amusing themselves in the most disgusting manner you can imagine. But you don't have to take my word for it. Allow me to introduce to you the actors—and actress—in the little drama that will shortly unfold: Captain Rodney Coleman, United Systems Special Security Forces; Zachary Radner, age sixteen; and Alessandra Rossini, age twelve."

In the communications center at Kings Dominion, Matthew cued up the footage of the interrogations of Captain Coleman by Zach and Sandy. He had already decided *not* to share the interrogations of Coleman by Sergeant Jameson and himself. *That* would stay secret. But the childrens' testimony would be quite enough, especially with other footage he had taken when he had liberated that camp.

"Now that I have your attention," Matthew continued, "maybe you will realize that all is not well in the society in which you live, nor with those who rule over you. And perhaps you should think about your support of yet another war in a far-flung part of the galaxy—a war against some of your friends. Pleasant dreams."

He didn't quite sign off, though he had no more voice or pictures to send. Instead, he sent Barry Sutton's "software update" for all the printers. Every printer so "updated" would itself update others.

The inclusion of the major tranquilizer in printed foodstuffs would stop.

Zach Radner, next to him, said, "Is that it?"

"No," said Matthew. "But we can expect to come under attack soon. Are you ready?"

"Ready in all respects—sir." And to make his point, he hefted his new DEW rifle and checked its charge, safeties, targeting system, and so on. Matthew did the same.

"Are you sure this is the most defensible position?" Zach asked.

"It might not be," said Matthew. "I suspect we could hold out longer in the maintenance shop. But this is the best place from which to send communiques—or a live stream of the battle, from our point of view. And that is precisely what I am going to send."

"They're going to take us, aren't they?"

"Yes. We cannot avoid that. Are you ready to make your speech?"

"You bet. Do you think maybe my parents will see it happening?"

"Since I mentioned your name in the last communique, the chances of that are higher. Not certain, but still—higher."

"That's enough for me," said Zach, a look of determination spreading over his face. Then he turned sober. "Too bad Ayelet—that is, Lieutenant Cohen—can't be here. Now *she* can make a speech."

"No doubt," said Matthew. "But she has her own mission to perform."

Just then, they both heard an explosion out on the employee/delivery road.

"They're here," said Matthew as he switched the camera back on. "This is Matthew Morrow," he began again. "I am speaking to you from the communications center at the Kings Dominion Amusement Museum in NRD-01-VA-Doswell. With me is Zachary Radner, to whom I have already introduced you. The authorities have chosen to attack. Understand this: we will fight to the death.

"My young friend would like at this time to say a few words."

Matthew nodded to Zach, who stepped in front of the camera. "Hello, out there in la-la land," he said contemptuously. "Four hundred thirty years ago, a popular song talked about 'sons and daughters rising up and fighting where we stood still.' And two hundred years before *that*, another song has children swearing to enlist when their elders were no longer around. This is it. Right here in Kings Dominion. I don't expect any of you hearing this to understand one thing of what I'm telling you now. But maybe, in the weeks to come, some small particle of what I'm trying to get through all your thick sheep heads will sink in.

"Copy this, and get this straight: the Elves are not your friends. The United Systems are not your friends. The United *Nations* are not your friends. You saw what some of them did to me. Maybe you didn't wind up in a pedo game preserve with me. But when you really think about it, that's where you are right now.

"For instance: did you know the food you've been eating has been drug-laced for the last fifteen years or longer? You wouldn't notice a thing like that, would you? Put a frog into a stewpot and turn on the heat slow and gradual, and the frog doesn't know he's cooking until he's totally cooked. Well, we've taken care of that, Commander Morrow and I. Don't ask how. Just know this: we fixed the printers for you. They're safe now. And if anyone tries to make them *un*safe, they'll meltdown and be no use to anyone, good or bad.

"But we can't do any more for you than that. *You* need to take back control of your lives—all of you. Just remember: the authorities are not your friends. If they felt they had to drug you, that means they're afraid of you. They might have taken your guns away. As a matter of fact, we think your ancestors just handed them over 380 years ago. But you have them outnumbered. That's why they drugged you. They're not going to do it anymore. So don't *you* keep on drugging *yourselves*."

Another explosion blew a hole in Admin Parking.

"Sorry," said Zach, "but we gotta go. We're gonna be busy here. But you can all watch what your authorities think they can do—and how you can fight back."

Matthew used his interfaces to issue another command. The autonomous television show director program now took over the surveillance cameras. From now on, this program would send the most dramatic feed to the pirate channel that Matthew, with Barry's help, had set up.

A maglev AFV, bristling with SSF, rounded the corner between Maintenance and Central. Or it was doing this until a land mine detonated beneath it and turned it into a fireball. A similar explosion took place in another driveway between Maintenance and the Canteen.

That's when the autonomous company commander program started directing projectile and DEW fire at the approaching SSF troops. Suddenly, the Canteen, Maintenance, and Central buildings became instant pillboxes. Bullets riddled the windows of several offices, shop rooms, and the canteen kitchen. Of course, more SSF started to arrive—and then three mortars opened up from the roofs of the administrative office buildings along International Street.

Zach opened his mouth to speak, but Matthew stopped him with a look. He *did not* want the SSF to get any word that they were fighting against a totally robotized defense force. Let them find that out for themselves—the hard way.

Even the mortars couldn't hold out forever. One by one, the SSF silenced them—at a frightful cost in battle damage. International Street might never again be as attractive as it had been.

Now more SSF began to approach the central blockhouse, this after Maintenance went up in a burst of brick, glass, and flame. Zach used his DEW gun on several SSF.

Then he took hold of the Negev and pressed its triggers. The big gun shattered the window and sent out withering projectile fire into the teeth of the approaching SSF.

"How many do you think they sent against us?" Zach asked.

"Likely a full troop," said Matthew—loudly enough for the microphones to pick up. "Make that a mixed company—infantry and cavalry both."

"Commander," said the boy, "they're getting closer. I don't think we can hold them off anymore."

Matthew tapped into the camera feeds and used them to survey the field. "I agree," he said after a few seconds. Then he caught Zach's eye and gave a significant nod.

Matthew slapped the raised patch on Zach's left shoulder. He felt the large workforce of nanobots disperse immediately. They would execute the capture contingency plan. For himself, Matthew just issued a silent command.

In another five minutes, the Negev was out of ammunition.

Five minutes after that, an SSF sergeant blew off the comms center door.

He then raised what must have been an EMP handgun—and fired.

The EMP charge knocked Matthew off his feet. Then everything went dark.

# Chapter 4

**H**e awoke on a stiff bed—not that its stiffness mattered to him. What mattered more was that this was not a real bed. It was a shelf, hinged at the wall to fold against it. Two heavy chains, at head and foot, fastened to that wall, held the shelf level.

He looked down at himself. Instead of his Naval uniform, he wore a bright orange jumpsuit, almost like a Navy pookie suit. Except this suit bore no accouterments at all, except a number in a dark orange box: 234675643R.

At the wall opposite the bunk stood a desk with a single chair. On this desk rested a crude writing tablet and—wonder of wonders—a graphite stylus. Above the desk hung a large flat viewer.

He eased himself off the bed/shelf and stood on the floor. Then he started taking stock of his surroundings. First, he grasped the viewer and discovered he could swivel it so he could view it from any angle within this room. No, not room. Cell. To his right reared a cinder-block wall with a small window overlooking what must be a large body of water. He reached toward the window and drew back at once from the electromagnetic force field protecting it. What might that body of water be? He couldn't tell— because it was daylight. The force field admitted no outside air, so he couldn't get that kind of fix, either.

Next to the window stood a charging alcove—obviously for him. He knew how to run a simple diagnostic on it. Everything checked out—no, it didn't. Something was a little off. Parts that didn't fit together exactly right, finish that was wearing thin—but how could industrial printers make that kind of mistake? Never mind—they had. Whoever built this alcove improvised it using a printer that was clearly failing. The signs were subtle—but unmistakable.

For that matter, that cinder-block wall was noticeably weaker than it should be. Not weak enough for him to make an escape—well, maybe he could, but the effort would slow him down. But still—the cinder blocks didn't fit together properly. Something was wrong.

In fact, something was wrong with a lot of things. The big monitor didn't *quite* fit in its wall mount. For that matter, someone had been careless in mounting the wall mount. Again, an organic might not notice, but Matthew did. The wall mount wasn't even level, and the swivel action was somehow … binding. What kind of building was he in that someone had been so careless in building it?

Either they didn't notice—or they had given up on improving on fit-and-finish and so on.

He turned around and beheld the open end of the cell. He crossed to it and confirmed that a force field barred this opening, too. Beyond and to either side stretched a hallway—no, a narrow gangway that gave out onto a light well.

The viewer flashed on.

In a fraction of a second, he confirmed the suspicion he had formed about the viewer. The spare furnishings, the writing stylus, and *paper* tablet, a shelf for a bed, and force fields keeping him in—all said one thing: he was a prisoner. And the wall-hanging viewer had no interactive features at all. It was a visual monitor, nothing more.

In the next fraction of a second, he ran a diagnostic over his systems. Again as he suspected, he had no working network interfaces. Whoever took him off *Bonaventure VII* clearly had disabled them.

Lieutenant Commander Matthew Morrow USN came to attention and faced the viewer. Or rather, he faced the small camera and microphone that could transmit any information out.

"Good morning, Commander Morrow," said a voice from two excellent stereophonic speakers. The voice belonged to a woman—human, Caucasoid, wearing long shoulder-length brown hair, and looking at him with nondescript brown eyes. She wore a white smock over a Naval officer's uniform. The partially obscured markings included the eagles of a captain—though not a captain of the line. The Staff of Life made her a medical officer—a very senior medical officer. She sat at a typical senior officer's desk, now holding several slim tablet devices displaying what looked like memoranda. The desk stood slightly off-center in what looked like a typical professional office—for Navy Medical. Except that office was anything but shipshape. Dr. Girard, aboard *Bonaventure VI* and *VII*, had kept a much neater office.

"And how are we this fine morning?" the woman continued in a patronizing tone. All doctors, even Dr. Girard, used first-person plural pronouns when talking to a patient. Matthew had never figured out why or who had started that custom.

He read the nameplate on the desk. Making every effort to be polite, he said, "And good morning to you, too, Dr. Folsom. I am fine, thank you—but I must ask why am I confined here."

"Oh?" she asked, with a quizzical expression and tone.

"I spot an anomaly in Protected Wild Space—roughly within NRD-01-VA-Lucketts. I report it to my commanding officer. And then I find myself subject to arrest and imprisonment, with neither charge nor explanation. And first to greet me is a medical officer, not a security officer. Why?"

"Do you really think," said Dr. Folsom, now beginning to sound a little hard, "that you can convince me that you have *no memory* of the events since your arrest?"

"I don't know what you're talking about, Dr. Folsom," he answered. "I make a report, then a squad wearing totally unfamiliar uniforms literally ambushes me and uses an EMP device to disable me. Then I awaken here. I demand to speak to my commanding officer. Such is my right under…" He continued by quoting article, section and paragraph from the Uniform Code of Military Justice.

"Games, must we, Commander?"

"That, Dr. Folsom, is up to you."

"Now you're being rude," she said in a steely tone. "Kindly remember where you are."

"How can I remember what I do not know? I have only one visual clue to the surroundings of this building, and it is clearly insufficient. I do not even know what planet I am on."

"For your information," she said, now definitely snarling, "you are on Sol d. To be more specific, you are in the Botany Bay Psychiatric Institute.

I am Captain Brianna Belle Folsom, MD, PhD—your chief physician, psychiatrist, and, as far as you're concerned, warden. You are in my hands now, and what I say, goes. Do I make myself clear?"

"My demand to speak to my commanding officer still stands."

"Your original commanding officer was relieved of his command immediately following your arrest. He subsequently retired at the rank of rear Admiral. I understand that he returned to his family vineyards in Bordeaux, in the French Republic. Why the UN will let a retired officer continue to make wine by such old-fashioned methods, for the benefit of lofty VIPs, doesn't matter here. What matters is that you have no commanding officer—other than myself. *Now,* do you get the picture?"

"No."

"I beg your pardon?"

"I said, *no,*" said Matthew, raising his voice for the first time. "I think you're lying to me, Dr. Folsom. Captain de Grasse would not behave as you describe."

"Retired Rear Admiral Jacques-Yves de Grasse had no choice in the matter, I assure you," said Dr. Folsom. "This matter was decided at the very highest levels."

"In complete violation of my rights under the UCMJ, if true."

And now Dr. Folsom did the last thing he would have expected. She formed her right hand into a fist and brought it slamming down on her desk. It was a miracle she didn't break several of the display devices before her; as it was, she scattered them and knocked one of them to the floor. "ENOUGH!" she bellowed. "You will start to tell me *right now* why you murdered half a section of Special Security Forces, took two hostages at Bethesda Naval Hospital, assisted an incoming patient at said hospital to escape, killed several hospitalmen in the process, and *then*—the kicker—infected every printer on the planet with a virus we *still* cannot eliminate, that has caused total disruption to food delivery, and followed that up with a lurid propaganda video with the obvious intent of subverting the governments of the United Nations and Systems!"

Was *that* what was wrong with printed construction and other materials? No—she was talking about food printing. Yet another mystery—or an act. "As I said before," he said aloud, "I don't know what you're talking about. And now I know even less."

The monitor abruptly cut to black.

Five minutes passed—during which Matthew acutely felt the loss of his interfaces. He *could not* explain Dr. Folsom's behavior. An interrogation-by-misdirection scenario had rapidly escalated to an uproar. But why?

Then he slowly started to replay the conversation in his secondary memory. Which, he discovered, was completely barren except for the recording he had just made—now how had that happened? That, and his *Encyclopedia Galactica*, current (as far as he could determine), but with a curious … addendum. Something about alternate values of the Seven Constants of the Universe, given in units he did not recognize. "Feet"? "Pounds"? And what was this "Rankine" for temperature? Or the "Elektra," for an electric charge? Whoever heard of units like these?

But that mystery could wait. Carefully, he reviewed the conversation. No clue there. Either she was a *very* accomplished actress or had earlier received a report that angered her clear through. Hostage taking? Multiple murder? Aiding and abetting the escape of a psychiatric patient? Why would he have done any such things? He simply did not know.

Then he concentrated on the best wide-angle view the recording had of the office. Carefully he examined every fixture, every wall hanging, even the memo tablets—wait—memo tablets. Memoranda always carried date stamps. The resolution left much to desire, but maybe he could zoom in on one of those memos and read the date.

And he did. The memo in question was actually an after-action report from something called the "Special Security Forces." So that much of Dr. Folsom's story checked. Now the date…

MJDN 204150.

Dr. Folsom must have staged that. Matthew could not bring himself to believe that *fifteen years had passed* since his arrest aboard *Bonaventure VII*.

All right. He had one way to figure out whether this date was at all correct. But about that method, he would keep scrupulously quiet.

The viewer lit again. It depicted Dr. Folsom at her desk, now considerably neater—in fact, it held none of the memo tablets. What it *did* hold, besides the nameplate, was a digital clock and calendar. The earlier clutter must have buried this. It held the date: MJDN 204153.

"Let's go over this again," said Dr. Folsom, now speaking in a deceptively normal tone. "Just what date do you think this is?"

Well, obviously, she meant the date of his arrest. So he gave that: "Em-jay-dee-en-one-nine-eight-six-seven-four."

"That's a lie," she said. "Look at the date on my desk calendar."

He did. "And I have only your word that that calendar date is correct."

"Why don't you check your *Encyclopedia Galactica?* Surely you know by now that it is fifteen years advanced from that ridiculous date you gave."

Now *there* he had her. "No, it isn't," he said. All perfectly true, except … but he would not mention that exception to Dr. Brianna Folsom.

She sighed. "Very well," she said. "I see that those lazy fools at Bethesda Naval Hospital forgot to update your encyclopedia chipset. But perhaps you can explain these pieces of evidence."

Again she surprised him with her seeming forthrightness—or maybe this was all part of the act. She began with surveillance footage from a place she advertised as the admitting office at Bethesda Naval Hospital. He saw himself clearly directing a battle aimed at freeing someone recently taken into custody. Except Dr. Folsom had clearly lied, or erred, in referring to his two companions as "hostages." For he would never have trusted hostages with DEW and EMP rifles, nor expected them to perform as well as they did. The after-action reports she showed next were at least consistent with the footage.

The next report mystified him. It listed an Elf named Elek, Ambassador from his world to the United Systems, and his VIP transport as "missing." But someone had heavily redacted that report. Or Dr. Folsom wanted it to *look* redacted.

And then the propaganda video she mentioned in their earlier interview. Actually, *two* such videos. In one, he made an announcement—no, wait. That video showed evidence of redaction also. But the footage of him and a sixteen-year-old boy actually defending the communications center at the Kings Dominion Amusement Museum showed no redaction. And something else about that teenager struck him. Something, almost like a command, that said he could and should trust that boy implicitly. He didn't know how he knew, but he knew it as surely as he knew he was alive.

Why would any interrogator, playing a mind game, make redaction part of that game? And who *was* that boy? If he should trust him, then he should recognize him. Yet, he did not. Or did he?

Could Dr. Folsom actually be telling the *truth?* The possibility boggled the mind. And maybe something had happened to him that even Dr. Folsom did not know.

Last of all, she showed the after-action report. He read the casualty figures and damage assessment, and whistled. If they were setting up a kangaroo court-martial, they had built a tremendous body of evidence. According to this, a mixed infantry-cavalry company of these so-called Special Security Forces had suffered *fifty percent casualties in armed effectives* to capture him. Twenty killed, fifty-five wounded. The damage to the museum's International Street would require an industrial printer to repair. Now *that* would be no small thing. And most of the casualties and damage were due to appallingly antique weapons—type redacted. But evidently, even nastier than standard Navy or Marine issue DEW weapons.

"You flatter me, Dr. Folsom," he said at last. "You understand that I still don't believe it."

"It doesn't matter what you believe," she said. "The Judge Advocate General's Office has remanded you to my custody. And here you will stay—for how long, depends on your co-operation. And if you *don't* co-operate, you will stand trial by drumhead court-martial—and that court will have the power to adjudge a penalty of death by dismantlement."

"You know better than that," said Matthew. "I can *demand* trial by a *regular* court-martial, as well, you know. And penalties of death are…"

"You, *Commander*, are in a position to demand *nothing!*" she said, raising her voice again. But instead of blanking out the viewer, she lowered her voice and began again. "See here," she said. "I can make your life as pleasant—or as miserable—as you desire. So you need to get on my good side. And making frivolous demands or other references to your *rights* is *not* the way. Do you understand?"

If he ever hoped to learn the truth of his situation, he would have to play her game. He disliked playing anyone's game on that other person's terms. But she left him no choice.

"Yes," he said. "I understand."

She smiled in satisfaction. "Good," she said. "It's so much better to get along, don't you think?"

"I wouldn't know," said Matthew. The one thing he could never be was obsequious.

"I shouldn't have expected you to know," said Dr. Folsom, "considering your service record. But know this: I am in charge of you now. And unless you want me to see fit to melt you to slag, you will cease this rudeness at once."

"You won't do that in any case," Matthew said as calmly and politely as he could manage. "Logically, you have a use for me in some highly valuable project you are running. Why else did you have someone bring me here and violate several Articles of Military Justice in the process?"

Her eyes narrowed further, and he could almost believe they were smoking toward the end. But then suddenly she started laughing! For at least a full minute, she howled uproariously. Finally, she calmed down and said, "Touché, Commander Morrow. I *do* want you for my latest project. And I *know* you will be quite valuable." Then she dropped her tone down an octave and said, "But I don't discuss things like that over the intercom or any form of communication subject to intercept. So I will send a guard contingent to escort you to my office. I'll want your word of honor that you will make no attempt either to escape, or on my life—or your own."

Matthew took ten seconds to compose a reply. "I will promise only to hear you out," he said. "After that, I will decide what to do long-term."

She took a few seconds to consider that. Then she said, "Your scruples about not lying do you credit. Your stubbornness does not. But I'm confident that, once you hear what I have to tell you, you *will* cooperate."

The screen blanked out again.

Five minutes later, Matthew heard the sound of marching feet. Then a squad—eight-strong—formed outside his cell door. The members of that squad—all-male—wore a black uniform with gold-colored accouterments. They included one corporal, one private-first-class, and three each PV2 and PV1 enlisted. All carried DEW rifles at the ready—except the leader. He carried an obvious EMP projector. Those square plate-like antennae gave it away.

So this is the uniform of the Special Security Forces, Matthew decided. The squad that had arrested him had also worn that uniform.

The corporal stepped forward and touched a pad on the left side of the cell (from Matthew's point of view). The shimmer of the force field vanished.

"Prisoner," barked the corporal, "fall in."

Matthew squared himself and "fell in," in the center of the squad. The corporal barked another order, and the squad moved down the catwalk.

Cells to the right side looked open. But Matthew knew they were not; their shimmering force fields were all active. These cells, furthermore, did not hold ordinary prisoners. Botany Bay was mainly an open-air rehabilitation colony. Most prisoners spent their days on relatively pleasant outdoor duty. Or such had been the case fifteen years ago. In this building and along this corridor, prisoners screamed, cackled, or whistled at him. One or two of them hurled themselves against their force fields as many as three times before desisting.

What kind of institution-within-an-institution is this? Matthew did not consider that question idly. Modern prisons did not feature such violent behavior among their inmates. Or they weren't supposed to.

Matthew had spent his entire career as an officer aboard three ships named *Bonaventure*. The fifth ship of that name had rescued him from the failed Berks World colony. He rose to his present rank of lieutenant commander before posting to the sixth ship in the series. And in his spare time, he studied the careers of the other ships named *Bonaventure* in the past.

In all that review of history, he found nothing—*nothing*—to equal this. The Botany Bay Psychiatric Institute was the only institute of its kind throughout the United Systems. Of course, every Navy ship had a clinical psychologist or psychiatrist on board, to counsel crewmembers or even officers who had trouble coping with the stress of a long-term cruise. The Marines, for their part, had their own customs for "bucking someone up." That aside, Captain Brandon Nelson's CMO aboard *Bonaventure II* once had described the Navy as one big psychiatric experiment. That applied especially to ships in *Bonaventure*'s league—whichever *Bonaventure* one chose to talk about. But *never* did any Navy doctor experiment on his patients as Dr. Folsom seemed to be doing.

Did she have full authorization for such experiments? More to the point: did she deliberately order him down this corridor just to rattle him?

Matthew and his guards passed beyond the more violent of the inmates and came upon four, two to a cell, segregated by gender. These inmates he *did* recognize: Andrew Blakely, Jonathan Polsen, Jennifer Evans, and Katherine Helmsley. The famous Misfits of Station Midgard. He had never met any of them, but he knew their faces from briefings during the Metamorphic War. So this was where the Navy had brought them. Like obsolete but still powerful ordnance. Which was how the United Systems must now regard him. Ordnance. Not a person.

Three of the four gave no sign of recognition or even acknowledgment of existence, of either Matthew or his escort. Jennifer Evans behaved a lot differently. She leaped from her shelf-like bunk and rushed to the force field—and stopped just short, as if from experience. And gasped at him, mouth open in surprise—and what looked like flirtation.

Then the party had turned a corner. Out of the corner of his eye, he saw Miss Evans back away from the force field in obvious disappointment.

Matthew and his escort approached a guard post. The corporal showed an ID to a camera. With a harsh, rasping buzz, an apparent force field flicked off. Matthew (and the SSF contingent) walked through the now-open passageway.

This corridor looked far more pleasant. No force fields here. Obviously, they were now in the administrative wing. About three doors down, he spotted the transparent, labeled wall that must be that of the warden's office. He read the legend:

BRIANNA B. FOLSOM, MD, PhD

MEDICAL DIRECTOR

BOTANY BAY PSYCHIATRIC INSTITUTE

UNITED SYSTEMS MILITARY FORCES

BUREAU OF PRISONS

A single, cold-faced, female chief yeoman—for this must be a Navy wing—rose from her desk. Her face wore an expression as severe as the tight schoolteacher's bun that bound her gray-streaked hair. "Corporal?" she asked in a voice that would match a contralto—if it were at all musical.

"Prisoner 234675643R to report to the Director, as ordered."

For answer, the yeoman touched the screen before her. Dr. Folsom's voice called out, "Yes?"

"The prisoner has arrived, ma'am."

"Send him in."

The yeoman nodded. "The prisoner may proceed." And she touched another place on her screen. Behind her, the door marked PRIVATE unfastened and moved inward on its right-sided hinges.

Matthew walked in and beheld Dr. Folsom, seated at her desk exactly as he remembered from the monitor in his cell. She didn't rise from the desk, but she did smile—a patronizing smile. "Sit down, Commander," he said, gesturing to the single chair in front of the desk. A chair with arms—well, perhaps that was an afterthought.

For want of anything better to do, he took the offered seat.

"I see your facial repair went well," she said.

Now that she mentioned it, he did remember watching the video of his capture. Someone had swung a metal club that had connected squarely with his left temple and torn away a portion of his thin gold-plated "face." Instinctively, he reached up with his left hand and felt the temple. He could detect no damage. "Another thing for which I should take your word, Doctor—or shall I address you as 'Captain'?"

"'Doctor' will do here. Since you insist on playing the retrograde amnesiac, I will tell you that I consider that of no moment. Except to congratulate you on the thoroughness and internal consistency of your imposture. But obviously, your memory, up to the moment of your arrest, remains intact. Or at least that's the impression you are striving to give. So I would expect you to remember a certain name."

"And that would be?"

"Natalya Fyodorovna Bronskaya."

The name struck him as forcefully as an EMP charge would have. He drew his lips tight. "Would you repeat that name?"

"I believe you heard me correctly the first time: Natalya Fyodorovna Bronskaya."

"And just how do you know that name?"

"She's here."

"What kind of sick joke are you telling?" he asked. "Did my commanding officer ship her body here?"

"Who said anything about a body?" she asked, almost cackling. "She's alive."

"That," said Matthew, making every effort to control himself, "is impossible."

"Why impossible?"

"Because I saw her die," he said, deliberately talking like an adult explaining an obvious fact to an obstinate child. He went on to narrate in detail the fateful mission that had claimed his friend's life.

"All right," said Dr. Folsom after he had finished. "Such is the official record, consistent with the logs of *Bonaventure VI* and the reports by Captain de Grasse and Dr. Girard. Now would you like to hear what happened *after* your ship made port?"

"I don't follow."

She grinned—a feral grin. "I think you do, Commander," she said. "But of course, you wouldn't know the details. Know then that Dr. Holger Tildblad, who preceded me in this office, ordered her body sent here—to Botany Bay—and in cryostatic preservation. Upon receipt of the body, Dr. Tildblad ordered the construction of a total-body prosthesis like yours, according to the designs recovered from Dr. Erich Frankel's laboratory on the failed colony of Berks World. The prosthesis differed from yours only in duplicating the body habitus and features of Lieutenant Bronskaya. When the prosthesis was complete, Dr. Tildblad and his team thawed her out, performed an axial craniotomy and spinal section, and extracted the entire central nervous system, plus the eyes, ears, and the endings of all the cranial nerves, except for the vagus and spinal accessory, of which the Frankel prosthesis provides adequate analogues."

"You do realize," said Matthew, who felt his gorge rising—or something equivalent to that, anyway—"that you violated her right of informed consent. Captain de Grasse would surely have informed me of any provision in her living will for any such procedure. He did not. Therefore this Dr. Tildblad stood in complete violation of every rule of medical ethics—"

"Spare me, Commander," she said with a wave of the hand. "Though you occasionally served as some sort of project officer on certain isolated occasions, you have no scientific training and therefore cannot possibly understand the special situations that can arise—"

And now Matthew Morrow did something he had never done in his career. He interrupted a superior officer. "Dr. Folsom," he said, in a thoroughly cool manner, "I must ask *you* to spare *me* the specious attempt to defend an unethical and morally repugnant decision—"

"*Shut up!*"

He stared hard at her. Clearly, he had, as his old friend Engineer Eric Shaka would have said, "struck a nerve." He nodded in grim satisfaction. He had found her weak spot.

At last, she said, "This discussion is getting us nowhere, so I will cut to the chase. Lieutenant Bronskaya is unable—or else refusing—to communicate. Indeed she has spent the last twenty-odd years in a catatonic state. And that's where you come in."

"I?"

"Yes, you. You, of all people, should be able to snap her out of her blue funk. And that is exactly what you are going to do."

The order froze Matthew completely, a state very like the catatonia Dr. Girard once had explained to him. Any organic being would have stayed frozen long enough for Dr. Folsom to notice. Matthew knew better than to let *that* happen to him.

Why did Dr. Folsom give a Merchantman's mite about Natalya's condition? How might Matthew be able to help Natalya? Did Dr. Folsom realize that *two* functioning Frankel cyborgs would prove more than a handful even for a regiment of these Special Security Forces, even if they *all* carried EMP guns? What orders might she have from an even higher authority?

As quickly as he posed the questions to himself, he arrived at an answer Captain de Grasse had used on more than one occasion: *there is not but one way to find out.*

He'd start with something simple. "What makes you think I, more than any other person, could bring Natalya out of her catatonia?" he asked.

"Don't be obtuse, Commander," she said. "There are witnesses to a certain shore leave that preceded the mission you mentioned. To say nothing of Dr. Girard's medical logs that mention her modifying your artificial digestive tract to neutralize intoxicating liquor and other such substances. Why would you even request such a thing? Unless that had happened to you."

"So, besides everything else," he said coldly, "you invaded my medical privacy."

"I repeat: spare me the platitudes. Do you agree, or don't you?"

He suddenly realized that, throughout his career, he had been under surveillance. And why should that be? Because he was special, that's why. And because someone, high in the Admiralty or higher, wanted a company of undefeatable warriors. And had committed the resources to build at least two prototypes. To serve what end? He couldn't begin to guess.

But this much he also realized: *that plan must not come to fruition.* A strike force of soldiers in Frankel prostheses? Even a platoon of them, he knew instinctively, could lay waste to an entire city. Imagine a company—a battalion—a whole *regiment* of such soldiers! This was the stuff of lurid fantasy born of pure power lust. Definitely not "on" for a society that pretended to be peaceful.

Matthew reviewed the full catalog of all the enemies the United Systems had ever had. He could think of no enemy, except maybe the Hive, that would rate this kind of counterattack. And come to think of it, turning a battalion of cyborgs like him on The Hive might prove dangerous. The Hive might turn them, as they tried to turn Matthew when *he* had gone up against them shortly before his arrest. Or else any strike force powerful enough to defeat the Hive might decide to turn on the Admiralty and the United Systems itself.

No—this had to stop. And the only way to stop it was to make revolution. Protesting to higher authority was useless—especially if that higher authority would place someone like Dr. Folsom in a position of authority. But to make that revolution he needed Natalya alive and functioning. Between the two of them, they could do it. They couldn't be dictators, and they couldn't do it all by themselves. But they could inspire others. *That* was the key.

So after a pause that he timed with exquisite care, he said, "I agree."

Dr. Folsom smiled that wickedly cynical smile. "I thought you might," she said, leaning back in her swivel chair. Oh, what a fool she was. She still didn't get it.

"I have certain conditions," he said next. It was a calculated risk. Everything depended on how urgently Dr. Folsom or her superiors needed his help with Natalya.

Dr. Folsom said, "What are they?" Good! Her need *was* urgent. Now to see *how* urgent.

"You have four other inmates, whose insights I will likely find very valuable—and to whom Natalya might respond." He named the Misfits.

"Out of the question."

"Why? I passed them on the gangway on the way to your office. They seem functional enough."

"They are all autistic savants," said Dr. Folsom. "As valuable as they proved to the Intelligence Directorate during the Metamorphic War, they are a positive menace to themselves and to society. Ms. Evans, in particular, can't seem to keep her hands off men. I finally had to make sure to assign all-female details only to handle her."

"Do you want my help, or don't you?"

"Commander Morrow, I told you before that you risk death by dismantlement."

Matthew ignored that—for now. "I repeat," he said, "do you want my help or don't you?"

Dr. Folsom stared at him for five seconds. Her look said *later for you.* Then she said, "Agreed. What else, though I'm afraid to ask?"

"Complete privacy in all my interactions with her, and in my discussions with my staff."

"Of what possible value can that be?"

"Dr. Folsom, you know better than to question the value of privacy between a man and a woman. As for my staff, we cannot plan effectively if we know someone is watching and listening. I've read the logs of the Station Midgard Experiment. Lieutenant Commander Udayan Thakur, as Medical Director on Station Midgard, kept very thorough records. He noted the diagnosis you just gave and emphasized the importance of privacy in all their discussions." And thank God he had done that … wait a minute. *God?* What kind of concept was that? Where had he heard it?

She smiled—or rather, smirked. "I agree to that, too," she said. Of course, Matthew harbored no illusions that he would have the privacy he now demanded. No matter—it would buy him time.

"And obviously I will need a suitable conference room and treatment room. I will gladly share quarters with those four so that our discussions can continue at any hour, day or night."

Now she smirked even more broadly. "I can definitely arrange that," she said.

Matthew nodded. "Then I can begin as soon as all is in readiness."

"Good," she answered. Then she summoned the guards to conduct him back to his cell.

* * *

Matthew abruptly woke up at 0037 hours that night.

Wait a minute. 0037? How did he know? Because the Network Time Protocol server told him.

*What!?*

He shouldn't have his interfaces. He hadn't had them after waking up that day.

*But they had come back.* How?

The reception was terrible, of course. Concrete walls, electromagnetic force fields—all conspired to limit his access. But NTP servers and bridges were more powerful than most.

Instantly he read the date: MJDN 204154.

Was that date correct? Or was this yet another bit of misdirection? Only, how would Dr. Folsom suddenly know how to misdirect him?

He eased himself out of his bunk, not wanting to trigger the lights. He managed to get a glance out the window.

The stars never lied to him. In comparison to the time stamp, their positions in the sky confirmed that the modified Julian day number was, indeed, correct.

So fifteen years *had* passed. And Dr. Folsom had let slip something vital: he had spent most of those fifteen years at Bethesda Naval Hospital. In a medically induced coma.

But how had he gotten his interfaces back so easily? What had the SSF missed when they picked him up? And did this have anything to do with those oddball Seven Constants values?

He suddenly realized he had a craving. Several cravings. He had never had cravings before, of any type; now he did. Why would he suddenly develop the urge to eat sand and metal? This was crazy—but if he didn't satisfy his craving, it would drive him to distraction—as it was already doing. He couldn't isolate the source of the craving. So, for now, he must satisfy it.

He reached for the lip of the metal bunk on which he lay. Carefully he gripped it between thumb and forefinger of his right hand—and tore directly through it. Now he had a flap of jagged metal, still attached to the bunk but in his iron grasp. He started working it, back and forth, back and forth...

And it broke off in his hand. Without the slightest hesitation, he placed it in his mouth. Chewed. Injected an entirely different kind of saliva from his usual custom. It created an odd slurry that, before tonight, he would have spat out as repugnant. Now it tasted almost sweet. And so he swallowed it.

He tore off another flap of metal, next to the notch from the first, and ate that, too.

That quieted the metal craving. The sand would be more difficult.

He looked at the wall next to him. Of course: the wall, made of concrete, would have silica as part of its aggregate mix. Even in this era of industrial printers, Portland cement concrete was a preferred wall material. So this would satisfy his craving for silica, the main ingredient of sand.

So he scratched out a small hollow in the wall, close to the bunk so that maybe a guard wouldn't notice it. He ate two scratchings before that craving quieted also.

Now he felt fatigue such as he had not felt for decades. He went back to sleep.

He awoke at 0700. The first trip he made was to the charging alcove. At first, he could draw only a trickle of charge—but then the alcove let him charge at the full rate. So he took on a full charge within five minutes. With that done, he returned to the bunk. He remembered his odd activities of the night before and was trying to work out a way to conceal them.

Then he froze in place.

He couldn't find the notches he had torn out of the bunk lip the night before. They had vanished as if he'd never made them. But something seemed odd about that lip. He carefully pinched it between thumb and forefinger. *It was noticeably thinner than before.* An organic wouldn't notice it— but he did.

Then he glanced at the wall—and found the secret.

The wall next to the bunk had a moving metallic mass covering it. He reached out to touch it—and it threw a spark at him. Then, as he watched more closely, the mass started to retreat from the wall. And leave a section with no visible sign of the damage he had caused. But he found he could detect a very shallow gradient in the wall, actually indented. Also too shallow for anyone but him to notice.

And then that quivering metallic mass moved directly toward his hand where he touched the wall. He was about to snatch his hand away when some urge—almost a command—told him to freeze. He did, remembering that a similar command had forced its way to his conscious mind when he saw the sixteen-year-old, Zach Radner, in the video footage from Kings Dominion.

The metallic mass moved onto his hand, covering it. Then it moved up his arm, across his chest, up his neck—and into his mouth. He almost started spitting it out, but that same command told him not to. Within minutes, he had somehow swallowed the whole mass, almost without effort.

Only then did he realize what composed that mass. Once, aboard *Bonaventure VI*, a nanobot plague had gotten loose on board. It had taken all of Matthew's own inventiveness, and that of virtually the entire engineering staff, to defeat the plague.

And that's what he had just now taken into his body. An army of nanobots. Had someone implanted them within him to lie dormant until last night? And why?

Fleeting memories crossed his consciousness just then. Someone offering him a beaker of a metallic suspension to swallow. A strikingly beautiful woman with raven-black hair and a warm smile. Then that same woman, on another occasion, locked with him in an intimate embrace. And at last—that boy again at Kings Dominion. Something he'd barely caught while reviewing the video footage. Matthew saw his hand giving the boy a comradely slap on the right shoulder. A calculated slap. Feeling a quivering patch under his hand, a patch that immediately dispersed.

Then it was over. He was standing in a cell—but now knew a lot more. Nanobots, in a large enough force, have the collective intelligence of a domestic cat. These had communicated with him. *We're friends. We're here to help. We fixed your interfaces and can do a lot more.*

*And where did you come from?* he asked silently.

*Sorry. Need-to-know.*

He ran a diagnostic on himself. All in order. But that silent voice communicated with him again: *You're capable of more than that, but it wouldn't show up on your diagnostics. Trust us.*

That would have to do until he solved many more mysteries. But one more question…

*My* Encyclopedia Galactica *seems to have an addendum. May I know what that is?*

*You are equipped to understand a system of measurement that has had many iterations since the ancient Roman Empire. You are likely to meet others on this continent who use a recent iteration of that system. When, and if you meet such people, you'll know.*

*I don't know what you're talking about.*

*Of course, you don't. We can give you this much of a hint: get yourself and Lieutenant Bronskaya out of this installation. Then we can brief you.*

That, Matthew decided, would have to do. He turned around where he stood. The viewer hung where he had found it the day before—with a small camera set in the top edge. And he realized he'd turned his back on that camera at a critical moment. *Dr. Folsom won't know about you, will she?*

*No. We made sure of that.*

Just then, that guard squad came back for him.

The cells that yesterday held the Misfits now stood empty. That could be a good or bad sign—depending on how subtle Dr. Folsom wanted to be.

The guards didn't take him to Dr. Folsom's office. This time they herded him into a lift, which took the whole group of them to the top floor.

The lift doors opened. He found himself at the end of a narrow passageway. The guards parted in an apparent signal to him to leave the lift. He did, and the lift doors closed behind him. He looked for a call button and found none, as he expected.

He turned and started down the passageway. First, he found what looked like living quarters. Five rooms, each with a bunk and a desk and a viewer. All empty. But the sixth room, he knew, lay behind a secure—and opaque—door.

The seventh door led into a conference room, where four people awaited him.

"Commander Morrow, we presume," said the oldest of the four. This man looked to be seventy years old, which fit the records.

"And you," said Matthew, entering and extending his hand, "must be Jonathan Polsen."

"How do you do … oh!" said Jonathan as he took Matthew's hand. "They told us you were metal, but I didn't really believe it. But please, you must let me introduce my friends. Jennifer, this is our project officer, Lieutenant Commander Matthew Morrow."

Jennifer Evans, her face framed in rich red hair that hung to her shoulders, looked at him and smiled. "We've met," she said, extending her own hand. "I hope you'll forgive my earlier display."

"Your reputation precedes you," said Matthew, taking the hand. "And yes, I'll forgive you." These two people, at least, were being truthful—on the surface. But something about Ms. Evans' attitude put him off. She was still flirting with him, though she was not quite as outrageous about it as she had been earlier. And yet … it all seemed … what was the word? Contrived. As if she wanted something.

"Katherine Hensley," said Jonathan again, "do you think you can say hello to Commander Morrow?"

At this, a younger woman, her long blonde hair hanging straight and halfway down her back, stepped forward. But she did not speak. Matthew remembered her file. That file described an extremely shy girl of about ten. Today she would be twenty-five. But she was still as shy and withdrawn as before—no, more so.

"Good morning," he finally said.

She looked up at him, and he, at first, saw fear in her eyes. But fear gave way to curiosity and, at last, to some semblance of trust. She offered her hand, and he shook it as tenderly as he knew how.

"And last of all, Commander," said Jonathan, "may I present Andrew Blakely, who actually is our leader—of a sort."

The younger man—forty years old by the records, having dark hair of medium length, and wearing the same bright orange jumpsuits they all wore—smiled and extended his hand. "Good morning, Commander Morrow," he said. "Now perhaps you can tell us to what we owe the pleasure of this change of routine."

"Quite simply," said Matthew, "Dr. Folsom needs my help. And I, in turn, need yours."

"The Dragon Lady asked *you* for help?" Andrew asked with a sardonic smile. "That, I would have loved to watch."

Matthew launched at once into a briefing about Natalya and what Dr. Folsom expected of him.

"So that explains that extra room," said Andrew. "We saw it when the guards brought us all here. But we can neither get in nor see inside."

"Then that's where they installed her," said Matthew. "Ladies and gentlemen, if you don't mind, let me see her first. Alone."

"Of course, Commander," said Andrew. "We'll wait. We've *been* waiting for more than fifteen years, and we're dying to know what's happening on the outside."

"That," said Matthew, speaking at least partly truthfully, "will have to wait. Now, if you'll excuse me, I have another acquaintance to renew."

All four nodded and found seats at the conference table. Matthew stepped out into the passageway and turned to the one remaining cell, the one with the opaque wall and door. It was latched—but, as he quickly discovered, not locked. As if Dr. Folsom meant for him to puzzle it out.

Which he did, in less than thirty seconds. He took hold of the latch mechanism, pressed in *just so*, and heard a satisfying click. Then he shoved the door aside into a prominent slot in the wall.

Natalya sat on a low-lying bunk along the right-hand wall as he faced in. At least, Matthew reckoned that this was Natalya. Whoever had crafted this body he beheld, had done an excellent job of imitating the body he had last seen. Instantly he recalled standing off to the side, watching while Dr. Girard and her team frantically tried to revive Natalya. Then he recalled her saying that fateful word: "Stop." After so saying, Dr. Girard had allowed Matthew to approach. He had memorized Natalya's round face, her hazel eyes, her red hair hanging just above her shoulders, and her expression of someone who had at last found peace.

Then he recalled his engineer friend, with whom he had held many earnest conversations. One fine day, a dam had broken within his mind. This was after Dr. Girard, with Eric's help, had removed a chip that had blocked his emotional response. The two had speculated endlessly—and in vain—about the purpose of this chip and why Matthew had any such chip in his system. The wardroom was therefore sharply divided on whether to remove the blocking chip and let Matthew "feel" for the first time in his adult life.

In the end, Captain de Grasse made the hard call. *"C'est son droit,"* he said. It is his right.

The first emotion he felt was utter hilarity—at a joke Eric had told him five years before. But the second was appalling grief. For only now was he allowed—or able—to mourn Natalya.

Now, staring at this likeness of a face he had never thought to see again except as a three-dimensional hologram, he felt that grief all over again.

Dr. Folsom had, evidently, spoken at least this much truth. Natalya stared straight ahead, almost without seeing. Her eyes—organic, behind prosthetic lids, like his own—were open. But they were totally vacant of expression. This was not peace. This was total, complete shock.

Matthew decided to try to speak. "Hello, Natalya," he said.

She turned her head and faced him. Her expression did not change— or rather, not so an organic would notice. But he read the *very* subtle changes and knew he was getting through at some level.

"You know who I am," he went on, walking in, closing the door behind him, taking the desk chair, and sitting on it, facing her. "I can guess that your experience has come as a profound shock. You know, of course, that your body is not yours—or at least, not the one with which you were born. I'm afraid I can't help you with any tales of adjustment. Yes, I went through something similar, but my memory of those days has never come back to me. Perhaps you and I can help one another—you to reconnect to the present, and I to reconnect to the past."

Now he saw an ever-so-slight tremor shoot through her.

"Natasha," he said, using the diminutive form of her name, "I know you're trying to reconnect with me. I don't blame you for shutting out Dr. Folsom and the rest of them. But if you and I are to help one another, we need to talk. So please—don't shut *me* out."

She shook again—harder this time.

Now he took a chance. He reached out and took her left hand in his right. "Natalya," he said, "it's me. Matthew Morrow. And you are

Lieutenant Natalya Bronskaya of the United Systems Marines. You were in action on Rigel g. I need an after-action report. Give it to me."

At first, she didn't respond, except that he now detected the fine tremor in her hand. The tremor became more pronounced. Then her fingers closed upon his with a grip that would have crushed an organic's fingers. As it was, it caused him a *very* slight amount of damage, and his nanobots were, he knew, already on the scene. He met her grip, strength for strength. And now her entire prosthetic body was shaking, gently at first, and then with jerks and spasms and short breaths.

Then she half-sobbed, half-howled—a long, drawn-out howl of anguish and outrage.

She let him go and held her hands before her as if they were claws. "Look at me!" she cried. "These hands aren't mine; these arms aren't mine; this *body* isn't mine! *Solkyn syn,* what have these blackguards done!?" Then she looked—really looked—at Matthew. She stopped screaming, but now her eyes were wild. For five seconds, she held her pose. Then she threw her arms around him and held him. Such a grip would have killed an organic. But Matthew sensed no intent to kill, but sheer, abject desperation. "Matthew!" she cried. "I've lost everything! I'm not a woman anymore! I'd rather be dead! Oh, Matthew, why didn't they let me die? Why? I never signed on for anything like this! What am I? A mere shell!" She then lapsed into Russian and spoke too rapidly for Matthew to follow. But her tone betrayed her feelings—outrage … and deep personal despair.

Matthew returned the embrace. "I'm here, Natasha," he said, trying his hardest to be soothing. "I'm here. And though I know you're outraged, you would otherwise be dead—and I am heartily glad to find you alive once more. Let it all out, and then we'll talk about setting it right." He repeated himself in Russian to make sure she could understand at any level.

Natalya sobbed. Loud, wracking, heart-rending sobs burst out from her voice box—and how like her original voice she sounded! As her crying continued without ceasing, the artificial tears started to flow over his own eyes. And he began to shake—with mingled sorrow and outrage at what Dr. Tildblad had done to his friend. What kind of monster did things like this? How clueless could Dr. Folsom, to all outward appearances a woman herself, be about how any woman would feel about a thing like this? No—

not clueless. Uncaring. Matthew did not pretend to know in what cynical world of her own Dr. Folsom lived. This—this woman in a fabricated body shaking and sobbing in his arms—was the real world.

Natalya cried for five minutes more. Then, slowly, her sobs began to subside. At last, she broke the embrace and brought her new body under some semblance of control.

"I'm all right," she said. "I think. And thank you, Matthew. Thank you for not insulting my intelligence by telling me 'everything's going to be all right.'" She smiled a crooked smile and said, "Matthew, I swear to you, that if you had said that to me, I would have knocked your head off."

"I know," he said. "And I couldn't blame you. Nor will I pretend that you—that we—are in good hands. In point of fact, we are not. Something very wrong has happened to our society, if the wrongness wasn't always at the heart of it. We are in the hands of a thoroughly unethical scientist who likes to experiment on her patients. She succeeded to her office from the actual person who did this to you." He was sure Dr. Folsom could hear every word, but right now, he was past caring. *That's for you, witch!* "I told you we would set it right. But to do that, we must work together."

"Why are we here? Why hasn't Captain de Grasse gotten us out of this?"

"Rear Admiral de Grasse has retired to his family vineyard in Bordeaux."

"What do you mean?" she asked. "The Captain wouldn't leave us in the lurch like this!"

"Natasha, I don't know how to tell you this, except straight-out," said Matthew. "No fewer than twenty-two years have passed since last we saw each other on *Bonaventure VI.*"

"*Twenty-two years!?* What … in … space!!"

"Twenty-two years. And as for our former captain, Jacques-Yves de Grasse never impressed me as the kind of officer to question the orders, or the motives, of his higher authorities. He would never regard his superiors, at the highest levels, as his enemies. But that is what they are. I am here, not because the Admiralty asked me politely, but because they placed me under arrest."

"Arrest!? First, you tell me that twenty-two years have passed, and now you tell me the Navy placed you under arrest? What's going on here? This is not the Navy I knew!"

"Let me brief you," he said. And he gave her the best briefing he could, first describing the missions of *Bonaventure VI* and *VII* after her … death. That included the removal of his emotion-blocking chip and his endless speculation as to its initial reason and purpose. At that point, Natalya laid her right index finger over his mouth. He stopped talking and stared at her.

"Matthew," she said, actually smiling a warmer smile, "I have to tell you this, so please don't take this wrong. You were very stiff when we knew each other last. You're not stiff anymore. I'd say that little 'surgery' on you did you a world of good."

"Thank you, Natalya," he said. "That means a lot to me."

"And something else," she said. "When I first met you, you were like a little boy. I wondered about that—wondered so much that I tried to check up on you. I found nothing, of course—ran into blocks that looked a lot thicker than my privacy blocks. And … when I told you before that I didn't want you to talk about it, that was from shame. I felt monumentally ashamed of myself for … for…"

"I know what you mean," he said, reaching out to touch her left hand again. "You don't have to apologize."

"But I do apologize. And you *don't* know what I mean. I wasn't drunk that night. I took a detox pill ahead of time. Even Dr. Girard didn't know a thing about that. I got *you* drunk just to see if I could get some information out of you. What ended up happening between us was more than I bargained for—besides being a stupid, careless, *rotten* thing to do to a fellow officer and utterly unbecoming of one. And it was worse than that! I told you that you were like a little boy. Well, what do you think that made me? A pedophile! If I looked at you funny on shipboard after that, it was because I felt … so … *sick* with myself for what I had done!" Then she smiled more warmly still and said, "But Matthew, I want you to know

... you're not a boy anymore. You're a man. A man I am proud to have known, even as intimately as that. The only thing is ... I'm not the woman you knew before."

"Yes," he said with a smile, "you are."

"Are you sure?" she asked. "Please don't say that to be kind to me."

"Natalya," he said, "right now, I cannot tell you all that I feel for you." To make his point, he pointed at the monitor she had in her room. She looked—and suddenly she growled, then roared. In a flash, she stood up, reached for the middle of the top edge of the monitor, and crushed it. Then she tore the monitor straight off the wall, crashed it to the floor, and ground it to powder beneath her feet.

"There!" she said. "That'll teach some people to watch what they shouldn't!" She clapped her hands together three times to shake the dust off them. Then she smiled. "You were saying?"

When Matthew recovered from his shock, he burst out laughing. Great gouts of laughter poured out of him in a torrent he positively could not stop. Nor did he especially want to stop it.

"What's so funny?" she asked.

*That* penetrated. "Now," he said, grinning, "I *know* it's you. They copied your hair, your face, your voice, and your body. But your brain—*that* they had to transplant, along with much else. Your personality shines through. They didn't—couldn't—duplicate that, nor take it away from you.

"But more than that," he went on more soberly, "I just saw the side of you from whom I need help the most. So you were investigating me that time. Okay. Say that I continued the investigation. And the results might make you furious all over again. I hope they do."

"For goodness' sake, Matthew, what could be worse than ... Oh, Matthew, everything I say is wrong. Please strike that from your memory."

"I can't do that. Nor do I need to—I sympathize. Believe me, I do. And here are the results of my investigation. They didn't do this to either of us out of any misguided notion of kindness. They have—or think they have—a use for people like us—what we have become. And the continued urgency of that use is the one reason they have not killed either of us out-of-hand. The bigger fools they.

"Our superiors, for their own reasons, seek to create a class of ultimate warriors. To deploy against whom, I do not know—yet. Dr. Frankel likely had such a goal in mind when he built me. And I am in deadly earnest about setting things right. I intend to make revolution on this world and throughout the United Systems. *I will not allow the authorities to complete their project and unleash untold death, misery, and destruction on inoffensive targets.* Nor put anyone else through what they separately put us through.

"And I'll tell you something else," he went on, warming to his subject. "I see signs of imminent economic collapse. Little things. Fit-and-finish problems on the bars of our cell, imperfections in the cell walls, that sort of thing. They don't mean much by themselves, but they add up to a much bigger problem. What happened on Novy Mir, the world of your birth, is about to happen again, this time throughout the United Systems. *The printers are breaking down.* When they do, chaos will take over. To forestall that, I need the warrior I came to know—and love—by my side. Between us, we shall be invincible—and we just *might* save the organics from their own follies."

As he kept talking, she smiled more broadly—then bared her teeth. When he spoke that last word, she rushed to embrace him again. This time was different. It was like their first interlude. Except, this time, neither of them were drunk, but clear-headed.

"I see they didn't leave out all the nerves of the skin," she said, smiling wolfishly. "You might be right, after all, Matthew. I hope our ranks won't make *too* much difference."

"No fear of that," said Matthew. "You and I make our own rules now."

"Tell me more," she said. "Bring me up to date. All the way."

Matthew described the Metamorphic War. He told of his arrest and everything he remembered since. Then he talked about things he did *not* remember—yet—but inferred from after-action reports, video footage, and other evidence. "That much, Dr. Folsom and her superiors know or suspect," he concluded. "But now—while we still have time before they come and make repairs to this room..."

"Are you sure we don't have any cameras other than the one I destroyed?"

"If we had, I would have felt their electric and magnetic fields. There's something else you need to know, and now." He explained about his nanobot army. "That army can split into as many teams as you and I or anyone else need. They can make sure you will always be in working order—or make repairs if you suffer damage. I don't know—yet—the full extent of their capabilities. But there's but one way to test them."

"Do it, Matthew," she said. "Give them to me. Just tell me what to do."

"Follow my lead," he said. Then he kissed her, full on the mouth—an open-mouthed kiss that she taught him more than a quarter-century ago. She sealed her lips against his, almost greedily.

Matthew felt the nanobots moving into his mouth, ready to make the jump. Natalya's eyes widened. But Matthew held her tighter. Then her eyes changed—became welcoming.

She broke the embrace first after the transfer was complete. "There," she said, licking her lips in satisfaction. "Now I want the true test. Are you game?"

"Yes," he said, without the slightest hesitation.

She reached for the zipper on the ridiculous jumpsuit he wore and started to unfasten it.

# Chapter 5

**M**atthew burst into the conference room. He carried some links from one of the chains that once held up Natalya's bunk in her cell. He looked for the monitor, found it, and threw a chain link. It flew straight at the tiny camera in the monitor's top edge and shattered it. Matthew, with his electric-field sensors, felt it die.

Andrew, who had been nodding off at the conference table, jerked awake. "Commander Morrow!" he said. "What's going on?"

"Everybody up!" Matthew ordered. "We are getting out of this building, and *right now.*"

Jonathan's eyes widened. "Just like that?" he asked. "But I thought we were going to try to awaken Lieutenant Bronskaya—"

"I have done that," said Matthew. "No time for questions. We have to be out of one of the ventilator ducts before the SSF show up, as they surely will. Miss Evans, I leave Miss Hensley to you. I need you all to follow me *on the double!*"

They did. Matthew led them back into Natalya's room. Natalya waited for them—with the ventilator grille in her hands. Several shards of metal and chunks of concrete lay scattered on the floor. Though not, he saw at once, enough to account for the destroyed grille and widened space. She had clearly been "snacking." *Good.* Her nanobot army would soon be up to full strength.

"Natalya Fyodorovna," said Matthew, "may I present Jennifer Evans, Katherine Hensley, Andrew Blakely, and Jonathan Polson. These four will be our staff."

"This opening is just wide enough for the four of you," Natalya said very quickly. "One at a time. Ladies first." And she braced herself against the wall, hands in the classic stirrup formation.

"Kathy," said Jennifer, "do as the lady says. We have to trust these people."

Katherine leaped into the opening and scampered out of the way. Jennifer, Jonathan, and Andrew formed into a queue to follow her in.

Matthew left them to it and immediately rushed back out into the passageway and into the room he knew they'd assigned him. He threw another chain link at the little camera in his own monitor to disable that. Then he ripped off the ventilator grille, tore a hole big enough for himself, pocketed enough material to "snack" on later, and levered himself in.

He came into a horizontal chase just ahead of Katherine. "Follow," he ordered and turned toward the main chase that ran vertically, parallel to the lift shaft. He could tell that the others were following—and in fact, counted five of them. *Good.* Natalya was bringing up the rear. Matthew was, in effect, leading a squad, with Natalya as the "chaser."

One thing occurred to him. *Am I carrying any kind of homing device?*

The collective voice of his nano-army came back: *You were. Not anymore. Yum, yum.*

He reached the shaft—and discovered that someone had provided it with handholds for maintenance access. They would make an excellent ladder, and he now used them as such.

He painstakingly instructed Katherine on how to use the handholds. Then he started down. All he had to do was get to the main cell block level. There, he could hack into the wireless network and open a few doors. None too soon—he could faintly hear the outraged calls of the SSF squad that must have responded to the monitor blank-outs. *Sorry, Dr. Folsom, but you really should have thought about what I could do. When you invaded the privacy you agreed to grant, you ended all bargains. As I knew you would.*

He found the cellblock level, three levels down. Once there, he felt the network carrier waves wash over him. The access code cracked easily, so he used it to stop all lifts in place and close all heavy doors.

He kicked out a grate that led over the gangway at the cellblock level. Dropping to the gangway, he called out, "Hurry!" He took hold of Katherine and lowered her, gently but quickly, to a solid grate. He did the same with Jennifer, Jonathan, and Andrew. Natalya didn't need any help.

"Someone's behind us," she hissed.

"Good," he said. "Let's you and I prepare to greet him."

Sure enough, an SSF corporal started to emerge from the ventilator opening. Matthew and Natalya reached up, took hold of him, and pulled him out before he could react. Natalya knocked him out while Matthew relieved him of the EMP gun he carried. Next, they knocked out a PFC who thought he could still capture them and acquired a DEW gun. But the third member of the pursuing squad hung back.

"All you SSF still in the shaft," said Matthew, "come out. Now. Or I start shooting at random."

"Oh, yeah?" came a voice from behind and above—probably the squad chaser. "Why don't you come in and get us?"

"Happy to oblige," said Matthew. Natalya gasped, but he was in the duct before she could do more than that. Sure enough, someone took a potshot at him—and instantly regretted it. What had made Matthew take a chance going back into the duct, he didn't know. One of those odd subliminal commands, he shouldn't wonder. What he did know—now—was that he had a body shield.

Now, at last, he remembered. On a mission against Hive raiders, he had picked up that skill while infiltrating a Hive crew. The Hive thought he would betray his friends—because they didn't know what friendship was. That was their fatal weakness. But they had taught him to construct a body shield. *That* was what he had just deployed when the SSF had shot at him.

He took hold of the wounded SSF guard and dragged him out of the duct, taking care to take his gun. Now the rest of the squad followed.

"Your uniforms, ladies and gentlemen," Matthew said without further preamble. Natalya understood at once and began stripping the men. The others followed her lead. Quickly, they stripped their erstwhile pursuers, then tied them up with torn strips of the orange jumpsuits. With eight pursuers, they had enough uniforms to go around for each of them. They let the wounded man keep his uniform, which was, of course, punctured.

Matthew looked at the insignia he wore. Two chevrons. From somewhere came a fleeting memory that he had recently worn another such uniform—with three chevrons, not two. Another mystery for later.

Natalya, wearing the chevron-and-bow of a lance corporal, came up to him. "You don't even have a beam burn," she said. "How did you manage that?"

"Body shield," he said simply. "Long story. I'll brief you later."

Now he turned his attention to the network and issued another silent command.

The restraining force fields for all the cells abruptly shut off.

"Prisoners, fall in!" Matthew ordered.

All the inmates came out of their cells. Two of them—the ones who had tried to rush their transparencies as he passed yesterday—proved a handful. But Natalya, Marine officer that she was, handled them easily.

Matthew and his companions were, of course, armed—though Katherine seemed uncomfortable carrying a weapon. Matthew looked to Jennifer, who smiled and said, "She'll be all right. She and I understand one another." Katherine smiled shyly back at Jennifer.

Matthew nodded and turned back to the other prisoners. "Listen up, people!" he said. "I am Lieutenant Commander Matthew Morrow, United Systems Navy. For now, you all may call me "sir." Follow me out of this building, and you will be free. Follow me further than that, and I will make you part of something much larger. The revolution has begun. Together we will build a society that never again does things like what Doctors Tildblad and Folsom have done to you. Are you with me?"

"Yes, sir!" they all shouted in chorus.

Matthew handed the two remaining guns to the prisoners whom he judged best able to handle them. It was a snap judgment, but it was all he had time to make. Then he gave quick orders to every member of his squad to take a specific position and take charge of a particular group of former inmates. Natalya, of course, would act as the rear guard. Matthew took point and said, "Forward!" and they followed.

When he arrived at the first heavy door, he waited for Andrew and Jonathan to join him. Then he gave it the command to slide aside. Of course, another SSF squad tried to attack. With Matthew's body shield and two DEW guns in practiced hands, the three-man fire team made short work of them. Matthew didn't bother distributing uniforms; he just distributed the guns to eight more prisoners.

One of the burliest of them—six feet tall, broad-shouldered, his red hair cut *very* close to his scalp—asked, "When do we get guns?"

"When I capture a gun worthy of a big, brawny man like yourself," said Matthew, "it's yours."

The burly man grinned at him and said, "Yes, sir."

They went on toward the lift bank—and ran into another squad, aiming a crew-served gun. Matthew and his team didn't give them any chance. They fired and killed them all.

To the burly man who had complained earlier, Matthew said, simply, "Your gun."

The burly man lifted it off its mount and cradled it as any of the rest of them cradled an ordinary DEW gun. "Thank you, sir," he said—and even managed a salute.

Matthew returned it. "What's your name?" he asked.

"Color Sergeant Sean O'Shea, United Systems Marine Corps!"

"And I," said Natalya, "am Lieutenant Natalya Fyodorovna Bronskaya, also of the Marines." As O'Shea managed to salute her in turn, she took stock of the rest of their new followers. "Color Sergeant," she said, "these people obviously look up to you. Take charge of your platoon, Sergeant."

"Yes, *ma'am!*"

"Now," said Matthew, "your orders. Lieutenant Bronskaya and I will take the first of these lifts to ground level. You will defend these lifts and get these people down to that level. Don't worry; I've fixed the call pads for you. I want our entire force at ground level, on the double."

"Yes, sir!"

At that moment, a lift opened its doors. A fire team of SSF started to come out firing. Matthew and Sergeant O'Shea dispatched them all. Matthew roughly hauled out the four members of the team. "Get those guns to people who know how to use them, Sergeant. I'll see you dirtside." And he, Natalya, and his four-member staff boarded the lift.

As the lift suddenly stopped halfway to ground level. Matthew sent orders wirelessly to override the stop order and another command to bring the lift down. When the doors opened, another squad of SSF greeted them. Matthew rushed out, body shield at full strength, firing as he went. Natalya brought up her own weapon and used it to an even more devastating effect. *But of course,* he told himself, *she's a Marine.* Within a minute, every member of that squad lay dead.

As he surveyed his fallen foes, Matthew listened carefully to the sounds his feet made as he walked. The lack of echoes told him he was walking on a solid foundation. Satisfied he was on the ground level, he set about looking for their means of escape.

That's when the building's public-address system came to life. "Matthew Morrow!" shouted a voice he recognized instantly.

"Are you talking to me, Dr. Folsom?" he asked, talking to the air.

"No, I'm talking to your friend, Natalya Bronskaya. *Of course,* I'm talking to you!"

"Well, make it fast because we're in a bit of a rush."

"Oh, you *are!?* Well, we'll see about that. You're in a cul-de-sac; you do know that, don't you?"

"What should that matter?" asked Matthew. "You must know by now that we will go where we please, when we please. You can't stop us. You've already taken several casualties. You'll only take more if you do not simply order your people to step aside. And if you do, it *may* go slightly better for you when you come before the revolutionary tribunal." As he spoke, several loads of inmates joined him. He could tell by feeling the vibrations from the lifts that more were on the way.

"Aren't we getting ahead of ourselves, talking about revolutionary tribunals?" asked Folsom in open sarcasm. Then she snorted. "The idea of *you* making revolution. Truth to tell, you're nothing but an overgrown kid. And an autistic kid, at that!"

"It's a little late to throw such canards at me," said Matthew, "considering the decorations I earned, not to mention the unit citation granted to *Bonaventure VI* while I served aboard her."

"*Mister* Morrow, it's time you learned who and what you are," said Dr. Folsom. "My predecessor had access to the complete records of Dr. Erich Frankel. He describes how he received two boys, aged eleven and twelve, the apparent victims of a traffic accident involving a bus in the Weizenland Tunnel, Schillingstadt Cavern, Cymru Complex, on Berks World. Dr. Frankel, looking for a source of processing power for the android proto-warriors he was building, took a notion of converting his android bodies into total-body prostheses. All he needed were brains. And he took yours for one, and that of one Stefan Weiss for the other. Since, after all, you both 'died' in the same accident, that decision was only logical."

Those names! Weizenland … Schillingstadt … and Cymru. German and Welsh place names. All of it came back to him in a flash. His life—his *organic* life—had ended that fateful day when he was eleven. And Stefan Weiss—yes, he remembered that name. Stefan Weiss had been chasing him—with every other boy in the street tunnel egging him on. Matthew had broken out and headed across Weizenlandavenue, seeing the school bus coming down the street after it had just dropped them off. If he could just get past the bus, he had reasoned, it might buy him some time. But Stefan had been too quick for him. He had bowled him over, and then the bus had struck them both.

Now he said, "If you know about Stefan Weiss, what happened to him?"

"Funny you should ask," said Dr. Folsom—who, now, was almost cackling at him. "He's here now and would be pleased to renew your acquaintance. He's told me all about you. How you bullied everyone in the neighborhood, and he was the only one to stand up to you. How you and he were in that accident because you tackled him in front of that bus. *And* how you opened the airlocks to let all the air out, after some *stupid* argument or other with Dr. Frankel!"

"Lies!" cried Matthew in fresh outrage at events he only now remembered. "All lies! The truth is the exact opposite—and if anyone opened those airlocks, he must have. Not that it matters. By now, I have all my forces assembled. We're getting out of this building, and you and Stefan can swap lurid tales about me all you want until my eventual revolutionary guards arrest you both."

"I don't think so," said a new voice—and not over the intercom.

Matthew whirled toward the lift bank opening. There, before him, stood a man-like creature, slightly taller than he. And Matthew could not mistake his features. Someone had built for him the face Stefan Weiss would have worn as an adult. Blond, curly hair, an almost triangular face— the face of a smirking angel—or demon. Golden skin, of course, like Matthew's own. And his eyes were the same shade of brown Matthew remembered all too well.

Behind him, he heard Katherine gasp in horror. What history did *that* indicate?

Matthew was sure he wore a baleful expression just then. "Maybe I'll arrest you right now, *Scheisskerl.*" he said and raised his EMP gun. This could bring down any cyborg, including Stefan.

And just as quickly, Stefan Weiss batted the gun straight out of his hand. Then he struck Matthew with a blow that sent him flying all the way to the far wall of the lift bank. He felt the wall give slightly as he made a man-sized indent in it.

*A sucker punch.* Typical of Stefan. Matthew tried to recover himself to return to the battle—and found that he could not. In fact, he couldn't do much of anything. Nor see the network, either. He could still see and hear things in the immediate area around him. But that was all.

His nanobots told him: *Multiple connections severed. Your spinal cord has been compromised; working on it.*

Stefan Weiss had retrieved the EMP gun. He raised it…

And Natalya launched herself at Stefan, wrapping arms and legs around him and bowling him over. Again the gun went flying. "Color Sergeant!" she cried. "Get Matthew and all these people out of here! Now!"

"But what about—"

*"GO!!"*

Sergeant O'Shea's voice sounded, snapping out rapid-fire orders.

Hands—gentle and caring hands, four pairs of them—lifted him up. He could render absolutely no assistance. He couldn't even speak—no, wait. Suddenly he could manage a sound, but no more than an inarticulate rasp.

Loud thumps sounded but grew more distant. The owners of those pairs of hands must be carrying him rapidly down the passageway. Then, footsteps, pounding on the deck next to him. Sergeant O'Shea's voice again: "Don't worry, sir. We've got this."

Then the sensation of movement stopped.

"Gangway!" bellowed Sergeant O'Shea. Then again, louder: "I said, *gangway!*"

"Not this time, Sergeant O'Shea," said a man's voice—a threatening voice. "Put down your weapons, and that android you're carrying, and surrender."

"Go … yourself," said the Sergeant.

"Oh-h-h-h," said the other. "You shouldn't have said that…"

*Network connections restored!*

And Matthew could see the network once again. That was all he could see just now, but it was enough. From sensors in the passageway, he made out the section of SSF behind the fugitives, and another section ahead of them, behind closed doors. Beyond *those*, he now saw, lay the landing area and hangars—and freedom, in the form of an LCG. It was likely fully charged and completely space- and airworthy—*if* his forces could reach it.

And in the lift bank, Matthew saw something that made his heart sink—or would have, had he been an organic. Natalya was fighting Stefan—and losing the battle.

Desperately he reached out with his mind, trying to reach her.

And he did! *Natalya! Can you make it?*

*No, Matthew. Get out. He who fights and runs away, and all that.*

*I love you.*

*And I love you, too, Matthew. Now get out while you still can!*

Matthew reached out with his will.

The double doors opened. And behind him, another set of double doors closed.

The SSF Sergeant-in-charge cursed. It was his last curse. Sergeant O'Shea burned a hole in his heart. That was the signal for every other armed effective in Matthew's force to open fire.

Reinforcements were on their way. That is, until Matthew, again through a few silent commands, cut them off.

The fugitive force made it through the doorway, though they suffered five casualties. Other members of the force took their weapons and moved on. As soon as all were through the double doors, Matthew closed them.

*Complete vocal restoration. You may speak.*

"Sergeant!"

"Yes, sir?"

"LCG."

"Ten-four!"

The SSF, or some authority, had thoughtfully provided signs leading to the landing area. All Sergeant O'Shea had to do was follow them, which he did.

When they emerged, everyone could see the LCG standing on one of the pads. Matthew reached out to it and made contact. *Good.* It was completely pre-flighted and armed. A standard-issue SSF model, built for prisoner transport—and carrying DEW cannons and even missiles. Obviously, the SSF, or whoever organized it, feared ordinary people greatly. And maybe with good reason—good enough for Matthew to use. But first, he had to get away from here.

Of course, the ship had a guard force around it and inside it. But those guards always assumed the ship would be friendly. And they always had at their disposal specific systems for neutralizing any insurrection on board.

Matthew concentrated on, for lack of a better phrase, *becoming the ship*. Suddenly, all those anti-insurrection defense systems turned against the guard force. Every guard inside and around the LCG perished. Some of the guards pursuing the fugitives escaped with their lives, but only because they could simply retreat.

"Whoa!" said Sergeant O'Shea, bending over Matthew. "Is that ship safe?"

"For us, yes."

Realization dawned on the Sergeant in a flash. He grinned. "Rog-*er!*" he shouted with glee. Then he raised his voice even more and said, "Everybody aboard the LCG. *On the double!*"

The *ad hoc* squad carrying Matthew now carried him up the boarding ladder built into the stern landing leg. Then they moved quickly to the flight-deck ladder and waited. They didn't wait long; Matthew could barely see another squad carry two corpses down that ladder. Then his team carried him up the ladder and into the cockpit. He half-felt, half-watched them strap him into the copilot's seat. Andrew Blakely took the pilot's seat and started into the pre-flight checklist. Or at least, he started into a sort of checklist he was clearly improvising on the fly. Twice—only—Matthew corrected him on something he'd missed.

Matthew accessed the navigational routines. Dr. Folsom had told this much of the truth; their ship stood in the former city of Sydney. *Now where to go?* And as soon as he asked the question, he knew the answer. His bots briefed him as quickly as he thought it. Now he knew the full layout of Botany Bay—things the bots must have run their own program to steal from the mainframe—and included details of a very special place.

Quickly he plotted their course. Having to do this without using his arms and legs annoyed him. But being *able* to do it *while working around this disability* fascinated him.

Andrew must have been reading the navigational displays as they changed. "Is that your course order ... sir?" he asked.

"Yes," said Matthew. "Out over Sydney Harbor, where we can spoof the automatic harbormaster into taking down the force field to let us pass.

Then south, to pass Tasmania on the ocean side. Then west-northwest to the Great Australian Bight. Our target is the larger of the Green Islands. We'll land there while we make further plans."

Sergeant O'Shea's voice abruptly filled the cockpit: "Ten-twenty-four, sir!" As good a code as any to indicate everyone—everyone alive, anyway—was aboard.

Andrew needed no further prompting. "Secure, all, for raising ship!" he shouted—and his voice reverberated throughout the craft. "Liftoff in five. Four. Three. Two. One. *Mark!*"

Matthew felt the ship rise—a bit of a surprise. What was with the artificial gravity? And Andrew had known to warn everyone to secure themselves. He would make an excellent second-in-command. But now Matthew had to concentrate on something more important: getting them out of Sydney Harbor. He was correct; the harbormaster accepted his recognition code as valid. The force field came down, long enough for the ship to slip through. After that, he sent silent orders to follow the roundabout course he had plotted earlier.

A sharp pang of regret shot through Matthew. He had just lost his subliminal connection to Natalya. Somehow, he knew she was not dead— just out-of-range—because *he* was out-of-range.

Sergeant O'Shea's voice sounded again, softly this time. "Sir," he said, "I don't know how your systems work, but I think maybe you could use some ten-seven time."

He was about to say, "Ten-seventy-four," meaning "no." But his nanobots interrupted him: *He's right. You need extensive repairs. We can do that best if you shut down. We can wake you later.* He tried running a diagnostic and found he couldn't even do that. He would have to trust the bots.

*Effect repairs,* he ordered the bots. Then aloud, he said, "Ten-four. Did you happen to retrieve the EMP gun?"

"Yes, sir," said the Sergeant. "Only … I'm sorry we couldn't use it to rescue Natalya. We weren't used to that weapon and could never get a clear shot without affecting her, too, and…" He trailed off.

"Don't worry about that, Sergeant," said Matthew. Useless to tell O'Shea that Natalya likely had a body shield; he wouldn't have known that, and even Matthew couldn't be sure. "You did well. Now send Miss Evans up here and have someone bring me down."

Jennifer came up the ladder. When she saw Matthew, she asked, "Hey, big fella, what did that big bully do to you?"

"I'm paralyzed," he answered. "I'll need…" *Two hours.* "Two hours for repairs. We are on course to the Green Islands, on the far side of the Great Australian Bight. We're not cloaked, but as long as we follow this course, no one will notice us."

"What will we find there?"

"Nothing but vacant land. But on the mainland, we will find a *very* special colony," said Matthew, now consciously "reading" those stolen files the bots had found. "Descendants of a country that got wiped out in the Great Climate War," he went on, marveling even as he said those words. "These people apparently never accepted full rehabilitation. The United Nations keeps them in the Western District of Botany Bay. Ideal people for a rebel force."

Jennifer grinned fiercely. "Then we're eventually going back to Sydney?"

"'Big ten-four.'"

Jennifer gave Matthew's inert left hand a squeeze. Then she touched a spot on the copilot's screen. "Sergeant," she said, "I am ten-twenty-three, and I'll be ten-eight at this console for awhile. Send medics to carry Commander Morrow below. Put Jonathan and Katherine in charge. They'll know what to do. And whatever they or Matthew tell you to do, you do. Ten-four?"

"Ten-four."

The bots sent Matthew a signal he could neither mistake nor fight. He went to sleep.

# Chapter 6

He awoke refreshed and immediately looked around him. The squad had put him into one of the secure infirmary beds. He tested his arms and legs. All in working order—and were they stronger than before? He felt his face where Stefan—or his enhanced Frankel prosthesis, anyway—had slugged him. Damage repaired—and in fact, his whole face felt "up-armored."

Now he ran a diagnostic. Whoa. He never before had that much data from a diagnostic. Not only did he have a body shield, but he now had onboard radar and IR sensors, and an extra nictitating membrane—an invisible eyelid—over each eye. No, wait—that was more than a membrane. It could give him night vision and a wide variety of tactical overlays over normal vision.

*Ingenious*, he thought. *My compliments.*

*Don't credit us. Thank your friends for making the suggestions.*

Now he looked to one side. Jonathan stood to his right. Katherine stood beside him.

"Jonathan," he said with a smile, "what did you do?"

"The logical thing, once we knew about your nanobots," said the older man. "We suggested every enhancement any of us would want to have when going up against a big bully. The enhancements we all wished *we* had, when we were kids."

"And just how did you establish contact with the nanobots?"

"Credit Katherine here," said Jonathan, nodding to the younger woman. She blushed and smiled a shy smile. Jonathan went on: "She just put out her hand when the bots started coming out of your mouth. Then she started signing, the way she always communicates with me. First, she told me to bring the usual raw materials—silicates and metals—starting with several metal shards and concrete chunks you must have carried out of the hospital. Sergeant O'Shea cannibalized the printer stocks for more. Then I suggested all the rest of the enhancements. The bots read her mind, or whatever it is they do, and did the rest. Which reminds me: how did they take?"

"Excellent," said Matthew, who sat up the rest of the way and dangled his legs over the bunk. He looked around, spotted the digital clock on the far bulkhead. "You've been busy," he went on. "Prisoner transports don't have bulkhead clocks."

"No, but Sergeant O'Shea pointed out that this isn't a prisoner transport anymore."

Matthew smiled again. "Point taken," he said. "I see that two and one-half hours have passed. Where are we?"

"Now entering the Great Australian Bight, on course to the Green Islands."

"Who's piloting us?"

"Andrew and Jennifer."

"Are they still on duty on the flight deck?"

"Yes, sir."

"Thank you, Jonathan—and you, too, Katherine. Your work has been exemplary, and I shall be glad to keep you on my staff."

"Thank you, sir. But ... Well, I have one more question."

"Ask away."

"Why *did* you have Dr. Folsom move us to that specialized ward? You didn't need us with Lieutenant Bronskaya, did you?"

Matthew smiled again. "Good catch," he said. "Of course not. But of all of Dr. Folson's experimental subjects, I could tell you were suffering the worst. I also knew that Naval Planning Staff had a reason for asking you four to help them plan strategy in the Metamorphic War. I already knew I was going to make revolution, and I would need the best staff I could get."

"But why? I mean ... Why revolution?"

"Because Dr. Folsom is carrying on a project to create an army of oppression," said Matthew. "Natalya and I—and Stefan Weiss—are the prototypes. I *must* stop that project. Add to it the circumstances of my arrest, *and* what they did to Natalya. Oh, it was easy enough for me to get used to a Frankel prosthesis. I was literally a kid then—you heard Dr.

Folsom, and about *that* much, she told the truth. And I now remember having sessions in my organic life with a child psychiatrist who gave me the whole battery of psychiatric tests—Rorschach inkblots, Wechsler Intelligence Scale for Children, the works."

"Yes, I can well imagine—sir. Then you *are* on the spectrum, as she said?"

"Yes, she *did* say that, didn't she?" said Matthew. "As I said, I had every psychiatric test in the arsenal. No one told me what was wrong with me. Or maybe no one had time—because the 'accident' happened just after that."

"I take it *you* were running from the *other* kid, not the other way round."

"Correct," said Matthew. "And there's much more. Dr. Frankel could not have picked a better subject than myself. I know that now. But for the longest time, I couldn't remember."

"What was that world name Dr. Folsom used … Berks World?" asked Jonathan.

"Yes. My father received a posting to the mining colony there when I was seven years old."

"Then you weren't born on it?"

"No. I was born right here, on Sol d, just outside the historical city limits of Richmond, Virginia, in Nuevo Aztlán. My memories go back to when I was three or four years old. In fact—now, here, is a very odd thing. Dr. Folsom showed me footage of a siege I supposedly tried to withstand at the Kings Dominion Amusement Museum in NRD-01-VA-Doswell."

"I know that place!" said Jonathan. "Did people really take thrill rides without the benefit of gravity manipulation?"

"Indeed they did. My earliest memories of that place—that have only just come back to me, thanks, ironically, to Dr. Folsom—are of visits to it when I was four years old. I remember spotting the tallest ride in the park…"

"The Intimidator?"

"The same. I watched the car train go up that ramp, then down. And I said, 'Someday…' But my horrified mother looked daggers at me for saying that. So, I never mentioned it again."

"And when did your psychiatric tests begin?"

"After I relocated to Berks World—no, wait a minute. It was after my father won admission to the Harvard School of Organization and Project Management in Cambridge, Massachusetts. We all packed up and settled in a high-rise in Belmont. I started seeing a child psychiatrist in Boston while I was also going to school."

"If you don't mind my asking, what was the … What do doctors call it … the indication?"

"I couldn't begin to tell you anything specific," said Matthew. "Most of what I remember of my childhood was a lot of yelling and seemingly endless punishments—detentions, face slaps, that sort of thing—and for the least infraction. The worst thing I could ever do was violate a safety rule. And more: I had no athletic talent at all, Throw a ball precisely so that another person could catch it? Strike it consistently with a cudgel and place it with that same precision? Utterly beyond my skill."

"I know how that feels," said Jonathan. "When the kids choose up teams, they pick you last—and then they rag even harder on the team captain unlucky enough to get stuck with you."

"Just so," said Matthew. "Hard to imagine today, isn't it? All that to show you that when I first received this Frankel prosthesis, I thought it was the best invention in history."

"Did you have any particular reason not to have athletic talent?"

"Oh, yes. My natural cerebellum is severely damaged. Hypoxia during the birthing process—something went wrong with my mother's anesthetic protocol. It would be left to Dr. Girard aboard *Bonaventure VI* to figure that one out. But my prosthesis carries a lot of extra circuits to give me the hand-eye coordination I never had as a child."

"But athletics wasn't your only problem, was it?"

"No. Have you ever noticed that neurotypicals do things according to a set of rules they never bother to communicate even to one another? But if you violate one of them, they shun you."

Jonathan nodded grimly. "You don't know how long I've waited to talk to someone who understands," he said.

"Doesn't Andrew understand?"

"Well," said Jonathan with a slight smile, "maybe he does but doesn't want to admit it."

"I'll have to speak to him about that," said Matthew. "We have to be scrupulously honest with one another in all things."

"Did you have *any* talents?"

"Yes," said Matthew in a more definite tone. "My mother, for all her faults, taught me to read. By the time I reached school, I already knew how. And mathematics—nothing is more logically consistent than mathematics. And from mathematics came music. I could never compose, but I could definitely rearrange. My mother seemed to think I had a future as a concert pianist. I'll never know whether I was ever *that* good. Mostly it was a chore—but it still had its attraction.

"But mostly, I remember those psychiatric tests. I wouldn't learn what those were about until the ship's psychiatrist on *Bonaventure VI* shared their basic theory. It wasn't something she would ever have done with anyone else—but somehow, she felt I deserved to know. Not that they all made any sense. Tell me, Jonathan: what does a Rorschach inkblot mean to you?"

"That somebody splattered ink on a piece of heavy paper, folded it over, let it dry, and preserved the pattern. That's it."

"Did you know that one of the patterns is supposed to represent a father figure, and another, a mother figure?"

That made Jonathan laugh. "Couldn't be!" he said. "There's only one design that has any part of it that looks remotely human—the third pattern. Two heads, looking at one another."

"And that's not the one I had in mind. Well, you can understand that I flunked the Rorschach Inkblot Test. The records of that test—and how

Dr. Conroy got access to them, I'll never know—show that the psychiatrists said I was too literal-minded for the test to have any value. The Thematic Apperception Test was something else. Ten ambiguous scenes, each of which could be something out of a play or film. And the interpretations I came up with, frankly, scared my examiners."

"Scared? How?"

"Violence, Jonathan. Half of them suggested violence to me—either its aftermath or a prelude. You know our society detests violence."

"Yes, but your own mother *did* attack you violently. So, of course, you would score that way on that kind of test. With all due respect to the medical profession, I think psychiatrists can be pretty stupid about things like that. Did they institutionalize you?"

"At least one authority wanted to do just that. But when we got to Berks World, the superintendent of elementary education said 'no' to that. He placed me in the Cymru School, in the second grade. Halfway through the year, they advanced me a grade. But there was just one problem."

"What?"

"Not *what*. Who. Stefan Weiss."

"So *that's* where you met him," said Jonathan.

"Yes, and what made it worse was that he was my next-door neighbor. Fortunately, it took only that one half-year to convince Mr. Carrington, the principal officer, never again to assign Matthew Morrow and Stefan Weiss to the same class. But I still had some behavior problems in my fourth grade—I got sent to see Mr. Carrington about them. Twice. But then, one day, he summoned me, Stefan, and two other boys to his classroom. And he read the Riot Act to the other three and in front of me. That must have really humiliated the three. Two of them got the message Mr. Carrington wanted to send. But Stefan—well, Stefan was Stefan."

"How soon after this did the bus collision happen?"

"About a month later. The fight started on the bus itself—the same basic trouble. Stefan was blocking my way, and I got tired of it and struck him, karate-chop fashion. You can imagine what he tried to do next. I say *tried* because immediately an older boy got between us. He was a member of the Bus Patrol—typically three sixth-graders assigned to each bus, all wearing badges and printed-canvas baldrics to give them the appearance of authority.

"So this Bus Patrol member—actually the leader—blocked his way. And Stefan said, 'Let me go! This punk hit me, and I'm going to get him!' So the other boy said, 'Not on the bus, you don't!' And the other members of the Bus Patrol took positions to either side of Stefan to back up their leader.

"So the leader seated Stefan up front. Worst mistake they could have made. Because we got to our stop, and he got off first, and lay in wait for me. He was going to settle matters right there, and it didn't matter that at least one member of the Bus Patrol got off on the same stop. Not only that, he had a gang to back him up.

"Well, when the bus started to move off, I broke and ran. Stefan was right on my tail, and the other boys were yelling, 'Get him, get him!' Then I turned in front of the bus. I thought I could gain some distance if I could just get the bus between him and me. So what do you think he did? He took a flying leap and bowled me over. The bus couldn't stop, so…" And here, Matthew balled up his right fist and slammed it into his open left palm to imitate a collision.

"The bus hit *both* of you?"

"You got it. The next thing I knew, I was wearing this fine new metal and plastic body. What I didn't know, of course, was that Stefan was wearing one just like it."

"Dr. Frankel?"

"Yes. He must have had some serious clout with the police and the hospital."

"But you didn't mind it, did you?"

"As I said," said Matthew, "it was easy for me to adapt to a new body. More than that—it felt positively glorious at first. I could do things with this body I could never do with my own. I have as much coordination as I could ask for and strength to match. Dr. Girard once told me I could win the Olympic Games single-handedly if they'd let me compete. And I believe it.

"Then one day, I went to sleep and woke up unable to feel any emotions at all. Dr. Frankel had installed an emotion-blocking chip in my head. For decades after that, I was an emotional cripple. Not only that, but the procedure—or maybe just the chip—blocked my childhood memories."

"Why would Dr. Frankel give you a thing like that?" Jonathan asked.

"Because of Stefan," said Matthew. "When I found out that Stefan was part of the experiment, I had the bad sense to complain about that. In fact, I did more than complain. I have this vague idea that I tried to destroy Stefan. Whatever I did, I blocked it out of my memory. *I* did the blocking. But the damage was done. So I wound up with the chip as a result.

"Or, so I thought. But now I wonder just how well Stefan himself adapted to the experiment. Maybe, out of an abundance of caution, Dr. Frankel tried to cripple *both* our emotions. He managed to do it to me. But Stefan—I think, now, Stefan killed Dr. Frankel before he could get around to giving him the implant. Broke his neck and just left him there. That's how I found him when I woke up to the decompression alarm. I barely got myself into a closet and clamped my eyelids shut before I heard the sound of the biggest vacuum cleaner ever invented. The next thing I remember was awakening years later, when the Marines of *Bonaventure V* found me. I was the only survivor of the disaster that was Berks World."

Jonathan shuddered. "I … I don't know what to say, Commander. If you don't mind my asking, what saved you from going totally over the edge?"

"My music," said Matthew. "Throughout the sub-adult education I got, then my classes in the Academy, someone discovered my musical talent. I already knew how to play the piano and sing—and though my voice had no inflection, I, at least, could carry a tune. All through my Academy years, I would play the piano, or the bass drum, that someone taught me to play.

"But my playing was never authentic playing. I just mimicked the most popular performers of classical music. I couldn't put my soul into it, because with that chip in place, I might as well not have had one. Until, aboard *Bonaventure VI*, the ship's surgeon and engineer proposed taking that chip out of my brain. It provoked some argument at first, but the Captain settled it fast. He said it was my right. So Dr. Girard did the operation. That's when the emotions of a lifetime crashed in on me at once.

"One of the first things I did, trying to get over Natalya's death—or what I thought was her death—was to find the ship's music room, run off the most heart-rending music score I knew, then sit at the piano and start to play it. *My* way, this time—no mimicry. I can remember distinctly what piece I played that day: Tchaikovsky's *Pathétique* Symphony, the Fourth Movement. You can imagine … sorry. I … give me a minute…"

The tears flowed afresh as he remembered pouring out his grief into the notes that, he learned later, the great Russian master had written to express his own emotional stress. According to legend, these were the last notes he wrote before committing suicide—at the orders of Tsar Aleksandr III—nine days after his last work saw its premiere.

At last, he could continue. "I can still remember Captain De Grasse coming in at that moment, with Dr. Conroy by his side," he said. "Both told me that was the most moving performance either of them had ever heard. Dr. Conroy—her full name was Diana Conroy—you're not going to believe this, but she had tears in her eyes. My Captain half-jokingly expressed his fear that he would lose me to the concert circuit. But of course, I had no sense of irony. I told him I would rather stay with the ship. But I also stayed with music—and discovered that I *could* compose at last. I wrote a theme for Natalya, all her own—I look forward to sharing that with her. I even wrote an anthem for the ship.

"But Natalya—now *she* woke up with her new body *as an adult*. And hadn't had time to adjust to that. But of course, Dr. Folsom doesn't understand that, or care. I almost strangled her when she told me what she wanted me to do. But that wouldn't help Natalya, and the authorities would just appoint another doctor in her place. I also wondered *why* they put Natalya's brain into a new body. Add that to the spectacle of you and those other patients on that cellblock, and I reached the only conclusion I could reach. I have to put a stop to this once and for all. Now that I had to leave

Natalya behind, I'm the only one who can do it. Revolution is the only way I know to stop it."

He stopped abruptly. For he saw Katherine beginning to shake. Jonathan turned to her but said nothing.

And then Katherine spoke. "Th-th-th-thank … y-y-y-you…" she said. And neither man could mistake the tears gathering in her eyes.

"Katherine," said Matthew, turning her face toward his, "*I* thank *you*. For being who you are and for helping me at a critical moment."

That only made the tears flow more freely. And then Matthew remembered something else critical. "Katherine," he said, knowing his voice was hardening, "did Stefan Weiss abuse you?"

That made Katherine sob even louder than Natalya had.

"I swear to both of you," he said between his teeth, "that I will take Stefan Weiss out if I ever see that artificial face of his again. Besides being a willing prototype, he is the lowest kind of criminal."

That statement had poured out of him beyond any effort he could have made to stop it. He suddenly realized that right now, he needed to offer comfort, not pledges of vengeance. He reached out with his left hand and cradled the still-sobbing Katherine in the crook of his arm. Then he reached out for Jonathan, too—for Jonathan displayed the red eyes of one wanting to cry but not wanting to show weakness. The three held that tableau for over two minutes.

Then Katherine broke it. Words poured from her in a torrent that continued for another two minutes. Matthew carefully recorded every word as evidence—for the historians would try the case endlessly in the future. They always did. He added to this record a mental note to discuss with them—later—how he could record live streams from his senses, and ask their permission before he shared it or published it. He could always seal it in an archive—revolutionary justice allowed that. For now, he sensed they needed to know they could trust him never to share anything without their permission.

At last, he said, "Jonathan, Katherine, don't worry. Your narratives will stay private with me—and if you prefer, I can keep them private for as long as either of you lives. But right now, we have a mission to plan. Andrew and Jennifer are still piloting us?"

"Yes," said Jonathan.

"Go and find Sergeant O'Shea. Tell him I want a conference, and I'll want him part of it."

"Yes, sir," said Jonathan. Katherine dried her tears hastily and smiled once more. Then they left.

Matthew walked briskly to the flight-deck ladder and climbed it. As he entered the cockpit, he looked at the viewing dome around him. It depicted a body of water with a nearby shore—the Great Australian Bight. Ahead, he knew, lay the Green Islands.

"Andrew," Matthew said, "take us down to near sea level. Lay in a course to put us down on the larger of the Green Islands. Set the sensors to look for any infrared radiation or any other sign of habitation—though I don't expect any. Mind your approach—you'll want to approach from the southwest, from the ocean side. The landmark near those islands is Sharp Point—our objective.

"When you've set everything up, put the ship on autopilot. Then I want both of you to join me in a conference. This ship does have a small briefing room. I want to plan our next operation."

"Yes, sir," said Andrew with a smile and turned to work.

Jennifer looked up then. "Matthew?"

"Yes?" Then he caught a look of half-reluctance in her eyes. Turning to Andrew, he said, "How's the setup coming?"

"Just about to engage autopilot, sir."

"Carry on, then. We'll join you later."

"Aye-aye, sir," said Andrew and disappeared down the ladder.

"You were saying?" Matthew said to Jennifer.

"I thought I heard a woman's voice a moment ago. Was that Katherine?"

"It was," said Matthew. "She told me a rather disgusting story. But, I would violate her confidence if I told you more."

"No, you wouldn't," said Jennifer. "I know that story." Then she growled, "Those—the guards back there made me watch."

"Then I'll want to discuss that with you—in private—later."

"But seriously … you finally got her to speak?"

Matthew swallowed hard, then said, "Yes."

"I'm more grateful to you than you can imagine … sir," she said. "I thought she would never speak again." While she spoke, Matthew took note of the seriousness of her tone and expression. The contrived flirt he had known before was gone. The *real* Jennifer had resumed her rightful place. Matthew would be sure to tell her that—later.

What Matthew said now was, "It was the least I could do for any member of my staff. Especially a senior member. Shall we join the others in conference?"

"Yes, sir. And thank you again."

# Chapter 7

**W**hen Matthew entered the briefing room, he noticed several of his guests sipping various beverages, cold and hot. "And where did you get those beverages?" he asked.

"From the printer," said Sergeant O'Shea. "Why?"

"Draw me a sample. Coffee will do."

The Sergeant turned to, then handed the cup to Matthew. He tasted it—and of course, with his analytical equipment, he could do far more than taste. Then he nodded. "Clean," he said.

"Wait, what? What do you mean, 'clean'? Sir."

"I was verifying something Dr. Folsom blurted out at me in our first conversation," said Matthew. "I think you'll find yourselves thinking with far clearer heads than usual, or maybe you already have. She told me a virus had infected all the printers, so that if you ask one to produce any food or drink, it no longer comes laced with a promazine derivative."

"Is *that* what happened?" Andrew asked. "I noticed something a little off in our rations. About a week ago, Dr. Folsom literally didn't let us use any printers. She said they had turned dangerous."

"She was lying, as was no doubt her custom," said Matthew. "In fact, all food printers lace their foodstuffs with a promazine derivative. Or they did. She alleges that I managed to infect the printers so that they can't do that anymore. Andrew, I'll want to disassemble that printer and examine its code after we finish here. I want to verify something else she blurted out in her rant.

"But first: to the briefing I need to give you. The name of this country that once existed, and covered the middle latitudes of a continent that today is called Aztlán, was the United States of America," Matthew said to his assembled staff. "Does that name sound familiar to anyone?"

"It does to me, actually," said Sergeant O'Shea. "The name survives in the fabled history of the United Systems Marines. Some give it as the explanation of why we have our headquarters in Quantico, Virginia, and not Portsmouth, England."

"Andrew? Jennifer? Jonathan? Katherine? Any of you?"

The four other occupants of the room shook their heads.

"Then listen carefully," said Matthew. "The history of the United Nations of Sol d, and part of that of the United Systems, begins with that country. The key event related to our present mission is the Great Climate War. I *know* some of you have heard of *that*."

"I should say so!" said the Marine Sergeant. "Lord Steele himself committed the Royal Marines to form the backbone of the United Nations Climate Force. We all learned about that."

"Then I assume you learned, also, that UNCLIFOR, under his command, conquered, laid waste to, and literally reconfigured most of the land south of *Inuit Nunangat*—the Abode of the Inuit—and even expanded the latter territory by gifting them most of a land called Alaska. Maybe you learned that some very fortuitous lightning and meteor storms gave the victory to Lord Steele and his forces. But this you might *not* have learned: the Earl and his successors supervised the reconfiguration and *also* captured over a hundred million Americans and removed them permanently from the land."

"Let me guess," said Andrew. "The 'Handsome Earl Steele' shipped them here, to the Western District of Botany Bay."

"No," said Matthew. "He merely handed them over to the United Nations Special High Commission on Re-education. Which, after a generation, did indeed ship millions of them here."

Andrew gasped. "Do you mean to say," he said, "that their descendants are still here, still maintaining their loyalty to that nation-state after all this time?"

"In a word, yes."

"But *how!?* Why didn't they simply sterilize the lot or seize their children and educate them in special schools?"

"You mean as Dr. Folsom might have done?" Matthew asked.

Andrew paused for three seconds. Then he said, "Well, yes. I mean, we all have some reason to suspect the government of far worse violations of intelligent life-form rights than they even accused the Metamorphs of perpetrating."

"Yes," said Matthew. "And immediately after the Great Climate War, that is exactly what UNSHCREÈD did. Most of the adults and their children accepted assimilation into the UN. Or at least that's what everyone assumes. But many refused. Of the adults who underwent forced sterilization, many simply disappeared. The Commission never heard from them again.

"But the children were the problem. When they grew up, their special education didn't always take. But the original commissioners had died, and their successors had no appetite for repeating the cycle. Of course, while all this was happening, the UN evacuated the Commonwealth of Australia and turned it into the vast prison system we know today. So in what was once Western Australia, UNSHCREÈD dumped the stubborn members of the second generation of Americans—in a reservation."

"And have kept those people penned in this district all this time," said Sergeant O'Shea. "How much room do they have?"

"About forty percent of the continent. They're next to the Northern Territory—which is nearly totally untamed wilderness. No one lives there today except the Aborigines—the original native population of Australia."

"Let me guess our mission," said the Sergeant. "We're going to lead all those people off their reservation."

"Exactly. We probably will not recruit the Aborigines. But we *will* liberate all of Australia."

O'Shea whistled. "I must say, sir, that I never thought, when the SSF arrested me, that I would be part of such an awesome revenge against them."

"I was wondering about that," said Matthew. "Why *did* the SSF arrest you?"

"Because, looking out the porthole of my heavy cruiser after the Anti-Hive Expedition of MJDN 198670, I spotted something in the wrong place," said the Sergeant. "Way west of Quantico, it was. In fact, I'd swear it was in Protected Wild Space."

Matthew jerked himself bolt upright. "Just a minute," he said. "What was the date of your arrest?"

"Why, four days later. MJDN 198674."

"And what was the name of your ship?"

"*Bonaventure VII*, Captain Jacques-Yves de Grasse commanding. Why?"

"*My* ship. They must have arrested us both on the same day."

"Well, I'm dashed! We're old shipmates! But why didn't Captain de Grasse speak up for us?"

"Captain De Grasse had a failure of imagination. They retired him and sent him to his ancestral vineyards in the southwest of France. We'll have to recruit him eventually—and perhaps very soon.

"But our problem is more immediate. Botany Bay—all of it—is going to be the headquarters of the revolution. For three reasons. One, we're here. Two, we have the makings of a rebel force; just beyond the force field that separates the prison districts from the reservation and the Northern Territory. And three … I want to break Natalya out of her confinement. With that force, we can do it."

"Yes, but first, we need to capture all the vehicles in the Perth complex," said the Sergeant. "That should help."

"It will, but we don't dare approach Perth directly over water or even over land. It's too well-defended, even from this vessel—alone."

"So, where do we land?"

For answer, Matthew called up a display of the Botany Bay continent, then selected a detail of the Western District, and the western end of the Great Australian Bight. Then he placed a marker on the two islands on the ocean side of a peninsula that encircled a fair-sized body of water. "Those," said Matthew, "are the Green Islands. We'll use them first as our base of operations. Our first objective is this land feature." Here he pointed to a part of the land that jutted out into the Southern Ocean, like a point. "That," he continued, "is Sharp Point, part of the Torndirrup Forest. If these maps are accurate, the authorities don't bother setting lookouts on this bluff. Doing so would cut them off from Perth, and they fear the New Americans too greatly for that. Instead, they've mounted a force-field generator on the bluff."

"And this time," said Andrew, realization lighting up his face, "instead of deceiving the network to let the force field down temporarily, we take it out."

"Yes," said Matthew. "The time for stealth has passed. From now on, we fight openly. First, as you said, we'll destroy that generator. Then we'll fly in, find ourselves some Americans—and start recruiting. Then as soon as we have a force ready to fight—we'll attack Perth overland.

"And now, I want to examine that printer. Sergeant, bring some tools."

Together, Matthew and Sergeant O'Shea removed the faceplate from the printer in the briefing room bulkhead. Matthew then engaged his interfaces and started to read the code.

It didn't take long to find the virus, exactly as Dr. Folsom had said. But he noticed something else. "That's odd," he said, almost without thinking.

"What is? Sir?" asked Andrew.

"The printer does have a virus, and, in fact, it bears some signature of my own writing. It has a comment code in my style. But I don't remember being able to write anything as sophisticated as this."

"Then who wrote it?"

"Well, obviously, I had help," said Matthew. "I must have gotten it from the same place I got … Well, that's neither here nor there. All you need to know is that these printers are reasonably safe. They add no poison—and neither do they add any drugs. But they're starting to make mistakes, so if anything from them tastes the slightest bit off, let me know."

"Sir," said Andrew, "if the printers are making any kind of replication errors, maybe I can track them down."

"Go ahead—if you can. But I'll tell you right now: the society I hope to build will go back to farming and animal husbandry. This," said Matthew, pointing to the printer, "represents a failed experiment. And in fact, that failure is going to bring the economy crashing down on our enemy's heads. That might even happen soon enough to make a military difference for us, though I'd hate to visit the attendant chaos on the civilian population. So, use the printers for now, but let's see about converting one or more of the holds of this vessel to cold storage for victuals. Those we might get from our allies—as soon as we can make a treaty with them. And don't forget to build a proper galley."

"Aye-aye, sir!" said Andrew with a grin. "In fact, I'll just take a look at these deck plans ... Say, Matthew, I think our job's already done for us. Or the big part of it, anyway."

"Which one?"

"Cold storage. This vessel already has that—in fact, half the holds are cold storage, evenly split between refrigeration and freezing."

"Now what could they possibly ... Andrew, I think we've discovered something about Botany Bay none of us suspected. Cold storage is for medicine or victuals, and nothing else. Certainly not in a prisoner transport. So what do you know? Botany Bay has an export economy, and the exports are victuals for the elite."

"The elite ... Oh, I get it. Of course, the elite wouldn't be eating anything laced with promazine. But what you're saying is that *they* don't trust the printers, either."

"Either that," said Matthew, "or else there's something about fresh produce and meat that printers can't duplicate. Very well. So we have our cold storage. When we contact our allies, we'll revictual. But we still need a galley."

"Right. I've got just the spot for one. I don't suppose any of our Marines are trained as shipfitters, though."

"Actually, I am," said Sergeant O'Shea, "and I'll check with some of the other soldiers to see whether I can coach them. Remember, Field Marshal, you and I served on a heavy cruiser, where we all had to bear a hand at shipfitting, occasionally, for damage control. Marines always see to repairs in their part of the ship, and that's not a skill one soon forgets."

"Excellent," said Matthew. "See that Andrew gets all the help he needs, then."

"Aye-aye, sir."

* * *

"'Land, ho,' Commander," said Andrew. "Two islands on the horizon, and the mainland just beyond. Those are the Greens, I'm sure."

Matthew stood behind the two pilot chairs at which Andrew and Jennifer were sitting. From that vantage point, he could see the tactical display that showed the landmasses.

"Visual," he said. The great wraparound display now showed the two islands—barely. Everything was dark, except for the extra light beginning to shine from behind them—the light of dawn.

"Very well, helm," he said, using a title he had used just once—on a much larger ship than this. "Bring us in at low altitude. Land among the trees on the landward side. I want to see the Point, but I don't want anyone on the Point to see us. Not until we're ready to attack."

"Aye-aye, sir."

Matthew went below. He entered the main assembly room, where the rest of his forces were gathered. He strode up to the central podium and turned on the address system. "Now hear this," he said. "We've sighted land. Take seats and strap in. Sergeant," he added to O'Shea, "you have your orders."

"Aye-aye, sir—Squad One, prepare to deploy. Everyone else, secure for landing!"

As the former inmates took their seats, the Sergeant walked up to Matthew. "Permission to speak freely, sir?" he asked, keeping his voice low.

"Granted."

"If anyone had told me, fifteen years ago, that I would be leading this kind of platoon, I'd have told them they were—well, crazy. Technically I'm too old for this job, but I still wouldn't trade it for anything. Just thought I'd let you know—sir." He finished with a salute, which Matthew returned.

Then Matthew gripped the podium—gently, for him—while the ship slowed, then settled down on Big Green Island. Once he confirmed landfall, he opened the boarding door.

"Sergeant," said Matthew, "deploy your recon squad."

"Yes, sir—Squad One, go!"

The eight-member reconnaissance squad picked up their kits, formed a line, and filed down the boarding ladder. Matthew, still at the podium, called up the feeds from the outboard cameras. He waited about a minute before he saw the squad moving almost to the timberline. Three of them then climbed nearby trees until they were out of sight.

Matthew switched on a radio channel to hear the back-and-forth chatter. Then came the message he most wanted to hear: "Recon calling ship."

Matthew nodded to O'Shea, who answered, "Ship to recon. Sergeant O'Shea here."

"Sarge, the Point has some lookouts on it, but I don't think they're hostile."

"What makes you think they're not?"

"They've set up a small camp with canvas tents. And they're flying a flag I don't recognize."

Matthew said, "Have them pipe it in."

The Sergeant passed the order on, and Matthew now got a feed from the high-resolution binoculars one of the lookouts was carrying. He fed that to the big screen. It showed a small camp with four lookouts—and a horse for each. And he saw the flag but couldn't resolve it as well as he'd like. "Sergeant," he said, "see that flag?" He pointed to it. "Have your man zoom in on that."

"Yes, sir." And soon, the view changed, with the flag growing larger.

Thirteen stripes, seven red and six white—and in the upper corner next to the pole, a blue field with fifty white stars on it, in five rows of six and four rows of five. "Sergeant," he said, "those are friendly." In fact, he recognized the Flag of the United States of America from history. Though why did it feel more familiar to him than that?

"Tell the squad to focus on this range and bearing," he said, telling them the location he picked up from the ship's sensors. He was directly plugged into those, so he knew approximately where the nearest force-field projector must be sitting. But he was determined to strike precisely.

The recon squad followed his orders. And there sat the generator, on the seaward side, just where he would have expected it. It was beyond the reach of an attack on land—and where no one would ever expect an attack from the sea.

"Flight deck. Range and bearing … mark!"

"We copy range and bearing, sir," came Andrew's voice.

"Fire one."

The ship rang with the vibration of a missile launch. Matthew picked the missile out on his tactical display. As he watched, the blip representing the missile moved toward the image of the force-field projector. The blip touched the image—and then both blip and image disappeared in a bright flash.

"Direct hit," Andrew reported. Then: "Target destroyed; local force shield down."

"Sergeant," said Matthew, "recall your squad. We're taking off."

"Aye, sir," said O'Shea, who gave the order. Five minutes later, Squad One came pounding up the boarding ladder. Its members found their seats at once.

"Flight Commander," said Matthew. "Take off and make for the Point."

"Aye-aye, sir!" And the ship did indeed take off. It crossed the channel between the Green Islands and Sharp Point, and landed on the lookout the reconnaissance squad had followed earlier.

"Touchdown confirmed, Commander," said Andrew. "We had a bunch of people on the ground, looked like maybe three squads of cavalry. They scattered, but they look like they're cautiously approaching. *Very* cautiously—those horses look ready to bolt any moment."

"Let me see them," said Matthew.

The big screen lit up and showed several men, all mounted, as Andrew had said. And, of course, their horses were skittish. An explosion close enough to see was something new to them.

"Is that them?" asked O'Shea behind him.

Matthew looked closer. They wore unmistakable camouflage-fatigue uniforms. Each man's right shoulder bore that same thirteen-stripe and fifty-star flag he had seen flying before.

"Yes," said Matthew, "these are the New Americans."

"Not play-actors, then?"

"The SSF are good, but not that good," said Matthew. "The SSF were expecting us to attack Perth—and might be wondering why we didn't attack Melbourne or Adelaide."

"Still," said O'Shea, "I'm making sure my platoon has full charges all around."

"A prudent precaution. Send out a single squad."

"Yes, sir," said the Sergeant, who issued the orders.

The squad walked down the boarding ladder and deployed around the stern landing leg. Not long afterward, they sent a signal up the ladder to the Sergeant, who passed it on to Matthew. "Their leader would like to see … Well, *our* leader, and that's you, sir," he said.

"Let's oblige them, then," said Matthew. And he led the Sergeant down the ladder. That might not be the safest procedure, but, remarkably, it was standard Navy protocol.

Matthew took in the party that now stood to one side of O'Shea's squad. He now confirmed his initial impression. Facing him was a three-squad section of what looked like the United States Cavalry. They wore far more modern uniforms, and carried projectile weapons more refined than the histories of nineteenth-century Earth depicted. A staff sergeant, their apparent leader, dismounted and stepped forward to greet Matthew.

"Do you command this ship?" the Sergeant said.

"Yes," said Matthew, not wishing to complicate matters too much. "Lieutenant Commander Matthew Morrow, late of the United Systems Navy, at your service. And you are?"

"Staff Sergeant Andrew Ewer, United States Cavalry, sir."

*Ewer.* Now, why should that name be familiar? It lay, as Eric Shaka might have said, on the tip of his tongue. Then it was gone. The Sergeant's name was just another name.

"I'm sure you have many questions, Sergeant Ewer," said Matthew. "Such as, why did I make a stealthy landing on an unused island, in a prisoner transport. And the nature of my mission."

"Well … Yes, Commander Morrow," said the Sergeant. "We see ships going in and out of Perth all the time. No one uses the Green Islands. This is something new. And your firing a missile and taking out that force-field projector is *definitely* new."

"And I am happy to explain," said Matthew. "This is revolution."

"*Revolution?* Commander, I hope you're serious about that."

"As serious as you can imagine," said Matthew. "First, we take over this continent and the surrounding islands. I don't know whether you know this, but this entire continent is a vast prison, with a central wilderness. As I said, we're taking it over. Then we conquer the Earth. No, not conquer. *Liberate.* And more than a hundred planetary systems in addition."

"Begging your pardon, Commander, and thanking you just the same and all that, but … I'm afraid we can't offer any technology to match yours."

"Technology I command, in abundance," said Matthew. "You have armed effectives, and horses. I need a fighting force that can move fast and strike hard. *We* will provide the technology. Together, we will win."

Sergeant Ewer grinned ear-to-ear. "Sounds like a plan!" he shouted with glee. "This will have to go up the chain of command, of course. But with your ship, I think we can expedite that greatly. In the meantime, I'm sure our Lieutenant will agree to share any recon with you."

"Wait," said Matthew. "How did you pronounce that rank name?"

"*Loo*-tenant, of course, sir," said Ewer. "How else?"

"In my service, we pronounce it *lef*-tenant. But that hardly matters."

"Actually, sir, it does to me," said the American. "The UN was using limey talk during the Resettlement. But you said something about the United *Systems* a minute ago."

"The United Systems," said Matthew. "is a United Nations of the galaxy—or at least our quadrant of it."

"And full of the same horse pucky, right? Sir."

"Semantics being what they are, yes," said Matthew. "Which is why I am determined to make revolution against it." Oversimplified, but it would serve.

"Just one thing, sir," said Sergeant Ewer. "Again, begging your pardon, and with all due respect to your having commandeered one of those armed prisoner transports and taking out that force-field projector, what else have you got? The Lieutenant and everyone on up will want to know."

"Well," said Matthew with a smile, "I see little need to classify that." And he shared with the Sergeant some of his capabilities, though not his history. Naturally, Ewer asked him to demonstrate some of what he could do. A pulverized rock and a cleaved boulder later, Sergeant Ewer stopped asking. "The Lieutenant needs to see you right away," he said and gave a set of coordinates.

Five minutes later, Matthew was sharing his proposal with Ewer's platoon leader. Then, with his LCG to speed him and his forces on their way, he met first a troop commander, then a squadron commander, then a regimental commander, and finally a brigadier general. He said, "Commander, I have my appointment from the President-in-exile, by and with the advice and consent of the Senate-in-exile—which means I can send you to talk to the President without further delay. And that's exactly what I propose."

He called for his aide-de-camp and dictated a letter, which the aide actually wrote with a graphite stylus on a sheet of flimsy paper. This he handed to Matthew. "If you take off now," he said, "you can be at New Washington, in the center of the reservation, in a few hours. We use flag semaphore, so the President will at least expect you. This message will give him enough details to convince him to listen to you. The rest…"

"Yes, the rest is up to me, General," said Matthew. "I'm accustomed to that."

* * *

"Commander Morrow, I presume?"

"Yes, sir. And do *I* presume correctly that I am addressing the President-in-exile of the United States of America?"

"You do," said the six-foot-tall man before him. He had black hair and beard, which he kept trimmed to no more than a half-inch in length. A broad-brimmed hat protected his swarthy face from the semitropical sun. He dressed with remarkable informality for a head of state—a shirt with short sleeves, khaki trousers, a brown leather belt, white socks, and brown leather ankle-high boots. "Jack Abrams, at your service," he said, holding out a hand.

Matthew took the hand and gave it a gentle squeeze—which still made the other man wince. "General Jackson did not exaggerate your physical strength, I see," said the President. "Have you got your credentials?"

"If you mean this letter of introduction from the General, yes," said Matthew, breaking the handshake and handing the letter over.

Abrams read it over quickly, then nodded. "Excellent," he said. "Absolutely excellent. Come—we will continue this discussion in private. This other officer," he said, indicating a balding man of average height, uniformed as a four-star General, "will accompany us. This is General Henry Harrison, the Commandant of the United States Cavalry."

"Pleased to make your acquaintance, General," said Matthew, who once again had to shake a man's hand very gently.

Abrams led them into a low-lying building—made of bricks, baked and stacked and held in place with mortar. Few indeed were the planets of the United Systems whose inhabitants used this kind of building material. And as they entered, Matthew noticed wood-burning fireplaces that had seen heavy use, and lighting fixtures holding wax candles.

"Our technology is, as you see, limited," said the President as he walked behind his desk and gestured to the chairs in front of it. "Your ship looks like something out of a novel by Jules Verne, or C. S. Lewis, or H. G. Wells. Since our removal to this land in the first century, the UN would make air raids and destroy any prototype dynamos we dared build. We're blessed to have our horses and our guns—but we literally re-created industries our ancestors had abandoned."

"Does the SSF ever reconnoiter your lands from the air or by sending in spies?"

"SSF? Who might they be?"

Matthew explained—not only about the SSF but also about his ship.

"So *that's* why your ship is armed," said the President. "Imagine arming a *prisoner transport* with lightning bolts and rockets! Not even H. G. Wells would have thought of that one. This SSF must be plenty afraid of their people."

"I suspect someone, among the powers-that-be who rule the United Nations and United Systems, is afraid of something," said Matthew. "*Very* afraid." And he explained about his own arrest, fifteen years ago, and some of his activities since.

"Commander, if I may," said the President, "let's get down to brass tacks. You're obviously playing a *very* high-stakes game. And you come to me, seeking a military alliance. Now aside from our supposed mutual hatred of the United Nations and all its works—and our only slightly different grounds for such hatred—what have we to gain? The Congress will want to know. In fact, they *have* to know. Congress, not I, has the power to declare war."

"Mr. President," Matthew began, "you and all your people are prisoners. You are as much prisoners as were those formerly miserable inmates I led to freedom in New South Wales. *And* other prisoners in other parts of the continent once called Australia and now known as Botany Bay. I offer you liberty—basic human liberty. Those electromagnetic walls that keep you in would vanish. You would gain access to all the technology the UN has denied you. Or if I can't deliver that, at least I can leave you free to redevelop it. If you wish, I could set the objective of restoring you to your original lands. You would gain partners in honest trade. No one would tell any of you to stay in some small district. Individual members of your people would gain opportunities to better themselves—and enrich the lives of others in so doing. All this lies beyond the force fields. But first, we must take them down. We—meaning you and I, your forces and mine, and any other forces we can rally."

The President received all this with open-mouthed astonishment. Then after Matthew stopped speaking, he brought his hands together in a clap. Clap—clap—clap—on and on, faster and faster, and smiling more broadly by the second. "Outstanding!" he said. "Commander—no, wait. 'Commander' is too tame a rank for you. 'Field Marshal' would be more appropriate. But at whatever rank—will you tell Congress what you just told me?"

"I will," said Matthew. "Since your Congress alone may declare war, I must address them, and the sooner, the better."

"Consider it authorized!" The President stood, walked to a rearward corner of the room, and pulled a dangling overhead rope cord. Shortly afterward, a messenger walked in.

"Send word to the President *pro tempore* of the Senate and the Speaker of the House of Representatives," the Chief Executive ordered. "Give them my compliments and say I would be pleased to have Congress assemble at once for a joint session. Tell them I shall ask Congress for a declaration of war against the United Nations and the United Systems."

"Begging your pardon, sir—United *Systems?*"

"This officer," said the President, indicating Matthew, "will explain that to the Congress. Include in your message my assurance that any necessary explanation will be forthcoming. Now get going! We haven't time to waste!"

"Yes, sir!" said the messenger, who left immediately.

* * *

"Mister Speaker, the President-in-exile of the United States, and Lieutenant Commander Matthew Morrow, late of the United Systems Navy!"

The echoes of the words of the Doorkeeper to the House of Representatives died out. Then all the assembled Members of Congress came to their feet and began to applaud. With President Abrams leading the way, Matthew Morrow passed through the door and walked down the gentle slope of the carpeted aisle. The faces of the assembled Representatives greeted their President with recognition and Matthew with curiosity and anticipation. In the distance and to the left of the podium complex in the Well of the House, Matthew saw two long rows of seats and the people who now stood next to them. These, the President had explained earlier, would be the Senate, now guests in this chamber. And above all their heads, Matthew beheld the galleries, now filled with more guests. They, too, stood and applauded.

As Abrams and Matthew mounted the steps toward the guest speaker's podium, a great rustle sounded. With so many people taking their seats, that was inevitable. Matthew glanced downward and saw the carbide-tipped javelin he had earlier asked for. That would make a good demonstration.

Another of those annoying, impossible-to-place memories shot through Matthew's brain. He saw himself taking a similar podium—in a room without galleries. A room, such as it was, featuring stalactites and stalagmites, many equipped with cameras. No cameras appeared here— because these people had no electricity to run them. Behind him sat the Speaker of the House and the Vice-President of the United States at their combined desk. On the wall to their left hung the vote-recording system— a complex system of sliders along horizontal tracks. Two hundred one of these tracks hung there, ranked in groups from one to forty-one. Each group represented a "State" these people carved out of the abandoned lands in which they found themselves, centuries ago.

And crowning this antiquated—but presumably effective—voting system was a display of the date. Matthew read it: November 3, 2417. Corresponding, of course, to MJDN 204157.

"Ladies and gentlemen," said the Speaker, "I have the high privilege and distinct honor of presenting to you the President of the United States!" And the applause began again, lasting at least as long—five minutes—as it had before.

Abrams took the guest's podium, with Matthew waiting behind and to his left side. "Mr. Speaker, Mr. President, Members of the Congress, and fellow Americans watching here," he said, "you don't ordinarily see me unless I am reporting on the state of our Union. This is not an ordinary circumstance. For we now have an opportunity to take back, from those who stole it from us more than three and one-half centuries ago, our most precious possession: *our liberty!*"

A smattering of applause greeted that last.

"I know you're skeptical," he said. "It seems incredible, does it not, that we, limited as we are to coal, candlelight, and horses, can fight a force that hems us in with an invisible wall that can kill anyone who approaches too closely. But two days ago, I received a report from our cavalry forces at Sharp Point. They reported that a gravity-levitating ship of the skies *destroyed a generator* of that invisible wall with an *explosive rocket*. Many of you might have seen that vessel—looking very like a serving platter—standing in this city. *Today you will meet the commander of that vessel.* And he will tell you why our liberty is once again within our grasp—and how to reclaim it!"

A murmur of astonishment sounded throughout the hall.

"And so, without further ado," Abrams resumed, "I stand before you today to make my own introduction! Ladies and gentlemen, *I* have the high honor, and distinct *pleasure*, to introduce to you Lieutenant Commander Matthew Morrow, late of the United Systems Navy—and soon to be *Field Marshal* Morrow, *Supreme Commander of the Revolutionary Forces of Free Earth!*"

The murmur rose to a half-gasp, half-shout. But when Matthew stepped forward to speak, the hall fell into absolute silence.

"Mr. President, Mr. Vice-President, Mr. Speaker, Members of the Congress, and all Americans admitted to these galleries," Matthew began, "I, too, sense your skepticism. For that reason, *I* count it a high privilege and distinct honor to address this body. You do me the courtesy of a hearing, which is all I have any right to expect. In the next hour, I hope to earn more than your courtesy. I seek to win your respect and willingness to join me in a war that all who wish to be free must fight.

"I could say to you that only subjects decline to fight for their liberty when the odds tell against them. But you know that already. So let me tell you what you do *not* know. And that is: today, you have a greater chance of victory than you've had since that Great Climate War that saw your ancestors removed to this reservation. This chance will not—I say again, *will not*—come again. Take it, and you will, at last, be free human beings. Let it pass, and you will remain the prisoners that you are.

"So much for general principles. Now I will tell you why you should believe in your enhanced chances of victory. I will justify to you your President's admittedly hyperbolic description of myself. Again I could simply cite my destruction of that force-field generator at Sharp Point. But what does that tell you? A mutinous officer stole an armed vessel—a small one, at that—and destroyed a target of opportunity. How does that make him a field marshal of any force that exists beyond his own imagination? Why should *you* order *your* military forces to follow such a leader? And by virtue of what special gift do I dare speak of liberation, not of Earth only, but of hundreds of 'Earths' you cannot even see, whose suns appear only as tiny points of light in your night sky?

"Ladies and gentlemen, obviously, you need more than what you have heard. And I am here to tell you more. And not merely to tell, but to *show*. I will begin … *now.*"

With that, he picked up the javelin. A gasp resounded throughout the hall, turning to horror as he aimed at the far wall. Then he let fly—and the javelin flew an almost straight course over the heads of the assembled Representatives. With a satisfying *thunk,* it buried itself in a wall panel—at eye level for one standing next to the wall.

"Will someone seated at the rear try to withdraw the javelin?" Matthew asked.

One representative did leave his seat. He crossed the rear corridor, took hold of the javelin, and pulled with all his might. He couldn't remove it. So he called for help, and two of his colleagues joined him. Even the three of them couldn't remove the javelin.

"Is there a problem?" Matthew asked with seeming innocence.

"Mr. Speaker," shouted the man who had first risen, "this javelin is buried about a foot in. We'll never get it out, short of asking the carpenters and masons to remove part of the wall."

And the hall erupted into applause and cheers. Matthew raised both hands, and the hall quieted. But their attitude had changed. They were rapt and eager to hear and see more.

"That," he said, "is a small sample of my own capabilities. And now, with the Speaker's permission, *I* will remove the javelin."

The Speaker nodded, and Matthew descended the podium, walked rapidly up the aisle, then crossed to the far wall. He took hold of the javelin with both hands and pulled. And it came out easily. He handed it to the excited representatives who stood by. "And now," he said, "observe."

He leaned against the wall, putting out his left hand next to the hole the javelin had made. His nanobots poured out of his mouth, down his neck, then along his arm. Reaching the wall, they at first disappeared into the hole. Matthew pulled out a small stick of metal and thrust it in. The nanobots quickly "consumed" it. After five minutes, they raced out of the hole—and began to repair it. They left only a small blemish as they raced back up his arm, his neck, and into his mouth.

"Your pardon, Mr. Speaker, ladies and gentlemen," Matthew said, trying to make his voice carry. "I had no wish to damage your hall without making *some* repair."

He nodded to the representative who still held the javelin. That worthy handed back the ancient-looking weapon, then put his right hand out and felt the panel. Then he turned and shouted, "Mr. Speaker, you can barely tell that anything happened to this wall!"

The hall erupted in even louder applause and cheers. Under cover of this, Matthew walked rapidly back the way he had come. As soon as he remounted the podium, the hall quieted, even more quickly than before. Handing the javelin to the excited President Abrams, he turned to speak again.

"That, Members of Congress, is but a small sample of my capabilities. Before I describe them further, I need to warn you of something no doubt some of you can guess. Which is: the United Systems, the polity from which I have defected, is trying to build an army of enhanced soldiers like myself. I have no idea of their intended targets. Perhaps *you* are the targets. The more reason to join me now, so that such a dreadful project never comes to fruition!"

For fifteen minutes, he delivered a lecture, not on the *full* extent of his capabilities, but enough to matter. Then he spoke about Directed Energy Weapons, their various sizes, and what they could do. Finally, he shared the full extent of the United Systems and their activities since these people's ancestors found themselves on a reservation.

"Which leads me to how we—together—can strike a blow for liberty," he said. "With the weapons your troops can already use, we can attack the reservation enforcement complex at Perth and capture it. We will find an arsenal of advanced weapons in it, which your troops should have no trouble training to use. We also will find more flying vessels like mine. I will select those among your officers whom I judge can learn to fly them and fight them effectively. My Sergeant will further train your troops to land on hostile ground from one of those ships. With that capability, we can move swiftly and strike—even behind enemy lines. We can then drive to the east, in a front stretching from the northern coast to the southern. Eventually, we will capture Sydney in New South Wales. And then this continent will be ours—*yours* especially.

"You heard correctly, ladies and gentlemen! We will say to your wardens and to the Special Security Forces that hem you in, '*We are taking over your prison!*'"

Again the hall broke out in cheers, louder than ever. And Matthew knew that the time had arrived.

"Mister Speaker," he turned and shouted, "what are you waiting for?"

"Will the gentleman—the Marshal—yield back the balance of his time?"

"Gladly, Mr. Speaker."

Anticlimax followed. The special session adjourned. The Senate filed out, its President *pro tempore* announcing their intention to convene in their own Chamber and "await the pleasure of this House." And then the representative who first had tried to pull Matthew's javelin out of the wall introduced the war resolution. Which then received a second. Several motions-to-waive-debate later, the resolution passed. Unanimously.

An eleven-year-old page took the resolution out of the room. Then he was back, with an invitation from the Senate for Matthew and the President to join it. And indeed, to attend in the Senate chamber itself, which the President said was a high honor indeed. The Senate also passed the resolution, also with a unanimous vote.

So the United States of America, as organized in the American Reservation, was officially at war with the United Nations—and the United Systems.

* * *

"That was certainly the fastest law or CJR I ever saw passed," said President Abrams as he led Matthew to the Capitol steps. "You certainly made an impression."

"I hope I shall make a similar impression on your people, Mr. President," said Matthew. "And more particularly on your officers and enlisted rankers."

"That demonstration you're planning next will impress them, I'd say," Abrams said. "Are you sure you really want to put on that kind of show?"

"In ancient Rome," said Matthew, "the senior consul—or Dictator, if the Senate appointed one—would receive a declaration of war by throwing a spear into a lawn they called 'Enemy Territory.' I have in mind a slight refinement on that ceremony."

The two men emerged into the open air and crossed to a vast portico at the top of a broad stairway. Below them stood a large throng of people. And beyond them stretched a set of green lawns. These people had almost replicated the city originally called Washington—but which Lord Steele had renamed Cornwallis. And this column of lawns and crossing streets was the perfect place for what he planned.

He held his javelin high, and the crowd went wild at the sight of their President and his guest.

"Fellow Americans!" shouted Abrams. "The moment we have long awaited, since the United Nations transported us here, has now arrived! In recognition of this fact, your Congress has now declared war against those who took us captive and the authority that appointed them! Give your hand to this officer, Field Marshal Matthew Morrow!"

Silence fell as Matthew stepped forward, still holding the javelin high. "People of America," he shouted, "I hold in my hand a steel carbide-tipped javelin. You may regard this as the spear of war. The Congress of the United States has just placed it in my hand. In so doing, they have imitated a far older Senate of a more ancient city and power. And now, to continue this ancient custom, I ask you, the *people* of the United States, to direct me! Where is our enemy? *Where are the Special Security Forces!?*"

The people started to point behind them—to the west. Where, coincidentally, lay Perth. Actually, Perth lay southwest, but here no one was quibbling. And they were chanting, too: "There! There! There! There! There!"

He raised his javelin and threw it at a forty-five-degree angle. It flew over the heads of the onlookers, almost out of sight before burying itself in the grass well beyond the rear of the crowd.

All broke out in wild cheers, gradually resolving to a chant of "USA! USA! USA! USA!" But even that chant gave way—for someone started to strike up a song. Matthew didn't recognize it immediately, but he heartily approved.

*"We will rally 'round the flag; we will rally once again,*

*Shouting the battle cry of freedom!*

*We will rally on the hillside and gather from the plain,*

*Shouting the battle cry of freedom!*

*Our country forever! Hurrah, boys, hurrah!*

*Down with the traitors, and up with the star!*

*As we rally on the hillside and gather from the plain,*

*Shouting the battle cry of freedom!"*

# Chapter 8

Matthew, astride his new war charger—tall, powerful, with a brown coat and white hair running down its legs—raised his binoculars. He didn't need any electronic field viewers, not to direct this force. The simplest technology that could achieve the objective was the preferable one. His new friend, General Kevin Carson, the Commandant of Cavalry, had said so.

Now, looking toward Perth, he could see the wisdom of his new friend's words. The enemy was trying desperately to reinforce its position. At first, they had tried to reinforce Sharp Point and repair the force-field generator there. But no mere engineering company could hold out against an entire brigade of cavalry! General Peter T. Jackson, commanding the Sharp Point Brigade, had rushed at once to hold the breach as soon as Matthew had arrived to introduce himself. For two days, he held that position, seeing no reason to let the enemy repair the invisible wall. Then, when the semaphore signal had reached him about the declaration of war, he changed from defense to attack. Two regiments of cavalry squadrons had driven the enemy off the Point, and then had galloped westward along the beach. In one day, they found the next generator and blew it up.

By then, the rest of the First Cavalry Division had arrived. That, then, was the new battlefront. Peter Jackson took his entire brigade onto the beach outside the force field. His boss, with the other brigade, paralleled his movements. Now, a week later, they were within sight of Perth.

Or so said their dispatches, which they sent by semaphore to the Second Division. Matthew was with that Division, having sent his LCG to assist General Jackson's brigade. And now, he could readily see that the First Cavalry Division had not exaggerated. They *must* be close. For the SSF defenders of Perth had given up trying to stop the American cavalry. They were throwing up a breastwork to the south of the city.

The best defense is offense; Matthew knew that well. So did his American friends.

Matthew made another test of his body shield. He was trying a new, further extension of it. He seemed to recall extending it to cover another person. That, of course, was another fleeting, hard-to-place memory. But it had given him an idea: could he protect his mount as well as himself? With the extra processors he had on board, he had run a simulation. The results had been good. So he had "snacked" on some more minerals so that his nanobots could improve the shield. And now—yes, the shield did cover his horse. Now he could ride even more confidently than could a medieval knight in the days of sword, lance, and arrow.

He handed the binoculars back to General Carson. "I'll be moving out now," he said. "Watch me closely. When I raise my fist, move. Fast."

"Yes, sir," said the General. "Good luck, Field Marshal."

Matthew gave a wave, then urged his horse forward. At first, he settled into a gentle trot. He knew he could outrun this horse even at a gallop. But he liked the high view a horse gave him. And he could feel the sheer power a horse had, power that could give him an edge in battle.

Now he was close enough to use his nictitating membranes. Among other things, they gave him the option of a magnified view almost like that from binoculars. The range wasn't as great, but now he didn't need the extra range. Nor the extra weight.

And he saw the dust of the battlefront. Close now—very close.

A slightly distorted voice sounded in his ears. Andrew's voice. "Commander Morrow! We have you on tactical. Can you read us?"

"Read you five-by-five, Andrew," said Matthew. "Except it's 'Field Marshal' now. Our allies will be expecting that." In fact, President Abrams himself had handed him two arrays of five stars, arranged in the points of a pentagon, before he had set out. "On my mark, break off from the front and attack at these coordinates." He gave them his best fix on the force-field generator now in his path. "Repeat that last."

"Aye-aye, sir." Andrew gave the coordinates with no mistake.

"Good. Stand by on this channel." Now he urged his horse into a lope. He would need to close the distance just a little more…

And now … gallop! As his horse leaped forward, Matthew signaled the ship again. "Prepare to attack! In ten! Nine! Eight! Seven! Six! Five! Four! Three! Two! One! *Mark!*"

A missile shot forward from the ship and struck the generator. It went up in a shower of sparks. Seeing that, Matthew raised his hand, doubled up into a fist.

Behind him, a bugle sounded "Charge." And thousands of exultant voices blended in with thousands of sets of hooves.

In the next instant, he was through the hole and plunging into the enemy line. Chaos erupted as he drew his DEW pistol and fired at the nearest SSF guard. The guard went down in a heap as the rest turned from their breastwork and fired on Matthew. All to no avail—for Matthew's shield was up. Most of the SSF succeeded only in killing themselves from the reflections.

Now Matthew caught sight of a heavy DEW cannon. He took one of his carbide-tipped javelins and threw it. Another shower of sparks flew up as the javelin found its mark. He might have liked to dismount the cannon later, so his American friends could drag it along. But it was too heavy, and right now, he needed it out of action.

And while the SSF tried in vain to stop Matthew, a series of shells struck the three remaining force-field generators between him and the battlefront. Then another shell sailed over his head and struck the generator beyond the one where he'd galloped in.

Now Matthew galloped north toward the next still-intact generator, for the Second Division had arrived. The first rank dismounted, of course, and let fly with an incredible barrage that caught the SSF unprepared. Canister rounds scattered hundreds of small round balls through the enemy defenders. The enemy panicked. Matthew kept his horse turned *away* from the scene.

The light cannons had the largest, most powerful horses drawing them. Each had one rider to draw the cannon itself and two more to help him service the gun when firing. Now they moved several horse lengths closer—and fired several shrapnel rounds.

That routed the enemy. The regular cavalry poured into the complex, then turned south toward the advancing First Division. Naturally, the cannon fire stopped—but now the two divisions had the SSF in a vise.

Incredibly, the commandant of Perth refused to surrender. So the United States Cavalry annihilated the enemy, to the very last armed effective.

But Matthew was not finished. He rode swiftly to the main administration building. There he dismounted and rushed in. The few defenders who had tried to defend—or shelter in—the building all fell before him. Using his network sensors, he plotted his way to the command center. Where, of course, no one could stop him. After dispatching the last defenders, he tapped into the network—easier to do on-site than with an infrared or radio interface.

He found what he was looking for: the routines that governed the force field. But he did not simply issue a stand-down order. Instead, he infected as many generators as he could reach with a virus.

Every remaining force-field generator on the entire continent began a countdown to self-destruction.

* * *

Matthew, General Carson, and Brevet Major General Jackson (now succeeded to command the First Cavalry Division) took inventory. The grim news came first: their losses—ten percent in armed effectives, and fifteen percent in materiel. Half the losses were from the kind of mistakes that come from centuries of inexperience in actual combat. The other half came because this army had engaged an enemy with vastly superior technology. And had still beaten it—a thing all agreed would boost morale.

Then the good news: in addition to taking the administrative complex, the New Americans had captured the enemy arsenals virtually intact. Directed-energy weapons, both small arms and big, permanently mounted guns, mostly overlooking the harbor. And lots of magnetically levitating armored fighting vehicles—autonomous, too. Plus the most valuable haul: gravity-driven craft, suitable for transport, air attack, and bombardment. The enemy had sent them in from Djakarta, with every available armed SSF effective on board. And now Matthew's new allies owned them.

Six days remained before all the force fields would come down. Matthew ordered that everyone use the time efficiently. Color Sergeant O'Shea took charge of training the Americans in small arms, and some of them in driving the maglevs. Autonomous they might be, but Matthew insisted that each have a sergeant to drive it, along with a crew. Matthew gave one other order: to de-sensitize as many of the horses as possible to the appearance of these vehicles. The SSF would no doubt use them in force, thinking to scare the horses. When the horses *didn't* scare, the Americans would have the advantage.

General Carson detailed a single platoon to train on Perth's big guns and watch the harbor. Matthew and his personal staff would keep control of the new aircraft—while offering to train any officer who wanted to learn how to fly one of them.

The strategy was very simple. Second Corps would push through the Northern Territory, all on horseback and carrying their traditional weapons. Since no one but aborigines lived there, the cavalry should have no trouble. First Corps would take the modern weapons and vehicles and enter the South Australia District. The troops would move when the force fields came down—and before the SSF had time to mount an invasion of their own.

* * *

On MJDN 204170, at twenty-three forty-five, the entire Army of the United States stood at the eastern border of what was still its prison-cum-reservation.

As Matthew had ordered, the cavalry stood in a long multiple rank in front. But behind them was a new force, freshly organized: infantry. News of the victory at Perth had flashed throughout all the communities of New America. So nearly every man, between the ages of eighteen and twenty-five inclusive, had rushed to enlist.

Matthew would have preferred to have soldiers behind him with more training than simply a lifetime of hunting and fishing. But using them made sense. The more experienced cavalry could move much faster if at least *some* soldiers would hold onto what they gained. Matthew did not spare them any of the new weapons. These soldiers were still green and must use the weapons they knew.

Now, standing atop one of the captured maglev vehicles, he swept the skies with his eyes. This was the most reliable way he knew to tell time. He could almost hear the ticking of the mechanical wristwatches his New

American officers carried. Primitive they certainly were, using centuries-old technology. But he had to admit they *were* accurate enough.

Twenty-three fifty. The border shimmered ahead. Only Matthew could see that—for two reasons. First, he kept his forces too far behind the border for enemy sentries to spot them. And second, he could see the most minute flickers no organic could ever see.

Twenty-three fifty-five. He climbed down from the roof of his vehicle and reached the ground. He knocked on the left-hand door—these vehicles all had right-hand drives. The driver—none other than that Sergeant Ewer he had first met when landing on the continent—let him aboard.

Happily, the windscreen of this vehicle was clean enough to see through just as well. It should be; he had cleaned it himself. The shimmer persisted. Just a few minutes longer…

And then the shimmer vanished.

"Go," he ordered. Sergeant Ewer started forward. Remarkable how quiet this vehicle was. He would depend on that kind of quiet.

As his vehicle moved, so did the entire first rank of the cavalry. A simple walking gait at first…

"Trot," he ordered. The vehicle sped up—to a speed he had calculated precisely. Sergeant Ewer knew what Matthew would want of him. And to either side, the cavalry ranks changed to the trotting gait, their riders moving up and down, up and down.

The vehicle passed a puddle of slag. "Is that…" Sergeant Ewer began.

"Yes, Sergeant; that's the generator—what's left of it. Go to lope."

Just in time, too, for the line now met its first opposition.

Standard practice with the SSF on Botany Bay was to keep a buffer zone between any two bordering districts. They would patrol within this zone, which had all the force-field generators on its side of the fields they generated. Now those patrols tried to raise weapons against a long line of men on horseback. A few of the enemy managed to get off some shots and kill some cavalrymen. But most of them fell where they stood.

Again according to plan, the second rank dismounted and stripped the fallen SSF of their weapons. The third rank passed them. The first rank had orders to stop for nothing.

"Another slag heap, sir," said the Sergeant. "Does that mean we're in the Southern District?"

"That it does," said Matthew. "Look sharp; we might see some more opposition any moment."

"None so far, Field Marshal—no, correction. Motorized cavalry contacts, dead ahead. Estimated range: a thousand yards."

English units, of course—or "United States Customary units," as the President had said. That was why someone—he still didn't know who—had installed that addendum to his *Encyclopedia Galactica*. With it, he could actually *think* in US Customary, saving several precious seconds.

"Plenty of time," he said aloud. "Flash your lights. Two flashes, then a pause, then five."

"Right, sir." And he did so.

"Now get ready to gun it. In a few minutes, the third rank—that used to be the second rank—will pass everybody to take the front position."

"And they'll be armed with those new weapons they picked up, right, sir?" Ewer said.

"Exactly."

The Sergeant grinned. Five minutes later, he was putting on more speed to keep up with the cavalry rank that was now passing the other two ranks.

"Range, five hundred yards and closing, sir," the driver said next.

Then: "Four hundred … three hundred … two hundred, and our boys have opened up."

"All according to plan," said Matthew calmly. "Stop here. Our troops will have to dismount soon if they're not doing so already."

Which they were. And as soon as everyone had taken cover, the cannon fire began—both shells and round shot at first, and then canister shot.

"The enemy is still coming, sir," Ewer said. "I can't imagine what's driving them."

"Greater fear of their own superiors than of us," said Matthew. "Their superiors must be very worried."

The fighting went on for another half hour. At last, Ewer reported, "That's it, sir. No one else coming. Wow—those guys fought and died to the last man. They must be plenty mad."

"Or terrified of something," said Matthew, more softly this time.

"Are they *that* afraid of their officers? Sir?"

"Maybe … or maybe something else. Sometimes an enemy will fight that way because he *can't* retreat. It's as if we had them in a vise. But what's the other half of the vise?" He caught himself wondering. Could it be Natalya? Well, if it wasn't, then…

"Shine your lights on a slow flash," he ordered. "I'm calling a conference."

In response to the slow flashing of the lights, Generals Carson and Jackson and their staff slowly rode up to Matthew's vehicle. Matthew got out and met them as they dismounted.

"General Carson, General Jackson, first of all, well done," he said. "Second: I have reason to believe we might have allies ahead of us. How far ahead, I can't tell. But that last wave of attack fought us as if they literally had no alternative. And maybe they didn't."

"But what allies could we have, Field Marshal?" asked Carson. "There's nothing but reformatories ahead—at least, that's the intel you gave us, begging your pardon, sir."

"Yes," said Matthew, the light suddenly dawning within his brain. "Reformatories—with force fields to guard them. Except the force fields are down."

"You mean *those* fields suffered from the same virus as the ones demarcating the Districts?"

"Precisely. I took them all down. Gentlemen, we're about to run into some prisoners in revolt. And I want them on our side, not opening up a front of their own. Pass the word down the line."

The two Generals saluted, remounted, and left.

* * *

Dawn had arrived.

The troops had been moving steadily for about six hours. Of course, the dawn came so quickly because the soldiers were moving eastward—directly into it. But Matthew knew he couldn't push those troops this hard much longer. They had kept themselves and their mounts going on the adrenaline flow from the excitement of battle—which didn't even apply to all the troops. The SSF didn't have the strength to oppose them all the way up and down the line. That could be both blessing and curse—for boredom could be a greater hazard than actual battle.

Nevertheless, Matthew wanted his troops to gain as much ground as possible. But not at the breakneck pace of an actual battle. Walk, then trot, then walk. That way, if anyone challenged them, the troops could better hold their ground.

"Got another sighting, Field Marshal," said Sergeant Ewer. "Estimate range: two thousand yards."

That was one advantage of moving by day, especially on a bright sunny day like today. They could see that much farther ahead.

"What do they look like?" Matthew asked.

"Just the usual moving target so far; hard to tell at this range."

"Stop," he ordered. The vehicle stopped.

Matthew stepped out. His built-in telephoto vision worked better without obstruction. He stared ahead, engaged the magnification…

"Use your binoculars," he told Ewer. "Tell me what you see."

The Sergeant did. Then he said, "Kids, Field Marshal. Definitely underage. I hope they're those reformatory inmates."

"Most likely, yes," said Matthew.

Ewer looked again. Then he said, "What do you know? They're waving a white flag. Now, if those kids are inmates in revolt, how do they know we're friendly?"

"Whoever is leading them is a *very* smart boy or girl," said Matthew. "They know the SSF would never field mounted cavalry. That's way too old-fashioned. They also know all the force-field generators melted down about seven hours ago, so anything's possible. So when they see a long line of men on horseback approaching, they know we're more likely friend than foe.

"Break out your flags, Sergeant. Give the signal to stop."

Ewer carried semaphore flags, the best substitute for the radios Matthew did *not* have in enough quantity. In theory, he could have had them printed. But he lacked the proper substrates. Besides, these New Americans had forgotten what radio was. So: flag semaphore.

The triple line of cavalry came to a stop. Of course, Matthew expected the ends of the line to swing slightly farther forward of his position. That was acceptable, so long as the line could hold. He would have liked to keep the line moving in the Northern District. But he didn't want to leave the SSF any gap to jump to attack from behind.

Now he watched as the small party—about the size of a squad—approached with the white flag.

And then he saw the boy in the lead.

"Rest easy, Sergeant," he said. "Walk with me. He's a friend, all right."

"You know him, Field Marshal?"

Did he know him? In fact, he recognized the boy from the footage Dr. Folsom had shown him. He had figured in the final battle at the Kings Dominion Amusement Museum. "Let's just say I do, Sergeant," said Matthew. He said nothing else.

Now they had drawn even with the squad. Matthew stepped forward, the Sergeant always at his side. He held out his right hand. "Zachary Radner?" he asked.

The boy, sixteen years old, stepped forward and extended his own hand. "That's my name … Field Marshal," he said, obviously reading Matthew's accouterments of rank. "Would your name be Matthew Morrow?"

"It is," said Matthew as he took the boy's hand and shook it—gently but firmly.

"Begging your pardon, Field Marshal," the boy said with a studied diffidence. "This feels weird. We should remember each other if we really did take part in a battle on another continent. But try as I might, I just can't remember you. Sir."

"Nor I, you," said Matthew, releasing the handshake. "I suggest we leave that puzzle for another time. You've correctly read my rank. These troops you see before you are part of the United States Army—representing the people in the Western District. They declared war against the SSF and agreed to be the nucleus of a new coalition. We are the Revolutionary Forces of Free Earth. I am the Supreme Commander. Does it suit you to join forces with us?"

"Yes, sir," said young Zachary, drawing himself up to full attention.

"Sergeant," said Matthew, "signal Generals Carson and Jackson. Give them my compliments and tell them I would be pleased to see them here. Now, if you please."

"Yes, sir."

# Chapter 9

"**I** have been a prisoner in the Botany Bay Reformatory Complex for three weeks," said Zachary Radner to the General officers facing him. "Upon my arrival, the Special Security Forces interrogated me. They wanted to know what I knew about … about Field Marshal Morrow. They had me watch footage of a siege at a … I don't suppose any of you know what an amusement park is?"

As it turned out, the New Americans did know, even though their technology was barely into the age of steam. Once his audience assured him they could follow his story, Zachary went on.

"Well, the SSF tried several times to find out what I knew about Field Marshal Morrow. I could tell them nothing, of course. So for three weeks, they kept me in isolation. Or they *thought* they were isolating me. But prisoners have ways of communicating, and we found such ways. Let's just say I have a natural rebel streak, for reasons I … well, would rather not reveal. I broached the idea of open rebellion. Enough of us agreed with that. We exchanged information on the plans of our detention facility and even found ways to communicate beyond it. We first made a plan for what we could do if something happened to the force fields. Of course, we had no idea how to make that happen, but we knew something *could* happen. Power failure, computer virus, any of a number of things.

"So after we laid such plans, I was just starting to think about how to defeat the force fields. And then, rather suddenly, at about zero-one-hundred this morning, they all came down by themselves. Naturally, I activated our plans for revolt. If I do say so myself, we made rather short work of our guards, suffering maybe ten percent casualties."

At that, General Carson's face went long. "Son," he said, "I'd call that the fastest growing-up any boy or girl should ever have to do."

"Well, sir," said Zachary, "some of us had 'grown up' already. We each had a reason for landing in the reformatory. I'm not sure I can expect you to understand all of them."

"I understand well enough that you were angry, determined, and would rather die than quit, no matter how many of your fellows died next to you," said General Carson.

"It might be more accurate, sir," said Zachary, "to say that even death was preferable to what the SSF were doing to us then."

Matthew had a sudden attack of not-quite-memory. He saw himself meeting this young man after straying into a facility where men hunted children. Now, what kind of facility could that possibly be? Then the memory was gone.

"Tell us more," he said aloud. "We just engaged some SSF who were acting as if they didn't dare retreat. What would you know about that?"

"Just this, sir," said Zachary with the bare hint of a snarl. "They were our former guards. We were chasing them. When we caught them, we were going to try them by our own tribunal—and likely execute almost all of them."

"For?" As soon as Matthew asked that question, he regretted it. Zachary suddenly looked ready to burst out shouting in boiling-hot rage. "Never mind," he said. "Forget I asked. Zachary Radner, as Supreme Commander of the Free Earth Revolutionary Forces, I invite you to join our coalition."

"And I accept with all my heart," said the young man. "I'm sure I can speak for all my friends."

"You must understand, however, that I must investigate the state of your training. From the very brief description of your … er … operation, you did well. But as we advance, we will be driving our enemies before us until they have nowhere to retreat. Then they will turn and fight us, like the cornered animals they will be. I want to know whether you and your followers are up to the challenge to come."

"It's fight or die, Field Marshal," said Zachary. "But we'll be glad to accept any further training anyone has time to give us."

"I'll hold you to that," said Matthew. "Very likely, though, your training will be that of direct battlefield experience. Now, as it happens, our troops need rest. We can advance a little farther, but then we must take what rest we can. Then we march. Eastward. To Victoria and New South Wales—while our other forces cross the Northern District and into Queensland. Though, very likely, New South Wales will be our last target…"

He paused, sensing an incoming message. "Your pardon, gentlemen," he said. "I have a signal from a part of my forces you haven't seen, Zachary. Specifically, my aerial reconnaissance squadron."

Zachary said nothing. But of course—he would be familiar with such craft.

Matthew withdrew to a corner. "Morrow here," he whispered.

"Marshal, this is Andrew. The Second Corps reports surprisingly easy going through the Northern District. No opposition. The Aborigines don't seem to want to join us, but they're content to let the Second Corps pass through, so long as they do it quickly."

"What does Queensland look like from your altitude?"

"Spread thin, sir. In fact, it contains nothing but penal farms."

"Did you say *farms?*"

"Yes, sir. Not nearly as productive as I think they could be. But productive enough. And not only farms but ranches, too."

"I think we've just found the source for Botany Bay's food exports," said Matthew.

"Yes … yes! Sir, I request permission to revictual our fleet when we capture this area."

"Permission granted. Now, what about Orpheus Island?" That was one of the largest land masses off the coast of Queensland.

"Completely re-wilded and uninhabited, sir."

"Very well. Pass the word to Second Corps. They have my permission to get across the Northern District as rapidly as they can. You will guard their southern flank. Make sure no SSF gets past any gap in the line. Have Second Corps anchor their line at the southeastern corner of the Northern District, and sweep clockwise across Queensland to form a line just north of New South Wales. You might have to split your own squadron to give air cover to the troops riding along the Great Dividing Range." That mountain chain ran north-to-south along the eastern coast of the continent. "There they are to wait until First Corps can reach the eastern border of the Southern District. Do you understand all that?"

"Yes, Field Marshal."

"Then pass it on. Morrow out."

He returned to the waiting Generals. "General Carson," he said, "the Second Corps will sweep through the Northern District and then capture Queensland and form a line north of New South Wales. We will drive the enemy eastward into New South Wales and Victoria. When we do, we'll have them in a vise. It is up to you to make sure our particular jaw of that vise will not break."

"What about the gap at the northern border of this district?"

"Good question," said Matthew. "You will send your best units to stop that gap and make sure no SSF get around it. The LCGs will provide air cover until you can get in place. But I suggest you select your units and move at once.

"Zachary, I want you and your friends to make yourselves available to General Carson to reinforce our main line. Your job is to make up for any units General Carson must detach to reinforce the northern flank."

Zachary nodded. "You can count on us, Field Marshal," he said. "We're ready."

"Good. Any questions?"

"Just one," said Carson. "What happens when the UN sends reinforcements from India and China and other points?"

"Then we deal with that when, as, and if," said Matthew. "But my assessment is, they don't dare. The minute they do that, people start asking questions they won't be ready to answer. And again: don't ask me how I know this, but these will *not* be normal times. If that footage of … let's see, how shall I address you, Zachary—ah, I have it. Senior command cadet—that's what you've become.

"As I said: if that footage of Cadet Radner and myself at that amusement park is accurate, we started a revolutionary movement among the general population. People will already be starting to ask questions. The more the UN acts, the more they have to explain or cover up. And we're going to give them a stark choice. We're going to make them pay, and pay dearly, no matter what option they elect.

"For that matter, remember: they already tried to reinforce Perth. We took it anyway. This limits their manpower, to say nothing of the rumors that surely are flying throughout the Indian Ocean region. Especially, I'll wager, in Vietnam and other regions in Indochina. The next reinforcement, if the SSF can manage it, will come from Vietnam."

Because no one had any further questions, Matthew dismissed the meeting. But Zachary hung back. "Field Marshal," he said, "I'd like a word."

"What about, son?"

"I don't know how to describe this, but … well, if I didn't know any better, I'd swear I had a really weird advantage. If I get cut, I heal very fast. And I'm stronger than I ever was. Why should that be?"

Matthew thought about that. Then he said, "I remember watching something else in that footage. I slapped you on the left shoulder—a precise blow. I wonder…"

"What, Field Marshal?"

Matthew told Zachary about his nanobot army.

"Do you think maybe I have things like that in me?" the young man asked.

"It's possible," said Matthew. "But let's keep that strictly between us. If it's important later, we'll both know."

"Yes, Field Marshal," said Zachary and saluted.

* * *

The march across the Southern District took another seven days. Zachary Radner's troops proved remarkably adaptable—and resourceful.

This allowed Carson to detach a brigade to close the gap in the broad front line.

Just in time, too, for the SSF did try to break through just as General Jackson's First Brigade arrived. General Carson later shared the after-action report with Matthew.

"Jackson's boys ran right into them," the General said. "Casualties, about five percent on our side—and fifty percent on theirs. They just flat didn't want to surrender. Zach Radner's Irregulars have a nasty reputation in the SSF, no mistake."

"In a way, that's useful," said Matthew. "But in another way, it's tragic. At this stage of the offensive, prisoners start to have a propaganda value. I've been thinking about how to exploit that—excuse me." He could detect a call coming in. He took this call where he stood. "This is the Field Marshal," he said. "Andrew? Is that you?"

"Yes, sir," said Andrew's voice, sounding slightly more excited. "We were just handing over the gap to General Jackson's forces when our tactical displays lit up like a group of fireflies. The SSF just landed troops in New American territory. They came, as nearly as we can tell, from Ho Chi Minh City in Vietnam. Intense fighting has broken out already. We're on our way to conduct some airstrikes. We might even have to do a bomb raid."

Bad. Obviously, the UN and United Systems were very worried—and now desperate. Making every effort to keep control, he asked, "Who is engaging the enemy?"

"Militia, sir. That's all they've got, and they're starting to be very hard-pressed. But if we can just get to the enemy landing zone in time, I think we can turn the tide."

"See to it," said Matthew.

"Will do. But there's something else you need to know. We read another formation of transports taking off out of Ho Chi Minh City. They seem to be headed for Brisbane, but they might split and send half their forces to Sydney."

"All right. Send one of the LCG transports to pick up some prisoners that First Brigade just captured. Then have them pick me up. I'll give them further orders then."

"Roger and out."

"You heard," Matthew said to his officers. "That stretches us a little thin, so I'm going to implement my propaganda gambit. Send a message to Cadet Radner. Have him detail some of his meanest 'Bad Boys' to the closest pickup point he can manage. One squad should do—no, on second thought, I want as many as he's got." Bad boys were like loose cannons, best secured as soon as possible. "Also: I want as many names of enemy dead as you can gather. And when you've done that, I want a plan to capture Adelaide, and I want it done yesterday."

"What's in Adelaide?"

"A network nexus and studio facilities," said Matthew. "Ideal for my purpose. The rest is on a need-to-know basis."

* * *

The transport arrived, bearing forty prisoners and a squad of American infantry. At least they wore the infantry uniform, but added a black left-shoulder armband with the white capital letters "MP." The squad leader saluted and made his report as soon as Matthew stepped aboard.

"Sir," he said, "Squad Six leader reports to the Field Marshal. Per your orders, we have names, ranks, and serial numbers for all forty prisoners. They refuse to say anything else."

"Acceptable, Corporal," said Matthew, returning the salute. "The enhanced interrogation will take place another time. And another place."

"Where will that be, sir? We have orders to accompany you to wherever."

"Adelaide. Which we are now about to take over. You and your squad, strap yourselves in. We're taking off."

It was done within two minutes. Three minutes later, the transport touched down at another point on the front. There, eighteen Irregulars boarded. Matthew smiled. Zachary had known what Matthew wanted.

These boys had the worst countenances Matthew had ever seen in ones so young.

And the prisoners caught it, too. Half of them were visibly shuddering as the boys found empty seats in the main assembly area and strapped in for take-off.

As the ship took off a second time, Matthew climbed up to the flight deck. Two American pilot officers made motions to stand. Matthew waved at them to keep their seats. "Don't get up; don't get up," he said. "Just raise your lead ship."

"Yes, sir."

A moment later, Andrew's voice filled the dome again. "Field Marshal," he said in a pleased voice, "we just made it. A few strikes with our DEW weapons were all the militia needed. Twenty-five percent enemy dead; the rest captured, with all their weapons. They want your orders for their disposition."

"Tell them to secure their prisoners where they are. But have them stow the weapons on four big transports among the prizes. The militia can't use them, but we can. I'm going to drop an entire squadron of dismounted cavalry on Adelaide, so send those ships to its outskirts." He gave coordinates of a precise position.

"Yes, sir. Any further orders?"

"Keep a sharp eye out for any other incoming vessels."

"Right, sir."

* * *

"Sir, General Carson offers his congratulations," said a mounted messenger. "Adelaide belongs to us. The Tenth Cavalry Squadron reports very little resistance—as if the enemy didn't even bother leaving a reserve. And without those force fields, they just flat didn't have a defense plan."

"There's something else, Sergeant," said Matthew. "I can tell. Out with it."

"Sir, there's a ... gentleman here to see you. He was wearing a weird kind of uniform, almost like an overall. Hard to describe. As nearly as we can make out, he's a 'trusty.' But this gentleman says he knows you; or at least knows who you are."

"That's more than peculiar, Sergeant. Suppose you just have him step forward."

"Yes, sir," said the Sergeant, who saluted.

A moment later, Matthew got a profound shock.

The man before him, a Caucasian, stood about five feet eleven inches tall and must have weighed 190 pounds. He had brown hair and green eyes. And Matthew understood the Sergeant's confusion. The man was indeed wearing, not quite the same thing as a prison jumpsuit, but something almost like an engineer's pookie suit—except that this man was no engineer. Or he hadn't been the last time he and Matthew had known each other—as first and second officers aboard *Bonaventure VI* and *VII*!

"Is that Bertram Kendrick, formerly of *Bonaventure VII*?" he asked.

"Commander Bertram Kendrick, at your service … Field Marshal," said the other, in an almost ironic tone.

"Yes, I am Matthew Morrow," Matthew answered. "And the last time we met, you outranked me. Now I outrank everybody. But suppose you tell me your exact role."

"Like you, I have been a prisoner of the Special Security Forces. Let's see … it's been ten years, I'd say."

"But *why?*"

Kendrick swallowed hard. "My … wife and I started to inquire into your rather abrupt arrest and seemingly total disappearance. Nobody wanted to say anything. Then we set out to recapture the visual and tactical logs of *Bonaventure VII*. Not easy, because BuShips scrapped her. But as the former executive officer, I had some clout—or thought I had. And I used it."

"And what did you find?"

"I don't know *what* I found," said Kendrick, his voice betraying exasperation. "Some anomaly in the Aztlán Protected Wild Zone—looked like some structures that weren't supposed to be there. Next thing I know, my wife and I are both arrested. They sent me here and sent her—I don't know where. I can only hope she's on this planet and continent."

"Back up a minute. Your wife?"

Kendrick smiled. "I married Diana shortly after they broke up the ship's complement."

"Diana … you mean Dr. Conroy?"

Kendrick grinned. "You got it," he said.

Matthew extended his hand. Kendrick shook it as if that were the most natural thing in the world. And let Matthew keep contact long enough to be sure of him.

"Pleased to meet you again, too, Field Marshal," said Kendrick softly.

"You may call me Matthew if you'll let me call you Bert, as we started to do after Eric Shaka and Dr. Girard yanked that silly emotion-blocker out of my head."

"This is more than a simple handshake, isn't it? It's a lie-detector test, right?"

"Yes," said Matthew, at last breaking the handclasp. "You 'check out,' as I believe the expression has it. You will understand that I need to be sure I can trust the people around me. Now, why do I find you here, in the administrative center of the reformatory district?"

"I'm going to guess that it started out as one other bit of meanness, to separate me from my wife. Whom, I regret to say, I haven't seen since our arrest."

"Any children?"

That drew a pained expression. "Yes," Bert said after five seconds. "A son and a daughter. Taken from us and consigned to the foster-care system. Probably adopted by now."

"We must endeavor to find them. But, as I'm sure you'll understand, that will have to wait. Among other things, I'm trying to reconnect with as many *Bonaventure* officers and crew as I can. So perhaps we ought to compare notes. What do you know of our former shipmates?"

"Jacques-Yves surprised the absolute hot out of me. He's retired! Imagine that—retired to his family vineyards in the French wine country. So naturally, he was in no position to help Diana and me."

"Nor me, apparently," said Matthew. "His retirement, or so my intelligence tells me, happened shortly after my arrest. Do you know what happened to any of the others?"

"Well, Warrant Officer First Class O'Reilly went from one ship to another, until, shortly before *my* arrest, he landed at the technical school. Teaching basic engineering principles to candidates for engineering ratings. A disgraceful waste of his talents, if you ask me. He belongs on shipboard."

"He belongs," said Matthew, "aboard a ship named *Bonaventure*. First warrant officers like him made all the ships named *Bonaventure* what they were, each in her day. What about Eric Shaka?"

"*He* landed at the Academy, teaching engineering classes to cadet midshipmen."

"Another waste. And Dr. Girard?"

"I totally lost track of her," said Bert. "I can only hope *she* didn't get arrested."

"And Karl?"

"He resigned from the Navy in monumental disgust after your arrest," said Bert. "He joined the Imperial Navy of the Morgens. Back with his own kind, you might say."

"Not that I can blame him," said Matthew. "The Morgens take things like honor very seriously. But now I have a surprise for you. There's one other officer you haven't mentioned."

"What are you talking about, Matthew? Of course, I covered them all."

"No, you haven't. You left out Natalya."

"*WHAT!?*" Bert's jaw dropped. "You've *got* to be *kidding*."

"No, I'm not," said Matthew. "I've seen her."

"You've seen … but blast it, Matthew, that's impossible! She was KIA on Rigel g!"

"And got a new lease on life for which she never asked and never would have asked. She is now an inmate of the Botany Bay Psychiatric Institute—wearing a total-body prosthesis, like mine."

"*You mean to tell me that they turned her into…!*" Bert stopped, took a deep breath. Then he said, "Strike that last intemperate remark. Believe me, I intended no insult of yourself."

"None taken, Bert," said Matthew. "I was extremely angry myself when I found out about it. It was bad enough in my case, but I must've been more adaptable."

"Why? I ask you, *why!?*"

"As nearly as I can analyze it," said Matthew, "the SSF, or whomever they answer to, want to create a cadre of indefatigable, undefeatable warriors. To attack what target, I do not know. It can have nothing to do with the Metamorphic War; I received my prosthesis long before that, as you know."

"And under what circumstances did you see her?"

"I woke up in that Institute," said Matthew. "I was an inmate there. My memory is somewhat confused on this next point; it seems I was initially at Bethesda Naval Hospital in Nuevo Aztlán, escaped from there, and found myself besieged within an amusement park in the Virginia District. How I got there or came from there to here, I have no idea."

"Never mind that. What about Natalya?"

"They—that is, Dr. Brianna Belle Folsom, the warden at the Psychiatric Institute—wanted me to snap Natalya out of a twenty-odd-year catatonia she lapsed into after they put her into her prosthesis. I managed to awaken her, all right—but when I tried to break us both out, something went wrong."

"I don't get that," said Bert. "As strong as you are, and if she's just as strong, what could have stopped you?"

"A third prototype."

Bert stared at Matthew, slack-jawed. "Just how many prototypes does this project have?"

"Only three: myself, Natalya—and one Stefan Weiss, who now is my most formidable individual enemy."

"But you did get out, and traveled to the American Reservation. Right?"

"Right."

"I understand why you're making revolution," said Bert. "That's what these 'New Americans' say you're making. And those SSF blackguards have earned it many times over. You can count me in."

"Thank you for that," said Matthew, with feeling. "That means more to me than you know. Now, you said you were here *in part* to enforce your separation. What other motive could the SSF have?"

"Believe it or not, it has something to do with my hobby."

"Your hobby?" Matthew asked. "I never thought to inquire into that."

"Well, I have one. Can you guess what it is?"

"No."

"Twentieth- and twenty-first-century aircraft."

"Did you say *aircraft?*" Matthew asked.

"You got it. Turns out the SSF have quite a collection of aircraft, here, in Melbourne, in Sydney, and possibly in Townsville and Brisbane, though I haven't gotten that straight. Most of them belonged to the Royal Australian Air Force before the Great Evacuation—except for one Boeing B-52 that belonged to the United States Air Force. Her logs say she was a leftover from the AUKUS pact."

"Bert, why is the SSF interested in vehicles that can never leave this world?"

Kendrick laughed. "You're not going to believe this," he said. "They've had a research project going on for centuries, trying to fit gravity compensators into these aircraft. Not so much the B-52, because she's such a big monster that she's extremely air-kindly. But the SSF have a total of seventy-eight F/A-18 Hornets, thirty F-35 Lightnings, six Boeing 737 airborne radar surveillance platforms, eleven Boeing EA-18G radar jammers, twelve Boeing P-8 anti-submarine patrollers, seven Airbus A330 MRTT tankers, and various fixed-wing transports. Plus fourteen Boeing CH-47 Chinook helicopters, twenty AH-64 Apache attack helicopters, and forty MRH-90 tactical transport helicopters. Not all in one place, of course—that's their total inventory. Except for some T-2 and TA-4 jet trainers right here in Adelaide."

"First, how did they trust you with this information? Second, why are they bothering with aircraft? Third, why haven't they been using any of them in action?"

"The answers are rolled into one," said Bert—and now he smiled more broadly. "The SSF inherited the lot from the original warders of the Botany Bay prison complex. And I happen to be the only one who can even figure out how to bring those aircraft into service. To say nothing of the stores of aviation kerosene—Jet Fuel A, they call it—in tanks wherever they keep these aircraft. It's taken me five years just to bring those aircraft into any kind of flyable condition. And even so—they're afraid to fly them! Without the gravity compensators, these guys are the biggest wimps I've ever seen. Hence that other research project I mentioned: to build a gravity compensator powerful enough to cancel out all acceleration, including angular acceleration—yaw, pitch, and roll—due to gravity or maneuvers, yet lightweight enough not to compromise performance. And as far as I've been able to determine, they've had no luck with that."

"I wouldn't expect it," said Matthew. "My *Encyclopedia Galactica* mentions all the aircraft you named. And you're telling me that no one even wants to *try* to fly these aircraft."

"Maybe they've got some cadets in Melbourne. I just flat couldn't tell you that. But none here in Adelaide. Except—now I think you'll really want to hear this. I just told you that the SSF were afraid to fly any of these aircraft. But they were perfectly willing to let me use some of the juvenile inmates as test subjects."

"What are you saying?" said Matthew. "Are you telling me you've started a flying school?"

"Indeed I have," said Bert, grinning. "I've got six students, whom I've put through two flying courses, six weeks in the T-2 and another six in the TA-4. Those kids are natural fliers. It must be those holo tank games kids that age love to play. Those SSF were real boobs, letting them play that kind of game. Going from the tank game to real flying, where you can actually feel what it's like to lean over or flip upside down—I'm telling you, those boys *love* it. Well, when all the force fields went down, I gently suggested to my students that they stick with me and continue their lessons. I had a hunch that a liberation force would arrive."

"And now here we are," said Matthew, grinning. "But you still haven't answered my other question: why bother? Can't they do just as well with gravmag hybrid fighters?"

"Matthew," said Bert, "you haven't studied the issue as I have. Have you ever really *looked* at a gravmag fighter? It has the worst aerodynamics of any flying object, living or non. Whoever designed it thought only of combat on a dwarf planet-sized body, like Sol d-1, or a planet with an ultra-thin atmosphere, like Sol e, or maybe in orbit around a super magnet like Sol f. It is highly overrated in aerial combat in any atmosphere thick enough to support life. Aerodynamic forces don't go away just because you stop trying to use them. And they can buffet you in a very annoying manner, one that costs prodigious amounts of energy to fight. When you look at one of those gravmag flyers, and then look at an F/A-18 … I'm telling you, there's no comparison. Matthew, an F/A-18 could fly *circles* around a gravmag fighter! I can feel it!"

"Bert," Matthew said, sensing another idea, "I want you to take your students' training to the next level. Can you teach them to fly the F/A-18?"

"Absolutely," said Bert. "And if we move fast, the SSF will never know what hit them."

"See to it, Bert," said Matthew. "And I want you ready to start training others."

Bert swallowed hard. Then his eyes seemed to light up. "Do I take it," he asked, "that you have targets to hit, places to go, that kind of thing?"

"Bert, you and I both know that those aircraft easily have the speed, range—including ferry range—combat ceiling, and armament to complete a full takeover of Botany Bay a lot faster than I was planning to do with horse cavalry augmented by ground-effect maglev AFVs. And I should *also* tell you that from here on in, we're going to meet some serious opposition, plus reinforcement from southeast Asia and New Zealand. We can't wait around. Those aircraft can make a difference."

"And you're talking about your Irregulars, right?"

"Yes."

Bert grinned ear-to-ear. "Send me your Irregulars," he said. "I look forward to this. In fact, I could use a couple of them right now as weapons experts in two-seat fighters."

"Good," said Matthew. "Because I'm appointing you Air Marshal in Chief."

"'Air Marshal in Chief' … I like it."

"Wear the title well, Bert," said Matthew. "Get your advanced students primed on the -18s. I might have an operation for them sooner than either of us thinks."

* * *

As Bert concentrated on turning his first students into an operational F/A-18 flight, Matthew commenced his interrogation program. For four days, the interrogation continued—while Matthew asked Zach to send a few more Irregulars to him. Zach had, by then, enjoyed good battlefield success—so he sent Matthew every Irregular who had scored above a certain threshold in holo tank gameplay. It seemed the SSF had used the holo tank games as a diversion—and as a reward for them to grant, or withhold, as a disciplinary tool. How wrong they had been!

After four days, Matthew was finally ready. Now he stood in Studio A of the main broadcast installation in the Adelaide complex. Of course, he didn't have a direct connection to the planet-wide network. He expected the UN to cut that off. But he had one of the radar surveillance planes (with Bert in the cockpit and a small crew of Irregulars working the radar and radio systems) to relay his signal to his fleet of LCGs, who, in turn, could relay it to the landmasses beyond Botany Bay. Andrew had made contact with several "pirate video" station operators in Madras, Calcutta,

Phnom Penh, and Ho Chi Minh City. So Dr. Folsom had been right—a revolutionary movement did exist. Better yet—they knew his name and respected it.

Andrew's voice sounded in his ear: "Field Marshal, you're live in ten. Nine. Eight…" Above his head, Matthew read the sign that said STAND BY. "…Three. Two. One. Mark." And the sign changed to read ON THE AIR.

"Good morning, ladies and gentlemen of the United Nations of Sol d. This is Matthew Morrow, speaking to you from Botany Bay—or, to give it its proper name, Australia. Today, I am speaking to you from the Special Security Forces prison-control complex at Adelaide. Which was, until recently, the chief landing port and control center for the United Systems Reformatory Complex. Those reformatories are now closed—and their former inmates are now enlisted in the Revolutionary Forces of Free Earth.

"Before I begin my manifesto, I would like to call your attention to the other portion of the split-screen you are watching. Those names you see, are the names of our prisoners. After those names finish scrolling, you will see a much longer list—of those we have killed in action."

He paused to let that last sink in. Then he said, "Allow me to introduce to you three of our most prominent prisoners." He gave their names and ranks. He had a warden and two prominent guard officers from one of the many reformatories of the Southern District. Not Zachary's reformatory; Zachary and his friends had killed their warden and chased their guards westward where they had met the First Cavalry Division. These three had been part of that force that tried to rush the gap and … Do what? Escape into the Northern District, perhaps? Take their chances with the dingoes and the crocodiles? That was the story they'd told to Matthew's young interrogators. It didn't make a particle of sense—until they confessed to their activities before the Great Liberation.

"And now," Matthew intoned, "it's time for them to speak to you. Warden Creighton, let's start with you. Would you please tell the television audience exactly what you told my intelligence staff and me yesterday?"

The warden—wearing a bright orange jumpsuit and sporting two black eyes and a cut lip—began to speak. It was a confession of a long litany of sexual, other physical, and psychological abuses of his former inmates.

"And how do you feel now, to recount these disgusting activities?"

"Ashamed. I shall be forever ashamed of my conduct. These children were in my charge, and I abused them."

Matthew produced similar results from the other two prisoners—both dressed like the warden and displaying the same evidence of recent facial trauma.

"That's fine," said Matthew. "You may take them aside." Five boys did so.

"I apologize for their state of dishevelment and obvious trauma," he said next. "But I'm sure you will excuse my young soldiers, seeing that these men had dealt worse with them when their situations were reversed.

"And now I must describe to you the other discoveries I have made." He went on to describe most of what he had seen in New South Wales. Not about Natalya—that could wait for a time more to his advantage. But he described the psychiatric hospital, and Dr. Folsom's experiments on her patients.

Then he narrated in some detail his actions since breaking out of that hospital. He chose his details carefully, to humiliate the UN and the SSF as much as possible. On the casualty lists he laid special stress. "Some of you watching this," he said, "are related to these casualties. What did the United Nations or the United Systems tell you about this operation? What sorts of desperate criminals did they say we are? And how easy did they tell you their victory would be? Who, indeed, has the victory? As you can observe, we have. We, who are fighting for no more than an intelligent being's absolute right to exist.

"Let's take inventory—no, not inventory—a manifest. We have the descendants of a society that first stood for an intelligent being's right to exist. The UN have held them in confinement on a reservation for nearly four hundred years. Furthermore, we have persons who might or might not be mentally ill. They have suffered experiments we would not countenance the performance of which on lower animals. And finally, we have children—children, ladies and gentlemen—subjected to the worst violations of their persons imaginable. Fifteen years ago, we accused one of our enemies in the Metamorphic War of this kind of abuse. And now the authorities ask you to 'honor' the 'sacrifices' of armed effectives defending *this sort* of activity?

"While I'm on the subject, I want to address an issue that I understand might trouble you. Some of you have noticed a change in the printers you were using to produce your meals and snacks. The authorities might even have warned you to stop using them. Not to put too fine a point on the matter, those printers were poisoning you." He explained about the promazine, and what "major tranquilizers" were. "For centuries, unenlightened psychiatrists gave these to people who, in their view, were divorced from reality and indeed considered none real but themselves. Even they understood that giving these drugs to persons *not* displaying signs of such divorcement was inherently dangerous.

"Yet the authorities were willing to give these drugs to you, without your consent or even your knowledge. Why? They can have had but one reason only. They sought to govern a population of sheep. Do you remember their long-standing accusation against the Morgenetic Empire of having similar ambitions? In light of that canard, their behavior toward you should strike you as ironical in the extreme. Now recall the eventual settlement of hostilities between the United Systems and what now calls itself the Morgenetic Confederation. In *that* light, the irony of their behavior becomes the more exquisite—or egregious.

"So what did we do? We introduced a virus program that would cancel the orders to drug you. And to make slag of any printer should anyone attempt to restore the instruction. They will tell you we compromised the food supply. We did no such thing. Instead, we made safe that which was unsafe. That is only a temporary solution, to be sure. For when our revolution succeeds, we will restore farming and animal husbandry."

"Field Marshal, we're starting to see some jamming," said Andrew's voice in his ear.

He went on: "I understand my signal might be degrading about now. Your authorities don't want you to hear from me. But this much I promise you and them: the world will continue to hear from me. And not only to hear from me but to see me. This is revolution. Now you know the causes of it and the cause I serve. It is up to you to make that cause your own. For only you can answer for yourselves this vital question: am I free—or slave?"

"Sorry, Field Marshal," Andrew was saying again. "Your message isn't getting out anymore. And those transports I told you about? They're turning westward. All of them. And they're coming with fighter escorts. I don't think we can hold them off."

# Chapter 10

"**T**ell Air Marshal Kendrick to switch to radar surveillance mode," Matthew ordered. "And patch him through to me."

"Aye-aye, sir!" came Andrew's voice.

Then another: "Weather-eye to Sunrise. Just got the order. What's the word?" It was Bert.

"The word has to come from you, Bert," said Matthew. "Tell me what's showing up on the radars."

"Stand by one … yes. A flight of gravmags escorting some large troop transports, headed westward, toward the American Reservation."

"Keep a close eye on them," Matthew ordered. "If they change direction at all, call me. Out." Then he turned to the six boys still waiting by his side. "Gentlemen," he said, "the order is: scramble."

The boys' eyes shone. "For real?" one of them asked.

"For real. Get your fight suits on. You need to go up right away. Take two of the two-seaters, and take your best-qualified alternates as weapons experts. Go."

They went.

* * *

Matthew watched as Bert Kendrick's first students climbed into their planes with two of Matthew's Irregulars to serve as weapons experts. He had moved from the studio to the director's room, the best place available to turn into an improvised command post. He looked at a cluster of screens before him—one showing a feed from each aircraft, from the flight line, each runway, Air Marshal Kendrick, and even one from Andrew.

"One to all fighters," Matthew heard the Irregular flight leader say. "Call off and report."

"Two, standing by."

"Three, standing by." And so on.

"All aircraft, taxi to the runway. Take off when ready, then join me in formation. Acknowledge."

They all did. Matthew followed the action through the flight line camera, then the runway camera. To his immense relief, it was evident that Bert Kendrick had trained these boys well.

"Sunrise from Weather-eye," Bert's voice said. "Be advised: enemy flight has turned abruptly. They've abandoned their troop transports and are aiming straight for Adelaide."

"Perfect," said Matthew. "Have Andrew intercept those transports. If the fighters have abandoned them, they are ripe for the picking. I want them intact, if possible."

"Ten-four."

"The battle is yours, Bert," Matthew went on. "Run it."

"Ten-four."

As Matthew watched, the flight leader lined up on the runway, applied his wheel brakes, ran up his engines, slipped the brakes, and barreled down the runway. A few seconds later, he was airborne. The rest of his squadron followed. Numbers Five and Six bounced once on the runway but eventually lifted off. The others made it up without incident.

"All ships, take formation," said the leader. Matthew watched with satisfaction as Numbers Two and Three took positions slightly behind and to either side of the leader. Four took the slot position directly behind One, with Five and Six to either side of Four.

Now the hard part. The leader turned north. And the other aircraft all turned as one to follow him. Bert had indeed trained these boys well. "Like the fabled Blue Angel US Navy Demonstration Squadron," Bert had explained.

"Gold One from Weather-eye," Matthew heard Bert say. "Uploading your targets in three. Two. One. *Mark*. Acknowledge."

"Roger, Weather-eye," came the young flight leader's voice. "We have them."

Matthew watched as the leader turned slightly to the right. Again everyone followed. Perfect formation flying.

"Gold One from Weather-eye," came Bert's voice. "Bandits dead ahead of you."

"Ten-four … One to all ships. Prepare to break and attack."

Matthew could only imagine what was happening in the air. But no one said anything about the bandits breaking off. Had they forgotten what air assets had fallen into Matthew's hands? Or did they simply not expect Matthew to be able to use them?

"One to all ships! Attack! Attack! *Attack!*"

Now Matthew could only watch. But this was how a battle should run. The burden of command: to hang back and watch others do what you cannot.

Number Two did a barrel roll and vaulted over Number One to take formation behind and to his right side—his right wing. Three and Four paired off, as did Five and Six.

Then Matthew caught sight of the bandits. They would have been too fast for any organic to watch and were almost too fast for Matthew.

The operation was far from perfect. Number Four took a direct hit from a DEW beam. *At least the young pilot had the presence of mind to use his ejector system*, Matthew noted. But when the bandit tried to fire on Number Three, he wasn't there. Then Three moved behind the bandit. "Fox One!" he crowed—and an air-to-air missile detached from his left wing, struck the gravmag fighter, and sent it to the ground—dropping it like a rock.

*What? No shield?* But of course—a gravmag fighter's electromagnetic shields could stop DEW beams—but not these air-to-air missiles closing at a relative speed faster than that of sound! Yet another reason Bert Kendrick had been so eager to field these aircraft.

Five and Six took the hint. As a result, they scored better against their bandits.

One and Two had their hands full with the one enemy pilot who was a match for any of them—the leader. Matthew watched approvingly as One went through every maneuver he could think of. The leader seemed to know them all, for he would never let One latch on to him. In fact, he managed to latch onto One—and launched a missile.

Overconfident and careless, it was the wrong move. A DEW beam would have produced far better results.One almost lost control evading the missile. But then he made a truly inspired move.

*He laid flak.*

The leader ran right into it, and it crippled him long enough for Two to take a positive loop, latch on behind him, and finish him off.

"Weather-eye to Gold Flight. Good kills, boys. You'll all make Ace yet. Return to base."

* * *

"What you are about to see," Bert told his pilots back at the studio, "is actual footage that your planes took during that last dogfight. They had only recently abandoned the celluloid silver-nitrate-impregnated film they had used before. And Number Four: your ship at least transmitted its impressions to the ground before it crashed. So we were able to process this footage much faster than we otherwise could have. Watch and learn, gentlemen. We were very lucky to lose one plane in this last action without losing the pilot. I don't want to lose another. Or any of you."

When the session was over, Number Four knew exactly how the bandit had fooled him.

"And what else did you learn, son?"

"I was afraid of him," the boy said. "It was almost as if I set myself up for it. It won't happen again."

"See that it doesn't," said Bert. "You're lucky in two respects: that you're still alive, and that we have another ship for you. But we can't build ships like that, so we can't go through them all."

"Furthermore," said Matthew, who had held his peace until then, "we will soon launch another operation. Not defensive this time, but offensive."

"What's the target?" Bert asked.

"Melbourne. The Victoria District—ah, excuse me. Another message from Andrew." He withdrew to the nearest corner and spoke in low tones. "Yes, Andrew?"

"Second Corps has a report, and it's a corker," said Andrew. "They report liberating one of the penal farms—one with an all-female inmate population. And among the inmates is someone I'm sure you know, if they have her name right. Diana Conroy. And she says she recognizes your name. I think they found your Dr. Conroy from *Bonaventure!*"

"Hold that thought!" said Matthew. Then he crossed the room again. "Air Marshal, come with me now, please. We need to talk."

"Any other questions?" Bert asked his young pilots. All shook their heads.

"Right with you, Field Marshal," Bert said next, then followed Matthew out into the hallway. "What's going on?"

"Save it for my office—ah, here it is." Matthew led Bert into what had once been the studio director's office, and closed the door.

"Well, Matthew?" he asked.

"We found Doctor … we found Diana."

"You found … excuse me." Bert staggered to a chair in front of the desk and collapsed into it. "Just … tell me one thing. Is she alive?"

"Alive and well, and eager to see us both, according to reports. My Second Corps found her on a penal farm in Queensland. One of my LCGs is going to fly her to Melbourne to meet us, just as soon as they finish revictualing from the penal farm and a nearby penal ranch. And they'll fetch fresh victuals for us all. That gives you an additional incentive to take Melbourne as soon as possible."

"Thank you, Matthew. Thank you, thank you, thank you. And I swear to you: I will do everything in my power to reunite you with Natalya."

"How did you know we were that close?"

"Are you kidding? Do you think I've forgotten that concert you gave us all after you lost that chip? Tchaikovsky's *Pathétique* Symphony, arranged for the piano by Matthew Morrow. I'll never forget that as long as I live.

Diana was right—it was the best Tchaikovsky either of us ever heard. And what you played next—*A Night on the Bald Mountain,* original piano score. *Fanfare for a Russian Marine,* an original composition. Yes, I remember. You paid tribute to her in music. Very heart-rending music, too, which goes to show how close you were. Am I correct in assuming you're still close?"

"Closer than ever," said Matthew. "Thank *you* for remembering."

* * *

The success of the Gold Flight against the SSF emboldened many more of the Irregulars. Bert Kendrick's flying school suddenly got a lot bigger. In a day, he had recruited enough new pilots for a second (Red) flight of fighters, plus three Chinook helicopters (ungainly-looking machines, each with two counter-rotating lift rotors, and big enough to carry a platoon!) and a squadron of the Apaches.

Not that Matthew's forces waited—they couldn't afford to wait. They moved out immediately—toward Melbourne, the next primary objective. Still, it would take them more than half a week to ride there.

"Perfect," said Bert Kendrick. "In those four days, I'll have those pilots as proficient as pros. And now they have real combat veterans to train them." He meant Gold Flight, of course.

Sergeant Ewer walked up to them then. "Sirs, pardon me, but I have the latest dispatch from General Carson."

"Read it," Matthew ordered.

"Very little opposition, and he's making contact with adult prisoners. They seem to be very well-led. And they report that the main opposition will be concentrated in Melbourne."

"As I thought," said Matthew. "The SSF have learned from their mistakes trying to defend the Southern District. Bert, that makes it imperative that your new pilots be ready."

"They will be."

* * *

A Troop, the most battle-hardened of the Tenth Squadron's forces, hadn't taken kindly at first to Matthew holding them back while the rest of their fellows rode on to Melbourne. But when he'd informed them that they would train to jump out of a low-altitude aircraft to hit the enemy behind his lines, they changed their attitude quickly.

That was four days ago. Now the training was complete. The time for battle was at hand.

The troop commander turned out his forces—all three platoons—on the flight line. Behind them rested the three Chinook helicopters in which they'd practically been living for the past three days. Next to them stood six Apache helicopter gunships. Their escort.

"You're about to make history," Matthew said in addressing them. "Your fellows will remember that you were the men who carried the day— by leaping over the enemy's line and taking their base from behind them. You have trained for this moment, and now it has arrived.

"I'm sure you have questions—after all, this is new to you. But that's why we have drill—so that you can play your parts well. Rest assured, you'll find the answers in the action to come."

He turned to the troop commander. "Put them aboard, Captain," he ordered.

The commander passed the word to his platoon leaders, who passed their own orders down to sergeants and corporals. In five minutes, three platoons were loaded aboard three helicopters.

Matthew, carrying one of several oversized PDDs his forces had seized at the Adelaide base, climbed aboard one of the six Apaches. He used his built-in comm circuits. "Weather-eye from Sunrise," he said. "Bert, it's your baby now. Take care of her."

"Big ten-four."

The three Chinooks took off first and formed a flying wedge, with the First Platoon leading. Then the six Apaches took off and flanked them, three on each side. Finally, all the helicopters headed southeast toward Melbourne.

Matthew watched the portable display as it repeated what Bert sent to him. Occasionally, he looked down and knew, from the line of slag heaps, when they had crossed into the Victoria District. Not long afterward, they passed over the heads of the cavalry—and met their first opposition.

Matthew ruthlessly suppressed the urge to shout orders on his own. Bert was managing this battle, and doing it well. It didn't take long for Matthew to realize that Bert had given the helicopter flight very simple orders: protect the transports and get to Melbourne fast, without worrying about killing every enemy soldier along the way. The cavalry would mop them up easily.

An hour and a half after take-off, Matthew heard Bert give another order: "Red and Gold Flights: scramble." The Red Flight took off first, then the Gold.

In fifteen minutes, Bert sent word that the fighter squadron, consisting of Red and Gold Flights, had crossed into the Victoria District. Then they passed the cavalry ... and passed over the heads of the helicopter squadron on a direct course for Melbourne.

Red Flight reached Melbourne first. They hit the spaceport, strafing it with missiles and rapid-fire cannons. The enemy immediately scrambled gravmags.

Gold Flight flew into the fray. As it arrived, Weather-eye sent feedback to Matthew so he could watch.

Matthew saw trouble from the beginning. The SSF had scrambled an entire *squadron* of gravmags.

Red Six: "There's too many of them! We're skunked!"

Red One: "Cut the chatter, Red Six! Attack! That's an order!"

Red Six, speaking with a desperate edge in his voice: "Fox One!"

The missile streaked out—and missed. But the gravmag, dodging it, veered to the left. And that was disastrous. Red Four screamed in horror before a sound of impact cut off his voice. Gravmag and F/A-18 both fell to the ground in bursts of flame.

Red Three shouted a string of curses, half of them at Red Six, the other half at the enemy. Then Weather-eye's voice sang out: "Watch it, Red Three! You've got one on your tail!"

Gold One, his voice exuding supreme confidence, crowed, "Fox One!" A missile streaked out, then found its mark. Suddenly the gravmag that had been pursuing Red Three vanished in a ball of flame.

That's when a single antiaircraft DEW cannon, the one that Red Flight must have missed on their strafing run, locked onto Red Five and fired. The energy burst seared off the outer third of Red Five's wing. Red Five at first tried to veer away, but the young pilot must have seen the antiaircraft gun looking for another target. So he veered straight for the ground gun, went full-throttle on his engines—and slammed into the gun, throwing up a shower of sparks.

Maybe that was all Red Three needed to see. "Red Six, join with me!" he shouted. And Red Six did.

The destruction of the last remaining antiaircraft gun and how it happened must have thrown the enemy into a state close to panic. The gravmags broke the coordination they had been displaying. Sensing this, the pilots of Gold Flight went after them in total bloodlust. Three gravmags went down in rapid succession. The remaining thirteen tried to regroup—but now the surviving elements of Red Flight shot up in a diamond formation, then down.

Breaking formation, they each headed to a different point of the compass. *Are they abandoning the fight?* Matthew wondered. *No*—suddenly, each plane in Red Flight took five-eighths of a loop, then a half-roll to correct themselves, and leveled out to fly back into the battle. Within seconds, all four fired missiles, resulting in four more gravmags going up in flames.

With those losses, the tide turned. With nine enemies to ten friendlies, the advantage belonged to Red and Gold Flights. Bert was right—craft for craft, jet fighters were totally superior. Each pilot calmly locked onto a gravmag and fired a missile, except that Red Three and Six struck together at one target. Then all the gravmags were down, and the F/A-18s landed on a runway that now belonged to them.

At that point, the helicopters arrived. The Apaches scoured the enemy's ground before they would let the Chinooks land.

In fifteen minutes, the spaceport belonged to Matthew and his forces.

* * *

Matthew and Bert stood side-by-side, watching the LCG transport drop in for a landing. Matthew could understand why Bert would be as nervous as he seemed. But Matthew had a different reason to feel apprehensive, for Diana Conroy had been a different kind of friend to him. Different, but no less special.

The transport landed, facing away from the two men. But that was exactly as Matthew had ordered.

Then … Yes, there was Diana Conroy. She wore penal-farm overalls but still projected the inner strength Matthew remembered from their many sessions together. Her hair was gray—obviously, her warders hadn't permitted her to color it. But she didn't seem to mind.

She was halfway down the boarding ladder before Bert broke and ran toward her. As he did, she descended the ladder more quickly. They met at the base of the ladder and embraced, holding that pose for several seconds.

Then they broke the embrace—and Diana walked toward Matthew. Their eyes met—and Matthew walked forward. When they were close, she held out her hand. "Commander," she said.

"Doctor," he said., taking it. And for a few seconds more, neither person spoke.

Finally, she found words: "I'm grateful to you for rescuing me," she said.

"Not your rescue only, Doctor," said Matthew. "Don't forget your husband. But more than that, this is revolution. The forces now taking over Botany Bay are under my command."

"Is this when the psychiatrist apologizes to her patient for doubting his warnings about persecution?" she asked.

"We never had that conversation," said Matthew. "The SSF didn't give us that chance."

"We can have it now if you like."

"Oh?" Matthew asked. "Have you further insight into my condition?"

"Yes. I never put this down into any record because I wasn't sure. But I have always suspected that you suffered—well, maybe *to suffer* isn't the operative verb—from Asperger's Syndrome. It is an Autism Spectrum Disorder, and like all such disorders, it features a lack of communication and social awareness and has the presence of behaviors some might find off-putting. All of which, you will forgive me for observing, you always displayed, along with this distinct feature of Asperger's Syndrome: you are very, very bright when it comes to jobs of work. The problem is that your symptoms could easily result from your transformation's trauma. Or from child abuse, which I always suspected from your Thematic Apperception Test results. But I don't know your childhood history. Neither do you."

"You mean, neither *did* I," said Matthew. "During my escape from the Botany Bay Psychiatric Institute, I encountered someone who brought back my childhood memories." He shared some of them.

"Then I regard my diagnosis as confirmed," Diana said. "But of course, I did not dare put down that diagnosis on your medical record. It would have raised a red flag at Navy Medical, and I did not want that. Even today, the Navy would not know what to do with an autistic officer. The very word *autism* connotes selfishness, self-centeredness, and self-righteousness and reflects the resentment all persons on the spectrum engender in their neurotypical peers. A vile, stupid canard, nothing more."

"But you don't share that resentment," said Matthew. "Neither did the Captain nor any other officer."

"I'll let Captain—or as I understand it, *Rear Admiral*—de Grasse speak for himself. The other officers, just so you know, came to me for advice on how to relate to you. All but Natalya, of course.

"For my part, I made it my personal mission to understand rather than merely react. I recognized the symptoms and signs in you from the day you and I became part of the ship's complement. So I spent a great deal of time researching Autism Spectrum Disorders. If the Navy Medical Bureau found that strange, so be it. I had a practical application for such continuing medical education, and that made it my business.

"So I come back to what I said earlier. You suffered persecution, culminating with murder. You suffered it again. But now … now you are rescuing others from it."

Abruptly her demeanor changed. She was no longer giving a clinical diagnosis. She was reacting on a human level—he could tell that much. "And I … I am ever so grateful to you…"

"And I to you, Dr. Conroy," said Matthew. "For all your kindness and understanding."

She took a deep breath, let it out. "And Natalya! Is it really true? Is she actually alive?"

"Alive, but, until recently, not very happy," said Matthew, who started to explain.

"Don't!" the Doctor said abruptly, holding up her hand for silence. Matthew knew better than to press; she was visibly upset. "Now I know why they didn't trust me enough to have me work at the Institute in Sydney," she said at last. "It sounds like Stanley Milgram's infamous Obedience Experiment, but squared and cubed with … I tell you, Matthew, it makes me shudder."

"I don't blame you," said Matthew. "More to the point, the wrongness at the Institute merely reflects the wrongness in the rest of society. Hence the revolution."

"Then count me in," she said. "I can only ask one favor."

"Your children?"

"How … how did you know?"

"A mother always cares for her children." *Even mine,* he didn't say. That could wait.

"Oh … forgive me … I…" She could say no more.

Matthew waited five seconds more. Then he said, "Let me assure you, Doctor, that I will give your children the highest priority among the hostages I am now trying to liberate. I'm sure you understand that Natalya has the highest priority of all. But I will not forget your children. I never forget a friend. But come. I've scheduled a war council in the control tower here. And I need you and your husband to attend."

Diana Conroy straightened up and looked Matthew square in the eye. "I would be honored to attend," she said.

* * *

Matthew stood in the four-sided glass-walled eyrie of the spaceport's control tower. As at the Adelaide airfield, his aerial and airborne forces had captured yet another arsenal of aircraft of all the types that mattered: fighters, gunships, and three more Chinook helicopters.

Matthew would guess four hundred years ago, the consoles he was looking at would have been crammed with dials, lights, and communications equipment. Now, only a fraction of that remained, which partly explained why the coordination of any defense of this spaceport had been so lacking.

Of course, the other part was how Bert Kendrick had taught his students the Delta Vertical Break and adapted it for aerial combat. Everyone in the fighter squadron was talking about that. It made the losses of two of their comrades easier to take.

The tower cab was thus the perfect place to have a war council, which he called as soon as the bulk of his ground forces arrived. Without any central coordination, the adult prisons had yielded with ridiculous ease.

He turned toward the lift as its doors opened. Out stepped General Carson, who looked slightly ill at ease in a room that moved up and down. With him came General Jackson, back from running the successful Battle of the Gap. Third to exit was Jake Boddicker—once a weapons trafficker, then an inmate, and now Matthew's latest unit commander. Then came Senior Command Cadet Zachary Radner. He smirked slightly—which Matthew could understand. Revenge must be sweet.

Last of all came Bert Kendrick and Diana Conroy.

"Gentlemen," he said to everyone else present, "these two officers are Commander Bert Kendrick and Lieutenant Diana Conroy, late of the United Systems Navy. They were, respectively, my old executive officer and ship's psychiatrist. Today Commander Kendrick is now Chief Air Marshal

Kendrick, who commands our new air forces." Matthew continued by introducing Generals Carson and Jackson and Senior Command Cadet Radner.

"If you'll each take one of these console seats," said Matthew next, "we can begin." Each man took one of the rolling swivel chairs, which usually faced outward, toward the tarmacadam that was still the favorite material for an outdoor facility. Diana, of course, sat next to Bert.

"Gentlemen and lady," he went on, "may I introduce Jake Boddicker, our latest member. Zachary likely knows or can guess how valuable General Boddicker will be to us. But you others likely will not. So without further ado, I will let him take the floor." And Matthew nodded to Jake.

When Jake stood up, everyone took a moment to take his measure. He stood about five-foot-nine, as did about half the former adult inmates in Victoria District. He looked to weigh 200 pounds and had black hair (growing only on the temples and back of the head) and brown eyes. Like Zachary, he smirked. Unlike Zachary, he seemed to smirk all the time, as if his face couldn't express any emotion but uniform contempt. But maybe, thought Matthew, his expression was beginning to soften. Only a beginning, but definite. Having discarded the orange prison jumpsuit, he now wore a freshly printed uniform, all in khaki. The uniform seemed to hang uncertainly on him.

"Gentlemen," said Jake with an ironic smile, "I am what the UN and United Systems call a failure. I represent the failure of the UN to create what they call 'New Man.' Now, you Americans, so Matthew tells me, are the ones the UN didn't even try to rehabilitate. They just dumped you in the Western District, threw a force field around you, and left you to yourselves." Jake grinned. "Big, fat mistake on their part, as you have so smashingly proved."

Now relaxing, he went on: "But I, along with the rest of us in Victoria District—and the penal farm system in Queensland—are products of the education system of the UN and the United Systems." He cackled. "Mostly, I remember getting one detention after another. If there's one kind of person their schools can't deal with, it's a boy, especially in middle school.

"None of the Academies were willing to accept me. They didn't even hand me a broom to sweep the streets. Robots sweep our streets. So they just stuck me in an apartment—in Los Ann-Jell-Leez, Al-tah Cal-ee-for-nee-ah—with a printer and gave me nothing to do. Yet, as far as I knew, I got the same rations of food stock, metal stock, and every other kind of stock a printer uses. Or, well, I got a basic ration, which I suppose is enough.

"And I noticed a few things. One fine day, I broke my first law. I picked an apple when no one was looking and ate it. Did either of you Americans know that our society makes that illegal?

"Why should it be illegal to pick an apple off a tree growing in a city park?" asked General Carson. "I can understand if it were part of an orchard, and the owner had to support himself with the apples he grew. But a park? In our society, eating the fruit of a tree is part of the price of admission."

"Already, you're expressing concepts very foreign to the leaders of my society," said Jake. "Am I right, Commander Kendrick? Dr. Conroy?"

Both these officers nodded.

"Well, Matthew here has told me what the issue was. You can print an apple, all right—but it comes spiked with some drug with a Greek jawbreaker of a name … wait a minute. Sound familiar?"

Diana Conroy stood up, obviously shaken. "Do you mean to say," she said, "that printers throughout the United Systems still introduce a promazine derivative into printed food?"

"Yes, ma'am," said Jake. "Or they did until recently. I'm going to jump ahead a little: something fixed the printers so they couldn't drug us anymore. That's what put me in good enough mental shape to organize a revolt when the force fields came down."

"For five years after my last ship was decommissioned," Diana went on, "I noticed the promazine adulteration. Matthew here had removed that program from all our shipboard printers. We all took it for a coding error."

"No, ma'am," said Jake. "No mistake. They *wanted* to drug us all. But now they can't.

"Back to how I got sent to the Big Rock—good old Botany Bay. Well, that apple I ate tasted better than any apple I'd ever eaten before. It also left me very clear-headed. So I made up my mind that, from then on, I was going to eat *real* food. That meant getting out to the frontier. And of course, I fell in with one of the two groups of people who would understand what I wanted and show me how to get it. One group, I won't describe further: the Merchantmen. Don't ask me who they are; I don't know, and even Matthew doesn't know. They don't look like much, but they think—really think—with clear heads; none of this 'New Intelligent Being' stuff for them. Only, I couldn't exactly mix in on a planet of short-statured people with big ears and crooked teeth—which is what all Merchantmen look like.

"The other group is more eclectic, you might say. They're the Syndicate. Or rather, *we're* the Syndicate. We trade in things even a Merchantman won't normally touch. Like drugs that can give you an escape from the namby-pamby drudge the United Systems have made of 'civilized' life. And exotic plants and animals, some of which I'd be careful handling or even approaching. The United Systems, let's say, frowns on moving life forms from one planet to another—something about ecological disruption. But that's also the only way to get real food—or it was. And then you have those who trade in, shall we say, personal entertainers."

When he said this last, he traced a feminine outline in the air with both hands. Generals Carson and Jackson made faces when he did. Zachary just nodded. So did Diana, with an ironic smile.

"And then," said Jake, "they have those who make, move, and sell weapons. Personal weapons and battlefield weapons—even ship's weapons. And that's what I became—one of the most notorious weapons merchants in the Six-o'clock Quadrant, which brings me to how I can help you. Weapons are in my blood. I can make a weapon out of anything—and I might surprise you with the weapons I can make. I can also use, break down, repair, and improve on any weapon you can name. And before you ask, I have even traded in projectile and explosive weapons like your pistols, rifles, and cannons. But more than that, I can help you with the directed-energy weapons the SSF uses.

"Matthew informed me that a program was making the rounds to fool a printer into making a projectile weapon good for maybe two or three shots. Naturally, I had to try that out for myself. That sort of thing is good for making a riot. But as an infantry weapon? Not so much. But I can set these printers up to duplicate your weapons or even make a crude—but effective—DEW weapon. That's pretty much how we in the Syndicate make just about everything. We take printers and do things with them the Elves never intended—or at least never intended the rest of us to do."

"Just a minute," said General Carson. "Who are these 'Elves,' anyway? Matthew told us something about them, but not nearly enough."

"The Elves," said Jake, showing even more of his teeth than before, "were the first otherworldly race that human beings ever encountered. In fact, we didn't go to them. *They* came to *us* even before the Great Climate War. At least, they were around long enough to intervene in that war—on the side of the UN.

"Well, *they* gave us printers to begin with. But of course, they also gave the United Systems the technique to restrict what you could make with them. In the United Systems, you can make almost everything—except what the United Systems doesn't want you to have."

"Like personal weapons, food that isn't drug-laced, or mind-altering drugs?"

"That, and lots more," said Jake with a swagger. "And that's the whole point of the Syndicate. You can get the goods the New Economy doesn't have. But: you have to give something in return. The Merchantmen don't like us, mostly because we're their competition. And because we can go places they can't go. Prejudice, you understand. But they respect us, and we respect them. Grudgingly, I admit, but still.

"But the United Systems doesn't respect us at all. When they catch us, they send us to ree-hah-bill-ih-tay-shun colonies like the Big Rock. Along with a few people we don't generally care for. Loose cannons, you might say—especially you Americans."

"What kind of offenders would they be?"

"The SSF calls them the Big Three. Murder, rape, and aggravated assault."

"Three?" Jackson asked. "Where we come from, there's a Fourth: robbery."

"Robbery?" Jake snorted. "In the United Systems society, if goods aren't contraband, robbery isn't worth doing. Why steal what you can print? You don't even have to steal the printer stocks. Printers are recyclers, too—you can recycle anything. And if goods *are* contraband, no one's going to prosecute you for stealing them. Oh, no—they'll prosecute the one who stole them *and* the one who had them to begin with. For possession—not wrongful possession, but merely possession."

"And just how many of those 'Big Three' categories of offenders do you have in your ranks?" Matthew asked.

"Of rapists, none," said Jake. "None of us take kindly to them. We executed them as soon as we revolted. Every last one. Starting with the pedophiles. And the serial murderers of women—oh, I'm sorry, Dr. Conroy." He paused after noticing that Diana was even more shaken than before.

She took a deep breath, then smiled a crooked smile. "Please go on, Mr. Boddicker," she said. "Compared to some of the abuses I've heard about, you guys are pussycats."

Jake cocked an eyebrow at her. Matthew caught it. Admiration, maybe?

"The rest," Jake went on, "well, we planned all along to send them on lone wolf missions. To kill the warden and the head guard, for example. They're good at that—working alone to eliminate someone who needs eliminating. But we have to watch them constantly. Even utopia has all kinds of stupid motives for murder—all of them coming down to personal dislike.

"Now sure, we in the Syndicate sometimes have to kill someone to make a point, or if someone tries to steal from us to go into business for himself. But that's different. That's not the same as just not liking someone and wanting him out of the way. Remember—there's no such thing as ownership in the United Systems, especially not the UN here on Sol d. So if someone wants an opportunity to be better than an intelligent vegetable, and they won't let him in the Navy or Marines or some such, he can always join the Syndicate. And when they don't, it's because they don't understand discipline. That's why they always create a problem. Everyone in the Syndicate understands that."

"But again," Matthew asked, "what proportion are we talking about?"

"Oh," said Jake, "maybe one or two percent."

"It seems to me," said General Carson, "that the revolution Matthew is making is going to shake things up for your Syndicate as nothing else can. What are you going to do when everyone *does* have the right to the kind of thing you peddle?"

Jake shrugged. "I imagine even the revolutionary government won't permit *everything*. The Syndicate will always find a market. But you're right, General. A lot of our trades will go legit. So maybe some of us will also go legit when everything shakes down. For that matter, the United Systems will tell everybody that Matthew is planning to turn all of society into one big Syndicate."

"Which is what I half expect them to say," said Matthew. "You see, General Carson, General Jackson, the position of the United Systems is to hold all things in common. They don't permit anyone to own anything. One doesn't have rights, but only allowances. The allowances look incredibly generous, I imagine, to those who understand a scarcity economy. But allowances are not rights. Then consider the rights the government denies: to food that doesn't come with a dose of tranquilizer, or to personal weapons, to name two. And most of all, the right to exist. You understand that. In fact, if not for your tradition of militia, the SSF would have taken your country over in our absence. But as I told you, the militia took care of the SSF intruders—with a little help from my aerial recon squadron."

"Still," said Jake, "I'm surprised you haven't had any further problems along that line in the last week. Why haven't they sent more reinforcements?"

"They have," said Bert Kendrick. "But they fly these clumsy gravmag hybrid fighters. *We've* got genuine twenty-first-century *jet aircraft* and the pilots to fly them. Shockingly young, I admit…"

"Do you mean to tell me," said Jake, smiling more broadly with every word he spoke, "that you have taught some of these Irregulars, here, to fly authentic *jet fighters* in combat?"

"Yes," said Bert. "And some of them have flown with great distinction."

"Well, son-of-a-gun!" said Jake. "Say, that's an idea. A lot of my fellow inmates were pilots, also. Oh, sure, they're used to the kind of rocket fighter or rocket whaleboat or LCG that has a gravity compensator. But you know, I think you're right. A craft that actually *uses* the air instead of fighting it … it's sounding better every second I think about it.

"Air Marshal, we're in business. I have men who'd love to train on your aircraft. That is, if you have any to spare."

"We have," said Matthew. "We captured more here than were available at Adelaide. And a good thing. You see, I haven't yet wanted to send any of my air forces over any spaceport city in New Zealand or Southeast Asia. For the moment, my plan has been to meet as many gravmag fighters or transports as the SSF think they can send, while attacking and capturing one administrative center after another. Now, however, we can be more aggressive."

"I'll say," said Bert. "Mr. Boddicker, we have more than jet fighters. We have helicopter gunships and transports. And something else: a very large jet bomber. I've wanted to put that in action, but I have a problem. Not enough ground crew to service it, and it has no tail gun. It has an emplacement for one, but the original Americans, who for some reason left this bomber in Adelaide, took the tail gun out."

"Just what kind of bomber are you talking about?"

"A Boeing B-52 Stratofortress."

"Wowww. And how much of a ground crew would you need to service it?"

"I could do with fifty if you could spare that many."

"Easily," said Jake. "And we can replace the gun. What other armament does it have?"

"Well," said Bert, "come to think of it, the SSF cataloged twelve AGM-86s back at Adelaide. That's a relatively slow-flying missile—or if you like, a flying bomb. We don't have nuclear warheads for them, but conventional high explosives should do what we want. And that's not counting the conventional bombs she can drop—enough for at least one well-timed airstrike."

"We can help you with conventional warheads," said Jake. "Bombs, too. It's getting a big-enough ground crew to Adelaide; that's the problem."

"I have that solved," said Matthew. "With the force we brought with us, and the aircraft we found here, we now have six Chinook helicopter transports. Each of them can carry a platoon."

"We are *definitely* in business," said Jake. "I'd take out the SSF bases in Auckland, Wellington, and Christchurch if I were you. They're the closest, and I'm sure the SSF have forces in strength at all three. For the rest, that's where stirring up revolt comes in. I take it you have something in mind along that line?"

"Indeed I have," said Matthew. "I want to send out another virus program to enable any printer to produce a simple, but safe, multi-shot weapon."

"Like the Colt Forty-five?" asked Carson.

"I'd recommend the Armalite AR-15," said Jake. "*That's* the weapon of choice for a revolutionary. It's not a DEW, but it's a lot easier to maintain and even to print ammo for."

"See to it," said Matthew. "I want that to go out by day's end."

"That's cutting it close," said Jake. "But you and I together should be able to manage it."

"Good. And please provide a list of the raw stocks any printer would need to make the weapon and its ammunition. I don't imagine basic stocks would cover it. We should start gathering that material, so we can make some of those weapons ourselves."

"What about those other revolutionaries that were making those plastic weapons?" Jake asked. "They could use the AR-15, too."

"True, but … well, this will sound strange to you, but I can't contact them. That part of my memory is gone. I literally woke up without it."

Diana Conroy gasped. "You mean … never mind."

"No, Doctor," said Matthew. "Anything is important. Remember?"

"You're absolutely right. You see … Field Marshal … it's just possible that you submitted to deep hypnosis to block out memories of certain associates you did not wish to betray. Those memories will return to you when you encounter a key—and I would guess that someone is actively trying to get that key to a place where you can see it. Now it's probably useless to try to unlock you ahead of time—I'm not *that* good a hypnotist, and I wouldn't want to risk burying your memories forever. But if you can't contact them, someone else will, and they'll be waiting for any message from you."

"What about that, Matthew?" said Jake. "Could that happen?"

"When we win here in Australia, yes, very likely."

"Good. We can share the secret with them when they do."

"Agreed—assuming I can recognize them. But we need something else: training. My colleagues here have never stopped complaining—with good cause—that their troops often lack training even on their own weapons, but *especially* on DEW weapons. Now that we've captured yet another extensive arsenal, I want to issue those weapons to everyone who doesn't carry them. And they will need training. On those weapons, and the AR-15, as many of those as we can make.

"Because we're about to move into the worst and most heavily defended district of all."

"New South Wales," said Jake. "Yes, I know. The Psycho District."

"I broke out of New South Wales with about fifty of the original inmates," said Matthew. "In the big experimental hospital in Sydney. I was lucky—among the inmates was a United Systems Marine Sergeant who definitely was *not* crazy. He and I were there because we each saw something we shouldn't have." *Well,* Matthew thought, *I was there for more reasons, but I don't need to elaborate just now.*

"Your point is well-taken about the mental condition of the inmates," Matthew went on. "These are some of the most dangerous inmates the United Systems has in its charge. The SSF always had greater strength in NSW to keep an eye on them. If they get any reinforcement, that reinforcement will go there."

"Which makes it a gilt-edged priority to deal with New Zealand ASAP," said Bert.

"Agreed," said Matthew. "Coordinate with Jake to get a crew back to Adelaide and get that B-52 ready for action. Load it with the AGMs and a full bomb load. It should then prepare to take off from Adelaide when we're ready to move."

"Will do."

"Now then," said Matthew, "I have to name one inmate—no, not an inmate, a *trusty*—at the Psychiatric Institute. He will be an extremely formidable foe."

"And who would that be?"

"I'm not sure even you know him," said Matthew. "Stefan Weiss."

Jake turned the name over in his mind. "No, I haven't had the pleasure."

"It would be no pleasure, Jake," said Matthew. "Stefan Weiss and I were 'brothers' of a sort."

*"You mean he has the same kind of total-body prosthesis you have!?"*

Diana Conroy gasped and put a hand to her mouth.

"That he has," said Matthew. "In fact, we originally came out of the same hospital. On Berks World."

"Holy …!! Pardon the French. Matthew, your name became famous throughout the Syndicate, along with *Bonaventure VI* and *VII.* We were always—always—afraid of running into you. Now you tell me the SSF has had someone else on ice all this time, having capabilities just like yours, and they are grooming him for … What, exactly?"

"Erich Frankel built us to be ultimate warriors. The difference is that I have a conscience, and Stefan hasn't. But happily, the differences go on from there. I have certain physical advantages that he does not." Matthew described some of them. "Where I got some of these extra features, even I don't know myself. Nor do we have to know. The point is: I have them, he does not, and if anyone sights him at all, they are to let *me* handle him. Me, personally. Let that be a standing order to all hands."

"Why don't you let one of my Apaches just strafe him?" asked Bert.

"I can't spare a helicopter gunship to destroy one cyborg," said Matthew. "Tempting, but no."

"Are you sure it would come to that?" Jake asked. "I mean, between our DEW weapons and the shells and canisters the Americans can shoot out of their cannons, I'm sure we could bring him down."

"He'd dodge any beam, shell, or ball," said Matthew. "He could overrun any position before the unit could do enough damage to slow him down. Do *not* underestimate him. No—you leave him to me—single combat. Trial by combat, for that matter—because he's got a few things to answer for. And only I can hold him to answer for anything."

His audience took a hard look at Matthew for several seconds. Zachary simply nodded. A few seconds longer, Jake nodded, too. "We Syndicate soldiers know a thing or two about honor," he said. "And discipline, as I said. Don't worry; we'll let you have at him. I'll make sure my boys know, too."

"And we'll take your word for it," said General Carson.

"Thank you," said Matthew. "Your men will do all I need if you can stop the SSF from backing him up. That, however, is for the future. For the present: let's get those new weapons issued at once. Coordinate with General Boddicker on training. Zachary, that applies to you, too. Any of your Irregulars who can carry one of these DEW weapons is to use one.

"Bert, see to that B-52 as we discussed.

"Jake, let's you and I get right on that virus program. And if you have any suggestions on how to improve the American weapons, large or small, feel free to pass them on.

"We'll move toward New South Wales beginning at 0600 tomorrow. But first, I'm going to make another broadcast. Unless anyone has any further questions, this meeting is dismissed."

Almost everyone else stood in line for the lift. Diana Conroy hung back. "Matthew," she said, "might I have a word?"

"Certainly. I was expecting that."

"Do I assume correctly that Stefan Weiss was the person you met in Sydney who brought back your childhood memories?"

"You do, and he was."

"This is personal between you two, isn't it?"

"And if it is?"

"Under any other circumstances, I would strongly advise you to let someone else handle him. But as I understand it, there isn't anyone else. Even Natalya must be helpless before him. Oh, *rot* professional ethics!"

"Diana, I threw the book away long ago. I had to. The book says to surrender."

"Well, unless you count a matter of not obeying an unlawful order," said Diana. "But that's the problem, isn't it? The law is twisted beyond recognition. Therefore, your judgment alone applies."

"Which, as you know, is the burden of command. Rear Admiral de Grasse would understand, I'm sure."

"And *I* understand. So I won't presume to advise you. I'll just express one wish."

"And that would be?"

"Don't let your personal animus compromise your ability to fight."

Matthew suddenly had another flash of memory. Of Stefan waylaying him in a corridor over some imagined slight, and Matthew trying to fight back using the methods of cartoon characters. That hadn't ended well. Aloud he said, "Acknowledged. And thank you again."

"Thank *you*, Matthew. For everything." And she turned and summoned the lift.

Matthew stood alone where he was, looking out over the spaceport. He reviewed every humiliating encounter he'd ever had with Stefan Weiss—things that even Dr. Frankel could never have erased forever. He looked for things he had done wrong, ways to improve.

After half an hour of this cogitation, Jake Boddicker came up the lift and entered the tower cab. "Well, Matthew," he said, "things are moving smartly. Bert's on his way back to Adelaide, flying an Apache and escorting a Chinook. That big banana is carrying fifty-five of my men—fifty ground crew, plus a five-man crew for the Stratofortress. Boy, they can't wait to get their hands on her. Bert's going to work everybody all night and send the Fortress up at 0500."

"Will that present any problem?" Matthew asked.

"No fear of that," said Jake. "My men have everything in hand. We need to talk about printer viruses. But first, I have to ask this one question."

"Go ahead," said Matthew, almost absently.

"Stefan Weiss means more to you than just an enemy, doesn't he?"

*That* brought Matthew up short. First Dr. Conroy, now this cynical blackguard. Making a supreme effort not to lash out at Jake, he said, "Those are burdens I, alone, must carry." Then he paused to take better stock. Stefan Weiss wasn't Jake's fault—and the issue was larger than Stefan, anyway. "All but one thing," he said next. "It is my deepest secret. But it might be important."

"I'm all ears."

Matthew told him about Natalya. As he did, Jake smiled ever more broadly. At last, he burst out laughing.

"Why, you son-of-a-gun!" he cried, clapping Matthew on the back—and instantly regretting it. "Ow—I forgot that your body is made of metal.

So you've actually got the girlfriend you deserve—and a gung-ho Marine, at that! Well, of course, you've got to take that metal psycho on yourself. In your spot, I would, too." Then he turned sober. "There's just one thing. Can she help us?"

"Jake, we both know that, if she could, she'd be doing it already. Any of a number of things could have happened to her. Leaving her behind was the hardest decision I have ever made. I won't know until I reach that hospital again. So I didn't want to engender false hopes—or harbor them."

"I get it," said Jake, suddenly almost crestfallen. "I'm sorry, Matthew— I didn't think about her not being able to help herself. Still, you gave her that nanobot treatment before you left. Man, I still can't wrap my mind around that. But you know what? I just got an idea."

"What idea?"

"Could your nanobots make up a squad that could carry a coherent message?"

*What about it?* Matthew silently asked.

*It would be more like a company than a squad. But, semantics being what they are, yes. Give us 'food,' and we can begin.*

"Yes, they could," Matthew said aloud. "And the unit they would require would fit inside a small vial. One of your lone wolf soldiers could carry it. It's risky—he mustn't drop it, and it would mean his going behind enemy lines. You know your men better than anyone. If you have any of your followers who can get into that hospital and get close enough, he need only open the vial."

"Yes, but that's the challenge," said Jake. "How close is 'close enough'?"

"Inside the building at least," said Matthew grimly. "And ideally into her new cell, wherever that might be. Likely on the top floor. But: if they have sources of silicon and metal, they can reproduce. That alone enhances their capabilities."

"I've got just the guy," said Jake with a feral smile. "Wes Ziegler's his name. I knew he would come in handy someday; I just didn't know how. He's a born liar and con artist, and he liked to play fast and loose with a woman's affections. And that usually involved pretending to be someone she knew, past or present, when he wasn't. By some definitions, that's rape, but it's still mighty technical." He snorted again, then said, "Even in a moneyless society, some men like to pull that trick just for the sake of pulling it, know what I mean?"

"I'll take your word for it."

"Well, the last time Wes pulled that trick, he pulled it on the wrong woman. I gather she was and is a ranking Naval officer, and he pulled his trick by impersonating another, more junior officer. Women in any kind of authority were always his favorite targets. I think the Navy sent him to the Big Rock just because he had conned one of their own, and someone important, at that. The Navy even said he killed her. I don't believe that because he really doesn't fit the profile of a serial murderer of women. So I kept him alive. My men still think I've gone soft in the head in his case, but now…"

"Now we both need someone to run a mission that happens to involve conning a woman in authority," Matthew finished for him. "In this case, Dr. Brianna Belle Folsom."

"You got it," said Jake, grinning even more widely. "Tell you what. Make up your vial, and he'll get it where it needs to go. Now: what do you wish done with or to any of the personnel?"

"Leave them strictly alone," said Matthew. "Except for Stefan, I want them alive—to face a revolutionary tribunal on-camera."

"That," said Jake, almost chuckling, "should make quite a spectacle. And an example."

"Which is exactly what I want."

"Don't worry," said Jake. "I'll make sure my guy knows that assassination is not part of the mission. Of course, your girl might feel differently."

"That's up to her," said Matthew. "But I think she'll want the same thing."

"Just one more problem, Matthew, and it's not a deal-killer, but it's significant. Can Natalya handle Stefan?"

Matthew winced. "That's the part over which I agonize whenever I think about her, back in that hospital—where he is."

"Then, if I may suggest," said Jake, "we distract him."

"Distract how?"

"Well, this might go to one of those 'burdens you alone must carry.' After all, I think you know Stefan Weiss a lot more than you're letting on."

"And if I do?"

"Oh, for Galaxy's sake, Matthew! Talk to me if you really trust me. Just how well do you know Stefan Weiss? What *exactly* is he to you?"

Matthew took a good hard look at Jake. This thoroughly amoral individual—for how else could he rise so high in the Syndicate?—might have something. "All right," he said. "I ask you to treat this the same as you treat my relationship with Natalya. Tighter, even."

"You have my word of honor, Matthew," said Jake. "Now, that might not sound like much, coming from a Syndicate man. But I told you before that we in the Syndicate understand honor."

"Very well," said Matthew. "To put the matter succinctly, we were boys together."

"And he was a bully, right?"

Matthew found himself swallowing for no reason—or maybe he had one. "Yes."

"And you're the target-of-opportunity that got away."

"What makes you say that?"

"Matthew, you told me about yourself, so *I'll* tell you about *my*self. I hate bullies worse than you do. And do you know why? Because exactly two kinds of losers join a dirty, stinking outfit like the SSF. One is the bully, and the other is the snitch. The snitch tells the bully his target, and the bully keeps the snitch in … well, whatever you can imagine. And I always hated both kinds. When I saw that our society rewarded those kinds of people—that's another reason I wound up joining the Syndicate, because the Syndicate has no room in it for either kind of loser.

"So that's how I know that Stefan Weiss must be a bully. He's just the type to become a *trusty* in an SSF mental hospital. So whatever you have to tell me, I'm sure I can guess. But I can't afford to guess. If I'm to be of any help to you at all, I have to *know.*

"So let's have it—all of it. How you two came to have your brains put into those bodies of metal and plastic, what happened in that laboratory, or hospital, or whatever it was, everything. The works. I have time."

So Matthew told Jake things he had only told Jonathan and Katherine. About the school bus, the accident, and the worst "accident" of all, that left him unconscious for years until a United Systems Navy heavy cruiser had found him. And then about their most recent encounter.

"As I thought," said Jake. "Notice how he and *Dr.* Folsom threw off on you? Bullies do it all the time. Of course, Natalya earned his rage by getting in his way. But that means you have *twice* gotten out of his grasp. Three times, if you count your resurrection and your survival of that airlock breach as two separate incidents, which I would expect of him—I know his type. And he is *still* the eleven- or twelve-year-old bully-boy who literally threw you *and himself* under a bus."

"And your point?"

"You like to make propaganda speeches," said Jake. "All right, here's my idea for your next one. You challenge him. Call him out. Appeal to his perpetually wounded vanity. Say anything you like, but get him to come out to the battlefront. Stick it to his ego deep enough, and he'll come. And while he's making his way here—my guy can be making *his* way *there.*"

"How, exactly?"

Jake put on that feral smile again. "That, Field Marshal," he said, "is for me and my guy to know, and you to find out later—when at least one of us can report Mission Accomplished."

* * *

"This is Matthew Morrow speaking to you again, from one of the liberated prison barracks in the Victoria District in what is now, once again, the Commonwealth of Australia."

Matthew paused, but only for a few seconds and strictly for effect. From his secondary memory, he called up the speech he and Jake had finished writing two hours before.

"The Revolutionary Forces of Free Earth," Matthew began, "are about to enter the last district in what you call 'Botany Bay.' This might interest you: Botany Bay, as a British Imperial place of exile, began with New South Wales. And Sydney, now our last objective, was the largest city in Australia before the United Nations evacuated it. Again, New South Wales became a place of exile, as did the entire continent. Only this time, New South Wales became the primary psychiatric commitment and treatment center, first for the United Nations, then for the United *Systems*.

"I am sure most of you within range of my voice, always believed the United Systems had at heart the best interests of those whom various authorities committed for treatment there. But I have proof positive, from my own *direct* experience, that this is *not* the case. Indeed it hasn't been the case for at least twenty years, and possibly longer. I have the testimony of multiple witnesses, who escaped with me on MJDN 204154, that for the last twenty years, two different Medical Directors of the Botany Bay Psychiatric Institute have been experimenting on their inmates. Experimenting in ways your schoolteachers have always assured you we do not accept on animals, much less intelligent life forms."

He gave some pointed and, he hoped, instructive examples. As he did, he hoped Andrew, Jonathan, Jennifer, and Katherine were listening and would understand. He wondered what Diana Conroy Kendrick must think about all this—for, of course, she would also be listening.

"And now I am going to share with you a story that I am sure has excited your curiosity. To wit: my own origin, how I became a revolutionary, and how I could succeed in that role. The fact of the matter is that I am wearing a total-body prosthesis. What you see before you—my head, chest, abdomen, and limbs—is all prosthetic. My brain, spinal cord, eyes, ears, and olfactory chemoreceptors are the only organic components I still possess. And indeed, I grew into this prosthesis over a period of six to seven years—because I acquired my prosthesis at eleven years of age."

He paused again to let his listeners process that item. Then he went on. "My story begins with my clinical death—and cybernetic rebirth—on the very first extrasolar colony of humankind," he said. "That colony is—or was—Berks World, originally known as Proxima Centauri b. There, Dr. Erich Frankel sought to create the ultimate warrior. A warrior impervious to most of the weapons an enemy might deploy. And one able to use any existing weapon and sense what ordinary organics never could.

"According to that portion of his records that USS *Bonaventure V* recovered at the scene of the Berks World Disaster, he first tried to build a completely cybernetic warrior. But he realized what many before him long suspected. Which is: you cannot duplicate the intelligence and rationality of humanoid species in the small space of a humanoid brainpan. So he changed his approach—radically. He designed a prosthesis that could accept an organic brain, spinal cord, eyes, ears, and olfactory receptors, and connect to cybernetic sensors—and motors.

"*I* am one of his *two* prototypes. The other is—or was—my next-door neighbor. A bully who literally threw me, and himself, under a moving school bus. And who, subsequently, destroyed Berks World in an effort to kill me. Of that, I am positively certain."

He gave very brief details of the bus accident. He intended to concentrate on the destruction of Berks World, and to that, he returned quickly.

"And how and why did Stefan Weiss come to destroy our world? In one small measure—only small, because we all must answer for the choices we make—you can lay the blame with Dr. Frankel. He never once considered the psychological shock of transplanting a central nervous system into an artificial body. The fact of the matter is that a neurotypical brain cannot adapt to such a prosthesis without intensive counseling. And Dr. Frankel, arrogant fool that he was, did not provide it to either of us. I adapted better—because I am *not* neurotypical."

He described the psychological tests he underwent, naming many of them for dramatic effect. Then he spoke of being the 'neighborhood weirdo' and his lack of athletic ability. Last of all, he named the diagnosis Diana Conroy had given him when they had met after all those years.

"Now consider the condition in which I found myself. To me, Dr. Frankel gave me a new lease on life—and a long-term lease. I accepted my fine new body as the vessel that kept me alive—despite Stefan Weiss' attempt to destroy me. I welcomed the enhanced physical strength and the eye-hand coordination I never had. And I welcomed the relief my new body would give me. I looked forward to my new life—as an *adult,* with the autonomy of one. I expect absolutely anyone on the Autism spectrum to understand—*fully*—what I am saying.

"But Stefan Weiss must not have been so able. *He* woke up in a body that was not his, a body he did not immediately know how to use.

"The rest of what I am about to say is part personal testimony, part according to the logs of *Bonaventure V*, and part conjecture.

"Dr. Frankel, shortly after awakening us, shut us both down. Then he equipped me with a microprocessor he designed to short-circuit my emotions and block the memories that provoked them. Which would leave me an emotional cripple for most of my adult life—until the surgeon on a ship named *Bonaventure VI* kindly removed it. That's a story I might tell you another time.

"For now, know this: Dr. Frankel did *not* have the chance to equip Stefan Weiss with that chip—because Stefan Weiss murdered him. I remember finding Dr. Frankel's body, neck broken, lying on the floor of his laboratory, when the decompression alarm sounded. The Marines found a trail of dead bodies and physical installation damage leading from the laboratory to the colony control center.

"As you probably know, Berks World was an underground colony. Proxima Centauri b does not weigh enough to hold an atmosphere. The original colonists won their license to settle it by stressing its mineral wealth. But official records state that some person, or persons unknown, opened the colony's airlocks. That caused an explosive decompression that killed every man, woman, and child on Berks World. Everyone, that is, except myself—because I woke up, found Dr. Frankel, heard the alarms, and got into a closet. There, I sealed myself against explosive decompression, then shut down almost permanently. In that state I remained, until the Marines from *Bonaventure V* found me.

"I never learned what happened to Stefan Weiss—until we met again at the Botany Bay Psychiatric Institute, w*here he is now a trusty—an inmate placed in a position of trust.*

"I will not share with you—yet—why I believe Stefan Weiss got that position of trust. But I will say that any psychiatrist who would trust such a person, particularly with the tasks with which Dr. Brianna Belle Folsom trusted him, is a quacksalver of the most disgusting order. Whoever would entrust *her,* with the authority she holds, deserves no office of honor, trust, or profit under any sound government. This is one of many, many motives I now have to make revolution—on Earth and beyond.

"And now I come to the point. Stefan Weiss, I know you can hear me. If you're not receiving the live stream, I expect Dr. Folsom to share it with you later. Stefan Weiss, I accuse you this day of three million counts of murder in the first degree and one count of rape in the first degree. And that's to list those of your crimes of which I have certain knowledge. These crimes are, in and of themselves, punishable by death. But of course, no authority on or off Earth can possibly bring *you* to account. No authority, that is, except one. *Me.*

"When last I saw you, I told you I was placing you under arrest in the name of the revolution. I stand here today to tell you that I'm not proposing to arrest you this time. Instead, I now offer myself as my own champion to decide your guilt or innocence by wager of battle.

"You heard correctly, Stefan. *Wager of battle.* If you have the courage to match your vile spite, I challenge you to a duel. Come out to the battlefront and face me, if you dare. In that personal combat, one of us will live or die. On the result will, in fact, depend the outcome of the War of Liberation of Australia and of the Earth that I am now waging. But more to the point, it will settle our quarrel.

"Tomorrow, my forces and I will invade New South Wales. I, myself, will invade from the Victoria District. You will find me doing something a marshal or General officer normally does not do: riding point. You need not bother sending any message. Just come. Come, or I will add *coward* to the epithets you so richly deserve.

"Until tomorrow—and may the best cyborg win."

He then sent a silent command to one part of this studio he had jury-rigged. It started to play the marching song of his forces—one that the New Americans had suggested to him:

*"We will rally 'round the flag; we shall rally once again,*

*Shouting the battle cry of freedom!*

*We will rally from the mountain, we'll gather from the plain,*

*Shouting the battle cry of freedom!*

*A Free Earth forever! Huzzah and hurrah!*

*Thus always to tyrants, we'll follow our star!*

*As we rally from the mountain and gather from the plain,*

*Shouting the battle cry of freedom!"*

NThe next day, at 0500, the B-52 took off from Adelaide, climbed to an altitude of fifty thousand feet, and set a course that would take it near Canberra and, if it needed to fly that far, toward Wellington.

Then at 0600, the massive combined forces of the New Americans, the Irregulars, and (for lack of a better name) the Syndicated Militia entered New South Wales on all sides except the sea.

The Special Security Forces had a division camped around Canberra. These came out—and immediately lost a good part of its strength and heavy weapons. The B-52 abruptly dropped to an altitude of nine thousand feet and dropped its load of conventional bombs as it passed overhead.

The remaining SSF engaged Matthew's ground forces on every front and fought them to a near standstill. Only their sheer numbers enabled the SSF to achieve even that much. They had trained for riot control, rounding up the usual suspects, and VIP security—not for active warfare.

While this was happening on the ground, the B-52 climbed back to its cruising altitude. Once there, it released its deadliest cargo: the twelve slow-flying missiles. Three groups of four flew toward Auckland, Wellington, and Christchurch in New Zealand.

But then, six gravmag fighters took off from Wellington. They didn't even try to intercept the missiles flying toward Wellington; even the slow-flying AGM-86 was too fast for that. Instead, they headed for the B-52, which had turned right, and headed back to Melbourne.

Matthew watched all this on various feeds from Bert Kendrick's airborne command post. So he took great satisfaction when the six gravmags suddenly had to contend with six F/A-18s, which had taken off from Melbourne.

Five of the gravmags engaged the Hornets straight away. They fired DEW beams, but of course, the fighter pilots knew how to dodge those. The only problem was that these five were a distraction. The sixth gravmag darted in toward the Stratofortress.

Then a hail of twenty-millimeter shells overwhelmed the gravmag's shields and sent it down. Jake had evidently replaced the tail gun, and the weapon had done its job.

One other gravmag broke for the Stratofortress. The M61 Vulcan tail gun spoke almost immediately and sent it, too, to the ground. Now four remained, and the six Hornets were too many for them. Two of the Hornets were two-seaters and thus had more versatile, and deadlier, weapons systems. They used these to devastating effect. Three of the gravmags took missiles from just those two. The one-seat Hornets caught the last gravmag in a crossfire and sent it down with four missiles at once.

Two and a half hours after the B-52 fired them, the twelve AGM-86s, four for each city, struck their targets. They made a mess of three airbases. The SSF would not be able to use them again.

At 1200, Jake Boddicker sent Matthew this cryptic message: OPERATIVE INSERTION SUCCESSFUL. EXPECT RESULTS 48 HRS.

Matthew didn't know *quite* what to make of that. But he already trusted Jake's good faith. Now he'd just have to trust that Jake and his operative knew what they were doing.

At 1800 that evening, he checked in with his recon squadron. "Talk to me, Andrew," he said. "What have you got on the tactical?"

"I don't know what to make of this, Marshal. I see an armored fighting vehicle just leaving the Sydney Psychiatric Institute. It's headed for your position. Doing at least 100 klicks—make that sixty-five *miles*—per hour."

Matthew noted with approval that Andrew was learning to use the units their American allies used.

"Just *one* vehicle? That doesn't make any sense."

"Nevertheless, Marshal, that's all I see."

"Estimated time of arrival?"

"Assuming it stops just once, it should intercept you in three days, sir. I don't know what difference they think one more vehicle can make. But every enemy unit is making way for it."

"I agree it's moving fast. Keep me fully posted on its forward progress. I want reports every hour, on the hour, unless I say otherwise."

"Ten-four."

"And keep the music playing. All hours."

Andrew chuckled. "Roger that!" he said.

The music, of course, was *Battle Cry of Freedom*. It alternated with *The Star-Spangled Banner*, another anthem the New Americans had taught him. Matthew admitted to himself he couldn't *quite* make sense of its every word. (Like, for example, "Praise the Pow'r that had made and preserved us a nation!" *What Power?*) But this much he understood:

*"And where is that band who so vauntingly swore,*

*That the havoc of war and the battle's confusion,*

*A home and a country would leave us no more?*

*THEIR BLOOD HATH WASH'D OUT THEIR FOUL FOOTSTEPS' POLLUTION!*

*No refuge can save,*

*The hireling or slave,*

*From the gloom of defeat, nor the doom of the grave.*

*And the Star-Spangled Banner in triumph shall wave,*

*O'er the land of the free and the home of the brave!*

# Chapter 11

Three hours later, Matthew got another call.

"Morrow here," he answered. "Who is this speaking?"

"Jonathan here, sir," said the older man—obviously standing the night watch. "Two things. First, the AFV that left Sydney is not stopping for anything. We're revising our estimated time to intercept. Make that two days, not three."

"And?"

"I need to share a finding with you that I've taken, frankly, two weeks to figure out. I didn't know whether I had anything, but Andrew told me you really should hear this."

"Jonathan," said Matthew sternly, "I thought I gave orders to consider *no detail* too trivial to share. But I commend you for sharing it now. Let's hear it, and let me judge its meaning."

"I do apologize, Field Marshal," said Jonathan. "It's just that I never expected to see any fleet of ships on the oceans of Earth. Maybe close to shore, but never in deep water."

"That alone is significant," said Matthew. "You know the UN scrapped all the wet navies and merchant marines of Earth centuries ago. Just tell me what you have seen," he continued.

"That's the strangest part of all, Field Marshal," said Jonathan, sounding more worried. "It's a small squadron of *wooden* vessels!"

"Say again? *Wooden?*"

"Yes, sir. Not only that, but wind-powered."

"Wind-powered vessels are still available for recreational use, Jonathan," said Matthew.

"But they wouldn't dare cross the North Atlantic Ocean in its tropical cyclone season. That's how I first picked them up. I was watching one of those cyclones—the authorities call them 'hurricanes' there. I tapped into some weather satellites to see it. And on the western edges of it, I spotted that little fleet. What amazing seamanship for them to get around it! Too good for recreational vessels. And nor would they be mounting cannon, would they?"

"Absolutely not! Are you sure of your findings?"

"Oh, yes, Field Marshal, no doubt about it now," said Jonathan—and Matthew read the excitement in his voice. "We first spotted them rounding the western bulge of Africa. Then they vanished from satellite tracking. They don't have tropical cyclones in the South Atlantic, so no one ever watches those skies. But I picked the ships up again, rounding the Cape of Good Hope. They were making directly toward Perth before your forces invaded South Australia and the Northern District. Specks on the ocean, spectrally consistent with wooden vessels. Then they turned away from Perth, heading for the Southern Ocean. Since then, they always kept just out of sensor range."

"Jonathan," said Matthew, "cut to the chase. What are those ships doing now?"

"That's why I'm reporting, sir. They suddenly turned north, directly toward Tasmania. Almost as if they want to land troops on that island."

"I gather you can resolve greater detail?"

"Yes, sir. The biggest one must be three hundred four feet long overall and forty-three-and-a-half feet in the beam. Three masts, and the tallest stands two hundred twenty feet above the water. And she's mounting fifty-two guns, including two bow chasers and twenty-five guns on each side."

"Now that," said Matthew, "makes that ship the most powerful and dangerous ship afloat. Now you mentioned a squadron. What kind of ships are accompanying this one?"

"Much smaller and wind-powered, like the lead ship. *Very* lightly armed in comparison. They look more like transports than real warships. Four in all."

"What sort of ensigns are they flying?"

"Sorry, sir. Too distant to resolve—and Andrew doesn't want to approach close enough for them to see us."

"Don't. You're not a cloaked vessel. Keep an eye on them, but maintain distance. If they break for the mainland or change course, alert me again. Do you notice anything else out of the ordinary?"

"Well, now that you mention that *any* detail is significant, well … wherever those ships go, we always seem to see a couple of shimmers, one ahead of them and one behind them. Weird. Almost as if the sea and sky themselves are rippling."

"I can't begin to imagine what those are. My orders stand."

"Roger that. Anything else?"

"All other standing orders to remain in force. Morrow out."

He cut the signal. "Sergeant!" he cried.

His Sergeant came up and saluted. "Field Marshal?"

"Find Generals Carson, Jackson, and Boddicker, Air Marshal Kendrick, Dr. Conroy, and Senior Command Cadet Radner. My compliments and I would be pleased to see them right away."

"Yes, sir!"

Ten minutes later, he had his war council reconvened. He shared with them everything Jonathan had reported. "What do you make of those ships?" he asked. "Anyone."

"I can't figure out the four smaller ones," said Carson. "The big one is definitely a wind-powered frigate. This is a wild guess, but that ship is either USS *Constitution* or a very good replica. Though who's sailing her is anyone's guess. Unless we have gained yet another ally."

"I learned in school that *Constitution* vanished in the Great Climate War," said Matthew.

"'Vanished' does not mean 'lost,' sir," said Carson. "Oh, I'd love to find out it's the real one."

"Then you don't evaluate that squadron as hostile."

Carson grinned. "Sir," he said, "wooden, wind-powered ships cannot be hostile."

"And what would they want with, or on, Tasmania?"

"Well," asked Carson, "does the SSF maintain any presence on Tasmania?"

"No," said Matthew. "It's totally re-wilded, like the Northern District."

"Force fields?"

"They should have come down with all the rest. But that island should have nothing on it but wild flora and fauna. The force-field generators were inside the field, not outside. Self-maintaining until I uploaded the virus to them."

"Then that squadron must plan revictualing, refitting, or both. *Especially* if they just brushed past a tropical cyclone and took any damage. We've not likely heard the last of them."

"That might be true, but for another reason," said Diana Conroy. "Matthew, those ships could be headed for us, or more specifically, you."

"Why me?"

"Maybe they know you. And—I admit this is a wild guess, but if you *were* once in Bethesda Naval Hospital, and escaped from it, maybe you were on that ship."

"I suppose that's possible since I don't know exactly what has happened to me," said Matthew. "But how could that possibly be relevant? And how would they know to find me here?"

"Matthew, remember that no one has found *that ship* for centuries. Maybe they *do* know you, and they're carrying the memory key we talked about earlier."

Matthew considered what the psychiatrist had just said. Finally, he said, "Agreed. But we have another, more important consideration. The SSF have sent *one* AFV this way—and it's not stopping for anything. Whoever's driving it must consider himself indefatigable. And I think we all know who it might be in that case."

Jake Boddicker nodded grimly. "Stefan Weiss," he said. "Your eyes in the sky said he'd intercept us in two days, right?"

"Yes, *if* we advance at our present overall rate," said Matthew.

Jake grinned. "Well, suppose we fall in and move out at four zeroes?"

Matthew looked at the rest of his war council. Everyone looked back at him with a resolute stare and a nod.

"Pass the word!" said Matthew, even managing to convey a little excitement. "Bert, can your B-52 make another bomb run?"

"That it can, Matthew," said the Air Marshal. "Bombs we've got, in quantity."

"I want a full bomb run on the enemy," said Matthew. "Send your bomber up with a full F/A-18 squadron to escort it. The rest of you: we will route our advance through the Mount Kosciuszko Forest. Our objective: Canberra!"

And his generals saluted and left.

* * *

Hundreds of years ago, Canberra, at the center of the Australian Capital Territory, was the capital city of all Australia. Now it was the administrative center of Botany Bay. It was, Matthew judged, the perfect place to bring Stefan Weiss to battle.

The wisdom of his decision to press on became apparent as soon as the massive force moved out. Matthew could see that his soldiers were all in high spirits. Best of all, most of them had forest training—which the SSF clearly had not. Twice, the SSF attacked their flanks, and twice they had to withdraw after taking heavy casualties.

At 0600, Andrew called Matthew again. "Sir," he said, "the enemy have all withdrawn from anywhere close to your position. They're making their stand at Canberra."

"Is there anything left of it?"

"Of the city, yes, Field Marshal," said Andrew. "Of the troops, not so much. Your jet bomber dropped its load on them. Very heavy enemy casualties."

"Where's that AFV?"

"Making straight for Canberra, approaching from the northeast. Same break-neck speed. He'll likely be there in twenty-four hours, give or take an hour. Assuming he doesn't stop."

"He won't," said Matthew. "I know who that is. Now, how about those wind-powered ships?"

"Passing Tasmania to the east. We all thought they were going to land there—until Jonathan finally figured it out. They've been catching the prevailing winds. They have to—that's what drives them. The ships have taken some storm damage, but they're coming on. We estimate that fleet is aiming for landfall in Twofold Bay. They'll reach that in about twenty-four hours. After that, if they land any forces, they'll have the roads available to them. The road passing the inlet makes a connection about fifty miles north, to another road that heads straight toward Canberra."

"Will our right flank reach that bay before that fleet does?"

"That's a negative. They're in the Great Dividing Range, moving through the Nadgee Forest. That's a slow slog. That fleet will make landfall about an hour before your forces arrive."

"Which means they're trying to hit the SSF from behind," said Matthew. "Assuming, of course, that they're friendly. But some of my other advisers are positive that they are."

"We can always overfly them closely to read their ensign."

Did he dare risk that? He absolutely did want to find out whether he had other memories locked away. Perhaps some had already surfaced, only to slip beneath the conscious level. But did he want to risk complicating his thinking while planning such a delicate operation?

"No!" said Matthew. "I want you to stay back. Do not let that fleet see you. Morrow out."

* * *

The combined armies moved inexorably forward. Occasionally the SSF would stand and fight—and lost every time. And then, as Andrew had led Matthew to expect, the armies met no opposition.

So they kept marching, or trotting, through the Mount Kosciuszko Forest, past Lakes Jinabyne and Eucumbene. From there, they crossed the Bogong Peaks Wilderness, Scabby Range, Bimberi Forest, and Namadgi Forest. On and on they went until they finally stood on the outskirts of Canberra.

And there stood all that remained, at least on Australia, of the Special Security Forces.

Only now the ranks were parting. Why should that be? And then…

"A chant, Field Marshal," said Sergeant Ewer. "I can't make it out. One word, over and over."

"What does it sound like?"

"Like the word 'vise.' But that doesn't make sense."

"Yes, it does," said Matthew grimly. "That's not a word. It's a name. It's pronounced as you say but spelled 'W-E-I-S-S.'"

"Is that the 'champion' you told us not to engage?" asked the Sergeant. "The one you said…"

"Yes," said Matthew. "Stefan Weiss. See how they almost worship him. Stop here, and hand me my javelin. I will take it from here."

The Sergeant obeyed. Matthew, javelin in hand, got out.

A maglev AFV broke from the crowd of SSF ahead of him and sped directly toward him.

Matthew raised his javelin, aimed for a precise spot, and waited. At the last possible instant, he let fly—and jumped to his left side as hard as he could.

The javelin struck home. The AFV fell—hard—gouging the ground for a distance of twenty feet.

Some of his cavalrymen started toward him. He waved them back.

Just in time, too—for the maglev exploded and sent shrapnel everywhere. The javelin must have created an electrical arc in the maglev's battery—what a simple hazard to leave uncorrected! Matthew heard a tinkling, like glass shattering. He turned to the right—and saw a jagged hole where his own maglev's windscreen had been. Fortunately, Sergeant Ewer gave him a quick thumbs-up sign.

Now Matthew turned to regard what was left of the enemy maglev. Sure enough, one bipedal figure was rising out of the ruins. Matthew recognized his old adversary.

"STEFAN WEISS!" Matthew made sure that name would carry as far as he could make it.

"Yeah?" said Stefan, standing upright and stepping forward, picking a shard of metal out of his right shoulder. "Last time we met, you said you were placing me under arrest. Here for a rematch?"

"Yes," Matthew answered. "I told you that in my broadcast, didn't I?"

"Yes, sure, *dork!*" Stefan cackled. "But you forgot about one thing." With that, Stefan reached down and picked up an EMP long gun. But the instant he raised it, a bolt like lightning froze him in place. He shuddered, roared in frustration, gripped his weapon with a death grip—and flew back ten feet as the weapon blew up in his hand. But he was already standing up once again as Matthew, without hesitation, raced forward, swung his fist, and dealt Stefan a frontal body blow.

His whole body seemed to ring with the blow he'd just landed. But he had knocked Stefan to the ground again. Matthew followed up his advantage, wading into Stefan and raining blow after blow to chest and jaw.

Stefan jackknifed his legs beneath Matthew's chest and shoved. Matthew shot backward and barely landed on his feet. He saw Stefan barreling toward him, fist upraised for a kill.

Matthew clenched his own fist, waited for just the right moment, then swung with every ounce of force he could deliver.

The blow connected. Stefan fell flat on his back—and bounced up immediately. Stefan's face might be made of metal, but it could still register the rage Matthew remembered from all those times Stefan used to waylay him back in Schillingstadt. But Matthew remembered other things, too. He remembered every blow a younger Stefan Weiss had ever dealt him—and remembered all the times he *wished* he had thought in time how to parry them and follow up with blows of his own. And now he was in the perfect position.

So when the next hit came—according to Stefan's usual pattern—Matthew caught Stefan's fist in his upraised left hand. Then he swung his right fist and connected again with Stefan's jaw. Stefan went down again.

Then it occurred to Matthew that Stefan had *his* pattern just as Matthew had Stefan's. So he needed to change it up.

Too late. Stefan aimed a vicious kick right between Matthew's legs.

That blow hurt worse than anything Matthew could imagine. But Matthew was just thinking how absurd it was that a total-body prosthesis would transmit the sensation of pain from reproductive organs that served none of their original purpose—when he got a subliminal message from his nanobots. *Turn off the pain circuits! You don't need them. We're on it anyway.*

He gave a thought—and the pain went away.

That alone gave him greater confidence. So, before Stefan could follow up any advantage, Matthew swung again and connected with Stefan's face. Stefan stared in open-mouthed surprise. Matthew followed up again with more blows.

But this had to stop. Stefan was learning and still absorbing the punishment. How to deliver a blow that would finish him?

Then he spotted his javelin, still part of that smoking ruin. The battery explosion had thrown it free! It wasn't much, but it was a weapon Matthew knew how to use.

And he had another weapon. Now, why hadn't he cataloged his enhancements before this?

He extended his right hand, not in a fist, but with a pointing finger—an exceedingly foolish thing to do in a hand-to-hand fight. But now he gave another thought … and a bolt of lightning shot out from his finger, aimed directly at Stefan's eyes.

The bolt struck home. Stefan cried out in pain—and this was a pain he wouldn't have been able to turn off even if he'd thought of it. Organic pain.

Matthew leaped for the javelin.

Curses! It was warped from the heat of the explosion! Must straighten it out!

Stefan was done crying out. Now he was roaring.

Was that javelin straight enough? Never mind—he couldn't repair it any further. So Matthew set himself and threw the javelin straight for Stefan's left eye.

The rod speared through Stefan's brain and came out through the rear of the calvarium.

Stefan Weiss—or the metal body that had held his brain and spinal cord all these years—stood frozen in place for several seconds. Then he—it—fell forward, never to move again.

"*Auf Wiedersehen*, Stefan," said Matthew grimly. "Punishment carried out."

He looked up at the two opposing forces that had watched the combat. The Americans, the Irregulars, and the Syndicate Men all held their breath.

"Well, what are you waiting for!?" cried Matthew. "Attack! Attack! *Attack!!*"

Then they rushed at the SSF, who broke and ran in a total rout.

Matthew did not move. He had to let his nanobots repair the battle damage to his body. But he was also trying to figure out who had fired the EMP shot at that critical moment. Matthew had left his stolen EMP gun aboard the prisoner transport Andrew was now flying and had not acquired another. So who had?

Matthew looked to the east. He saw someone he knew he should recognize. An African, dressed in what looked like a Marine uniform, with sergeant's stripes, stood holding another EMP gun. So that's where that bolt had come from! The Marine smiled at him. "How're you doing, Commander, *sir!*" he said, resting the weapon on the ground and bringing his right hand up in a smart salute.

Matthew raised his arm—he could still do that—and returned the salute. Then he looked behind the other man and saw a tracked vehicle with a heavy gun turret. A tank. And one that ran on battery power. Beside it, Matthew saw several lighter AFVs, not levitating but wheeled. Where had he seen vehicles like these before? And why were they water-streaked?

And then he spotted the flag these vehicles flew. That flag had the thirteen alternating red-and-white stripes of the flag his American friends flew. And the blue field with its white stars—but these numbered only forty-one, in five rows of five and four rows of four. Why should it be one column short?

Three things happened at once. First, it was as if a vault swung open in his mind. *Now* he knew the mystery of his arrest. He knew that no one had staged the scenes in that footage Dr. Folsom showed him three months ago. Nor had he taken any hostages—for Sublieutenant Ayelet Cohen and Chief Information Technician Barry Sutton had followed him willingly. Together, they had rescued Hospital Corpsman Andrea Riley as the Special Security Forces brought her into Bethesda Naval Hospital—in a straitjacket.

He remembered first smelling the pollution in the air of Earth. That pollution existed here, too. It was of the same chemical signature but worse. And it was coming from the north, where China lay. He must ask Andrew to scan for it.

He remembered fully leading that escape from that hospital and into Protected Wild Space. There he had met the Americans—the *real* Americans, who *had not* left their land but had burrowed underground when Lord Steele had led the United Nations Climate Forces into their heartland. They had presented him with evidence that the Elves played a perfidious game with humanity for nearly two centuries at least, until Juan de Cuellar first demonstrated faster-than-light travel. And the Elves *weaponized meteoroids and lightning* to help Lord Steele complete his conquest.

Matthew had, in fact, been on the scene when the Elfin Ambassador, Elek, had died at the hands of a twelve-year-old girl who had just escaped a sacrificial knife. That installation in NRD-01-VA-Lucketts, the sighting of which had led to Matthew's arrest, was a pedophile game preserve. Was—but no more. For he, Matthew, had liberated it. And Zach Radner, who had led the prisoner revolt in the Reformatory District, had assisted in that action.

So much else did he remember. The fateful meeting with an acting president, where he had concluded that war against the original United States had been the object of his construction all along. Then, addressing a joint session of the United States Congress in the Hall of the Mountain King in Cumberland Caverns. Capturing the Kings Dominion Amusement Museum—and staging its operations of four hundred years earlier to break an SSF captain. And, when he broke, he had told him that Natalya still lived—if you could call it that—and was a prisoner in the Botany Bay Psychiatric Institute. Which was where the SSF had brought him—as he'd known they would.

At the moment the SSF prisoner at the Kings Dominion Amusement Museum had made his confession, Matthew had formed the resolution that would bring him to this continent, for the Americans knew about their long-lost cousins in the Western District of Botany Bay. This explained the wooden fleet, too. Their flagship must be the original USS *Constitution*. And the others must be *Mayflower II*, *Susan Constant II*, *Godspeed II*, and *Discovery II*. Replica colony wagons, all. And all armed, exactly as their originals had been, with authentic chaser guns. Except for *Constitution*, which bristled with twenty-four and twenty-pound guns.

The "rippling shadows" had their own explanation because the United States Navy had two twenty-first-century ships, centuries ahead of their time when the Americans first launched them. Stealthy ships. And now … cloaked ships.

Why had he forgotten all this? Because the Director of Naval Intelligence, Vice-Admiral Sean Vincent USN, had offered Matthew Morrow and Zach Radner a regimen of deep hypnosis. Under its influence, in the event of capture, each would forget everything that had happened to him beyond a certain event. In Matthew's case, that event had been his escape from Bethesda Naval Hospital. In Zach's case, no doubt it was Matthew's rescue of him from that game preserve. But one glance at the new American flag, with its thirteen stripes and forty-one stars, would bring back all their memories. Zach hadn't seen the flag yet, but he would.

Matthew even remembered the forty-one stars and what they represented. The United States now had only forty-one States. The Senate that had watched him receive the Purple Heart had consisted of eighty-two members, not one hundred.

Then the second thing happened. An internal connection, much too small to see even if he could look at it, re-established itself. What he had thought was an addendum to his *Encyclopedia Galactica* turned out to be part of a parallel reference work: the *Encyclopedia Patriae*. With full particulars on the history of the United States of America, including the origins of those wooden, wind-powered ships. And the history of the United States *Patriotic* System of Units. Of course, he hadn't known why he carried new values of the elementary charge and luminous efficacy constants. His New American hosts from the American Reservation never used them. But the original Americans, in the undergrounds that lay beneath Protected Wild Space in North America, did.

Finally, the third thing happened. A long-dormant program awakened in Matthew and reached out to any network answering to a pre-set code sequence—and found it—in the tank. The tank, bristling with antennae, carried an information server—which carried Matthew's secondary memories. And now, at last, his network connection restored those memories to him. Memories of many enhancements—including ROM chips to preserve his most vital combat skills and furnish him with the *Encyclopedia Patriae* and all its secrets—were now restored.

Matthew also received a complete briefing on the voyage of the USS *Constitution* and the four replica ships across a vast ocean. Catching the prevailing winds, exactly as Andrew and Jonathan had guessed, except for the equatorial crossing. The doldrums. To cross those, those two modern, cloaked ships must have taken them in tow. No doubt those two ships would reveal themselves—in Sydney Harbor.

"Field Marshal?" Matthew turned. It was Sergeant Ewer.

"Not to worry, Sergeant," he said. "These are more than friendly. May I introduce you to the original Americans, of whom you are a long-lost cousin."

"Say what?"

"Perhaps you'll someday introduce yourself to Representative Ann Archer Ewer, from the Commonwealth of Pennsylvania."

"Wait a minute ... You mean the *original* Pennsylvania?"

"Yes," said Matthew. "And your distant cousin is the Speaker of the House of Representatives."

Before he could explain further, he had company. Out of the north, running hard at an incredible sixty miles per hour, came Natalya. Barely managing to slow down, she rushed up to him and embraced him. "Matthew!" she cried—not a bit out of breath; obviously, she knew her new body well. "Oh, it's so *good* to see you again. But listen—you have to raise your body shield *now*. There's going to be a thermonuclear explosion any second now, in the northern sky."

"Say what?" That was Sergeant Ewer.

"I'll explain to you later," said Matthew. "For now: *take cover*. And don't look up."

He led Natalya over to the platoon of metal vehicles that must have just landed. And to the platoon's leader—and the fresh Sergeant who had saved his life with that EMP shot.

"Lieutenant Natalya Fyodorovna Bronskaya, formerly of the United Systems Marine Corps," Matthew said, "may I present Second Lieutenant Benjamin Walston, United *States* Marine Corps, and Sergeant Peter Jameson, *also* of the United States Marine Corps. That's United States of America, by the way."

"Pleased to meet another Marine, ma'am," said Walston, holding out his hand.

Natalya shook it—briefly. Then she said, "Lieutenant Walston, I can already sense you have some highly sophisticated electronic equipment. I suggest you and your men shield it—*now*—against electromagnetic pulse."

Walston's eyes widened. "Did someone launch a missile at us?"

"You got it."

Walston turned to Sergeant Jameson. "Get to it, Sergeant," he said.

"Yes, sir ... *All right, let's raise those EMP shields to max! On the double!*"

Matthew wanted to ask Natalya to brief him further, but he immediately sensed an incoming call. "Morrow here," he said. "What is it, Andrew?"

"Field Marshal, we're tracking an LCG that literally popped in out of nowhere! Since when do anybody but the Far-elves have cloaked ships?"

"Our familiar Elves have them," said Matthew. "That will be a long brief. But that ship is most likely friendly. What's it doing?"

"Well, it dropped down very briefly and let someone aboard. It looked like Natalya … By the way, is she with you?"

"That's affirmative. Go on."

"Well, while you and Stefan Weiss were duking it out, that LCG made for your location, doing about 150 knots. Then suddenly, it slowed and dipped. Then Natalya *jumped* from the boarding ladder and took off on foot for your position. And making sixty miles per hour—I had no idea either of you could run that fast. And the LCG headed up north. Now we read an intercontinental ballistic missile taking off from the Manchuria region, and the LCG is on an intercept course!"

"Say *what!?*"

"I say again, the LCG is on an intercept course—make that a *ramming* course—toward that missile."

"Take all defensive measures against electromagnetic pulse! Pass the word to the squadron!"

"Roger that, and we'll be okay. But if that LCG hits that missile where I think it will, it will detonate over Manchuria. It will be too low to spread an EMP much further than that.

"Stand by one … Field Marshal, we're getting a forward camera feed from the LCG."

"Pipe that down to me," Matthew ordered.

He used his nictitating membranes to watch the view forward from the LCG, then a tactical display showing the missile. The POV changed again, now showing a close-up image of the missile. Matthew read the missile's name in Chinese characters: *Dongfeng 40*. He would have to check that out with Robinson and his team. But, he noted grimly, he could readily guess: the UN knew exactly where most of the old missile fields were and had just launched this one out of Manchuria. The tactical display confirmed a guess he'd already made: that missile had Canberra as its target.

Then he heard a sound that made him freeze. A woman's voice. A voice he knew.

*Ayelet!*

And it was, indeed, former Sublieutenant Ayelet Cohen. When last he saw her, she had become *Segen* Ayelet Cohen of the *Tzva HaHaganah LeIsrael*—the Israel Defense Forces. Now she was singing, "A Free Earth forever, huzzah and hurrah; thus always to tyrants…"

He turned to look at Natalya, who clearly caught the stricken look his eyes must be registering.

"Matthew," she said, taking his hand, "please draw away with me."

She led, and he followed, too befuddled to do anything else.

Ayelet was now singing a different song, this one in Hebrew: "*Kol od balevav panimah, nefesh Yehudi homiyah…*"

Natalya stopped. "Sit with me, Matthew," she said, still in that sober tone.

He did.

"*Ulfa'atey mitzrach kadimah, ayin le-Tzion tzofiyah…*"

"Close your eyes, Matthew," Natalya was saying. "It won't be long."

Matthew closed his eyes—just in time, for the tears were beginning to flow. But that meant he could see only the view from Ayelet's stolen LCG, the one that had belonged to the Elfin Ambassador, whom Sandy Rossini had filleted like a flounder in that raid on the pedophile camp. And he could hear Ayelet as she continued to sing: "*Od lo avda tikvatenu, ha tikvah ha noshana…*"

"I'll tell you when to raise your shield, Matthew," said Natalya, now beginning to sound a little upset herself.

"*La'shuv le-eretz avoteynu, le'ir ba David, David hana.*"

"Now, Matthew."

He took a chance. Maybe he could block all but the radio signal he was getting from Andrew. He tried it, and it worked. So he could still see himself, as it were, rushing toward the missile—except that it was Ayelet doing the rushing.

Ayelet's voice said one more thing. "Matthew, if you can hear this … *ani ochevet otch. Shalom.*"

The missile rushed toward him faster than he could follow.

And then, for the briefest instant, Earth gained a new sun. Within three seconds, the new sun burnt itself out.

# Chapter 12

**M**atthew lowered his body shield, and Natalya likewise lowered hers. Then he shut down his commlink circuits—all of them—and opened his eyes again. For five seconds he sat, looking into the high northern sky. The bright light from the detonation of the Dongfeng 40 missile had faded. So now the only sun in the sky was *the* sun.

Of course, Matthew could predict what the Americans would say. Ayelet had just "taken one for the team." This was an overwhelming victory on many levels. The enemy had tried the most desperate measure imaginable to defeat him and failed. Better yet, he had propaganda footage to prove to the world that a counterrevolutionary force had used *a weapon of mass destruction*, of the type the United Nations would never acknowledge having.

So why did this victory seem hollow just now? Because he didn't have Ayelet to share it with. Ayelet, she of the raven-black hair and arresting figure, who had freed him from his captivity in Bethesda. Ayelet, who had declared her love for him and comforted him when he thought Natalya was dead. Even decades after that loss, Ayelet had done wonders for him.

Of course, as he soon learned, he had *not* lost Natalya after all. So he had let the SSF capture him, knowing they would bring him here where he could free Natalya, and with her, an entire continent. But at what a terrible price! How could he bear this loss?

"Matthew," Natalya said softly.

He turned to face her.

"Please don't hold this in. I understand—perfectly. Ayelet was a wonderful woman in many ways. I'm glad she was there for you when you thought I was dead and had every reason to think that. I'm especially glad she set you free because otherwise, I'd still be in never-never-land.

"But, Matthew, we're alone here. I made sure of that. It's you and me now. Let it go. You can't be the stalwart, always-in-control commander all the time. Not even Captain de Grasse could do that. Those five stars on your shoulders—I still am dying to learn who gave you those—haven't frozen your heart. This is your moment—our moment. Take it."

The tears began to flow again. Then his chest began to heave—what would Dr. Frankel have to say about *that?* And then he did cry. Great, wracking sobs burst forth from him, as they had done from Natalya, three months ago. Now Natalya wrapped her arms around him. "Matthew," she said, "I'm here. Just as you were here for me. And we're going to set it right. Just as you told me. You were right, then, and you know I'm right now."

Matthew continued to sob and weep for five minutes more. Then, at last, he regained some semblance of control. He stood up and gently helped Natalya to her feet. "Thank you, Natalya," he said—and at least he could say it with dignity. "Thank you for that. And I believe you grieve for Ayelet just as I do."

"Believe me; I do," she said. "She told me everything. Even about your last night together. Before you ask, yes, it was awkward to hear—at first. But we didn't have time to get into the awkwardness. She told me how she had found you—she, a psychiatric nursing officer. Imagine that—a nurse who taught herself to be a pilot."

"I trained her in that," said Matthew.

"Even more remarkable," said Natalya. "She told me something else, too—the State of Israel has an Institute of Genealogy. They traced her ancestry clear back to a great historical figure—Elie Cohn, the most heroic covert operative in their modern history.

"Anyway, we spent half our time talking about me. She seemed to understand instinctively how I felt. You taught her that, didn't you?"

"If only by my own association with her, yes. She told me once that I was still a man, even if I wear a machine body."

Natalya smiled. "Of course you are," she said. "Don't think I've forgotten that." She kissed him full on the mouth. He responded. It felt very good, better than he expected. Then she said, "It's so much better this way, knowing that we're both free."

"I'll say again what I said before," said Matthew. "We make our own rules, in this and in any other context. Speaking of which: I could use a covert operative. Are you willing?"

"Whatever you'll entrust me with—Field Marshal," she said jauntily. "I want this revolution to succeed every bit as much as you do. And you've been making it a lot longer. I have some serious catching up to do. Beginning with those new units of measurement I heard you use."

"They're not so new as that," said Matthew. "Not all of them, anyway. In any case, that shouldn't be a problem. One more thing: did you get the other part of my message? About how every revolutionary with access to a printer could be his own gunsmith?"

"Oh, yes," said Natalya, still smiling. "That part was urgent enough for me to tell Ayelet about, first thing. She got the message off—before she saw the missile."

"That missile will have a lot of propaganda value," he said. "But come—let's check in with our staff. Before they wonder whether we're both malfunctioning."

Natalya nodded soberly as they returned to the site of Matthew's single combat. The ruined body that had once been Stefan Weiss lay where it had fallen. Lieutenant Walston stood next to it, looking a little uncertain—until he saw Matthew and Natalya. Then he snapped to attention and saluted.

Returning the salute, Matthew said one word: "Report."

"We didn't suffer any EMP, Field Marshal," the Lieutenant said. "Actually, you can thank Sergeant Jameson here for that. He was the first to figure out the secret of an Electromagnetic Pulse weapon. He wrote the whole thing up and gave the secret to Captain Robinson. That's how we came equipped with shielding."

"Congratulations, by the way, on graduating from OCS."

"Thank you, sir," said the young platoon leader. "You could have knocked me over with a feather when my first orders after I graduated were a posting to the Seventh Cav's Recon Platoon as its permanent leader, and *then* orders to ship out aboard *Constitution*. That must have been one helluva report you wrote to the OCS commandant. What did you do, send for me by name?"

"Something like that," said Matthew. "You proved yourself a good officer in all but name, back at Kings Dominion. I knew where I was going next and could think of no better officer to back me up, except maybe Captain Robinson—but that job would have been one or two grades below his bars. So I needed to make sure that you would graduate, then be the one to come after me.

"Anyway, that was a good shot Sergeant Jameson fired. Jameson obviously knows EMP weapons very well. I might have known that Stefan would cheat at our little boxing match. Sergeant Jameson made sure he couldn't. But, bottom line, you were already protected."

"Yes, sir. In fact, I don't think any of us got blinded, even partially. That missile went off too far away. It's those poor Chinese I worry about."

"So do I," said Matthew. "I assume *Constitution* landed you on the shore of Twofold Bay?"

"Yes, sir. The fleet will be on its way to Sydney."

"Which is where we should all be heading. Lieutenant Bronskaya will ride with you to Sydney. I have my own driver."

"Are you sure you don't want to travel with us?" Walston asked. "After all, we can provide better protection."

"Better that we travel separately," said Matthew. "Besides, she will want the opportunity to debrief you."

"Thank you, Matthew," said Natalya, smiling again.

"We will meet at the Botany Bay Psychiatric Institute. Which, as you will find, is near the harbor. I want to capture the Medical Director of that Institute, and I want her alive. You are not likely to find any more effectives on my level—if you catch my drift."

Walston grinned ear-to-ear. "Oh, I do indeed, Field Marshal," he said. "By the way, I like saying that. What about him?" he asked, indicating Stefan's remains.

"I'll take care of him," said Matthew. "I'll see you in Sydney."

Lieutenant Walston saluted. Then, after he and Natalya climbed into his vehicle, the Recon Platoon moved out. Matthew walked over to Stefan, threw the non-functioning body over his shoulder, and carried it to his own vehicle. Sergeant Ewer helped him stow it inside.

"Take me into the city," Matthew ordered. "I have a broadcast to make."

"Yes, sir," said the Sergeant, with more than the usual feeling.

* * *

"This is Matthew Morrow, speaking to you now from the Canberra Administrative Center of the former prison complex of Botany Bay," he said inside the usual warden's studio. "This soon will be the capital city of a reconstituted Commonwealth of Australia.

"But that can wait. I have two announcements that will be directly relevant, I'm sure, to most of you following my broadcasts.

"First, Stefan Weiss is dead. That champion of iniquity that the Special Security Forces hoped to pit against me fell before me in trial by combat. It was a combat long in coming, as I told you before. I have footage of that event, which I will transmit later.

"But now I need to transmit something else. About two hours ago, some authority or authorities unknown made the decision to attempt to destroy me, using a thermonuclear intercontinental ballistic missile." He explained about the Dongfeng 40 missile and its thermonuclear cargo and how Ayelet had destroyed it. He even sent his best holographic video of Ayelet's last moments.

"Do not let anyone tell you," he went on, "that no one knew about those silos. How could such a missile launch in the middle of my combat with Stefan Weiss if no one had those missiles primed and ready to launch on command? I, or rather *we*, have them dead-to-rights. And you have *them* to blame for the damage to countless cities in China from the launch of that missile.

"Do not let Ayelet Cohen, Lieutenant in the Israel Defense Forces, Heroine of the Revolution, die in vain. You know what to do. When next I speak to you, I will speak from Sydney, the last objective in Australia.

"A free Earth forever! This is Matthew Morrow, signing off."

He gave a signal, and then the "on-the-air" light above his head winked out. Then, at once, he heard some very loud applause.

Natalya strode in, still clapping. "Excellent, Matthew!" she said. "Very inspiring. I've never heard you speak that way before, and it was good to hear."

"I'm glad you like it," said Matthew. "More to the point, I *hope* my other listeners like it."

"Oh, they will. But Matthew … I don't know how else to put this, but … we need to talk."

"About what?" he asked, smiling.

"About Ayelet Cohen. Matthew, are you sure she's dead?"

"Why wouldn't she be? Natalya, I watched the camera feed. It was unmistakable."

"But, Matthew, it didn't include her being seated in the cockpit, did it?"

He opened his mouth—then closed it. "What are you driving at?" he asked.

"Matthew, you have to listen to me. Lieutenant Walston gave me a full briefing about her. Remember, she served as a guide for that little task force. And as strike force leader, Ben Walston would have as much reason to communicate with her as the task force commander. He is absolutely sure that Ayelet Cohen was—is many things, but 'suicidal' is not one of them."

"Then how does he explain what she did?"

"Matthew, you and I both know that an LCG transport can take a detailed flight plan and follow it without pilot's intervention. The earliest guided missiles could do that. And that's what she turned that ship into—a missile. Or maybe an anti-missile."

"But what do you mean that she did? Bail out in a lifeboat?"

"Matthew, have you forgotten already? A transport that size has a gig that's larger than any one-person lifeboat."

Of course, it did. And equally obviously, the detonation of the warhead would preclude any examination of the wreckage because it would destroy it. "Now, why didn't I think of that?" he blurted out. "Why didn't *I* think of that?"

"Because you were too close to the situation … *Shofet* Matthew."

"And where did you hear that title?"

"Lieutenant Walston told me. After *she* told *him* where that title came from and what it means."

"What else did Lieutenant Walston tell you?"

"Just this," said Natalya. "It was obvious to him that she was trying to prove something to herself—and to a bunch of other people. I couldn't understand all of it, but he mentioned the word *Zealot*. Was that part of your restored memory?"

"Indeed it was—and is. Now I know why Ayelet did what she did. You're right, Natalya. The Zealots are an organization she began to recruit long ago. Now she intends to join them and lead them personally. I told her once that she and they would know when the time was right. So she finally figured it out."

"And leading you to believe she was making a suicide run?"

"Partly for our benefit," said Matthew, reaching for Natalya's hand. He gave it a quick squeeze, and she returned it. "But more because she knew I would give her a good eulogy. Few things can inspire soldiers more than a leader they revere, whom they think has died in action, suddenly reappearing before them. And for that matter, nothing scares an enemy more than an apparently resurrected general or flag officer. The Moors found that out, to their dismay, when El Cid's staff propped his body up on its war charger for the final action. Now the SSF will have to learn."

"What was that last song she was singing?" Natalya asked. "Before she said she loved you?"

"The National Anthem of Israel—the old version, the one they sang *before* the State of Israel formed."

"And the version Jews sing today," Natalya said. "Imagine that—the State of Israel beneath the North American Protected Wild Space!"

"Yes," said Matthew. "But wait. If you know she told me she loved me, then you know Hebrew. Where did you learn it?"

"Novy Mir had a small Jewish population," she said. "A Jewish family tried to shelter me. They taught me Hebrew and even their *Tanakh*. I must find out what happened to them."

"Ayelet introduced me to that work," said Matthew. "I had time to speed-read and memorize it. I still carry it in my secondary memory. Especially the stories of the *Shoftim*."

"My Jewish hosts certainly take the *Tanakh* seriously enough."

"So does Ayelet," said Matthew. "And so do the people of the State of Israel, exiled though they are. They really treat It as an Historical Record. They even claim to know where the Elves came from—though even they aren't *dead* sure about that. But they describe their current living arrangement as a Second Diaspora, made pleasant only because they have better hosts this time."

"How in the name of … no. Matthew, you and I are *not* going to swear by the Five Ladies. Never again. No 'ladies,' they."

"I know," he answered. "And I concur. But right now, I ask you to bring me up to date. How did you escape from the Institute this last time?"

"It was those nanobots you sent," she said. "Very clever of you—and Wes Ziegler, your chosen delivery man. Do you know what he did? He *swallowed* them. Then he let the SSF capture him—maybe knowing they'd bring him to Sydney. Where exactly did you find him?"

"In the Victoria District, of course. He was an adult prisoner convicted of murder. The one who recommended him to me doesn't believe he killed anyone, by the way."

"Neither do I. Oh, he's a psychopath and a con artist, as he freely admitted to me later, but *not* a killer. He actually conned Dr. Folsom. It mustn't have been too hard because I gather she wanted to use him for a fourth prototype. The situation must have seemed urgent to Dr. Folsom, too. You were on the loose; I was acting catatonic again…"

"You mean you shut yourself down?"

Natalya grinned. "That's exactly what I did. That way, I didn't have to care what Dr. Folsom or that cyborg maniac trusty of hers did to me. Only Stefan Weiss had taken himself off! We learned later he decided to come after you. And right after he went off half-cocked and ran out on his own, is when Wes was admitted.

"So naturally, she wanted him for another prototype. Again, that's what he told me, and … Well, I believe him. It gave him bragging rights, and it fits with everything else that happened. He asked what kind of project Dr. Folsom had in mind, so she told him all about Stefan, you, and me. She even took him to see me."

"And?"

"*And,* Wes actually convinced her that maybe *he* could snap me out of my blue funk!" She burst out laughing. "He said Dr. Folsom could watch all the action on her monitors, and *that* seems to have sunk the hook. Besides everything else, Brianna Belle Folsom is a pervert, if you want my honest opinion."

"Then she also is a stupid, arrogant fool," said Matthew. "So she put him into your cell, and the nanobots he was carrying gave you my message."

"That's right. After that, it was a simple matter. He let the bots crawl over my face and into my mouth. Then he waited—while my bots chewed away the manacles and leg irons that held me against the wall of my cell. Once they were finished, I woke up, searched out all the bugs in the room, and smashed them. Then I just concentrated on getting us both out. Stefan was gone, of course, or so Wes told me. Even if he wasn't, I figured if I ran into Stefan again, I'd deal with him when the time came, as best I could. In fact, those new bots carried a lot of suggestions for enhancements, in addition to the message about how to print guns. Which meant Wes had to wait patiently, for hours. But it was worth it. Matthew, this new upgrade is great. I know Dr. Folsom is sorry for her initial experiment on me. As far as she's concerned, it was and is a total failure— from her point of view."

"But not from yours." It was more of a statement than a question.

"Definitely not," she said, with that same feral smile he remembered. "Anyway," she said, more seriously, "Wes and I interrogated Dr. Folsom's yeoman and screwed out of her that Stefan had rushed out to meet you in Canberra. So we grabbed the first AFV we saw and headed there ourselves. We encountered some Syndicated troops, and I let Wes rejoin his outfit. He looked very happy—as if maybe he had finally taken the revenge he'd been seeking all his life."

"Revenge? Against whom?"

"Who can tell? His mother, a woman teacher who didn't like boys, or maybe some warped female psychiatrist who took a shine to him and then blamed him for whatever happened afterward. Believe me, Matthew, I know all about wanting revenge, and I'm sure that's what drove him."

"You don't suppose," said Matthew, feeling another idea dawn on him, "that it was Dr. Folsom herself?"

Natalya took no more than a second to think about that—she must have learned well how to use her auxiliary processors to aid in cogitation. Then she said, "You know, it's funny. For just a moment, I thought it *might* be. But Wes didn't tell me, and didn't want to talk about himself, and besides, neither one of us had time."

"Don't ever expect a man to tell a woman a secret like that," said Matthew. "He's likely to regard all women as suspicious. That he trusted and worked with you is because you were just as much a prisoner as he had been. But go on."

"Anyway, after I dropped him off, I kept going—on foot, figuring my friend could use the AFV better than I. Then I met Ayelet's ship, so she picked me up, and we compared notes. I briefed her on the gunsmithing solution, and she briefed me on certain engineering secrets—like how to cloak another ship. You know the rest."

"Quite a story," said Matthew. "Especially about your escort. Had I known that Wes Ziegler and Dr. Folsom had a previous history, I never would have approved the mission. But I did, and he brought it off."

"Matthew, his conduct was exemplary, and I would recommend him for immediate promotion—if I could speak to his commanding general."

"You'll get that opportunity soon. You'll attend my war council. Where, among other things, we'll plan your first mission. But first, you and I have an appointment."

"An appointment I've been looking forward to keeping."

* * *

From that moment on, the offensive moved at lightning speed. Reports from the northern and western fronts told the same story: SSF were either in a total rout, or, in some cases, surrendering.

The SSF prisoners didn't present too significant a problem. But sometimes, the liberated psychiatric inmates did. They must either have suffered greatly from Dr. Folsom's experimental program or had genuinely serious mental problems.

Matthew summoned Jake and told him the problem. "If you have any suggestion," he finished, "I'd like to hear it. But we have to do it fast."

"I see what you mean," said Jake. "Well, offhand, I'd say that the best person to handle psychopaths is another psychopath." He fell silent for a few seconds, then said, "I know! Wes Ziegler! He's perfect! He just put one over on the one they all call the Dragon Lady. They'll respect him."

"And I can't think of a better man or a better assignment for him," said Matthew, smiling. "Natalya recommended him for promotion."

"And promotion he will get!" said Jake, smiling back. "That settles that. Any other problems?"

"Just one. The SSF should have gotten reinforced a long time ago. They haven't, and I don't know why, and it worries me. But that's my problem, not yours. Give Mr. Ziegler my compliments and put him in charge, as you said."

"Right!" Jake saluted and left.

Matthew ordered Sergeant Ewer to drive him to Sidney to rejoin the battlefront as fast as he could get there. And for the next three days, Matthew managed the offensive personally. It was more a tightening of a noose, first around Sydney, then around the Harbor. There, the very last of the SSF made their stand, with the sea at their backs. In the harbor floated USS *Constitution* and her replica colony-ship escorts.

Matthew was just trying to decide how to finish them off when he noticed two distinct ripples, not only in the air but in the water, one on each side of the wooden flotilla. Suddenly those ripples seemed to turn into two metal ships, with inward-sloping hulls. The numbers on the bows of those ships told him which ones they were: 1000 and 1001. Each of the new ships carried a long-barreled gun. Those guns took aim, then spoke with a deafening combined shot. Two shells struck in the midst of the SSF and exploded, sending bodies flying like dolls.

The remaining SSF surrendered. Only one installation remained—a once-imposing rectilinear structure not far from the Sydney Opera House.

"And now," he said to Natalya, now by his side once more, "we go to keep our appointment."

# Chapter 13

Lieutenant Walston and Sergeant Jameson greeted Matthew just outside the Institute.

"You won't find but one occupant inside, Field Marshal," said Walston. "She refuses to come out."

"She would be Dr. Folsom?"

"That's the name on the office door, anyway," said the Sergeant. "She answers to it—sort of. She won't come out, and you did order us to let her be."

"Yes," said Matthew. "Because, like Stefan Weiss before her, *I* wish to deal with her." He smiled. "Well done, gentlemen. You, Sergeant Jameson, have earned a field commission."

"Thank you, Marshal, but I think I'll follow the Lieutenant's example and try for OCS."

"A wise decision. Lieutenant Walston briefed me on your unique contributions. I'm sure you will qualify. And now, if you'll excuse us, Lieutenant Bronskaya and I have a visit to make."

"Just the two of you, Field Marshal?" Jameson asked. "I'm not sure that's safe…"

"For ordinary organic beings, it would probably be most unsafe," said Matthew. "Not for us."

Jameson burst out laughing. "Point taken, sir," he said. "Still, the Colonel would have my head if I let anything happen to you after all this."

"Is Colonel Campbell on this continent?" asked Matthew, arching an eyebrow.

"Not on *this* continent, sir," said Ben Walston. "He detached the Seventh Cav Recon Platoon for this mission, which makes me the senior American officer present on Australia. *But,* the Third Regiment drew the assignment to spearhead the invasion of the  Four Bore Tunnel. Its elements should be coming out in China and Vietnam."

"Excellent," said Matthew. "So my little diversionary action at Kings Dominion really did serve that purpose. I'll be convening a large assembly in the Opera House. You can meet some of your distant cousins then. For now, I'll call you if I need you. I have your number."

"Yes, *sir!*" said Lieutenant and Sergeant, snapping to attention and saluting as one.

Matthew and Natalya both returned the salute at once. Then they entered the Psychiatric Institute.

The cells in the main cellblock stood empty, of course. In any event, that cellblock was not his target. His target was Brianna Belle Folsom, MD, PhD, whom he fully expected to find in her office.

As he and Natalya entered the outer office—now empty—they heard her voice from behind the PRIVATE door. "Come in, Commander Morrow," she said. "I've been expecting you."

"What game is she playing?" Natalya hissed softly in his ear. "Doesn't she realize she's lost?"

"That kind of person can imagine neither shame nor defeat," Matthew whispered back. "And if my theory is correct and Wes Ziegler actually scammed her twice, she'll be in total denial—and could crack at any moment. Wait outside—but use your interfaces. Tap into my recorder's input monitors, as I showed you." It wouldn't be real mental telepathy, but between those two, it would more than serve.

"Right," she said.

Matthew moved to push the door aside—and it came off in his hands. Deftly he propped it against the wall and entered.

The office was even less shipshape than when Matthew had first seen it. Debris lay everywhere. Yet, there sat Dr. Folsom at her nearly ruined desk, in the classic "boss pose." He used his interfaces to check the wall monitor facing her. At least *that* was intact and ready to receive.

"As commander in chief of the Revolutionary Forces of Free Earth," he began, "I hereby place you under arrest. You will stand trial before a military tribunal for crimes against nature, abuse of your patients, and aiding and abetting a known rapist and mass murderer."

She yawned in his face. "Please stop with this boring pedantry," she said. "You and I both know you have *no* competent authority before which to bring me for any kind of trial."

"You are mistaken," he said. "*I* am your judge. The revolution is proceeding now, and neither you nor any other powers-that-be can stop it. I also have the Americans to help me."

"The Americans!" she said and spat. "A rag-tag force, living on idiotic dreams!"

"That 'rag-tag force' has helped me take over your prison, as well you know," said Matthew. "But they're not the only Americans I have as allies. Surely you know about the two very powerful ships that have taken over Sydney Harbor and defeated the last of your forces?"

"Your talents seem to have no end, Commander Morrow."

"Don't be absurd, Dr. Folsom," said Matthew. "I did not build those ships. And I think you know who did." Now he activated the display behind him. "Do you see that flag?"

"The American flag," she said disdainfully. "So?"

"Count the stars in the blue field."

"I don't have to count them. Fifty stars."

"Count them again," said Matthew.

He could hear her telling off the stars in her head. At first, she said, "That doesn't make sense…" Then enlightenment seemed to dawn on her—and sudden rage.

"*Traitor!*" she roared. "*Fool!* So the High Command was right: the original United States *did* live on. And underneath North American Protected Wild Space. Forty-one stars—I guess that's how many States they now have. *That was supposed to be your target!!*"

Although Matthew knew that already, hearing her say it aloud still rocked him. "What did you say?" he asked slowly.

"*That was the purpose of the project! Fifty years of work, all for nothing!*" And for fifteen seconds more, she called him several kinds of names. Then she said, "I hope you're satisfied. Since you captured the Canberra Center, *I* have been taking all the briefings. At first, I didn't know whether to believe them—riots in China, Vietnam, Myanmar, Bangladesh, and India. Highly coordinated riots, too—as if the rioters had experienced military advisers. And this—the Brazil-to-Vietnam Four Bore Line, totally shut down. And at least one branch line. Those idiots in the High Command should have anticipated that. That's how your American allies did it: they tapped into the tunnels and sent troops through them to come out on this side of the Pacific Ocean. And you—you aided and abetted them!"

Matthew waited for five seconds after she fell silent. Then he asked, "Are you quite through confessing the purpose of the cyborg project and your role in it?"

Now her eyes widened.

"That's right, Dr. Folsom," Matthew went on. "I deduced the purpose of the project before I came here. But you just confirmed it. This evidence will prove a sensation at your trial."

"How ... how..." She fell silent again.

"How did I do it?" asked Matthew. "I'll tell you. Integrity. Integrity and honor; both survive even when someone loses his memories—or, as I did, puts them away for safekeeping."

"What did you do? Submit to deep hypnosis?"

"Yes, and a lot more. You don't need to know the rest. Just know this: that flag above our heads was the key. And you're right—those forty-one stars *do* represent the number of States *now* in the United States of America. As for the rather ingenious war plan to invade the Eastern Hemisphere by capturing tunnels that run under the Bering Straits, I didn't need to remember that. You will, of course, realize that capturing Kings Dominion was a diversion for that very operation. I had to know to trust young Zach Radner, but a simple post-hypnotic command took care of that.

"But the point is: integrity. You have none, so you would never understand. My *integrity* kept me focused on two objectives: to rescue the woman I love and to stop your project." Let her think he meant only

Natalya. Ayelet would make her mark when she was ready, Matthew was sure.

Brianna Belle Folsom seemed to deflate. She sank in her chair and heaved a sigh. "Men!" she said dully. "They have always been my downfall, especially that con artist, Wes Ziegler—whom I should have known better than to trust a second time—and you. Why don't you just kill me right here and get it over with?"

"Well, well, well. So Wes Ziegler *was* taking his revenge on you. Anyway, killing you now would be counterproductive. You and all those like you must stand a military trial. And stand it, you shall. No matter how long you, *or I,* have to wait. Natalya!"

Natalya came in.

"Secure the prisoner. Then get the Recon Platoon in here. They are to seize all the computer equipment and start analyzing the files."

* * *

"It's good to greet you properly, Field Marshal," said Zachary Radner, offering his hand. "It's nice to remember that other battle you and I fought together."

Matthew shook the young cadet's hand. "I'll second that," he said. "Only, I hope the recovery of those other memories didn't hit you too hard."

"Victory is a great salve for any wound," said Zach, grinning. Then he frowned. "Only, I heard about Ayelet Cohen. I feel terrible that she can't enjoy it."

"I'll want to brief you in greater detail on that," said Matthew. "Top secret. Oh, by the way: Lieutenant Bronskaya, may I present Senior Command Cadet Radner."

Natalya smiled and extended her own hand. "I've heard many things about you."

"Good things, I hope." asked Zach with a wink as he accepted her hand.

Natalya smiled even more broadly. "*Very* good things," she said.

Matthew and Natalya moved on along what was almost a reception line. The next person he greeted was Chief—now *Senior* Chief—Barry Sutton, USN.

"And what assignment did you draw, Senior Chief?" Matthew asked.

Grinning ear-to-ear, he said, "Chief of information handling and electronic defenses aboard USS *Elmo Zumwalt,* sir. I run her shields, cloaking system, and her computers."

"And there's none better for that job, I'm sure," said Matthew. "And you, Hospital Corpsman Riley, how are you this fine morning?"

"*Chief* Hospital Corpsman," said Andrea, smiling almost as broadly as was Senior Chief Sutton. "In charge of corpsmen and hospitalmen aboard *Zumwalt.*"

Next in line were Bert and Diana Kendrick. When Diana saw Natalya, she gasped. "I hardly dared believe it," she said. "Oh, Natalya … is it … Oh, may I?"

Natalya smiled. "Why not?" she asked. And the two women embraced. A short embrace, but long enough. "Yes," said Diana, "it's you. Just as I remember you. But, oh, Natalya, are you all right?"

"It was hard to take for more than twenty years if that's what you mean," said Natalya. "But my man, Matthew here, gave me all the encouragement I needed."

"I just now realized how much I missed you since Rigel g. You saved my life, and for those twenty-plus years, I really thought you had given your life for mine. To see you again is more wonderful than I could imagine."

"I'll second that," said Bert, standing next to Diana. "Welcome back to the land of the living, Natalya. And Matthew, thank you again. For everything. Here we thought we could try to do you a favor, and now you've repaid us both far more than we deserve."

"Not entirely, Bert," said Matthew. "Your kids are still out there. This revolution is as much for them as it is for us."

"And I'll second that, too."

Next was Jake Boddicker, who grinned that ironic grin. "Found her again, did you?" he asked.

"Yes, indeed. Natalya, meet Jake Boddicker, weapons merchant, 'organized criminal,' and highly irregular general officer."

Natalya smiled and held out a hand. "Greetings, Mr. Boddicker," she said. "And thank you for sending Wes Ziegler to me."

"Happy to oblige," he said, taking the offered hand.

With all the greetings finished, Matthew led the way onto the concert stage.

Generals Carson and Jackson were also present, as was Captain Ronald Jones, CO of *Zumwalt*. (And likely soon to wear two stars, since he had commanded that task force.) But when these last three officers took the stage, the great hall erupted in deafening applause. This soon faded into a chant of "Mor-row! Mor-row! Mor-row!"

Matthew raised both hands above his head and waved at the crowd. Gradually it quietened and then fell silent as he strode to the podium.

"Generals, officers, and enlisted of the Revolutionary Forces of Free Earth," he declaimed, "today we mark our first victory!"

Again the crowd roared its approval. Again he had to gesture for silence.

"And as long as you are giving loud hails to me, I want you to recognize someone else, someone just as capable as I. Give your hand to First Lieutenant Natalya Fyodorovna Bronskaya, late of the United Systems Marines!"

Yet again came loud applause.

"Today, we also observe something else," he said when the crowd could hear him. "We have allies—allies of which even I had no knowledge. I didn't know them, but they knew me. They have been aiding us all this time, or else moving into position, waiting to strike at precisely the right time.

"You, Americans, will appreciate the first group. Centuries ago, Lord Steele and his successors removed you to this continent. They *thought* they'd removed everyone. He didn't. You left behind cousins, who literally burrowed underground." He explained how that came about and the kind of society in which the original Americans now lived. Then he explained what he had confirmed about the breach of the Four Bore Lines and the fleet that now rested at anchor in the Harbor. "Their flag served as the one thing that could remind me of their existence—at a time when I could *not* betray them."

He explained about his decision to lock away his memory in the event of capture and how a forty-one-star flag could trigger it. "I counted on my instinct for justice, and my own integrity, to impel me to make revolution, allies or no. As you can all appreciate, I'm sure, my instincts were correct." More applause broke out, then subsided.

"And now I come to the second set of allies I have." He explained about the network of like-minded people still in the "Civilized Footprints" on Earth. The cell system took a little longer to explain, but not much. "Those allies," he went on, "denied reinforcement to our enemies here on Australia. And now, together with the original Americans, they will press the revolution throughout the rest of Earth. And they include a very dedicated cadre indeed, representing a faith older than modern civilization. I refer to the Zealots. You will all hear of, and from them, soon enough!" Yet more applause.

"But we have a third group of allies, whom we might or might not contact. Two decades ago, the United Systems fought a long and costly war in the far reaches of the galaxy. Fifteen years ago, that war ended. But it ended with the United Systems debt-ridden and with pioneers and settlers of new worlds building another society *free and clear*. And as often happens, the debt-ridden society sought to tax the free-and-clear one." A murmur began to build at that. "Yes," said Matthew, "I hear you Americans realizing already what I am about to say. Many more centuries ago, your ancestors fought a war for independence against the very power that produced Lord Steele. And you fought that war for the *identical reasons* that are playing out again. *In the Nine-o'clock Quadrant of the Galaxy, a new freedom movement has arisen, identical to yours!* I cannot prove this, for I have not observed it. But I have every reason to deduce it.

"And if this is true, then our enemies will find themselves pressed on *two* battlefronts, not one! Two revolutions, in different parts of space, but stretching our enemies' resources to the breaking point! Therefore, we can confidently press on until we achieve our objective: *total victory and complete restoration of freedom!* And not on Earth only, but throughout a galaxy!"

This time, the applause was louder than ever as his followers came to their feet. As Matthew looked around the room, he saw Natalya, her eyes shining as she smiled back at him. Then the assembled troops—a fraction of Matthew's total forces—broke out into song: *Battle Cry of Freedom,* once again.

THE END

# The Admiral's Choice

*The Terra Prime Series*

## Book Three

Terry A. Hurlbut

# Chapter 1

Jacques-Yves de Grasse turned away from the sun, now setting over *la baie archachon* far away to the west. He faced his visitor squarely. "Would you care to say that again?" he asked. He had unconsciously slipped into a voice he had not used for fifteen years. The last time he'd spoken this way had marked the beginning of his retirement.

No, not retirement. *Exile*, said a voice in his mind. He ignored it.

Vice-Admiral Ramón Ordoñez-Pizarro USN frostily replied, "I believe you heard me the first time, Rear-Admiral de Grasse. A dangerous revolutionary movement has sprung up, right here on Sol d. And one of *your* former officers is at the heart of it."

"I won't bother asking you why don't you just say 'Earth,' if you still say 'Sol.' Instead, I will proceed to the next question: why come to me?"

"For the obvious reason that, if anyone can reach Lieutenant Commander Morrow and persuade him to stand down, you can."

*Sacré salaud,* he didn't say. "You fellows—or at least the Admiralty as then constituted—didn't seem to want my help fifteen years ago, when it might have mattered," he said. "They as much as told me, 'Go back to your family vineyard and be happy. This matter is in the hands of top men.' Well, obviously, your 'top men' have failed you. So now you come to me and say, *'Amiral-arrière,* we need your help!'

"*Connerie!*" he shouted. He was a vintner, not a rancher, but still a man of the country, and swore like one. "I ought to tell you and your superiors what to do with yourselves," he went on. "And before you upbraid me for a lack of manners, let me remind you: I am retired. For fifteen years have I been retired, and not by my choice, either. And as it happens, you are standing on the land of my ancestors, which belongs to me by the direct guarantee of *les cinq dames* themselves. So I don't have to accord anyone an ounce of respect who has not earned it. And you, *mon vice-amiral,* have not."

The Vice-Admiral made a big show of clearing his throat. Then he said, "I read the brief. So I understand how sensitive a subject this is to broach with you. But a moment's sober reflection—perhaps over a few glasses of the excellent wine for which your vineyard and winery are famous throughout the Galaxy—will, I am sure, convince you of both the urgency of the situation and your value to us in resolving it."

That part about the fame of his wine struck home. His father had often regaled him with the diary entries of his *multi-arrière-grand-père* Alain. In them, he described how he obtained the guarantee of which the Vice-Admiral had just spoken, from Mdlles. Francisca Ordoñez-Pizarro, Kanesha Preston, Ruqayya Tamraz, Jawahir Otayf, and, of course, Mdlle. Secrétaire-générale Gunilla Thorsell, their leader. And very lucky had his multiple-great-grandfather been to obtain it nearly four centuries ago. Everyone else forfeited his land, which then underwent *le rendu à rétro-sauvage*. Now, to look beyond the borders of the De Grasse 400-hectare holding, none could tell that the surrounding lands had ever been anything but wilderness.

Of course, his guest knew all these facts. Best, therefore, not to antagonize him *too* much.

*"Touché, mon vice-amiral,"* he said. "By all means, let us continue this dialogue at my house."

The two walked to where the Vice-Admiral's magnetically levitating vehicle, his flag lieutenant, and his Marine chauffeur waited.

* * *

Jacques-Yves didn't have to ride with the Vice-Admiral. After all, he had his own mag-lev car. But that car, like every car on Earth (very few of which existed), was fully autonomous. So all he had to do was dispatch the car to the garage, where it would find its own stall, at least as well as a horse would. Then he mounted the Vice-Admiral's vehicle.

Once aboard, he closed the passenger door. Then he took off his hat, revealing his perfectly bald and shiny head. He needed a hat, and a light coat, against the slightly nippy air.

The trip back to the main house took about fifteen minutes. Jacques-Yves spent the time enjoying the scenery. Though actually, the view was less enjoyable now. How forlorn the vineyard looked at this time of year!

The wine was long since laid down, and wine that had finished aging had gone out to the nearby town of Cadillac. There, stevedores loaded it onto barges for the trip down the Garonne to Bordeaux, as had happened for centuries. All this had happened two months ago—in the month *Vendémiaire*, the month of wine-pressing. At least now, he could better appreciate the view than he could have a month earlier. *Brumaire*, the month of fog, always shrouded his vines.

At last, they arrived at his house. Upon arrival, Jacques-Yves alighted first and acknowledged his butler, Michel. He then snapped rapid-fire orders to draw wine and serve it to him and his guest in the library.

The guest, upon entering the library, immediately fell to scanning the shelves that lined the walls. "Impressive," he said. "You're one of the few people in all the United Systems who keeps cloth-bound books. Vice-Admiral Brandon Nelson did the same following his second retirement, from command of *Bonaventure III*. Why do you do it? Surely you can access even texts like these on the Network."

"Not all of them. Besides, like wine, a true book is best appreciated when one can hold it in one's hand and turn its pages."

"Is that a Christian Bible I see on your shelf?" the Vice-Admiral asked with a faint note of disapproval.

Jacques-Yves ignored it. "Yes," he said. "A *Louis Second* edition, translated from the original Authorized Version of the British Royal Commission on Bible Translation, which they issued in … wait, wait, wait … em-zhee-day-enn minus nine zero six double zero, give or take a couple hundred."

"Did you just calculate that?" asked Ordoñez-Pizarro, now sounding impressed.

"Actually, no," said Jacques-Yves. "I memorized it long since. I'm far more accustomed to converting between MJDN and French Republican. For instance, today is MJDN 204195, is it not?"

"Of course."

"Well, to my way of thinking, it is Primeday, first day of the Third Decad in the month *Frimaire* in Year 626 of the French Republic."

"Why use such a calendar?" his guest asked. "The Gregorian calendar, that I might understand."

"Not when you reflect on the memories of war that attach to that calendar."

"But they attach to the Republican Calendar, too, no?"

"Yes, but the French Revolution is more remote. Besides, the month names are ideal for a farmer—or a vine-dresser and winemaker. They tell the seasons of weather or agricultural or horticultural or viticultural activity. And quite accurately, too—as these last fifteen years have confirmed. But all that suffices—and forgive my manners. Please seat yourself."

The Vice-Admiral sat in one of the two cushioned armchairs in the library. Jacques-Yves took the other. Just then, an underbutler arrived, bearing a wine carafe and two glasses on a silver tray. He set this on the small table between the two armchairs, then left. Jacques-Yves opened the carafe and poured for himself and his guest.

Taking one of the wine glasses, Ordoñez-Pizarro said, "Rear-Admiral, I offer a toast. We can drink to the resumption of your sadly interrupted career."

Jacques-Yves took his own glass and touched his to his guest's, but with considerable deliberation. "That's almost as provocative a statement," he said, "as your broaching to me that you need my help in quelling revolution." He paused to sip his wine, then said, "You do realize, I trust, that, thanks to the Admiralty, I have received no briefings since they relieved me of my command, arrested my second officer, scattered my last command from one end of the Quadrant to the other, and even decommissioned my ship. Almost as if they wanted to bury not only Lieutenant Commander Morrow but myself and my command as well. Are you now prepared to tell me why?"

"Why your relief and retirement and the decommissioning and the rest of it, no," said his guest. "Mainly because I know not these things myself. And by the way, we're going to be working very closely with one another. Can we not call one another by our first names?"

"Very well … Ramón. And I am called Jacques-Yves."

"Thank you a thousand times … Jacques-Yves." Well! Now Jacques-Yves could be impressed. Though they were speaking Standard, Ramón had just used a French idiom. Most Standard speakers would have thanked him a *million* times, through a misreading of the French phrase.

Taking another sip, he said, "It's not important. What is important is this 'revolution' my former second officer Matthew Morrow is supposed to be making. As I said, I have received no briefing."

"True," said Ramón, sipping from his own glass. "That is why I, not some more junior officer, am here. I must emphasize the extreme sensitivity of what I am about to impart to you. I am the eyes, ears—and voice—of the Admiralty and even of the security council and first secretary."

"More provocative still," said Jacques-Yves. "Just what has Matthew Morrow done?"

"He has conquered completely the prison and reservation complex of Botany Bay," said the Vice-Admiral. "In the process, he has gathered to himself not only the prison population but also the entire population of the American Reservation on the western third of that continent."

"*Cinq dames!*" Jacques-Yves cried. "The American Reservation—and how quickly *that* demonym rolled off your tongue. Surely you don't think I have forgotten that the name *America* is a name with which to frighten small children. And the American Reservation … the prison of the descendants of the last Americans who refused rehabilitation. You are telling me that Matthew Morrow has recruited *them* to aid him in his … quest, whatever that might be. Now, *just* when were you going to brief me about this!?"

"I am doing so now, Rear-Admiral, and that is the important thing."

"How did he accomplish this feat?"

"He escaped from the Botany Bay Psychiatric Institute in the New South Wales District."

"And why was he confined there?"

"That's not important. What *is* important is that, in the process of that escape, he hijacked an LCG prison transport. Using that, he traversed the Southern Ocean, then attacked the force-field generator at Sharp Point and introduced himself to an American cavalry force—horse cavalry, if you can believe it! —that was reconnoitering that generator at the time. After that, it was a simple matter to recruit the Americans. The Special Security Forces had restricted their technology to pre-electric inventions. How, is unimportant."

"You seem to regard a great many things as *unimportant* to which I would assign a great deal of import," said Jacques-Yves with a tone he almost regretted using.

Ramón seemed to take no notice. "The point is that the Americans had cavalry and mobile artillery. I must observe that the SSF were fearfully lax in this regard. They ought never to have permitted the Americans to reorganize their society as they did. But, *tacaños* that they always have been, they didn't want to expend effort building barracks, reformatories, or mess halls, and did not want to mix the Americans in with the regular populations of adult and juvenile inmates in the Victoria and South Australian districts. They insisted on leaving the Americans to their own devices, to fend for themselves. Oh, what can they do? We'll just raid them once in a while if they ever try to develop electric … ah, sorry. Forget I said that."

Jacques-Yves smiled thinly. *"D'accord,"* he said.

"And now see what! The Americans had built an army, and your former second officer recruited them. With them, he swept Botany Bay from Perth to Sidney and every installation in between."

"A moment, Ramón. How could he do that, given the force fields that, I'm sure, demarcate the various districts of Botany Bay?"

"By creating, almost as if he had done so immediately, a virus program that took down every force-field generator at once."

Jacques-Yves sighed. "Pray, continue," he said.

"Worse than that, in the administrative centers in Adelaide, Melbourne, Townsville, and Sydney, he has captured all the ancient aircraft that once belonged to the Royal Australian Air Force, plus a B-52 Stratofortress that once belonged to the United States Air Force. The SSF were conducting research on them, trying to design a gravity generator that would enable one of our pilots to fly them without risking vertigo or blackout from the accelerations attendant on air-to-air combat. But your second officer recruited, if you can believe it, *adolescent boys* to fly them as they were!

"And fly them they did, to embarrassingly good effect. Those SSF who did not die in action, now languish in the prisons they once guarded. And Matthew Morrow has made sure to confine them the old-fashioned way, with physical bars and fences, not force fields. All the produce from the penal farms and ranches of Queensland is now lost to us. He has set up a 'capital city' in the Canberra Administrative Center, and makes regular propaganda broadcasts from, as nearly as we can tell, the ancient Sydney Opera House. Thanks to him, riots have broken out in Mumbai, Rangoon, Phnom Penh, Hanoi, Ho Chi Minh City, and lately in Beijing, Shanghai, Nanjing, Chunjing, Auckland, Wellington, Christchurch, Seoul, Pyongyang, and Tokyo."

"Have any riots broken out in France?"

"Not yet, Admiral," said Ramón. "But the Latin Quarter in Paris is getting restive. I stopped in Bordeaux on my way up the Garonne to see you. No riots yet, but a whispering campaign. My sources also report more whispering at Alise-Ste-Reine. My staff suggested to me that the Five Ladies perhaps ought to have removed the statue of Vercingetorix," Ramón paused. "Ah, well," he said, "that is of the past. The present is our most pressing problem."

"Which could be worse," said Jacques-Yves. "I take it that's why you haven't moved against Matthew in force."

"You are pleased to joke, Jacques-Yves. We can't possibly land any troops on Botany Bay. First, that B-52 carried air-launched flying bombs with which he destroyed the spaceports of New Zealand. Matthew Morrow's rioting gangs have taken over every other spaceport from which you could cross to Botany Bay over water alone. We tried once to drop troops into the American Reservation—and the American militia killed or captured them all. Trying that again would give his revolution more publicity—and more fire-power and transport capability—than the

Admiralty would care to risk. And there are other reasons, which I am not authorized to disclose, why the Marines *and* the Navy are stretched thinly at the moment."

"Do you mean to say," said Jacques-Yves, "that we are under attack from The Hive, or the Far-elves, or some such enemy?"

"No," said Ramón. "At least we have no attacks from *those* quarters. More than that, I cannot—must not—say."

"But what you *are* saying," said Jacques-Yves, "is that you don't want to assault Matthew Morrow's position with main force. I suppose you also hope you don't have to destroy him. You do know that I know exactly what he is and how formidable he can be. The Five Ladies know how he saved a key mission for me. Two, in fact. Except the second one happened shortly before his arrest."

"All perfectly true, Jacques-Yves. Believe me; we don't want to destroy him if we can help it. That's why we need you. But you need to know more about the arsenal he now appears to have at his command."

"Meaning *more* than aircraft of the twenty-first century? Do tell."

"We know that he has acquired at least five LCG prisoner transports, in addition to that twenty-first-century 'air force' he now has. And we suspect—and this is the most sensitive intelligence I have to share—that he now possesses a wet navy."

"A wet navy?" asked Jacques-Yves. "Ramón, just how long has he been operating?"

"Since MJDN 204154."

"And within forty-one days, he has constructed a number of ships of war that can float on the water? Impossible."

"I never said he built a wet navy," said Ramón. "Only that he possesses one."

"How? And where did he get it? The United Nations decommissioned every ship of war it possessed more than two centuries ago. You know that. No vessel that could possibly serve as a warship is even permitted on the oceans of Earth today."

"These photographs show us what he has," Ramón said. He then snapped his fingers. His flag lieutenant, a slight-looking gentleman wearing two silver lieutenant's bars and the shoulder lanyard of an aide-de-camp, walked to the table where his superior—and his host—sat. He carried something Jacques-Yves thought he'd never see again. It was a genuine *porte-documents* or "briefcase" in Standard. Holding this out in front of him, the flag lieutenant opened two snaps and flung open the lid. Ramón reached into it and drew out another incredible set of objects—hard-copy photographs.

"You said this was a sensitive matter," said Jacques-Yves, soberly. "For any other matter, you would hand photographs like these to me on a microdrive."

"You never saw these photographs," said Ramón with emphasis.

Jacques-Yves nodded and took them. And goggled at the first one. *"Incroyable!* This is the United States Ship *Constitution*—or as perfect a replica of that vessel as ever I could imagine."

He stopped abruptly as he noticed Ramón turning pale. "How would you know what that vessel looked like?" he asked, voice dropping to a near-whisper.

"Now *you* are pleased to joke, Ramón," said Jacques-Yves. "I built a model of this vessel as a boy. She's a legend in Earth naval history. Surely I needn't tell you of the most famous sea battle of the Anglo-American War!"

"We had wondered whether that was the original," said Ramón, still whispering. "And I assure you, this is no joke. Look at the rest of those photographs, if you please."

Jacques-Yves did. And goggled again. "Why, these are priceless!" he said. "They are perfect replicas of four of the first colony ships to carry settlers from Great Britain to what became the United States of America. I recognize them. *Mayflower. Susan Constant. Godspeed. Discovery.* Do you realize the value of these vessels? All five! No civilized human being has set eyes upon any of them since…"

He broke off. Then he asked, "Ramón, how closely in your confidence do you keep your flag lieutenant?"

"As closely as my own person," the other said. "If a flag officer cannot trust his flag lieutenant, whom can he trust?"

"Just as well," said Jacques-Yves. "I was about to say that none have laid eyes upon these vessels since the Aztlán Climate War. *Constitution* remained active, as a museum ship, ever since that other war in which she figured. As the Climate War broke out, she vanished. Along with all these other vessels—replicas all, belonging to two different historical societies. Now, how in the Five Ladies' names did Matthew Morrow acquire them? And if he did, then he commands a crew for each! Where did he recruit them? I tell you frankly, Ramón, that you have a very serious problem on your hands, to be sure."

"But that's only the half of it, Jacques-Yves," said the Vice-Admiral. "Look at the last photograph."

Jacques-Yves didn't know quite what further shock to expect. But in that last photograph, he got the worst shock of all. It depicted two block-like ships with the oddest shape he'd ever seen. Hull and deckhouse sides alike sloped inward. A word came to him, a Standard word: *tumblehome.* Even L'Académie Française still had trouble with that one. Tumblehome referred to the inward slope of the upper part of the hull—if a ship had such a slope. But these two vessels had tumblehome extending to the very waterline, even below it! Even the ships' bows had inward sloping edges! Then he noticed catalog numbers on their bows: 1000 and 1001.

Unbidden, the phrase came to him: the *Zumwalt* class. Then he looked again at the vessel numbered 1000 and could plainly see signs of some kind of repair—repair of battle damage that might have occurred centuries ago—to a vessel without access to a proper drydock.

"Ramón," he said, "your problem is more severe even than I first imagined," he said.

"Why? As if the Admiralty knew not."

"Because these are the very vessels—USS *Zumwalt* DDG-1000 and USS *Michael Monsoor* DDG-1001—that sank the third member of their class, NAS *Lyndon Baines Johnson* DDG-1002, and then vanished, like the other five. *Zumwalt* must have taken the brunt of the battle damage; she's had repairs that still show. The only reason such modern vessels as these could survive, other than their power plants running on natural gas instead of uranium, is that they must have made port—somewhere." He broke off. "Where have they been hiding all this time? And how could Matthew Morrow have found them?"

"I have one idea," said Ramón.

Jacques-Yves looked up in surprise, for his guest was almost *snarling.* "Would you care to share?" he asked.

"As you might guess from my last name," Ramón began, "I have a famous ancestor."

"Francisca Ordoñez-Pizarro?" Come to think, the Vice-Admiral certainly looked it, with his jet-black hair, round face, and slightly darker-than-suntanned skin. All attributes *la directrice générale du Nouvel-Aztlán* had possessed. Not to mention fiery black eyes, like those that allowed Francisca to rise so high. Those eyes were flashing just now.

"Well, of course, she, too. I can understand that you would think first of the first Director-General of New Aztlán. But I have a more recent ancestor, her lineal descendant, Bernardo Ordoñez-Pizarro. The last commandant of the United Nations Climate Force. He begged the Security Council to let him keep searching for any more of *los estados-unidenses* who might have escaped the grasp of Lord Steele, the first commandant of that Force. The Security Council waved him off, called him paranoid, and disbanded his force anyway. Well, *now*, at last, they can apologize to my family!"

"Ramón, surely you don't think the original United States of America still exists?"

"It's not what I think, Jacques-Yves. It's what I know. What I feel in my bones."

"Ramón," said Jacques-Yves, doing his best to sound patient, "the entire region between the two coastal strips that make up *le Nouvel Aztlán* underwent the Retro-Wild Rendering … excuse me, Re-Wilding, after the Climate War."

"Then how do you explain these ships, eh?"

How *did* one explain how seven vanished ships could suddenly turn up? "Well," said Jacques-Yves, "I could speculate endlessly about how the original crew of each became a 'generation' crew, literally training generation after generation of their descendants to take over vital crew functions. Including some of the best shipfitters in the history of naval architecture. Keeping those wooden vessels afloat for nearly four hundred years was certainly an achievement. Those two *Zumwalt* class destroyers are even more remarkable—for *Zumwalt* herself obviously underwent considerable repair.

"I'll admit that I cannot explain their reappearance. And I have already observed that the Admiralty has a problem. There shouldn't be any wet-navy warships afloat in the oceans of Earth.

"But something's missing here, Ramón. What does Matthew Morrow say? I admit it might seem an idle boast, but a rebel's boast is another officer's lead, is it not?"

"We *hope* that's their entire Navy," said Ramón. "But there's more with which to scare the Admiralty—*if* they can wrap their minds around it."

"And what is that? After all, what you've shared with me already suffices to shock."

"That last photograph? Look at it again. Look closely."

Jacques-Yves reached for his antique magnifier. A crude substitute for the "zoom" function on an *écran moniteur*, but effective. "What am I looking at?" he asked. Then he said, "Wait! Each of those vessels is firing its big shore gun! But those guns were supposed to be useless! The last government of the United States never appropriated the funds for the special ammunition those guns were to carry."

"And how did you know *that*?"

"Ramón," said Jacques-Yves, "look behind you. That shelf," said Jacques-Yves, pointing.

The Vice-Admiral turned to look. "What about it?" he asked.

"What series of bound volumes do you see?"

Ramón leaned over to look more closely. Then he said, "Is that *Jane's Fighting Ships?*"

"Yes, in the editions of the twenty-first century. Elsewhere I have a copy of every other edition I could get my hands on. From the last editions, I know all about that fiasco with the Advanced Gun System and the too-costly ammunition they never made. Except that someone *has* made it, or at least a serviceable substitute. Clearly, Matthew is engaged in serious business."

"Exactly. But there is more. Our satellites were lucky to snap that photograph. For in the next instant, there was … nothing to see. Only the wooden flotilla remained. Of those two ships, the satellite could detect no sign!"

"That's impossible!"

"Nevertheless."

"Then do you mean to imply that those vessels are cloaked?"

"Again, you score."

"Well," said Jacques-Yves, "if anyone would ever cloak a wet-navy vessel, these two ships would be the perfect candidates."

"Does *Jane's Fighting Ships* give you that historical insight?"

"It does. Even in their heyday, vessels of the *Zumwalt* class would typically appear as fishing vessels on the sensor systems of that day. Add to it that those shore guns, originally useless, now have ammunition they can use. And now, total cloaking. I can see why you regarded Matthew Morrow's movement as dangerous. But what can possibly have driven him to do all this?"

"That," said Ramón, "remains classified."

"*Pardon?*" Jacques-Yves said, lapsing into a string of French. Then he took a deep breath and went on in Standard, "Excuse me, Ramón, but I must insist that you and the Admiralty be totally candid with me. How can I get through to Matthew if I know not all that he is saying?"

"Trust me on this," said Ramón. "He is making a lot of incredible accusations, most of which are false. As such, their substance need not concern you."

"*Need not concern me?* Ramón, that *substance* has convulsed more than a dozen cities on the oceans immediately surrounding Botany Bay and a few thousand miles inland. It has reached the city of Paris and likely reawakened the memories of the original national hero of France—going back to before France existed. As you, yourself, now admit. And you come to *me* for help in persuading him to stand down. How can anything he says *not* concern me?"

"All you need to know is that he has gone, quite simply, insane. And he might very well have allied himself with a nation-state we all thought destroyed."

"Which, need I remind you, Ramón, is your unsupported hypothesis, nothing more."

"I know I can't expect you believe that. Nevertheless."

Jacques-Yves sat where he was for ten seconds. During that time, he tried to process all the information he had received and identify the information he had *not* received.

"Will you stay for dinner?" he asked. That might be one way to find the missing pieces.

"Thank you, no," said Ramón. "I have other matters that require my attention. For one thing, we are still trying to establish a two-way channel of communication. Matthew Morrow has cut off all communication with Botany Bay except the broadcast stations, which he is now operating to make pirate broadcasts. But as soon as we can be sure he'll listen, we will call upon you. Never fear."

"I promise you," said Jacques-Yves, "that *fear* is not the word—not in this context. I will eagerly await your further communications."

* * *

"The *vice-amiral* has taken his departure," the butler said about half an hour later. "At what hour does *mon amiral* wish to dine?"

Jacques-Yves looked up from his copy of *Jane's Fighting Ships,* edition 2016. "I will dine at seven hours, Michel," he said. "My habitual meal will do."

"Thank you, sir."

Michel turned to go. Jacques-Yves got up from his armchair, tucked *Jane's Fighting Ships* edition 2016 under his arm, and started for his study. After two steps, he stopped and raised a hand. "Wait."

"Sir?"

"I'll need some references in my study—*Jane's Fighting Ships,* editions 2013 through 2021. You will note I have the 2016 edition already in my hand. Have someone pull the rest from their shelf and bring them to me directly."

"Yes, sir. Will that be all, sir?"

"Yes, thank you."

Michel walked to the shelf, obviously to pre-select the volumes in question by pulling them partway out. Jacques-Yves left him to it and walked briskly to his study. Here he kept the records attendant on running the vineyard and winery. Here also, he kept the records of his naval career and the research projects he had begun upon his retirement. Those things, quite simply, kept him sane. The project that excited his interest now was his history of naval architecture. He hoped to publish it someday. In this New Economy, he couldn't hope to recoup any remuneration. The Five Ladies had abolished copyright and patent, along with much else. But there was always satisfaction. Satisfaction that someone would always know the truth about some things, as only a naval officer could see them.

Two ships interested him most of all now. Thankfully he didn't have to wait long before a valet brought in the books he had asked for—nine weighty landscape-style books.

"Set them on that table, if you please," he ordered, pointing to a simple four-legged table. The valet knew his job well. He set the books down and waited. At a nod from Jacques-Yves, he left.

Jacques-Yves continued to read the 2016 edition. Here was the treasure trove. For in that year, in the Gregorian Calendar, the United States Navy commissioned *Zumwalt* and launched her sister ship *Michael Monsoor.*

He knew instantly where to find the information he now wished to review. Outboard profile, top and bottom plan, bow and stern elevations, inboard profile, and deck plans. He had studied these only briefly before, though slightly more carefully than usual. The curious histories of those two vessels had prompted the extra study. But now—now he must study those vessels far more closely. For here was his best clue to Matthew's intentions, until Ramón Ordoñez-Pizarro cared to reveal more.

What was the Admiralty hiding? Surely Matthew had published some sort of manifesto. Why not share that with him?

Jacques-Yves thought about Ramón's fantastic theory about the original Americans. *Could* they have survived—and in sufficient numbers to service these two vessels? These vessels were the key. They were, without a doubt, the most powerful ships afloat today.

And how could Matthew have fashioned ammunition for those shore guns? Even the Americans didn't do that before the Climate War. *Zumwalt* fought her battle with *LBJ* alone, using the low-altitude, terrain-following guided missiles the Americans had developed long before. That much, a court of inquiry later established. *Mansoor* left her station, and everyone assumed she went to *Zumwalt's* aid. Of the three vessels, the hastily assembled United Nations Navy recovered the wreckage of one: LBJ. The other two apparently vanished off the face of the oceans.

And now they were back. Only Matthew—or someone else—had made them capable of shore bombardment and taken over all of Botany Bay, which once had been the continent, and Commonwealth, of Australia.

But why, why, *why!?* What did Matthew hope to gain? Botany Bay was as isolated as was Cruria Australis, the cold, snow-blown continent that lay beneath the Southern Cross. Jacques-Yves still had the old world portrait globes that identified that continent as Antarctica, the continent opposite the Bears' Ocean—the Arctic Ocean. The Five Ladies had changed the name, saying no geographical feature should ever have to self-identify relative to another. They had also renamed North and South America, assigning the names *Aztlán* and *Amazonia*.

The United Systems had changed Australia to Botany Bay and evacuated the entire civilized population from the Commonwealth that once held sway there. They had done it by the oldest expedient of all: loading them aboard a colony ship to settle another world. That suggestion had come, actually, from the Elves. Only the Aborigines remained in their Northern Territory. Tasmania had undergone *le rendu*. And each of the remaining "states" of the old Commonwealth had gotten a particular set of United Systems rejects. Western Australia had become the American Reservation. South Australia had received the juvenile offenders; Victoria and Queensland the adult offenders, with Queensland given over to penal farming. And in New South Wales, once the nucleus of Botany Bay? There, the United Systems dumped the dangerously insane among their people.

But now … now that entire continent was hostile. Matthew Morrow had done this. But what did he plan next? What could he do, staging out of an isolated continent, with seven wet-navy ships? Five wooden, and two metal—and heavily armed, and cloaked. Plus a B-52 Stratofortress, with fighter escort, and all those other aircraft! Did he have Chinook helicopters? He seemed to remember that the Royal Australian Air Force did once have them. Those banana-shaped troop carriers with the dual counter-rotating main rotors could easily jump from Queensland to New Guinea and hop their way across Indonesia to Vietnam. Any ground forces using them would thus have access to three continents. To say nothing of *Constitution*, which could carry a platoon at least and escort the other four wooden vessels, each of which could act as a transport.

*What are you after, Matthew?* he could only wonder.

A sudden commotion in the *foyer* broke through his reverie. *Now, what was going on that Michel couldn't handle better than this?* He heard Michel's voice … and a woman's voice. From the cadence, slightly artificial. And yet, somehow familiar. But at five hours of the afternoon?

He rose from his desk and strode to the *foyer*. Unconsciously he affected the stride he once used in the passageways of his last ship,

*Bonaventure VII.* He didn't often affect that manner, except when something annoyed him—as it did now.

"What passes?" he barked in French as he burst into the *foyer.* "What is this noise? Forget you that I am at home to no one at this hour…"

He froze. Michel turned from the argument he'd been having with the female visitor—or intruder. "My excuses, my Rear-Admiral," the butler said. "I tried to tell the *mademoiselle* that you are not receiving, but…"

Jacques-Yves silenced him with a quick hand gesture. For he had eyes only for the woman.

*"Bonjour, mon capitaine,"* she said. And, of course, she called him *"captain."* For that's what he had been to her when last he saw her. She stood one hundred eighty meters tall and had the same bright red hair and hazel eyes. She wore what looked like Marine camouflage fatigues, and the silver bar on each shoulder marked her rank. But they also bore an insignia he did not recognize: a stylized symbol of Earth, depicting the Eastern Hemisphere, but sporting dove's wings. In her hand, she carried the single-visor canvas hat, also in fatigue colors. And that voice identified her convincingly.

But it did not change the fact that she was supposed to be dead these twenty-five years. Yet, here she stood … No, wait. Her skin was gold—like the skin of an officer they both knew.

Barely able to speak, he answered, "Hello … Lieutenant."

# Chapter 2

**T**he gold-skinned woman held out her hand—not continental socialite style, but Marine style. *"Comment allez-vous, mon capitaine?"* she continued in flawless French. "Or … pardon me. It's Rear-Admiral now, is it not?"

"That's exact," he said, taking her hand. Hard, artificial, likely strong enough to crush his fingers. At least she knew that incredible strength she now possessed; she squeezed just enough. Matthew would have done the same.

Turning to the butler, he said, "Quite all right, Michel. Allow me to present Lieutenant Natalya Fyodorovna Bronskaya, late of the Corps of Marines of the United Systems—and formerly a ranking officer in my last command." He couldn't help noticing that Natalya seemed faintly awkward to hear him mention her old service. Did that winged-globe insignia have any bearing on that?

"Lieutenant Bronskaya is my guest this evening," he continued. "Carry on with your duties."

"Yes, sir," said Michel. "Shall I set another place at the table?"

Jacques-Yves turned to Natalya, who nodded. "Yes, definitely," he said. "The same meal. I will notify you of any change. Carry on." At least, he *hoped* that would be satisfactory—to her.

Michel left down one hallway. Jacques-Yves turned to his latest guest. "Pray, come with me," he said. "We will continue in my study."

"Thank you, Admiral," she said, turning to follow him.

As soon as they arrived in his study, he brusquely said, "Pray, seat yourself," gesturing to an armchair. "And by the way: *can* you dine, in human fashion?"

"Yes, thank you, Admiral," said Natalya, taking the offered seat. "Since Matthew could, I can."

"Of course," said Jacques-Yves ruefully as he sat behind his desk. *Jane's Fighting Ships* still lay where he'd been reading it. He closed it and shoved it to his left side. "No, there's no 'of course' about it," he said. "Lieutenant, what *bizarrerie!* First of all, that's not a standard Marine uniform. What's that insignia that you wear? What does it represent?"

"The Revolutionary Forces of Free Earth."

"*Les forces révolutionnaires!?* And what can that want to say? Do I infer that *you* have turned revolutionary?"

"Yes, Admiral."

"*Quel bizarrerie,*" he said again. And then, *"Quel! Biz! Zarre! Rie!!"*

"Admiral," said this … this metal-and-plastic body that looked so like Natalya Bronskaya and spoke with her voice, "when I tell you *why* I have turned revolutionary, you will not find it so bizarre. And more than that, you will join me."

Jacques-Yves de Grasse stared at his erstwhile security officer and strike-force commander for a very long time. Then her voice—or rather that chillingly accurate facsimile of it—broke upon his reverie. "A sou for your thoughts, Admiral," she said softly.

"Eh? Ah, yes—back to the days when we had something called 'money' to spend. I was just thinking of when we first met. I was a junior pilot officer, on my first deep-space posting."

"USS *Napoléon Bonaparte* CC-65," said Natalya. "How could I forget? I suppose you would think back to that first time, after all," she sighed, and her eyes—at least they looked real—took on a faraway look. "Novy Mir," she said. "And a polity calling itself *Soyuz Sovyetskikh Sotsialistichyeskikh Respublik.*"

"Or in my language, *l'union des républiques socialistes soviétiques.* Yes, I remember. What foolish rosy-eyed idealists those were, who petitioned *le conseil des colonies* for permission to settle a new colony world, and reproduce—and without benefit of printers—the economic model of the polity with that very name, that once stood for Russia and several other countries in eastern Europe and central Asia. And it took that polity about as long to fail as the old one did."

"Seventy years," said Natalya. "And I was there for the last sixteen years of it. Sixteen years, during which I learned how to survive. As I had to."

"It's not as if they didn't pick a good spot," Jacques-Yves went on. "Kepler-438 b. Twenty percent heavier than *la Terre* and eighty-eight percent similar. If that experiment could have worked on any world, it would have worked there. But of course, the Navy lost contact with it and sent our ship to investigate and, if necessary, evacuate. I still remember the officers who served with me—including First Lieutenant Warren Maczak of the Marines, our strike-force commander. He was aboard my LCG, leading the First Platoon and also commanding the whole company. You know, of course, that they rewrote the doctrine on urban warfare while pacifying Novy Moskva. What an appalling disaster that was—half the buildings burned, and gangs occupying the other half."

"One of which," said Natalya grimly, "was holding *me* captive at the time. My father was lying dead in the streets, his body only then turning cold. I trust we don't need to go into the ways that gang used me."

"No," said the Admiral hastily. "Lieutenant Maczak briefed all the officers. After which, Captain de Gaulle charged us all never to disclose anything we saw or heard in that action."

"Funny that you should think back all that time."

"I am trying very hard," said Jacques-Yves, "to understand what has driven you to such an extremity."

"Admiral," she said with a smile, "aren't you the least bit curious to find me alive … and changed?"

That brought him up short. "Yes," he said after three seconds, "indeed I am. I rendered your remains, as I thought, to a funereal transport after that dreadful business on Rigel g. No one ever told me what was so urgent about shipping you off to Sol d. And in cryonic stowage, at that! What can Dr. Girard have overlooked? And what is this change in you?"

She merely smiled.

Jacques-Yves sighed. "I mean, more than the obvious physical change, Lieutenant," he said. "That gold skin—your incredible strength—and for what it's worth, they reproduced your voice exactly. That's a Frankel total-body prosthesis you are wearing, is it not?"

"Yes, Admiral," Natalya said. "Containing not only my brain but my entire central nervous system, plus my eyes, inner ears, and all twelve cranial nerves on each side."

"Actually, I start to wonder why no one saw fit to tell me at the time."

"Don't ask me, Admiral," she answered. "The Botany Bay Psychiatric Institute did this."

"*That* name again!" he cried.

"You've heard of that institution before?"

Jacques-Yves took a deep breath, then said, "Yes. This very day, in fact."

That caused her to sit bolt upright. "What!" she cried. "From whom?"

"From Vice-Admiral Ramón Ordoñez-Pizarro, Director of Naval Intelligence."

"*Der'mo,*" Natalya growled.

"*Pardon?*"

"Oh, excuse me. *Merde.*"

"I know what the word means," said Jacques-Yves, drily. "Lieutenant Maczak said that was your every other word on Novy Mir. I gather the Vice-Admiral's visit presents a problem?"

"And how! It means I have less time than I thought I had."

"Time to do what?"

"To recruit you, of course."

"You are pleased to joke," he said with deadly calm.

"I assure you, Admiral, I do not joke."

"Tell me this," said the Admiral. "Do I infer correctly that you are here as Matthew Morrow's ambassador?"

"Well, it's none too soon for you to grasp that! Of course I am. And I tell you frankly: he would be absolutely furious to see you in this mausoleum in which you have installed yourself."

"Mausoleum?" Jacques-Yves caught himself. He mustn't shout; that would bring Michel asking how he could be of assistance, which was the last thing he needed now. More quietly, he said, "Lieutenant, this happens to be my home and the land of my ancestors."

"Ancestral land or no," Natalya said, "a mausoleum it still is. One would think you came here to die—except that you didn't. I know you didn't. Which means you don't belong here. You were never meant to be a vine dresser and winemaker. I don't care if your wine is the best-tasting Bordeaux in the Galaxy. Nor even that you inherited some land patent with tenuous tenure at best. This is not the life you were meant to lead. You belong in your conning chair on *Bonaventure*, whether it's the sixth or the seventh, makes no difference. You commanded a capital ship; that's your life. Or at least, you belong on the deck of a capital ship, in command of a task force. They took that from you, just as surely as they took Matthew's liberty from him."

She now leaned forward and actually held out her hands toward him. "Admiral," she said, "please join me. Join *us*. Take your life back."

"I cannot promise any such thing," said the Admiral. "Not until I hear much more. All right, then. So Matthew Morrow sent you, and you have confirmed it."

"What finally gave you the key?"

"The Botany Bay Psychiatric Institute. Matthew Morrow was confined there."

"Did Vice-Admiral Ordoñez-Pizarro tell you that?"

"He did indeed. But never mind that. How do you propose to recruit me—and what has gotten into you and Matthew both, that you contemplate such a drastic step as revolution?"

"Well, tell me this, Admiral. You have acknowledged the change in me. Why do you think it came about? And why should the Botany Bay Psychiatric Institute be in charge of a program to develop the Erich Frankel prosthesis for widespread use?"

"All right," said Jacques-Yves. "I confess, I had wondered about that. That Institute is a place of confinement and treatment of the criminally insane. I can barely understand Matthew winding up there, but not you. Never you."

"But why Matthew?"

"*Zût alors!* How should I know? These black-clad security personnel board my ship one day, take him off, and then announce that I am to retire and my ship is to go for scrap."

"And you never thought to ask why?"

"Lieutenant, one does not question the orders or the motives of officers of the Navy."

"And that's the problem, isn't it?"

"And what do you want to say, *'that' is the problem? What* problem?"

"The problem of a society that is inherently unjust and is about to collapse."

"You stack enigma upon enigma. Pray, come to the point."

"Well, I scarcely know where to begin. But I'll begin with the printers."

"What about them? Other than, they can't make good wine? My ancestor got a land patent from the Five Ladies on the strength of that, by the way."

"I mean, Admiral, that whatever the printers were supposed to be able to make, they are making less well every year. And in the last fifteen years, the problem has become noticeable—and worse."

Jacques-Yves paused to reflect. He steepled together the fingers of both hands and rested his chin upon them, then reflected on several interesting expansions he'd made over the years. Like expanding into textiles …

"You might be right at that," he said. "I must ask Michel to review for me all the substitutions he has made these fifteen years. Now and again, he'd mention to me something about 'real things' being of significantly better quality." He broke off as he noticed Natalya taking a certain alarm. "Lieutenant … No, may I call you Natalya?"

"I wish you would, Admiral," the rebel officer said. "I did, after all, come here to renew an old friendship."

"Then tell me right now, if you please, Natalya: what do you have? You look alarmed."

"Admiral," she said, "does any of your food come out of a printer?"

"Odd that you should ask," he said. "Michel has lately sought my authorization to hunt wild game to put food on our tables. Or at least to take some of the excellent two-meter-long Atlantic sea sturgeon that breed in our river, the Garonne. Naturally, I can't countenance such a thing. But more to the point, long ago, we started to grow flax and establish a textile mill. Now he wants to grow wheat, rye, corn, and such things and rehabilitate an ancient water-driven mill."

"Admiral," said Natalya, "I don't know what your Michel … your butler?"

"Yes. What about him?"

"I don't know what he knows or suspects. But if you value your life and your sanity, you will at least start planting food-staple crops, even if you can't bring yourself to hunt."

"And why should I have to do that?"

"Because … Oh, pardon me. I had forgotten. Admiral, I'll pose you another question. Might you have noticed, perhaps forty-five or so days ago, your thoughts becoming clearer?"

*That* struck home. "Yes," he said. "Natalya, again, you score. You were right—perhaps I *am* in a mausoleum of my own making. At about the time you name, I began to resent my present situation. And I know not—knew not—why. After all, this is my home, as I told you. Yet every day, I hear a voice in my head telling me I am in exile. Again, I know not why, or from where, that voice comes. But how would you know that it happened forty-five days ago?"

"Because that's when Matthew released a virus to all the printers of the world, to cause them to leave out a certain ingredient in any food or beverage."

"And that ingredient would be?"

"A derivative of a major tranquilizer called promazine."

Jacques-Yves was suddenly very glad he had been seated before he heard that. He actually felt his heart race. "Do you mean to tell me," he said, "that the people of this planet, and possibly every member of every ship's crew, has been taking … a *toxin*, and not by their choice?"

"On the button, Admiral."

"I … I am without voice. I literally cannot believe what I'm hearing. I distinctly remember Matthew bringing a serious programming error to my attention—along that very line. I told him to correct it. Now you tell me it was no error, but the *intent* of the authorities…" Then something else occurred to him. What was that time span? "Wait, wait, wait. Forty-five days?"

"That's what I said, Admiral. Is that important?"

"Yes," he said grimly. "Ramón told me," said Jacques-Yves, very deliberately, "that Matthew Morrow had regained consciousness, at the Botany Bay Psychiatric Institute, on MJDN 204154. Except that was forty-one days ago, not forty-five. So how could Matthew have acted earlier?"

"Simple. Your Admiral Ordoñez-Pizarro lied to you. Matthew Morrow first regained consciousness on MJDN 204109. And not on Botany Bay at all, but at Bethesda Naval Hospital."

"Bethesda … Maryland? In New Aztlán?"

"That's the only Bethesda I know that has a naval hospital."

"Now *that*," said Jacques-Yves, who now stood up from his desk and began to pace, "is an entirely new pair of arms. If Matthew Morrow has, in fact, been conscious for nearly ninety days, why should Naval Intelligence keep *that* from me?"

"I can explain that, Admiral," said Natalya, "when you agree to join me."

"And that, Natalya," he said, "is blackmail. And you have yet to answer my question: how come *you* to get mixed up in revolution?"

"It's very simple," said Natalya softly. "I owe Matthew Morrow my life."

Jacques-Yves froze in place and stood that way for a quarter of a minute. "All right," he finally said, "at least tell me this much. How comes it that you owe him your life?"

"Gladly," said Natalya. "But first: did Vice-Admiral Ordoñez-Pizarro mention me?"

"No."

"Well, we already know he's a liar," said Natalya. "He surely knew that my, for lack of a better term, *resurrection* would be difficult to explain."

"Why don't *you* explain it, then?"

"Certainly. I need not go over that last rescue mission. By the way, how did that mission go?"

"If you mean, after the hospitalmen evacuated you to the ship and your second-in-command took over, then it went well. No further casualties among the officers—though a few more Marines won their listings in Memorial Hall." He named them. "So, what do you remember next?"

"Waking up in a body that was not mine, holding up hands that were not mine, and speaking with a voice that was not mine, though, at least it sounded right," she said angrily.

"And next?"

"What do you think? I was so shocked; I simply shut out the world and everything and every*one* in it. Matthew tells me that lasted for twenty-five years."

"*Dégueuelasse,*" he said. "And how did you get out of that state?"

"Matthew brought me out of it."

"How?"

Natalya's eyes actually seemed to sparkle at that. "Admiral," she said, smiling, "all I can say is that the fairy-tale collectors and composers were right. When a woman loves a man, as I loved Matthew and now love him all over again, his voice can reach her in the deepest depression. All he had to do was talk to me."

"So you're telling me that you loved Matthew?"

"You can put that in the present tense, Admiral," she said. "Though, I suppose, I must apologize. I never told you when it happened."

"I think I know. On shore leave, was it not? And a month into our first cruise," said Jacques-Yves. "Your manner underwent a definite change at the next wardroom meeting—and I remember Matthew's almost studied ignorance at that same meeting. So now you admit that you broke discipline, to say nothing of taking advantage of…" He couldn't speak.

Natalya smiled again. "Admiral," she said, "I've already made my apologies to Matthew."

"I should certainly hope so," he replied frostily. Then he took a deep breath and sat down again. "On second thought," he said more calmly, "if Matthew accepted your apology, that ends the matter. And would, even if I were still in command and you two were still in my wardroom. But that is of the past. So, he said some things to you that recalled whatever had passed between you twenty-five years ago."

"And that was all I needed to hear. Of course, he let me cry for what I'd lost, and then assured me that I hadn't lost the most important thing, as far as he was concerned." She smiled again, "Admiral, you cannot know what that meant to me."

"I'll take your word for it. And what did he tell you next?"

"At first, only that he must have seen something he shouldn't have," said Natalya. "Something the Admiralty didn't want known. That, and how Dr. Folsom had informed him of your retirement."

"Dr. Folsom? Who's he?"

"*She*. Director of Psychiatry at the Botany Bay Psychiatric Institute."

"I see. And what is her role in this affair, other than her position?"

"Her predecessor had sought to duplicate Dr. Erich Frankel's work. It was he who placed my central nervous system in this body. She was his second-in-command and eventual successor."

"You spoke correctly about Vice-Admiral Ordoñez-Pizarro," said Jacques-Yves, grimly. "He would not have dared speak to me about what happened to you. I might have strangled him if he had. I swear to you, Natalya, that I knew nothing of this. Certainly not what happened to you."

"But why did you leave Matthew where he was?"

"I told you before: one does not question the orders…"

"Or the motives of one's superiors. Matthew told me … and forgive me for saying this … that this was your worst failing. Only that's not quite true, is it? Do you think I don't know the direction your career took after I had to leave your command? Matthew shared all with me. Including the other missions you ran between my apparent death in combat and his arrest. For instance, he told me about your fielding an improvised task force to establish a blockade during the First Morgenetic Civil War. Matthew was not likely to forget that incident. You actually let him command one of those ships. And a good thing, too, as it turned out. Do you remember what you told him after he delivered his after-action report? And submitted himself for discipline?"

"Yes," said Jacques-Yves. "I told him no commanding officer should ever apologize, even to his officer-in-tactical-command, for acting on a piece of intelligence that he could not report up the chain by … how does one say it in regulation-ese? Ah, yes…'because of the delay involved or for other clearly obvious cause.' And that went double when his quick action saved the operation—and that is no exaggeration.

"But how does that apply to my case? I wasn't in the field then. We were in orbit around this very world!"

"Oh, Admiral," she said, almost wistfully, "does your duty really require you to be so trusting? Don't you want to know what Matthew saw that was so sensitive?"

Jacques-Yves took a deep breath and let it out. "All right," he said. "What was it?"

"First, I'll tell you what he reported: an anomaly in Protected Wild Space, west of the Bethesda complex. In NRD-01-VA-Lucketts. That report led to his arrest."

"Was *that* all? No, Natalya, there was something else."

"Indeed, there was, Admiral," she said, with that grim tone returning. "It was a game preserve."

"A game preserve? In *Protected Wild Space!?*"

"But not only that, Admiral," she said. "The game was not wild animals. It was children."

"*Impossible!*"

"Quite possible," said Natalya. "And with evidence to prove it." She reached into a pocket of her fatigues and pulled out a microdrive. "A complete copy, Admiral," she said, tossing it onto the desk. "Only, I wouldn't play that before bedtime if I were you."

He picked up the microdrive and stared at it for a good long time. Then he pressed a button in the kneehole of his desk. The one bare surface he maintained turned into a computer workstation, which, of course, had a jack for inserting a microdrive. He inserted this one, navigated the file-management display that came up, and selected a video file at random.

Afterward, he didn't know what shocked him more: that such an installation would exist or that the Elfin Ambassador would be involved. For among the scenes that played out was the killing of that ambassador by his intended victim—a twelve-year-old girl.

"*Nauséabond, en effet,*" he said, feeling nauseous. "But you said he did not tell you all this at first. Why not?"

"Because he didn't remember it just then."

"What does that want to say, 'he didn't remember it just then'?"

"He escaped from Bethesda Naval Hospital," Natalya said. "Three people escaped with him, including a chief information technician. That person helped him slip through the Barrier into Protected Wild Space. There he reconnoitered that installation."

"I sense that this recording is redacted," said Jacques-Yves.

"I regret very much that I must 'compartment' certain information. Let it suffice that he found some valuable allies. They helped him capture that installation and rescue the children in it, and took charge of those children afterward. But they also enhanced him. Greatly. And equipped him with a program by which he could erase his secondary memories and lockout his primary memories in case of capture."

"That explains the discrepancy between the two dates," said Jacques-Yves. "So he escaped from Bethesda Hospital on MJDN 204109, and then encountered you on Botany Bay on MJDN 204154."

"Correct."

"Then what if I were to tell you," he said slowly, "that Vice-Admiral Ordoñez-Pizarro has formed the theory that the original Americans, who once occupied the middle part of the continent called Aztlán today, still exist, and have maintained their society even in the face of the Re-Wilding?"

Natalya almost—but did not quite—take that without flinching. After three seconds, she said, "I will neither confirm nor deny an account of events I did not witness. I prefer to let Matthew Morrow tell you about that himself—again, if I can persuade you to join us."

Then it was true. But that did not begin to tell him exactly where his duty lay. Aloud, he said, "I will consider it. By the way, does he still call himself a lieutenant-commander these days?"

"No, Admiral. He holds the rank of Field Marshal."

"How appropriate," said the old Admiral. "I knew he was ambitious, but I knew not how much."

"Would that *ambition,*" said Natalya. "explain why a rocket force, unknown to me previously, tried to destroy us with a thermonuclear missile?"

"*WHAT!?*" He stared back at her in literal open-mouthed astonishment.

She started to repeat that last. Jacques-Yves, cutting her off, said, "I heard you, I heard you, I heard you, I heard you!" Now he buried his head in his hands.

For five seconds, he held that pose. Then he raised his head, took a deep breath, and let it out. "All right," he said. "Come over here." He got up again and crossed to the corner of his study where he kept his world portrait globe.

"What is this artifact?" Natalya asked. "It's very attractive."

"It is a three-dimensional map of this Earth."

"Really?" Natalya gasped, and her eyes widened in wonder. "But why not simply call up a holographic display?"

"I happen to like solid objects," said Jacques-Yves. "I think I'll show you my library. Now let us see." He spun the globe until he could see the continent marked *Australie*. Then he spun the frame on which the globe was mounted so that he was looking directly at the landmass.

"Now then," he said, "from where did that missile launch?"

She pointed to a spot in the Manchuria region of China.

"And how do you know that?"

"Matthew has acquired an air force of sorts," she answered. "Including LCG prisoner transports, easily capable of seeing such a launch."

That confirmed what Ramón had told him. "And the target?"

She pointed to the old capital city of Canberra.

"*La vache*. What kind of other secrets is the Admiralty keeping? Come to think, Ramón was very evasive with me. Imagine keeping a brace of missiles within striking distance of Botany Bay and not telling anyone! But why Canberra?"

"Because that's where Matthew and I happened to be standing at the time," said Natalya. "It will be a very long brief. For now, let it suffice that there were three of us cyborgs on Botany Bay at the time. The third … well, of him, the less said, the better. Like Matthew, he came from Berks' World."

"The failed colony on Proxima b?"

"The same. And we can now solve an important mystery about that colony."

"Are you telling me this other person was the one who opened all the airlocks and killed everyone?"

Natalya nodded. "Everyone but himself and Matthew," she said. "The fact of the matter is that they knew one another as boys. Stefan Weiss—that's the name of this other cyborg—was the bully and Matthew was his target. The two of them died in an accident involving a school bus. Dr. Frankel made cyborgs out of both of them, not Matthew only."

"Let me guess," said Jacques-Yves, "Stefan Weiss went insane."

"Or simply drunk on the power Dr. Frankel gave him. He couldn't tolerate Matthew surviving with him. So he destroyed the colony."

"And lately," said the Admiral, "*both* of them were on Botany Bay. *La vache*, what was Dr. Frankel, and what were those officers on Botany Bay, trying to do? Create some new kind of ultimate warrior?"

"That's what Matthew and I believe. But I've been digressing. Matthew started with the American Reservation, in a campaign to sweep across Botany Bay. As he was closing in on the New South Wales District, he used the official announcement station to call out Stefan Weiss. The two fought their last battle outside Canberra."

"And Matthew won."

"Yes."

"And then," said Jacques-Yves, now feeling angry again, "the enemy—that is, the Special Security Forces—passed an alert that Matthew had won the fight. And the Admiralty—or someone in high authority—decided to destroy Matthew by any means necessary. How in the name of every officer under whom I ever served did you survive? Are you that robust?"

"Happily, we never had to test that," said Natalya. "A truly wonderful woman ... a heroine of our revolution ... flew an LCG directly at the missile and rammed it. We believe the missile had at least one warhead with a contact fuse."

"Which blew the others up. And at what altitude?"

"Four hundred kilometers."

"*Zût*. No wonder all those Chinese cities are running riot. Electromagnetic pulse effects, a flash bright enough to blind, plus radiation effects … and all of them happening over Manchuria. I tell you, someone is going to pay for this."

"Not so, Admiral," said Natalya, more soberly still. "We've already figured out that the Admiralty, or the SSF, or whoever gave that order, has already found a scapegoat. The pedophile game preserve alone would justify revolution. The missile makes all other courses impossible."

"Are you sure about that?" asked Jacques-Yves. "Are you truly sure? You're telling me that absolutely no one in the Admiralty or the Security Council is trustworthy."

"Admiral," said Natalya with a sigh, "think. Who would appoint a monster like Holger Tildblad to direct the Botany Bay Psychiatric Institute?"

"He's the one who gave you this … er … body."

"Yes. And how could he get away with a thing like that? Why didn't Brianna Belle Folsom, his successor, intervene and lay information about the project? How could she get away with the atrocities Matthew and I have documented, and in some cases, suffered? Who put a promazine derivative into everyone's food and drink if anyone was trustworthy? Surely you know that things like these must have had approval at the very highest level."

"Heads-of-state have had ranking subordinates run their own projects before, without the knowledge or authorization of those same heads-of-state."

"All right, then! What about Dr. Frankel on Berks World? Who covered up the full extent of that project? They even tried to erase Matthew's earliest childhood memories. But by the time he revived me, he had recovered them. Admiral—face it! He has information sufficient to embarrass the entire government! You already know the Admiralty is lying to you. Why shouldn't the corruption go as high as the Secretariat? As old as this secret is, do you really think anyone could become first secretary who had not even knowledge of these things? No—a first secretary must support them with all his heart!"

Jacques-Yves turned away. Burying his head in his hands, he walked across the room to the far corner. For several seconds he held that pose. Mercifully, Natalya kept silent until, at last, he could lower his hands, turn, and face her.

"Natalya," he said, "I apologize. You must think I regret to see you again, after these many years. I assure you, I am very glad to see you. You were an officer under my command. I thought you killed in action. To see you alive once more … Why, it's as if I had lost a daughter and gotten her back. But what you have brought me, I find extremely difficult to believe."

"I comprehend, Admiral," she said soberly. "But ask yourself: what have I to gain by lying? And have I ever lied to you?"

"Nothing, and no," the old Admiral said. "But a lie is not the same as a misinterpretation. A logical explanation, far less dire than you have brought me, might still exist."

"It might, Admiral," said Natalya, shaking her head sorrowfully. "But it does not."

At that moment, Jacques-Yves heard Michel's discreet knock. "Yes?" he asked.

"Dinner is served, *mon amiral.*"

"Thank you, Michel," Jacques-Yves said. "Natalya, let us leave this for later. After dinner." And he crooked his right arm toward her.

"Delighted, Admiral," she said with a smile as she took the offered arm.

* * *

"So that's what you meant by not being able to countenance hunting or fishing," said Natalya. "You turned vegetarian, even vegan, did you not?"

"Yes, I did," said Jacques-Yves. "I will not even *pretend* to eat meat."

"But this food is still printed, is it not?"

"Yes. But didn't you say that shouldn't present a problem?"

"Admiral, if you please, let me act as your taster."

"Are you sure?"

Natalya smiled. "Remember, Admiral—this is a prosthetic body. Promazine and its derivatives can't harm me." She picked up her soup spoon and scooped up a sample of the *vichyssoise* before her. She carried it to her mouth and swallowed as Jacques-Yves waited. Finally, she smiled. "It's safe, Admiral," she said.

"*Bon.* Then I shall play the host from now on. Michel, the wine."

Michel produced a bottle of white wine—the de Grasse vineyards grew grapes for white wine as well as red. He uncorked it and poured some into the glass that Jacques-Yves held out for him. The old Admiral sniffed it, then nodded to Michel, who then poured full servings for Jacques-Yves and Natalya.

"Will that be all, *mon amiral?*" the butler asked.

"Yes, thank you," said Jacques-Yves. "Pray, leave us now."

The butler withdrew, leaving the two old friends alone.

"May I offer a toast?" said Natalya. At her host's nod, she raised her wine glass. "Let us drink, then, to old friendship—and comradeship-in-arms."

"*Oyez, oyez,*" said Jacques-Yves, who touched his glass to hers. As she sipped her wine, he watched her closely. He was used to the wines from his winery, but …

"Truly, your wine is excellent, Admiral," she said. "I can readily see how your ancestor managed to get a land patent for this vineyard."

"As my ancestor wrote in his diary," said Jacques-Yves, "only a few glasses of wine sufficed to convince the Five Ladies that even the new printers from the Elves could *never* produce wine as good as any that came out of the soil. The *terroir* of good Bordeaux wine is simply non-duplicable."

"But if I may so observe, Admiral, that applies also to the fruits of the land," said Natalya. "Michel is correct. This soup tastes as if made from mutant ingredients. Believe me—I can tell."

"I can just imagine," said the Admiral. "And to what do you attribute that 'mutant' taste?"

"Simple errors of copying built up over time," said Natalya. "Like actual mutants one occasionally encounters in the wild."

"See here," said Jacques-Yves, "if the food is not to your liking, then…"

"I don't mind," she said. "I apologize for seeming to find fault with everything. It's just that Matthew has taught me to question *everything* I encounter. Without exception."

Jacques-Yves took a deep breath and slowly let it out. Then he said, "Natalya, obviously, you could not leave the discussion until after dinner. I ought to have expected that. But if I may ask, are you sure you're accounting fully for all your emotional reactions?"

"I'm not sure I understand."

"Simply this," said the Admiral. "I accept that your waking up 'wearing' a total body prosthesis came as a profound shock. But perhaps you've let your shock cloud your judgment of other matters. Like these apparent printer errors. And while I cannot condone the introduction of an anti-psychotic drug into everyone's food, I remain hopeful that the right person will, if we inform him, correct the problem."

"Is Matthew letting his own emotions cloud *his* judgment, then?" asked Natalya.

"Yes, he is. And I lay the blame squarely with the Naval Criminal Investigative Service. How they, and those Special Security Forces, could have treated him as they have, is beyond my comprehension. Had they not, we would be having a far different conversation."

"Or maybe we wouldn't be having any kind of conversation," she answered. "Because I would still be catatonic. I am quite desolated, Admiral. I must reject your notion that Matthew and I are not behaving logically. But I recognize that you could not see the justice of our cause as clearly as do we."

"I have fear that I cannot see at all the justice of your cause."

"Admiral, I'm going to tell you a story. It's a story from Novy Mir, before the *Napoléon* came to rescue the survivors of our 'great experiment.' Pardon me for describing this, but … well, since we didn't print anything, we ate as humans everywhere ate before the Elves came. We took lots of flora and fauna with us—or at least the founders did. Frogs among them. And sometimes, I would stew them."

Jacques-Yves made a slight moue of disgust at that thought.

"Yes, I know how you feel about that. But I needed to set some background. Sometimes when I was foraging for food, I would capture a frog to eat. But I didn't throw it into boiling water. I did at first, and found that was the fastest way to lose one's meal. So I started lowering the frog into a pot full of lukewarm water, and *then* lighting the fire underneath it. It was very effective. I could easily cook a frog before it even knew it was cooking. Heating the water slowly and gradually made things much easier than heating the water to a boil before throwing the frog in."

"You are telling me," said Jacques-Yves, "that the authorities are stewing me slowly and gradually, like your frogs."

"That's exact, my Admiral," said Natalya softly. "And not you alone. Everyone."

"And to what end?"

"To an end as old as civilization itself, Admiral—to maintain control. As I told you: the grand experiment is failing. They ought never to have authorized the Novy Mir colony. That exposed the central weakness. The printers compensated for that weakness—until now. Matthew, of course, captured hundreds of them as he conquered Botany Bay. From the errors they are already making, he calculates that the system will fail catastrophically in five years' time—six at the outside. And already the air is polluted again."

"Is that another subtle change I'm not supposed to notice?"

"Yes, indeed. Matthew noticed it immediately upon his awakening in Bethesda. At Botany Bay, it's worse. And he's traced it down."

"To where?"

"To China. Which is now the seat of industry."

"There is no industry on *La Terre!*"

"Oh, but there is, Admiral," said Natalya. "A *munitions* industry."

Sighing, Jacques-Yves said, "Well, Ramón did tell me about a 'classified' reason that the Navy and Marines were stretched thin. I don't suppose you or Matthew have the key to *that* mystery."

"Indeed we have, Admiral," said Natalya, who suddenly sounded grim. "Revolution has broken out in the Nine-o'clock Quadrant."

# Chapter 3

"**Y**ou don't want to say that the Metamorphs have regained their strength?"

"No, Admiral. The Metamorphs didn't start that war, or so our informant tells us."

"Who could possibly inform you of doings in the Nine-o'clock Quadrant?"

"Dr. Udayan Thakur," said Natalya. "Former Base Surgeon aboard Station Midgard, and now—well, his story is almost as interesting as Matthew's or mine. He's a 'renegade augment,' through an 'arrangement' his parents made. It made him capable of realizing any career goal he chose, or even more than one. So when revolution broke out, he decided he wanted to act the part of a 'secret agent.' He literally parachuted from orbit into Sidney after Matthew and I, and our allies, secured it."

"And how exactly did your Dr. Thakur parachute down to Earth from orbit?"

"In a personal re-entry capsule."

"I did not know the Marines were deploying that at scale!" said Jacques-Yves.

"They aren't. It's still experimental," said Natalya. "Then-Captain Medea Mercouri of USS *Argo* developed it during her passage across the Twelve-o'clock Quadrant."

"Are we talking about USS *Argo* CLG-711? The light cruiser that can land on a planet's surface? The ship that vanished into an uncontrolled wormhole shortly before the Metamorphic War broke out? And then returned from the Twelve-o'clock Quadrant seven years later?"

"The same."

"Do I take it the *Argo* is in our Solar system as we speak?"

"Yes, Admiral. Holding station near Ultima Thule, so Dan tells us."

"I remember him," said Jacques-Yves, drily. "He put us all to shame when we visited Station Midgard, and he examined Matthew. He treated Matthew as just another officer, not … well. That's of the past, of course. So Dan Thakur is now involved in another revolution—about which the good Admiral Ordoñez-Pizarro refused to brief me. I gather you can?"

"Yes, Admiral," said Natalya. "Relax. This will be a long brief. First: did you know that several humans and Midgardians established settlements in the Nine-o'clock Quadrant, after the Metamorphic War ended?"

"Only what I read on the popular news networks."

"Then this you might not have heard. Two years ago, that quadrant fell out-of-contact."

"*La vache.* That *would* have been less than comfortable to explain. So that's how long this other revolution has been proceeding in the Nine-o'clock Quadrant?"

"Yes. I'll tell you what Dan Thakur told Matthew and me. Four years ago, the United Systems started to levy taxes on these new settlements. You have to remember: the United Systems was and is debt-ridden. Printer stocks are not infinite, and at the end of the Metamorphic War, they were scarce. While the settlements—which now call themselves the Free Systems—are free and clear."

"So the United Systems tried to tax them."

"That's exact."

"And how did Medea Mercouri get mixed up with the Nine-o'clock Quadrant?"

"Well, when she brought her ship, the *Argo*, back to Six-o'clock, the High Command debriefed her on a rather striking set of adventures deep in Hive territory. How she managed to get through that space without the Hive totally assimilating her crew, even Dan found it too difficult to explain. But for her reward, they assigned her as CinC9, in charge of all Navy and Marine assets in the Nine-o'clock Quadrant. She always considered that an insult and a waste of her talents and intelligence—both the gathered kind and the in-born kind.

"Well, when the Security Council passed those new taxes, she rebelled. She absolutely refused to enforce them. Even when a cadre of Beringians from the new world of Oklahoma—under the leadership of her old ex-oh, by the way—destroyed a shipment of tea from Earth, she refused to take any enforcement action. So then the Navy recalled her to Earth. Not only would she not go, but she declared the Six-o'clock government illegitimate and threw in with some civilians on the colony world of Terra Nova who were already urging independence. Dan estimates that one-third of her forces, including the crew who inherited the *Argo*, went with her. The rest remained loyal and now answer to a new CinC9, an Admiral William Howe.

"Two years ago, things came to a head. Admiral Howe sent down an LCG to a city on Terra Nova called, believe it or not, Lexington, and..."

"A 'shot heard round the Galaxy' rang out. Exact?"

"Exact. The Nine-o'clock Quadrant has been at war ever since."

"And do you believe this account from Dr. Thakur?"

"Implicitly."

"It would explain," said Jacques-Yves, "why the Navy and Marine Corps are 'stretched thin.' And it might explain why the Admiralty are afraid to take any further overt action. May I assume that Matthew has been 'sharing' this account in his 'propaganda broadcasts'?"

"That he has."

"And Ramón told me that Matthew had gone insane. *Quel bizarrerie, en effet.* Then again, your very appearance is bizarre in itself. If I can accept that, I have to accept much else. The question is how much I *can* accept."

"Admiral, I say again: think. What was so special about Matthew, the late Stefan Weiss, or me, that anyone should go to the trouble to outfit any of us with total-body prostheses? Didn't you ever wonder about Matthew himself? Let me tell you, Admiral: I did."

"Why should you? Beyond being, and forgive me for saying it, pruriently curious about him?"

Natalya chuckled. "I deserve that," she said with a smile. Then, turning serious again, she said, "But remember, Admiral: as commander of your Marine strike force, I also was in charge of security. And it always struck me funny that anyone would invest such resources in a project of that kind. I tried investigating the project but kept running into dead ends. Privacy locks I could understand—but these locks had 'top secret' or worse labels."

Natalya paused for a second or two.

"What have you?" asked Jacques-Yves.

"I never told you this, Admiral," she said. "But I went on that particular shore leave boiling with frustration because I couldn't figure out where Matthew came from. I let you believe I just plied him with drink to test how he would respond. And got drunk myself on the strength of it. But what I didn't tell you was that I was interrogating him. I was never drunk, either—I took a prophylactic alcohol antitoxin before I even went down on that shore leave. That's how it started; what you called a 'prurient curiosity' developed in the course of the evening."

"If you're trying to shock me, Natalya," said Jacques-Yves, "you've failed. What's that, next to having you show up on my doorstep when I thought you dead? So tell me: did your 'interrogation' succeed?"

"No, Admiral," said Natalya. "Because he knew even less than I'd been able to find out. It left me burning with shame, though, for more than one reason."

"We discussed that quite sufficiently long ago," said the Admiral, who suddenly paused again.

"Now, what have *you*, Admiral?"

"Nothing. Just…" He trailed off.

"Admiral," she said, voice hardening, "with all due respect to your rank, talk to me. Please."

Very deliberately, Jacques-Yves said, "The after-action report from your second-in-command contained a few hints that I dismissed at the time. Lieutenant Kress was even more obsessed with security than were you—which made him a most worthy successor to you. I suppose it comes with the territory, he being a Morgen himself." Leaning forward, Jacques-Yves went on, "He told me that the enemy dispositions on Rigel g always struck him as indicating advance knowledge, not only of our presence but who would be commanding the Marine detachment. He swore that the enemy commander must have received detailed intelligence about you personally. We could never prove that, of course, and obviously, he won the battle anyway. But he mentioned other things. Like how those evacuees got themselves into such a strife that they would need rescue."

"What was so strange about that?"

"They violated several security protocols to get into that situation. Or so Lieutenant Kress wrote in his report. I still have it. Would you like to read it?"

Natalya surprised him. She made a very angry face. "Yes, Admiral, I would like that very much," she growled. "It rather sounds as though someone set me up. And why not? Someone who had survived a failed colony, then became a Marine, and qualified for OCS faster than ... well, than most." Abruptly she stopped growling. In a softer tone, she continued, "In fact, my background is very close to a few things about Matthew's background that he only recently remembered. That's how he could sympathize with me when I finally put my shame aside and told him everything about me." Now she bowed her head. "Excuse me, Admiral, I ... I…"

Then she did something he would never have expected, something that changed his entire outlook on this affair. She reached up with her left arm and wiped her eyes. Her breath came out ragged, and that's the *last* thing he would expect from a cyborg …!

"Pardon ... pardon me, Admiral," she finally said, her breathing settling down. "I should have expected to find out something like this eventually. But that doesn't make it any easier."

"I should think not," said Jacques-Yves, grimly. *"C'est absoluement dégueuelasse.* I owe Kress an apology; I knew your death upset him, but now I know why, and I blame myself for that. I never followed up on his report. My fault entirely. And I owe *you* an apology. And Matthew."

"Why Matthew?"

"For more than the reasons you think, Natalya. You see … I never briefed him on Lieutenant Kress' suspicions. Lieutenant Kress briefed me directly, as was his right as a Marine, not a Navy, officer." Again he clawed at the air. "*Zût encore!* Perhaps if I *had* briefed Matthew, we could have stopped all this!" Then another thing occurred to him. He went on, more softly, "Of course that might have meant…"

"It might have meant that my death would have been permanent," Natalya said when Jacques-Yves didn't finish his sentence. "Have no fear, Admiral. I've struggled with that thought myself. Matthew told me from the first that he was heartily glad to find me alive. And since then, he's made me feel just as glad."

"Which does not alter the fact," said the Admiral, "that I failed both of you."

"Does that mean you'll join us?"

"Not yet," said Jacques-Yves sharply. "I could never make such a decision merely to expiate my self-disgust for a bad decision. I need to meditate on everything else you've told me."

He hung his head. What else could he say, knowing how he had really put his finger in his eye? Words were totally inadequate. He was still searching his mind for *anything* to say when he heard something that made him look up. She was whistling a tune. He had heard that tune before … but not from any celebrated composer.

He looked straight into her eyes. "Did Matthew share that with you?" he asked.

"Yes," she said, smiling. "I never knew he could compose…"

"He couldn't," said Jacques-Yves. "Not, at least, until *Débora* operated on him to take out the chip that had been blocking his emotions. He well and truly loved you, as I'm sure he's told you. The first thing he did, when your loss crashed into his mind, was to go to the ship's music room and play the most heart-rending interpretation of Tchaikovsky's *Pathétique* Symphony—specifically, its Fourth Movement—that I or anyone else on board had ever heard. And then … then he wrote that music. He called it your theme."

"You should hear it with a full orchestra playing it," Natalya said.

"I have," said the Admiral. "We had enough instrumentalists on board to make at least a small orchestra. Matthew arranged it."

"Ah, but you likely never heard it played on wind instruments with real reeds or stringed instruments made of wood, drums made with real membranes, and so on."

"And you have?"

"The New American Symphony played it for me in the Sydney Opera House," said Natalya, her voice now seeming to swell with pride. "I recorded it. I can record anything now and upload it, too."

"You almost persuade me to join your revolution, just for that," said Jacques-Yves. "Even that will not suffice, however—but do upload it. I should like to hear what a real orchestra sounds like."

"Only too pleased."


They finished their meal in silence, after which Jacques-Yves had Marcel conduct Natalya to the guest bedroom. He himself retired to his own bedroom. Only instead of taking *Jane's Fighting Ships*, edition 2016, with him, he took some far more pertinent reading matter. To wit: the after-action report by Lieutenant Kress, USMC, concerning an action on Rigel g.

Neither he nor Kress could have known where events would take both men. Kress had changed the gold bar on his shoulder to a silver one, thus becoming *First* Lieutenant Kress, after taking over permanently as company commander. Then had come that dreadful mission that had ended in the wreck of *Bonaventure VI*. Lieutenant Kress had jumped two grades and become *Major* Kress, commanding a full battalion of Marines on Station Midgard during the Metamorphic War. Jacques-Yves understood that Major Kress had found his own love interest, an affair that ended tragically when the other officer was killed in action.

Then, incredibly, he had figured in the second of two civil wars that convulsed the Morgenetic Empire. Jacques-Yves had run a little side action in the first—and during that time, Kress had laid down his Marine commission and taken part in the fighting within the Empire. After all was over, Kress had taken up his commission again. But after the Emperor had made some thoroughly bad decisions that almost lost the war for the United Systems/Morgenetic Alliance, Wolfgang Kress had done something Jacques-Yves still couldn't get over. He actually *challenged the Emperor to a duel*—and won. With the eventual result that Jacques-Yves' old officer was now Emperor.

What would his old friend think, knowing that Natalya had lived? The more Jacques-Yves thought about this after-action report, the more sense it made. Why had he not seen Kress' logic before? Because it led too close to home, perhaps?

*Jesu-Christ* once said that a prophet was not without honor, save in his own hometown. Did an enemy risk detection, save only when said enemy was always in charge?

Jacques-Yves was still pacing his room, the after-action report in his hand, when again, he heard a commotion from another part of his house. He donned a robe, belted it, and reached for the intercom. But before he could touch it, a hall boy knocked at his door.

"*Entrez,* he ordered.

The hall boy entered.

"What passes out there?" the Admiral asked.

"*Mon amiral,* Marcel gives his respects and rather urgently requests your presence in the *foyer.*"

"For what cause?"

"*Monsieur,* we have an intruder."

"Lead the way," said Jacques-Yves, and followed the hall boy down the corridor.

The noise got louder with every step they took. At last, they emerged into the *foyer,* where Jacques-Yves beheld a scene he scarcely expected. He saw Natalya, still in uniform, holding a man about thirty centimeters off the floor with her right hand locked around his throat! The prisoner wore an outfit that looked a little like combat fatigues, except for being black as jet. At Natalya's feet rested a black balaclava-style headdress and a pair of black gloves. Taking in the outfit, Jacques-Yves saw a jacket with many pockets in it. Natalya held him up effortlessly and snarled, "Are you going to talk, or shall I end your miserable existence right here and now?"

"*Cela suffrira!*" Jacques-Yves bellowed. Everyone, except the hapless prisoner, turned to look.

"Put that man down," he ordered. "But hold him securely. *I* will question him."

Natalya let the prisoner's shoes touch the floor but still held him in that same neck grip.

"Marcel," said the Admiral, "report. How came you and Natalya to take this prisoner?"

"*Mon amiral,* he entered the house surreptitiously," said Marcel. "We found on his person the most sophisticated burglars' tools anyone ever carried. I suspected at once that he was no ordinary burglar. So on my own cognizance, I had Lieutenant Bronskaya awakened so that she could at least give her opinion. What she found … well, if you will permit, perhaps she can explain."

"Well, Natalya?"

"Admiral," she said in her no-nonsense Marine voice, "this man is a spy. The equipment he was carrying would be available to no one other than Naval Intelligence or, as I strongly suspect, the Special Security Forces. I was just about to ask this *crotte* about that when you appeared."

"And now, whoever you are," said Jacques-Yves, now thoroughly angry. "What are you called? To what service do you belong? And how came you to enter my house without an invitation?"

The man glowered and said nothing.

Then Jacques-Yves remembered that he had spoken in French. So he tried again in Standard, "What is your name, rank, and service? Why did you break into this house? This is private property, and you are trespassing."

"*Nothing* is private in our modern society!" the prisoner spat. "Maybe you don't understand that anymore, *Admiral* De Grasse. In any event, if you let me go, it *might* go better for you in court."

"Court? You wouldn't mean a court-martial because you know I'm retired."

"I mean the special tribunal set up for hard cases like yours. And I'm not going to tell you another thing."

Jacques-Yves considered that for a few seconds. Then, switching back to French, he ordered, "Search him."

With an efficiency Jacques-Yves would not have expected from his staff, four servants bore the prisoner down and held him fast. Natalya let go of the man's throat, took hold of his jacket in two handfuls at the neck, and pulled. She continued to tear his jacket down the middle. Within five minutes, she had laid out a rather impressive kit—a Personal Digital Device, another crude-looking device that looked like nothing so much as a hand-held antenna array—and several black canisters.

Jacques-Yves bent down and picked up one of the canisters. He hefted it, looking carefully at the prisoner as he did. The prisoner's eyes bulged.

"*Tiens, tiens!*" he said. "This frightens him. I wonder why?"

"*Mon amiral!*" cried Natalya. "Pray, handle that canister carefully! It is an aerosol."

"How dangerous can that be?"

"Very. Considering the other equipment this man had on his person, I think you would find that it contained an aerosol solution of cyanide of potassium. Except that I would not test that if I were you!"

Jacques-Yves' blood ran cold. He handed the canister to Marcel, who set it down as delicately as if it were a grenade. Then the Admiral picked up the hand-held "antenna array" and looked it over more carefully. And his blood ran colder still.

"Natalya," he said, handing her the device, "what do you make of this?"

She took it from him and seemed to examine it more closely still. Then she looked up with a very grim expression. "This," she said, "is an electromagnetic pulse projector. Why Dr. Folsom at the Botany Bay Psychiatric Institute didn't try to use that on us, I'm not sure. But someone obviously thought they could paralyze me with this."

"Could they?"

"I think I have a defense against this sort of thing about which its inventors knew not," she said, still speaking French. "Perhaps I'll keep this, to analyze it and make sure I could defend against it. But everything should be obvious now. The Special Security Forces traced me here—and intended to kill you all and capture me."

"Is that correct?" the Admiral asked the prisoner in Standard.

Again the prisoner stood mute.

"Marcel," he ordered next, this time giving the order in Standard, "if you had to defend against a gas attack, could you?"

"Oh, yes, my Admiral. It just so happens…"

"Never mind what 'just so happens.' You will break out some of your defenses, enough to protect yourself and as many men as you need. Then you will take the prisoner outside, to the rear garden, and test that canister on him."

"NO! I'll talk! I'll talk!"

Jacques-Yves looked the prisoner in the eye. He stared into the other's eyes for a long time.

"Never mind," he finally said. "You have already told us everything we need to know from you, from your reaction alone." Then to Marcel, speaking in French, he said, "Take him outside and dispatch him. Don't bother with the canisters; I want you to take care of the matter quickly. And then … then I have much fear that we shall have to abandon this house."

Marcel, in the same language, said, "*Mon amiral,* if I may?"

Jacques-Yves looked his butler in the eye and caught an expression he'd never seen before. This man obviously knew something and had not shared it with him. Something sensitive. Aloud, Jacques-Yves said, "Continue."

Marcel, as Jacques-Yves half expected, countermanded his order—to a degree. First, he ordered the hall boy, who hadn't said a word since rousing Jacques-Yves, to summon three other members of the staff. When they arrived, Jacques-Yves noticed that these were three of his burliest hired hands. "This man is a prisoner of war," Marcel told them. "Take him into the rear garden, at least one hundred meters distant from the house. Be sure to take with you something you can use to signal me at need. Wait there with him for further orders—but keep him alive. *No molestation.* Do you comprehend?"

"Yes, sir," said their obvious leader. And with an efficiency Jacques-Yves had thought to see only in Marines, the three took the prisoner away.

"And now, Marcel," said Jacques-Yves, "exactly what was that in aid of?"

"You were correct, *mon amiral.* This house and these lands could never withstand siege, and we shall have to evacuate. But I have a plan, for I have been preparing for such a moment for some time. Long ago, I came into contact with a revolutionary group who call themselves the 'Zealots.'"

Natalya gasped. "What did you just call them?" she asked.

"The Zealots, *ma lieutenant.* Their leader is one we know only as the 'Lady of the Lamps.' She has taken an interest in the Admiral and wants to make sure that, if ever he comes under such an attack as this, he can evacuate. And that his property, or as much of it as we can preserve, we will preserve."

"And she will want to interrogate the prisoner, is that not so?"

"Yes, *ma lieutenant.*"

"Admiral, I recommend you trust these people implicitly," said Natalya. "I think I know who this 'Lady of the Lamps' must be. Though I have not heard that name, I have heard of the Zealots. We can safely assume that this is the same group."

"And what is your plan, Marcel?" Jacques-Yves asked.

"That we pack as many of the historical artifacts as we can safely move. Every member of your staff knows the plan; have no fear. But the plan also calls for your own evacuation."

Now Natalya spoke again. "You may tell your Lady of the Lamps that Lieutenant Natalya Fyodorovna Bronskaya thanks her a thousand times—but that Rear-Admiral de Grasse has an important mission to perform that necessitates his evacuation to a place of my choosing, not hers."

Marcel bowed. "At your pleasure, Lieutenant," he said.

"And what," said Jacques-Yves. "is *that* in aid of?"

"Admiral," said Natalya with a tight-lipped grin, "it is time for you to join the revolution. And to meet at least some of my other allies."

# What Did You Think?

Enjoying *The Admiral's Choice?* Head on over to Amazon to follow me so you can pick up your copy. And, please leave me an honest review on Amazon, letting me know what you thought of *Matthew's War*.

## Thank You For Reading My Book!

I really appreciate your feedback about my books; your reviews make my books better!

Visit my online store at https://www.cnav.store/ to purchase patriotic gear and see my latest books and merchandise.

Thanks so much!
–*Terry A. Hurlbut*
www.conservativenewsandviews.com
https://www.cnav.store/

# Acknowledgments

First and foremost, the character of Matthew Morrow has its basis, not in "case histories" of "persons on the Autism Spectrum," but on my personal experience. In that light, I couldn't possibly acknowledge everyone in my life who taught me a valuable lesson on what neurotypicals really think of persons on The Spectrum. Some of those lessons have been positive, some negative—but all have been valuable. In addition to which I acknowledge God, Who never fails in love or honor.

Next, I must acknowledge the "giants" on whose shoulders I have the privilege of standing. They start with men like C. S. Lewis, H. G. Wells, and Jules Verne. But they also include some less obvious names—like William Shakespeare and C. S. Forester. And perhaps even less obvious names, like Julius Caesar.

I must also acknowledge many, who would ask me not to identify them, who have apprised me of certain evils in the world in which we are now living. This applies equally to the ugly side of modern allopathic medical research, education, and services, as it does to certain criminal activities.

Next, I must acknowledge Jeannie Culbertson, who served as an invaluable guide through the weeds which every writer must travel.

And last, I must acknowledge my dear friend Andrea, without whose guidance and inspiration this work would not have been possible.

*Terry A. Hurlbut*
March 7, 2022
(MJDN 59645)

# About the Author

Terry A. Hurlbut has been a student of politics, philosophy, and science for more than 45 years.

He is a graduate of Yale College and has served as a physician-level laboratory administrator in a 250-bed community hospital. He also is a serious student of the Bible, is conversant in its two primary original languages, and has followed the creation-science movement closely since 1993.

For more information and to read more of his writing, please visit Conservative News and Views at this link:

https://www.conservativenewsandviews.com/author/temlakos/.

www.ingramcontent.com/pod-product-compliance
Lightning Source LLC
Chambersburg PA
CBHW020053310726
48970CB00002B/302